THE
GLASS
PALACE

THE GLASS PALACE

KATHRYN TRATTNER

for you - my reader

Paths cross in perfect time.

— SEEKER

PROLOGUE

"Tyhr Valter."

The name filled the sick room—pushing on the walls, working to expand the forced boundaries of floor and ceiling. It spoke of the world, of the unknown, of mystery, and things the future held.

Astrid's father, weak after the heart attack and fading quickly, reached for her hand—fingers trembling, skin waxen. She took his clammy palm, wondering when he'd become so thin—a man devoured by grief and impossible anger. A consumption that occurred while she'd been busy, focused on the garden or lost in a book, ignoring her own sorrow. She should have paid more attention. She should have cared.

"Do not believe for a moment that he has forgotten about you, Astrid."

"Who?"

"Your husband. Tyhr," he said, swallowing, voice dry.

"Yes," she said, patting his arm and bringing a cup of water to his lips. "We don't need to talk about it now."

Astrid held it as he drank, only a few mouthfuls—not

enough to keep a man alive. But it didn't matter. She could see the end in his face. There was nothing she could do to stop it, to delay the final moment, so she'd resigned herself to it—waiting patiently.

"The contracts were signed many years ago. You were married by proxy. It will hold up in any court."

"I know—"

"All of this time," he said, continuing as if he had not heard her. "All these years. He made sure you had everything you might desire. Tyhr paid for your lessons and books, for the diamonds in your ears, for the life we've had here."

Astrid failed to keep a flash of disbelief from crossing her face—how could this man have paid for everything all these years? How old was he that he'd been able to provide for her since childhood? None of it made sense.

Her father sighed, familiar with her expressions— reading her as easily as he always had.

"Then why are we in debt?" she asked, raising her eyebrows.

"My fault entirely. I gambled. I needed more funds for your mother. I had to try everything I could. I sold it all to Samuel in the hopes it would be enough to cover the treatments she needed. But life happened so fast."

Of course, his efforts hadn't been enough. All the money in the world was worthless when it came to human life. Nothing could return the life of a mother, a wife, a woman with a soft smile and laughing eyes. No amount of money could have saved her, and it meant nothing if she were gone.

"I know Tyhr will send for you," he insisted. "And when he does, you must go."

She nodded, patting his hand, working to soothe him

and smother her own roiling emotions. Her eyes drifted to the bureau where a black-and-white photograph of her mother sat—a relic of their early years together, a younger version of the woman she'd known so well. Elizabeth, the charming beauty, who fell head over heels for Michael Stern.

"Astrid, look at me."

She searched his watery, pale eyes. Astrid saw the earnestness in his expression and nodded again. "I understand."

"I always thought we'd have more time. I planned to explain later when you were older and might be more understanding. When you might sympathize with the man I was when the choice was made. It is a matter of honor." He reached for her, grasping at her hand, his movements clumsy.

"I know," she said, patting him, offering comfort.

Astrid told him he didn't owe her an explanation. But that wasn't true—his honor and her life were connected, entwined in such a way that there could not be one without the other. Astrid loved and respected him. She trusted and believed her father—believed that when he said there had been no choice, it was the truth. But it was her life he'd bargained with and a part of her, buried deep, resented him for it.

He sighed, gaze drifting away. His watery brown eyes searched the room for something—for someone who would never come through the door again.

"I will honor the promise," Astrid leaned forward, placing her hand on his shoulder, feeling the thinness there —skin and bone, flesh and blood.

She wanted to recall him to this moment, to the minutes that remained to them. Time was precious. Even as they sat here with each other, it was running away—running out—and soon would be gone forever.

"Do not give up on him," Michael Stern whispered. "Tyhr won't give up on you."

————

A LETTER ARRIVED AS THE LAST OF THE FURNITURE WAS REMOVED from the house.

The men tasked with moving the items for the antiques dealer had worked quickly, shouldering the smaller items, and sharing the weight of the others. Each familiar piece passed over the threshold, out to sturdy wooden carts pulled by gray draft horses.

The men took the mirrors from the walls, the silvered surfaces still covered in black muslin. The collection of watercolors—by an obscure artist her mother had enjoyed —left shadows on the plaster. Antony's wardrobe had been packed still containing his clothes. Her father's desk still contained his letterhead. Her mother's dressing table left the house still smudged with rouge.

All of it was being sold.

The debt was too high. Her father's business partner, Samuel Porter, had done what he could, but between the family trouble and the collapse of Porter and Stern—the shared shipping company—there wasn't much that could be salvaged. Everything they'd possessed had been put toward the doctors for her mother. Then in the end, what remained went toward keeping her comfortable. Then her brother Antony died. Then her father.

Astrid wasn't sure when the company crumbled. It might have happened well before her mother became ill.

Their losses happened in quick succession, one failure feeding another, until there was nothing left.

She'd stood in the church to hear services for each one and made sure they were properly buried. One right after the other—mother, brother, and father. It was hard to believe. A small part of her held out hope that if she sat at the window in the dining room long enough, she would see her father coming down the street—her mother would come up the front steps of the row house in a flurry of cheerful words.

But if they returned, Astrid would never know.

There was nothing left for her to live on. No inheritance. No small stash of paper bills was discovered as the house was emptied. No distant relative had stepped forward to offer guidance. She was truly alone now—without a home or purpose.

Mr. Porter, the business partner, offered to cover her passage back to England. There she might find employment as a governess. Something suitable for a young woman alone in the world. But she knew nothing of England. They'd arrived in Sweden well before her fifth birthday and though her mother and father carried the marked English accent of that island, Astrid did not. England was as alien a place as the moon.

None of that mattered. Moving to England was speculation—what could and might have been. Her fate lay in another direction. A would-be husband waited in the wide world for Astrid. She had no idea where he might be or when their paths might cross but her father had promised Tyhr was out there.

The ring on her left hand caught the light, bending it—a circle unbroken.

Astrid pulled the envelope from her skirt pocket, paper

rustling against fabric, the sounds of the street filtered through the open door. There was no return address and no postage. It had been hand delivered while as the furniture was taken out but now, she could not recall the face of the person who'd put it in her hand.

The envelope was thick and heavy, the seams stretched by the contents—poised to burst. It opened easily as if the paper waited for her touch before giving up. Astrid pulled out a stack of currency from different countries and a series of train tickets in various languages—Swedish, French, and Russian. A letter accompanied these items, simple and straightforward.

You have my deepest condolences.
Come to Siberia.
I'll be waiting.
Tyhr.

The name was familiar. More than familiar. Her father spoke Tyhr's name many times—a prayer or curse, her mother shaking her head as the syllables passed over his lips. Astrid's husband-to-be. A man Astrid never met. A stranger she'd begun to suspect had forgotten about the woman out in the world who wore his ring.

She'd been half convinced Tyhr was fiction, a story woven together by her father for some mysterious reason. When she'd been ten, Astrid asked her mother if she was secretly a princess in hiding. But no, not a princess. Simply a young woman promised in an old-fashioned arrangement between two men of the world.

It had happened hundreds of thousands of times, and it would continue to go on—her situation was not new. She'd gone to school with several girls who had been married off in such a fashion. It didn't bother Astrid, maybe because she'd never come across anyone who'd managed to crack the hard case that surrounded her heart, maybe because she'd enjoyed the freedom it afforded her until this very moment.

Finally, he'd summoned her.

Tyhr.

There was nothing left for Astrid in Amsterdam. Nothing in England aside from the promise of safe passage and life in obscurity. Why not travel to Siberia—to meet a man she'd been engaged to since childhood? Why not have an adventure instead of withering and shrinking like fruit on the vine?

Astrid would go. She'd cross the continent to seal the promise made by her father.

She would see what kind of man this Tyhr might be.

PART ONE

THE OTHER SIDE OF PARADISE

CHAPTER ONE

The train took Astrid as far east as it was possible to go.

Beyond this point impassable mountains rose, steep and dark, colossal figures against the night—giants and masters of the landscape. Novgorod stood at their feet. A small town huddled together in the snow, lights flickered here and there—a fallen constellation scattered across the valley.

Astrid pulled her glove off—the brown leather worn and soft with age—and placed her hand against the cold window. Her ring tapped the glass, an audible *tick* as the two connected. She focused on the gold band, the promise that brought her to this point.

How much farther would she have to go?

Against the night, her hand was pale and slender, the nails buffed to a shine. She'd scrubbed the dirt mercilessly from beneath them, rubbing her skin raw, working to remove months of time spent in the garden without gloves. Her efforts paid off. You would never know from looking that Astrid spent more time outside than in, more time with books and plants than with embroidery or music lessons.

The reflection in the glass showed her the familiar lines of her face—a pale oval with sharp cheekbones and a slim nose, dark eyes fringed with long lashes, and straight brows. The dark red color of her hair, braided and pinned, looked brown in the station light. On the bench beside her, an anonymous traveling hat waited patiently to be pinned back in place. Barely twenty-two and, on the surface, the kind of young woman any man might admire in her fine traveling clothes.

She pressed a finger to her cheek, where a dimple appeared with each smile. But it had been a long time since she'd smiled, even longer since she'd laughed. The stern-faced woman in the reflection was one Astrid recognized too well.

With a sigh, she leaned back, replacing the glove, ignoring the way the ring felt warmer and heavier on her hand. It was nerves, excitement and fear rolling together, bubbling beneath the careful calm she cultivated like a delicate plant.

Beyond the train window, the world continued, the station warm with yellow light and humanity—the noise only slightly muffled by the glass. The platform seethed with activity, even in the middle of the night. She'd been surprised by the number of people riding to the very end of the line.

Porters laden with luggage wove through the crowd on the platform. Groups of young men in uniform shouted and laughed, one tossing a blue scarf to another as a pair of gloves exchanged hands—bets were placed, honor put on the line. A big man with a handcart pushed stacked crates covered in Cyrillic labels she couldn't read. A pair of older women wrapped in heavy fur-trimmed coats swept by, bundled in floral scarves, trailing maidservants and trunks.

A family in muted colors crossed the window. They were caught for a moment and framed perfectly—a living painting. The husband smiled, putting his arm around his wife's waist and pulled her close as she laughed. Two small children walked behind them, a boy and a girl, holding hands and clutching toys. An older boy followed dutifully behind with his arms full of paper-wrapped bundles, urging the two smaller children to keep moving.

Astrid watched as they moved together down the platform and out of sight. She touched her cheek, overcome with memory, then pushed it away, refusing to give the pain space. The station was busy and loud, full of noise and movement, but none of it seemed to be for her.

He'd said he would be here. Tyhr. A stranger.

What had she expected? A man holding flowers on the platform? A driver with her name on a placard?

Astrid wasn't sure. So, she'd wait until the crowd thinned before abandoning the warmth of the cabin. There would be time enough for the two of them to come face-to-face.

If he wasn't in a hurry to meet, neither was she.

She picked up *Tundra Flowers of Siberia - a Botanical History of the Region*. His letter from two weeks earlier marked where she'd left off. The only letter she'd ever received from him, dated January 1890. Not even a day, only the month and year, as if the exact date were unimportant. Perhaps it was, considering Tyhr didn't seem to be here to greet her in a timely fashion.

Clearing her mind, Astrid focused on the pages and soon everything else was forgotten. It was easy to lose herself in the book, reading by the weak electric light thrown by the wall scones in the cabin—wrapped in the whisper of paper and the growth rates of lichen.

The door to the cabin slid open with a squeak—sharp metal on metal—cool air rushing inside. The pages of the book rustled, and she smoothed them flat without looking up. Though the space was meant to be shared, she had been the only occupant for the entire journey—alone with her thoughts and expectations. Astrid wasn't ready to release the solitude yet.

"This cabin is occupied," she said.

"The train has arrived."

The man spoke in a low, smooth voice, his English touched by an unfamiliar accent. It would be a porter or some other person working to clear the train. He was probably curious as to why she lingered instead of getting off the train.

"Yes," she said, eyes on the page. "I'm waiting for the station to clear a little before I disembark. There's no rush. I'll be off your train very soon."

The sound of a turning page filled the cabin, leather glove to printed paper, a deep quiet following her words. The man remained in the doorway, a dark figure at the corner of her vision, a temptation to take her gaze from the book.

"What if someone has come to collect you?"

"He won't mind waiting," she said.

Another page turned as she followed the findings of the botanist—the carefully tracked spread of a specific lichen over a year detailed in a graph. The book, a companion to another tucked into the case at her feet, was part of a larger collection. The whole of it had made the journey with her, going north and then east, arriving here with a sigh in the dark. Her trunk must be on the platform by now, waiting to be picked up—waiting like Astrid.

"He?"

"My husband. He'll be here any moment."

Astrid wanted the man to go away, and she refused to look up or make eye contact, not wanting to encourage him. Another slow-turning page, another paragraph. But she wasn't reading now. The sounds of the station receded—the platform forgotten. She watched the tall stranger out of the corner of her eye, breathless, refusing to look up and validate whatever thought he might have had about a young woman sitting alone on the train.

"Maybe he got tired of waiting for you."

There was an edge of laughter in his voice. With a sigh, she closed the book and set it aside. As she did, the man moved into the cabin, taking the seat opposite. It brought them closer, his knee brushing hers, and she made a small noise of irritation. Astrid looked up, ready to tell him to leave, and stopped.

A mask—a snarling silver animal—watched her.

CHAPTER TWO

The light moved over it in such a way that the metal looked alive, separate from the man who wore it. The black clothes and silver mask, came together, giving him an air of frost—a rival to winter beyond the glass.

But his eyes were a warm gold, a shade unlike any Astrid had ever seen. The expression in them sucked the breath from her lungs and sent a shiver racing across her skin. Compelling, everything about him pulled her in and scared her at the same time.

"Who are you?" she whispered.

The golden eyes slid away, going to the window; people passed, unaware of the pair in the cabin. She wondered how they could miss him, how he had gotten on the train without someone stopping him.

"Why are you wearing a mask?"

"Maybe I don't want to be recognized."

"It's a fierce mask to wear if you don't want to be recognized," she said, glancing at the open door, wondering if someone would hear a call for help. "You're very hard to miss."

He studied Astrid—up and down—lingering on her left hand before going back to the window. "I think you'll find the opposite is true."

"Will I? I don't know why I would. As I said, I'm waiting for my husband."

Those eyes, piercing and magnetic, pulled her gaze back. "Tell me about him. Maybe I saw him on the platform, and I can direct you."

There was an edge of humor in his voice, the accent, the inflection. He sat forward a little, watching closely. She wondered if he smiled behind the mask—if he was enjoying how uncomfortable he made her.

"I don't have to tell you."

"Does he live here? Maybe I know him."

"I think I should be going."

She stood in a rustle of skirts, shoving the book into the case, before retrieving her hat. With fingers that shook a little, and mostly from anger, she pinned it in place. The case at her feet was heavy but Astrid lifted it with both hands. She looked down at him, amazed at how big he seemed even with her standing.

"Enjoy your evening."

"You as well," he said, remaining seated, seemingly content to stay.

Panic settled in her bones and tension pulled her shoulders back, as a feeling of wrongness overtook Astrid. She walked quickly down the narrow hall, passing empty compartments, putting distance between herself and the man, pausing only at the exit of the train car to adjust her coat and scarf. A cold wind blew, driving a light snow, eddies of white whirling across the platform. Even with all the layers she wore, it crept in, making her shiver.

Astrid hoped that her husband would be the one waiting in the cold, not her. Tyhr. The name on the bottom of the letter had seemed so foreign—an ancient weight on her tongue. Eyes were on her—hot and searching. She turned and the man in the mask stood watching her from the door of the cabin they had shared for only a few minutes. An unreadable, impossible, expression in his golden eyes.

Turning away, she stepped from the train, taking in the platform, and scanning the small crowd. She had no idea what to expect and didn't even know what he looked like. But the area was emptying out—no one lingered and those left moved with purpose. She walked swiftly to the ticket office. Astrid hoped for warmth and wondered if maybe Tyhr would be there.

She pushed the door open, the wind coming in with her, swirling into the well-lit but empty building to rustle notices tacked to the walls and a forgotten newspaper before settling. The ticket windows were closed, the space behind the counters empty—the benches and chairs around the large room vacant. With a sigh, she set the case down. Astrid wondered where she might find someone to move her trunk and wondered where this so-called husband might be.

The doors opened behind her, the wind returning, snow following. She felt him there, the man in the mask, and unease stabbed through her. Astrid turned, determined to deal with him once and for all, fear becoming a tight ball of anger in her stomach.

"What do you want?" she asked.

In this larger space, in the stark electric light, she realized how tall he was with broad shoulders and long, black hair tied back at his neck. The fur coat he wore added bulk, everything black on black right down to his polished boots. But there was nothing extra on his frame. Everything about him spoke of strength and power.

"I didn't get a chance to introduce myself before," he said.

Yes, of course. Realization slammed into her, stomach falling as a wave of resignation swept through Astrid, leaving behind defeat.

"My name is Tyhr Valter." He gave her a small bow—such a formal gesture—watching her closely for a reaction. "It's my ring on your finger."

Her hand tingled, and Astrid removed her glove. A simple gold band, delicate traces of an engraved floral pattern that had been worn away over time. The metal had grown warmer as the train brought her north, carrying her closer to him. Expectation had radiated from it. An alive feeling, if objects could live—a magic vibration if magic were real.

"You sent no portrait or photograph with your letter. My father never told me what you looked like. He said I would know you when we met, that I would have no doubts."

"Was he right?"

"Yes."

He nodded and glanced around. "I will collect your luggage and bring it to the sleigh. Did you bring much else?"

Was she really going to do this? Follow this strange man into the night when she hadn't even seen his face? But where would she go otherwise? There was no one left—no money, no safety net, no family. Astrid was alone in the world. Alone except for him and a promise made by her father.

"Take off your mask," she said, taking a step forward and reaching out.

Tyhr caught Astrid's hand—stopping her—golden gaze searching her face. Her eyes narrowed with displeasure and curiosity. She wondered if he was malformed or disfigured beneath the silver face of the tiger.

"There are things you will learn in time. At this moment, I need you to understand that this is not something I can do for you," Tyhr said, voice low and soft.

"And you expect me to accept this and go with you?" Astrid asked, pulling her hand away.

"I do." He reached for her, wrapping a large hand around her upper arm. It was a firm grip but gentle, the touch electric, sending a shock wave through her. "You came to keep a promise. You've already made your decision."

"It was made for me years ago. And circumstances have enforced it. But you," Astrid said, pulling free, "will have to earn it."

Tyhr chuckled. Strangely, the mask didn't distort it with no echo or altered sound. "How many trunks? Bags? We shouldn't linger. If you go through that door there, you will see a sleigh pulled by a black horse. You can wait there."

"There's this," she held up the case with her books and a stash of seeds from the garden she had so carefully culti-vated for years. A small piece of home—almost weightless. "And an old trunk with dark wood and brass bands on the platform. My father's name is on it."

"Go and wait then. There is a foot warmer and furs. Or blankets if you prefer."

Tyhr left her without another word, the empty station

office ringing with the sound of his boots on the stone floor. Astrid gasped, feeling as if she'd run for miles, breathless and exhausted from their conversation—this first meeting.

The sleigh was where he'd said it would be. A dark wood polished to a high shine with touches of silver and covered in carvings—tigers leaping, sitting, flowing over the surface, caught in the light thrown by the outside lamps.

But the horse stopped her. It was huge, bigger than any she'd seen before, and looked and moved like a swirling cloud of coalesced smoke—as if shadows had gathered around an unseen heart. The horse stamped a front leg once, snow splattering up, and snorted at Astrid. It was as real as any other horse she'd seen, alive and breathing here in this city square before the train station while at the same time being beyond anything she'd ever imagined.

One dark eye rolled to study her, considering her as she considered this strange creature. Slowly she stepped forward, breath held, and pulled the glove from her left hand. The ring on her finger was a golden thread in the night, catching the light from the street lamps. The horse lowered its nose to her hand, the contact brief and slightly whiskery.

His ears came forward, listening intently. She could see the light shining through the edges of its form, where shadow met atmosphere and reality. Astrid reached out slowly, giving him a chance to understand her intention, and she ran a hand down his neck. A solid horse. A real horse. And yet, not fully realized, not really here.

"It's nice to meet you," she said. "My name is Astrid."

It snorted, accepting her greeting, and she hurried to get in the front row of the double-rowed sleigh, placing her case at her feet and tucking rich brown furs around her. The cold crept under her clothes and into her shoes. With a grateful sigh, she put her feet on the warmer Tyhr had brought for her.

Thick snow fell quickly now. Flakes caught in the lights, catching on her eyelashes, and settling on the sleigh. The small square had been swept and shoveled, but there were banks of snow collected at the edges, built high against the walls of the shops. Large windows reflected the station lights. The streets leading off the square were dotted with their own lights. Snow piled up everywhere—narrow side-walks had been carved out in others. Astrid looked up into the night—low clouds, small, cold flakes touching her hot cheeks.

She didn't have very long to wait before Tyhr was there with her trunk, carrying it easily, though she knew it was heavy—so heavy she hadn't been able to lift it by herself. The porter at the station where she'd boarded the train had used a cart. He'd grunted as it was loaded, shooting her a look of irritation.

Everything left to her in the world was inside that simple box—letters and books, more seeds. Her favorite dresses and small items—a pearl necklace that had belonged to her mother, the silver cuff links that had been a birthday gift to her father, a small flower enamel pin from her brother. At the very bottom was a portrait of the four of them, stiff and formal, taken when she was in her teens. A black and white world forever frozen in that instant so many years ago. A box of memories of a past life.

Tyhr placed it in the seat behind them, coming up around the side and getting in—sleigh dipping with his weight. He adjusted the cover on his lap, looking very much like a bear in all his furs.

"What kind of horse is this?" she asked, watching his golden eyes, wishing she could see his face.

"One that comes when called and vanishes when not needed."

"But is it magic? What kind of—"

"Are you ready?" he asked, picking up the reins.

If Astrid said no, if she got out, and decided to throw herself on the mercies of the world, what would happen?

The world was a harsh place.

"Yes," she said instead, and Astrid was surprised to discover she meant it, and accepted it.

Tyhr nodded, flicking the reins.

"Let's go home."

CHAPTER THREE

They traveled in a bubble of light. The glow thrown by an oil lantern attached to the front of the sleigh shivered, the edges of the circle trembling. The black horse moved swiftly, and soon Novgorod fell away—a blink and it was behind them. The trees came closer, curious and ready to watch their passage. The sled made a hushing sound as it moved across the snow, the crisp surface cracking and shifting as the horse pulled them forward.

Astrid was grateful for the warm furs and the light. Without either, it would have been a much colder ride—the darkness too complete with this stranger beside her. But the light from the lantern did not stretch to Tyhr. Somehow. He was outside of it, set apart. The mask—the animal face—remained shadowed.

Overhead, stars filled the sky as the snow stopped and the clouds faded away. A river flowed to her right, a way to navigate through the night, leading to a place Astrid had yet to discover. But then even it was gone, abandoning her to an unknown land. How long would it take to reach his home?

Her home.

She glanced behind them, expecting to see the last glimmering of city lights—golden halos—and hear the sounds of life being lived at a distance. Nothing but the dark forest greeted her. Huge trees crowed in—tall and thick—the only way through them the narrow track they followed. It stretched on in either direction, unblemished, as if they had been picked up and transported whole to this place.

"Where are we?" she asked, searching his eyes behind the mask, the color so similar to the glow of a fire.

"This is the Black Forest," he said, keeping his gaze forward, intent on the path they traveled. His tone made it clear, not any black forest, but *the* Black Forest.

She studied the trees, dressed in thick snow, huge drifts at their bases. A midnight-green and white world. But the Black Forest was not a real place. It was a myth. A fairy tale. The Black Forest was home to lurking monsters, villains from the stories, witches, and trolls. In the stories, it was a shadowy place full of danger. An ugly forest full of knots and twisted undergrowth, fallen trees, sinkholes, and traps. A place you saw once from a distance and understood these were not borders and boundaries to cross.

"You're joking," she said, watching trees glide by, the bubble of light unable to penetrate the darkness or push back the shadows. She turned to him, pinning him with a glare of defiance. "The Black Forest isn't a real place."

"How do you know?" he asked, eyes flashing to her face and away.

"It's a story." She paused, trying to unravel the expression she glimpsed in his gaze, the tone of his voice. Was that amusement? Or disappointment? "My mother used to read me stories about it from children's books."

"A place can be real and be a legend. They are not mutually exclusive ideas."

She shook her head, half ready to reply when a noise stopped her. A branch cracked, shocking the quiet surrounding them—the sound of snow sliding and hitting the forest floor boomed out, a physical striking force. The horse flicked its half-transparent ears forward and back as its pace slowed.

Tyhr clicked his tongue. "Come on, no stopping now."

Astrid tried to see beyond the first row of trees, searching for anything that could be skulking, anything that would make this place other than what he said it was.

"What was that?" she asked.

He shrugged without comment, and she glared, willing him to answer.

"There were no large forests on the maps I looked at before coming here," Astrid said, crossing her arms, gripping herself tightly. "We should still be able to see Novgorod behind us. It was only minutes away, a handful. If the Black Forest were an actual place, it would be on a map."

"This place isn't on any maps." He glanced at her, some emotion she could not name flashing in his eyes. "Don't worry. As long as you're with me, nothing can touch you."

"I'm not worried," she lied.

Something crashed in the forest, another branch breaking, more snow sliding. The horse's ears swiveled; his head whipped to the left. Astrid followed his gesture, searching for what he sensed, a slowly spreading dread taking over.

Above the tall trees, a shape moved against the stars, wading through the forest. A thin creature, straight-backed with long limbs, with a head covered in long matted hair. The darkness made it impossible to make out more detail— only a thin humanoid figure with its head turned away, searching the trees.

Giant.

Astrid stood in the sleigh, gripping the front and staring, mouth open. Tyhr clicked his tongue, urging the shadow horse forward. The animal began to trot faster, the hushing crunch of their passage almost drowned out by the snapping of broken branches as the giant moved through the forest in a parallel line.

"Tyhr," Astrid said, reaching for him, gripping Tyhr's arm.

"Yes," he said, taking her hand and pulling her back to the bench. "I see him. Sit down and be quiet."

She eased back, unable to look away from the colossal figure shambling through the forest, head and shoulders above the trees. It paused—stretched out and poised to catch something. She held her breath, heart hammering against her ribs, wondering what it might be looking for and why. It was so close—the trees were so tall, and it rose high above them all. If it turned, if its gaze shifted in their direction, it would see the sleigh racing down this narrow road.

"What is it?" she asked softly, unable to look away.

Tyhr made a shushing sound—so soft, barely there— and flicked the reins. The horse's shape shifted, edges blurring, as if at any moment it might dissipate like a cloud of smoke. He glanced up at the creature and away, something so strange and unusual already an accepted part of his world. Not new, not extraordinary, like it was to her.

Ahead and to the right, a branch cracked, the sound like a shot in the forest—sharp and hard. Astrid made a noise of surprise and slapped a hand to her mouth, the glove warm against her cold face—solid and real in the moment of unreality.

The giant stopped, turning with inhuman speed, and for the first time, Astrid saw the creature's eyes—pale, icy blue burning like fire. It saw them. She felt found—how clearly they had been caught—and bit her lip, not knowing what to expect but terrified to find out. It took a few steps closer to the road, peering over the treetops, tracking them as the sleigh continued forward.

Its face was still hard to see clearly—long and stretched out, humanoid like the rest of it, with a frigid fluorescent stare. It stopped to watch them pass. Astrid turned in her seat as the distance between them grew, unable to look away, watching it for as long as it would watch her. She froze that way for several heartbeats, then more, until the giant did not seem as large as it had been before.

Then it turned and began to move away in the opposite direction—branches snapping and breaking—leaving the jingle of the silver harness and her own panicked breathing behind.

"What was that?"

"Something that lives in the forest," he said.

"A giant?"

He didn't respond, possibly waiting for her to elaborate or perhaps not caring. She studied the mask, the set of his shoulders. There was nothing she could read, no hint at what might be going on inside his head—no tell, no give-away. Her gaze shifted to his gloved hands. He gripped the reins tightly. That was the only hint that he might have been as worried as she'd been. The horse's ears were back, listening to them or straining to catch some hint of the giant behind them.

"What else is in the Black Forest?"

"You said you'd heard stories?"

"Yes," she said, gesturing with her hands, trying to express how strange the world seemed now that something she'd believed true for so long was revealed as a lie. "When I was a child. I don't read fairy tales now."

"If you don't read fairy stories, what do you read? You had a book/"A lot about gardens usually. Plants. Biological studies. Nothing about giants with glowing blue eyes out in the middle of a forest. What else is out here?"

"I have some books you might be interested in then," he said, a hint of a smile in his voice.

"Stories about his place?"

"No, books about plants."

"I'm not talking about plant books. I'm talking about these woods."

He didn't respond, throwing her a glance, another she couldn't read.

She sighed. Tyhr was talking around her, ignoring the question she most wanted the answer to. In some of the stories her mother had shared—brightly bound tombs with rich illustrations—there had been an equal mix of good and evil, the fairytale world spilling carefully on a central point. There had been a balance.

But others had come from an in-between place, the characters rarely one thing or the other. A mix, a point of gray where black and white met, bleeding into one another. Nothing was predictable in those stories. Those were the stories where the hero died and the villain lived a long and fruitful life.

"What else is in these woods?" she asked again, for the last time.

"We are."

———

WOLVES HOWLED. ONE LONG MOURNFUL CALL TO ANOTHER—a third picking it up, a fourth carrying it on. Then a dozen or more sang to the night at once—a serenade to the moon and stars twinkling overhead, voices full of pleasure and recognition of their beauty. The howls began far away, at a distance, but they were growing closer, nearing, until the calls came from only feet away but out of sight.

"Will they attack us?" she asked, eyes wide in the dark, working to penetrate the night beneath the trees, searching for a shape that said *wolf*.

"Not if you're with me."

"And if I wasn't?"

"Don't leave the sleigh, and you'll be fine."

They continued on and overhead the sky moved—the earth turning beneath them. To Astrid it seemed as if they remained in place, traveling without moving forward as the hours passed. The night never receded, and the sun never rose. A land of endless darkness, populated by giants and wolves.

She had been on the train for a long time; awake as they passed through other stations and crossed borders. At the time she'd been unable to sleep, intent on watching as her destination approached. Now, Astrid wished she'd slept. It would have been better to be rested and alert in this place; with the wolves an arm's length away and giants wading through the trees.

Sleep touched her, gentle and caressing, soft fingers on her cheek. It promised many dreamless hours, deep peace, and true rest. Her eyelids drooped, closed, and she jerked up, blinking.

"Sleep," he said. "We've got a long way to go still. I'll wake you when we arrive."

I'm not tired," she said, adjusting her hat, the drape of the scarf around her neck.

But it was impossible to keep her eyes open, exhaustion catching up with her to demand its due. Even with danger threatening a few feet away, it was getting harder and harder to keep her eyes open.

"I won't let anything happen to you."

CHAPTER FOUR

The sleigh had stopped.

The cessation of movement pulled her up from the ocean of sleep; up from where she slumped against the wooden bench with the furs tucked tightly around her. She blinked, rubbing her eyes as she sat up to look around.

Astrid was alone.

The man in the mask and shadow horse were gone. There were no tracks in the snow around her. The night carried on, the same as it had been before—a ribbon of thick stars traveling across the sky. But the forest was not the same. An ice cliff rose behind her, taller than anything she had ever seen, stretching up to meet the sky. The surface was smooth as glass, and it reflected the night—not only the night, but the shadow of the sleigh, even her figure as she stood, looking around. But there seemed to be some glimmer of something farther in.

Astrid was in a circle made by the trees and ice, a solitary clearing. No footpath or road leading out of it, nothing that could have brought her here or taken her away. The bench behind her was empty, the trunk gone, and she searched the area at her feet only to discover the carrying case was missing as well.

"Hello?" she called, turning, wondering what had happened to her traveling companions.

Her voice carried, the word radiating out, bouncing off the ice and shooting out across the trees. Instead of muffling the sound, the forest took it up, a strange echo coming back to her.

Hello.

Snow slid off a nearby branch, thumping into a drift, branches rustling.

Astrid sat, digging into the blankets, searching for something she could use to defend herself. Nothing. Nothing but furs and damp wool. Softer sounds came from the trees—the big, dark old-growth woods, where the light failed to penetrate, where shadows stretched from forest floor to sky.

Had Tyhr abandoned her? Would he leave his wife? *No.* She didn't think so. Her father would never have left her mother unless it was necessary. But her parents had been unusual, without secret love affairs and groups of gossiping friends. Her father had had her mother; her mother had had her father. They were a matched set, complete only when together. So close, in fact, that when one had gone, the other had followed shortly thereafter.

The cliff was impassable—sheer and wide. There were no handholds that Astrid could see, no way that Tyhr could have taken her things up the face of it. Maybe he'd meant to be kind, to let her sleep while he moved her things to some unknown place, and he planned to return for her. But whatever small kindness Tyhr meant, it irritated her now. Below that, fear lurked, and Astrid refused to acknowledge it or give it space.

When he came back, she would make sure Tyhr knew this wasn't an acceptable way to treat a wife. And she would make sure he never left her alone in the forest again.

A dark shape moved to her right. She caught the movement out of the corner of her eye and spun to face it. A figure stood at the back of the sleigh—a black shadow of a child, barely tall enough to see over the curved back, watching her. The child's eyes glowed pale blue, a color similar to the giant, intense as fire.

If sleep had lingered at all it was gone now. A wash of icy fear slipped down Astrid's back, chasing away whatever heat and comfort sleep had given her. She was wide awake, still as stone. The child, the creature, watched her with curiosity—she could feel the interest, the thrill of discovery.

Astrid turned slowly, facing the figure, trying to scan the tree line without taking her eyes off it. But the child-size form moved with her, coming around the sleigh, gaze fixed on her face.

It was all shadow—a body made of solid smoke and darkness—eyes glowing blue embers in an indistinct face. Its pace was smooth, and it moved without breaking the crust on the snow. Not a child, or even child shaped, as she'd first thought. It had made itself small at first, to get closer, to watch her. Now the shape grew as it came toward her.

Astrid stepped to the opposite side of the sleigh, wondering how far she might make it into the trees before it caught her. The Black Forest. It was full of wolves and giants, full of things without names, full of creatures like this one coming for her.

Don't leave the sleigh, and you'll be fine.

But Tyhr also said she would be safe with him. Where was he now?

The creature grew—long-limbed and thin-bodied—a swirling, shifting wave of long hair waving around its head. No clothes, nothing but a black, shapeless body, lacking definition and detail. It was taller than her now, and in another step, it was taller than Tyhr. With the next step, it towered over Astrid, coming to stand directly before her, so close she could have reached out, and poked a finger into the darkness to discover how real and solid it might be.

It stared at her with unreadable eyes.

The creature leaned forward, over her, and she had to tilt her head back to maintain eye contact. It put its hands on its knees, easing into a crouch, coming closer without touching her or the sleigh.

Astrid swallowed, unable to think, helpless beneath the stare.

"What do you want?" she whispered.

It lifted one hand, reaching out slowly to touch her face.

A cracking sound, ear-splitting and deafening, broke the moment, cutting it short. Astrid covered her ears, blocking out some of the noise. The creature turned to the cliff, shrinking as it moved, pulling away from Astrid. The ice split, breaking in a jagged line, a fissure opening at the top and racing down, distance growing between the two sections. It grew second by second and the world throbbed with the sound of splintering ice.

The shadow slunk away, shrinking as it retreated, much smaller now than when she'd first seen it. It hurried into the trees, disappearing beneath the branches, turning only once to look back. She caught a flash of blue eyes as it moved deeper into the forest and away from the cliff.

The earth continued to shake, ice cracking, a low rumble Astrid felt in her molars and stomach. Chunks of ice fell, crashing at the base of the cliff, breaking into smaller pieces and shattering. Out of the widening crevice came Tyhr, walking calmly, as if nothing could touch him.

"Where were you?" she asked, fear putting an edge in her voice, anger biting through her words. "You left me!"

"You were sleeping," he said, coming up to the sleigh, holding out a hand to help her down. "You've had a long journey. I had to return the horse, and you had still not woken up. I let you sleep."

"But—" She stammered, glancing at the forest, searching for a pair of blue eyes. "There was a creature. A child, but it wasn't, it grew, it looked like the giant we saw before. It reached out to me."

"Did you let it touch you?"

"What? No. Let it? Would I have had a choice?"

"Desire is a powerful thing. If you had wanted it badly enough, if you had been firm in your *no*, it would not have been able to touch you. Words have power here. Emotions, wants, desires, wishes, those things are only powerful once spoken aloud. But it doesn't matter. It would not have touched you unless you'd left the safety of the sleigh."

"Maybe if you hadn't left me alone, I wouldn't have had to deal with this at all." Her tone was sharp, irritation and fear mixing, overriding whatever wonder or curiosity there might have been in watching an ice cliff split or a creature made of shadow.

"Well," he said, holding out a hand, waiting for her to take it, "I'm here now."

CHAPTER FIVE

I ce tumbled from the cliff, a pitter-patter of small pieces hitting the snow, larger shards disappearing beneath the surface with a thump. Astrid flinched back, but Tyhr remained motionless as the crevice widened further. The hair on the back of her neck rose when the cliff shuddered to a halt, an open mouth before her, a hungry tongue of a path waiting to taste their feet.

"What is this?" she asked.

"The way forward." Tyhr squeezed her hand, a comforting gesture that she found herself returning.

"And then?"

"Home."

She looked down at his hand—how solid and warm he was, the strangeness of it all—and followed him into the ice. The way was too narrow for them to walk side by side and the ice continued to shiver around them.

"What about the sleigh?" she glanced back at it sitting in the clearing under a full moon. As strange as the ride had been, it was the only familiar landmark in her life at the moment. "Aren't you worried about it?"

"It will be there if we need it."

"Won't someone disturb it?"

"No, that won't be an issue."

"And the horse?"

"So many questions," he said, an edge of what might have been amusement in his tone.

"And no answers."

He glanced back at her, golden eyes flashing, but remained silent. With no response, she turned her attention to the ice. It was old—deep blue and green—water frozen for centuries, from another world. Lights moved deep within the ice—a full spectrum aurora curling and flashing. The walls leaned toward each other, narrowing as they walked on, the sounds of their steps bouncing back, the sharp gasp she let out amplified.

A shadow within the ice moved, twisting through the solid form. Astrid reached out, placing her palm to the surface, cold instantly shooting through her, engulfing her. The surface vibrated beneath her hand. Other creatures moved, more figures, indistinct blobs of color and shape within the glacier. The creature closest to her, only yards away in the ice, shifted a few millimeters. She gasped, leaning forward, stunned by the impossibility.

They were alive.

"Don't," Tyhr said, taking her hand from the ice. His voice held a warning, the faint shadow of concern.

"What are they?"

"I don't know." He watched the form within the ice, but it didn't move again. "I don't want to find out."

"You aren't curious? Or worried?" She waved a hand around them, at the split in the ice he'd created. "You come and go, aren't you worried this will wake them up? Or release them?"

"It hasn't in the past. But I've never touched the wall or called them to me. I don't tempt fate."

"I didn't call them," she protested. But the ice had trembled when she'd placed her palm against it, the light flickering like a heartbeat. Whatever was there had reacted to her. "How do you know something hasn't already escaped?"

"I've used this way for years. That's the first time I've ever seen them move."

"How many years?"

Astrid narrowed her eyes, searching for a giveaway, something in the way he held his shoulders or how he stood that would betray his thoughts. She felt blinded by the mask, his features hidden, expression invisible. But she needed information—was desperate for it. The need to piece this story together—how she'd crossed a continent to marry a mysterious stranger in a mask and the obvious magic surrounding it all—was all-consuming.

"Come on," he said, keeping her hand, pulling her gently forward. "We need to get to the door before the ice closes."

———

ASTRID WATCHED HIM, STEALING GLANCES WHEN SHE THOUGHT Tyhr might not notice, taking in every detail of his clothes and hair that was visible in the strange light surrounding them. The mask. A tiger. She returned to that again and again—smooth lines and snarling mouth. The voice that reached her, coming from inside and spreading out, was deep and firm, the accent softening the edges.

It had only been a few hours. From the train station to here. In that time, he'd changed Astrid's entire world. The clear lines of her life, the way things had gone and the way she had assumed they would continue to go, had vanished. A vast expanse of possibility lay ahead. Anything was possible. Here, in this place, he had proved the impossible things in the stories were real.

"How did you meet my father?" she asked.

"I'll tell you over dinner sometime," he glanced back at her. "Now is not the time to talk or linger."

The ice walls loomed around them, jagged, vibrating with the possibility of snapping shut like a jaw—sharp teeth closing. The backlit figures in the ice were gone. Only the stars above remained, unchanged, so near she might have pulled them one by one from the sky.

Underfoot, the path began to zigzag. New were sections revealed while concealing where they had been. They moved slowly—the incline so slight that she hadn't noticed it before. But now Astrid could feel the upward tilt of the rock beneath her feet. A sharp cry stopped her, an inhuman sound that echoed down the crevice, bouncing on the ice before crashing into her.

"What was that?"

"Come on," he said, walking quickly, dragging her along.

Astrid went, watching the path behind them, looking back until she stumbled. The darkness behind them seemed to be rising slowly, moving with them, keeping pace.

"It's ahead," he said.

"What is?"

"The door."

The cry came again, closer now, the tones of it different, altered.

"Is it like the thing by the sleigh?"

They turned a sharp corner, then another, the lights in the ice receding.

"Everything here is alike and unalike," Tyhr said, voice soft.

"What does it want? The thing at the sleigh wanted something from me."

Tyhr's silver face flashed in the dark, eyes curious. "What did it want?"

His voice was so soft—almost not there.

She opened her mouth but paused. What had it wanted? Could she say for sure now that it had meant her harm? Would it have taken blood or bone or sight or flesh from her? It might have wanted a kind word or a moment of time. It could have wanted anything in the whole world.

The cry came again.

A hungry cry.

Tyhr stopped, and Astrid crashed into him. "What?"

But then she saw it, an opening in the ice, a clear area, and a sheer wall of rock. Ice clung to it, the two coming together in a glittering swirl—a geode of frost crystals and solid stone. In the wall was a tunnel, a perfect oval mouth waiting to swallow them whole.

"Give me your hand," he said, taking a folding knife from his coat. Tyhr grasped her fingers, pulling Astrid toward him even as she leaned back and away.

"What're you doing?"

Her voice was sharp with fear. The creature behind them called again, mimicking her cry.

"A little blood. A price. One you must pay to pass."

Astrid struggled to break his iron grip, but Tyhr held firm. It was like fighting the rock wall—immovable and solid. Astrid twisting, the high pitch of her voice, the

pleading that didn't even sound like her—none of it
stopped him.

The blade flashed, silver steel, catching the stars and
the faint glow of the moon; it caught her gaze, and she
watched, transfixed, as it was drawn across the palm of her
left hand. A sting. A line of warmth, her breath coming in
and out in sharp gasps. Blood—black in the moonlight—
followed the blade.

"It's not very much," she said, chest tight, searching the
tiger's face and hoping for a human reaction.

"No."

His eyes flicked up to her face and away, to a point
beyond her shoulder. He dragged her toward the opening in
the rock, the mouth yawning wide, and smeared her palm
against the stone. Her palm tingled against the smooth
surface. When he dropped her hand, the rock was spotless.
It had soaked up her blood, the offering, drinking it as if it
were life.

"It's done," he said with a nod.

Astrid looked down at her palm. No blood. No cut.
Nothing but a faint line across her palm. Behind them, the
glacier rumbled as the ice ground together, the stone
around them vibrating. The cry came again, racing toward
them from the crevice, out of sight but not far behind.

With a deafening crash, the glacier moved, the walls
slamming together, falling into each other and sealing shut
with a shudder. She jumped back as ice exploded outward,
a piece striking her cheek, pain stinging across her senses.

"This way," Tyhr said, pulling her into the tunnel, dragging her away from the crashing wall of ice sliding toward
them.

Astrid clung to him, gripping his arm tight, and
followed him into the dark.

CHAPTER SIX

Moonlight softer than daylight hit Astrid's face, but still, she had to shade her eyes after the complete nothingness of the tunnel. The darkness had lasted an instant—the cold replaced with warmth, and the green scent of growing things—muggy heat, insect conversations ceasing with the sudden arrival of Astrid and Tyhr.

Hello.

Who are you?

Where did you come from?

The insects picked up their abandoned songs. She shivered, looking around, wanting to pull the moon down from the sky and hold it like a lover—a companion to keep away the night. Between the glacier and jungle there had been a darkness so complete, she'd thought there would never be light again. As her skin warmed and the chill faded, she tried to come to terms with the sudden change in their surroundings.

"Where are we?"

"The opposite side of paradise."

They stood on a rocky outcropping overlooking a deep valley filled with trees and the sound of water—everything a rich, velvety green in the moonlight. A world of tropical plants, not the species she would have expected to find so far from the equator, surrounded her. The jungle swayed in the warm breeze, the trees reaching gleefully for the sky— huge trunks shoulder to shoulder, smooth bark gray in the light. It reminded her of the glacier—different material but still an impassable wall.

"What happened to the door?"

"It's gone."

"How does it open?"

"Are you wanting to leave already?"

Something inside said *yes*. She tried to squash it, to hide the flare of emotion before it crossed her face. "No. But I would like to know. Does it take more blood?"

"No." He shook his head, stepping around her to touch a tree. She watched, expecting to see something, for the plants to shift and change. But his hand sank into the tree as if it were a mirage.

"How?" she asked, starting forward, reaching out for the spot. Cold shocked her, the cold from the Black Forest and the glacier.

"You just step through," he said, looking down at her, studying her face. "It will remember you."

"It?"

"This place," he stepped away from her, gesturing to the trees, "this door."

"It's a door?"

"That's the best way to describe it."

Astrid nodded, pulling back, and crossed her arms over her chest. The cold had gotten under her skin—the threat of it there, unseen but waiting. She didn't want to go back to that endless night. Instead, she turned to the jungle, going back to the overlook, and wondering what the muggy heat might be hiding.

The valley stretched out before them, narrow and deep, the floor hidden by trees, the sides rising to rocky peaks. The edges of dawn touched the east mountains, the sky beginning to glow, starting the slow business of pushing out the night. High in the sky, the moon had begun fading, ready to step back for daylight hours.

"Is it the same moon?" she asked, surprised she'd spoken aloud, unable to pull her eyes from the full glow.

"I've never seen more than one moon anywhere I've gone."

"That's not the same thing as saying yes," she sighed.

He shrugged, watching her as she took in this new place.

The jungle swayed around them as a fresh breeze passed, branches creaking—the air filled with the rustle of a million leaves. She turned gratefully into it and let it push wisps of hair out of her face. Astrid's hair had slipped out of the proper bun and her hat had vanished. When had she lost it? Moving from one world to the next? She thought about her traveling case then, the few things left to her in the world. It felt silly to long for things—for items that were just objects and nothing more.

But Astrid would have given anything to hold the last book her father gave her, the last dress her mother had said made her eyes sparkle.

"Where do we go from here?" she asked.

"There."

His arm came into her line of sight, finger pointing to another outcropping directly opposite. A house, indistinct and blurry, with one lighted window, overlooked the valley.

It sat perched on the rock, built directly into the stone, and clinging to the cliff. The house seemed to be part of it, coming out of it and formed by it—natural and unnatural all at once.

"Home?"

Wistfulness touched her voice—longing for familiar faces, the sound of their laughter, the beat of their hearts. This place might be called home, but it wouldn't *be* home. Maybe it would in time. If she gave it the chance. If she said it out loud enough times, maybe it would become true.

"There's a path along the rim of the valley," Tyhr said, extending an arm to the left. "It's a shorter way than going down into the valley and back up. We've got more walking to do."

————

DAY HOVERED, POISED TO SPILL INTO THE VALLEY, BREATHLESSLY waiting for them to reach their destination before cresting the rise and spreading out. She wished it would come. After walking in the half-light, having spent all that time in the Black Forest, she wanted nothing more than harsh daylight.

Tension radiated from Tyhr. He moved quickly ahead, several paces faster, and Astrid tried to keep pace—urgency nipping at her heels. They walked in a tunnel of trees, a narrow path worn smooth, and to the right, the ground dropped down, brush and trees clinging to the steep incline. It was still full night here, shadowed and concealed beneath the canopy. The air, which had seemed so warm at first, was cool in the pre-dawn hour.

"The house is there," Tyhr said, pausing on the path and gesturing for her to go ahead of him. "Just ahead."

Astrid moved past him, giving him a questioning

glance, and continued on the path. It narrowed further and then disappeared beneath her feet, leaving her facing a wall of vines and bushes. She pushed through it, a thorn catching her cheek and digging in, and she stumbled forward. Smooth flat stones caught her, dirt giving way to a formal terrace, the small square on the verge of daylight.

The house rose over her—white stone, several stories high, with wide shallow steps leading up to a pair of huge green doors. Lanterns glowed on either side, throwing circles of warm light. The doors were open in invitation, and she half expected someone to rush out to greet them— to say her name in recognition and pleasure.

But no one came. The house sat silent.

"Go in," Tyhr said from behind her, gesturing at the lacquered door, the deep carvings of the animals covering it. "Chinook will meet you and take you to your room."

Astrid hesitated, studying the masked face and glancing back to the house, the almost palace. It looked warm and inviting, despite the lack of greeting. It called to her, a comfortable place at the end of a long journey—offering rest after crossing continents and worlds to stand beside this man.

"You're not coming with me?" she asked. Something in her twisted—disappointment, disbelief. Had she come all this way for him to leave her at the front door?

"Not yet," Tyhr said.

He glanced away, to the east where the sky was more than gray, going yellow and orange, only the brightest stars remaining overhead. Surprise touched her; after so little conversation and his ring on her finger, she wondered why he'd leave now. She had questions. She needed answers. It was hard to believe Tyhr wouldn't have questions of his own. Didn't he want to know her?

"I thought," she said, moving to stand in front of him, meeting his gaze, "you would want to spend time getting to know me."

Tyhr looked down at her, going over her face, searching for something she could not name.

"I do. I will. Tonight."

He turned away, taking a step back into the jungle.

"Why didn't you write to me?" she asked suddenly, blurting out the question that had bothered her for years, that had become an unscratchable itch as they went from winter forest to humid jungle.

"I did."

"Once." She held up a finger, accusation in every line of her body—vibrating with it.

"It wasn't enough?"

She shook her head, pressure building behind her eyes, heat touching her cheeks. It had all been too much. She wanted comfort. She wanted things she couldn't put a name to. She wanted to be held while she cried and mourned—needed this man to keep his side of the promise made so many years ago.

"Come inside with me," she whispered.

"I can't," he said, voice low to match her tone.

"If you can't come inside with me right now," she hesitated, chest tight, uncertain and hating the way Tyhr's rejection made her feel. "Don't bother spending time with me later."

Tyhr turned without a word and slipped back into the jungle. Gone. In an instant. The trees and underbrush swallowed him whole, leaving her speechless as her heart hammered.

"Tyhr?"

The jungle was silent.

Blowing out a sigh, Astrid turned to face the house, blinking fierce tears away.

Sunlight hit the house—caressing moss-covered tiles, picking out imperfections, and highlighting decay. The pale stone was pocked with age, older and more worn than it had first appeared in the forgiving night. Intricate stone lattices covered the windows and balconies, a riot of carved flowers and geometric patterns. There were ferns growing between stones. A small yellow lizard skittered into a suddenly sunny location.

An old house, living in the jungle, surviving this strange place.

Astrid went up the steps one at a time—an unexpected heaviness in her heart. She paused when she saw the arched doors and their carvings. They were covered in tigers. Tigers leaping and snarling, some sitting with their backs to the viewer, others turned toward the jungle with an air of watchfulness. Astrid touched one, tracing the line of its back, feeling the roughened texture of stripes.

A light inside the house snapped on, falling across the steps, beckoning for her to enter.

———

ASTRID STEPPED INTO A LARGE HALL WITH PALE MARBLE FLOORS, her steps echoing through the space. She paused beyond the threshold, transfixed by the opulence. Overhead, a mosaic followed the curve of the ceiling—colors bright with streaks of silver and gold, the glint of copper here and there. The heavens, night and day meeting, the sun and moon at opposite ends, unknown constellations strung like jewels between them.

Delicate tables hugged the walls, displaying tall vases

and alabaster figures, with shallow dishes filled with colorful fruits and flowers. Between the tables sat large painted pots holding small trees and flowering bushes. The jungle hadn't stopped at the door, even here it was creeping in—contained in small pots and obviously a welcome guest.

She crossed to the nearest table to touch a flower, caressing the delicate white petals. A Eucharist lily, with glossy green leaves, common in South America. Not here, not in the far reaches of the European continent.

There were other flowers, varieties she had never seen in person—only flat and illustrated on a page. A bergamot tree pruned and bearing bumpy fruit. A squat container with a large gardenia, and beside it, a fuchsia and a bleeding heart. On another table sat an alpine snowbell and a red elderberry, and on the floor beside the table sat a pot of heather—scrubby and gray green with purple spikes of flowers. All of them blooming together, out of season, and filling the space with life.

A rustle of movement caught her attention, and she looked up. On the carved arch over an entryway to a room filled with low silk couches and chairs sat a small bird. Small and glossy black, with a flash of white on the wings, bright eyes staring back at her—intelligent and sharp. Astrid had the distinct impression he was considering her place in this house.

"Hello," she said.

She smiled to herself, a little surprised by her desperation for contact. Here she was, talking to a bird.

Good morning.

The words arrived in her head, there and as solid as if they had come through her ears. She stepped back, startled and eyes wide, bumping into a table. The pot trembled, flowers jumping, releasing a sweet green scent.

Do not look so surprised.

The bird dropped to the table and hopped closer, inspecting her—small head going side to side.

You cannot expect a normal house at the end of such an adventure.

"I'm not surprised." She shook her head, steadying the pot. "I don't think there's anything that could surprise me now."

The bird made a noise of derision. *We will see.*

"Who are you?"

Chinook.

"Tyhr said you would be here. It's a pleasure to meet you." How did you greet a bird? Shaking hands was out of the question. Nod? Curtsey? When was the last time she'd dropped a curtsey? Childhood. In some awful formal drawing room. She shuddered at the memory. "I hope that we'll be friends."

I am sure we will be seeing a lot of each other. There really is not anyone else around.

"Oh? I thought such a large house would be full of people."

The house is full. But there is little chance for conversation.

"No?"

The bird looked at her, and she struggled to read his body language, the unspoken thing he was conveying. *How much has he explained?*

Tyhr.

"Nothing."

The bird tilted his head and gave her a quick blink.

Come with me. I will show you to your side of the house.

"Side? I'll have a whole side of the house to myself?"

Would you rather have the whole house? Chinook asked tartly.

"No, it's not that." Astrid looked down at her ring and continued carefully. "I thought maybe I would be closer to Tyhr."

Without hesitation, he'd walked away, giving her nothing, leaving her with nothing. His reaction—the feeling of disinterest after everything—stung. Her cheeks burned at the thought of him turning his back on her.

What she didn't say was that part of her had expected their marriage to be official, to be consummated. This limbo made her anxious, knotting in her stomach, a ball of sadness that was quickly becoming anger. But still, she craved certainty. Instead, she found herself in the odd state of a continued engagement with no real idea of when she might no longer be a fiancée but a wife. Not one on a page and by proxy, but a promise sealed and delivered on.

The wide golden band on her finger, etched with flowers that were nearly worn away with age, hints of vines, a delicate petal. She watched the way light moved over the surface, caught in the smoothness. It fit her finger as if made for her, passed down through generations until, discovering her, this object had found its home. Maybe there had been a past life—a flash of fresh etchings, fresh flowers, but here and now, it belonged wholly to her, destiny clinging firmly.

In a hurry?

"What?" She looked up, startled out of her thoughts, blushing. "No, I'm not in a hurry."

You have plenty of time. You do not even know him.

"It's not that," she said, voice soft as she twisted the ring on her finger. "I thought Tyhr would be different. I thought he'd be here. I thought he would want something different."

Perhaps you should give him some time.

She nodded, grateful for the time to herself, for the understanding. It had never occurred to her that he might feel as she did—that they needed time to know more about each other beyond names. But that wasn't all Astrid knew. Tyhr wore a mask he refused to remove and lived in a house beyond the world, through the Black Forest populated with monsters, and opposite paradise.

And he lived with a talking bird.

"You said you'd show me to my room?"

CHAPTER SEVEN

Past large rooms, tall ceilings and walls covered in murals of the world beyond the windows, comfortable looking sofas and chairs, fireplaces with potted plants on the mantles. No artwork, no portraits. A beautiful house without a face in it, full of a cultivated jungle. Chinook led the way, moving from table to stair, up to a railing, waiting and watching as Astrid followed. Chinook led her up two flights of wide marble stairs. Her boots rang out against the marble as she followed, the sound hard and clipped.

The hall at the top of the stairs was completely dark, and she paused, looking around. "Is there no light?"

Not here. Your room is all the way down on the right.

"And the other way?"

"Tyhr's rooms."

Light from the stairway lit the way a little but there were no windows or lamps, only the gray light coming up from below. Thick carpets covered the hall, the colors dark and swirling, the pattern indistinct. Chinook was invisible, the sound of his wings the only thing letting her know that he was with her. Astrid followed the sounds he made, listening to him pause, the quiet seconds as he rested, and then the rushing sound as he took off again and moved farther along.

Here, he said.

His voice in the dark, in her head, startled her, and she nodded, feeling silly when she realized he couldn't see her. She held out her hands, tentative, searching for the door, grasping in the dark. Then she felt the frame, a carved door, and gripped the smooth metal knob. It opened onto bright sunshine and a light-filled room—mirrors reflected sunshine, doubled it.

Chinook flew in ahead of her, sweeping around the room, coming to a stop on her worn trunk. The leather traveling case sat beside it, both looking shabby in the glinting space. It was a relief to see them, and a part of her relaxed, releasing tension she hadn't realized she'd been holding until now.

"How did those get here?"

Magic.

"That's not a real answer."

Magic. As if it were real. As if all the stories from books were fact and not inventive fiction. But what else could this be? A journey full of trials, a man in a mask, and now a bird who spoke only in her mind. She'd been practical and accepting all of her life, raised to trust her own eyes and instincts, to believe what her gut told her was true.

And this? There was no doubt that magic lived in this place.

"Still," she said aloud. "Magic is not a real answer."

But of course, it was.

Chinook ruffled his feathers, the movement better than a shrug and just as clear.

"Fine," she said, turning her attention to the room.

The room was part bedroom and part sitting room, the area divided by a carved wooden arch—tigers leaping at the corners, birds perched at the apex. Two low sofas, pale gold with soft rose-colored pillows, faced each other and filled the space. Between them sat a table with a bowl of flowers. There were more tables at the edges of the room holding other kinds of plants—more flowers and sweet scents. A perfumed and beautiful space, the rooms of a princess. The kind her mother had sworn she had never been.

Astrid smiled to herself as she took in the murals on the walls—more jungle here. But no faces, no animals. Only a tangled mass of vines and trees, flowers and leaves curled into pleasing shapes.

Opposite the door was an enclosed balcony—door open, a soft breeze blowing through the sheer curtains. She crossed the room, stepping out onto the narrow space to peer through the carved lattice. Shadows crisscrossed her arms, sunlight heating a pattern into her skin, the bright day unreal after the night. The balcony stretched in either direction, following the curve of the house to the left and leading to another door on the right.

Turning her attention back to her rooms, she went to inspect the bedroom. More soft colors, blues in varying shades, more gold, and splashes of pink. It made her think of dawn, the colors melting into each other, becoming something more together.

The large bed with pillows mounded together was perched on a dais beneath a silk canopy. A warm brown wardrobe stood against one wall, and more plants bloomed in shades to match the room. A dressing table with a small seat was on another wall, a trifold mirror tripling the space, catching the silver brushes and a bowl of fruit on its surface.

Astrid moved to another door leading out of the bedroom, curious about how far her suite of rooms stretched. The next room was a washroom filled with white porcelain and plumbing. She hadn't expected to find this here—a bathtub and sink, a water closet, and a small cart full of soaps and oils. A bathtub. And warm water. Astrid shivered with delight.

Shutting the door, she turned back to the sitting room, going past Chinook and through another carved arch. A small office, a desk and chair, bookshelves, and a window looking out over the front door and stone terrace. Thick carpets beneath her feet, sunrise and bright days, a place to sit and write letters, a chair beside the bookshelves to read. There was paper and pens on the desk and a gold ticking clock.

The space reminded her a little of her mother's morning room—where she had written letters at a small desk and entertained close friends. A private space—her own space in a busy house. Even though the colors were different, the feeling was the same.

Turning, she walked back through the rooms, over-whelmed, stunned, and trying to take it all in. Astrid sat on the bed, looking at it all, staring. Everything was light and soft—the colors, the room, the feeling of the whole place. These rooms felt like a retreat, a place to gather her thoughts and restore her peace.

Tyhr had gone to a lot of trouble for her, to give her this space. Its beauty didn't feel accidental. Thoughtful atten-tion to detail—the way the curtains moved in the breeze; the way light reflected off the curved, painted surfaces of the pots. Even the plants themselves, delicate and fragile, unusual specimens each one.

Chinook watched her from the sitting area, quiet and alert, taking in each reaction. She smiled at him, hoping he would share, tell Tyhr how pleased she was with it all. It was more than she had expected, more than she could have hoped for.

Lunch will arrive later when you have had time to refresh yourself. The house is yours. When you are ready, I will complete your tour. Unless you would like to continue now?

"Some time to get settled will be lovely, thank you. I would like a tour, but that can wait."

He nodded and added, *Dinner at nine.*

"And Tyhr?"

He will be there.

Another small part of her unwound, soothed. Chinook blinked, an impossible bird expression she couldn't read, and made to take off and leave her alone.

"Wait," Astrid held up a hand, wondering how she should phrase her question. "Chinook, what kind of bird are you? Are you real? Or?"

Dark glossy eyes fixed on her as he sat motionless.

"I'm sorry," she said, waving a hand. "That was rude. I've never seen a bird that looked like you. That spoke."

Chinook flew to the dressing table, landing among the silver brushes and crystal bottles, knocking one over, gripping it with tiny, black-clawed feet. He turned, looking at himself in the mirror, head to one side. He opened his wings, flashing the band of white feathers, watching the reflection thoughtfully.

I never thought about it.

"Have you always been a bird?" she pressed, wondering

again how he was speaking to her, how his conversation seemed so human.

A white-shouldered tanager.

"A what?"

She could recite the Latin names of plants for hours—could see a specimen and recognize it at once. But when it came to animals, she had no idea.

A bird, he said, tone sour, leaving her room in a rush of feathers.

A bird. Just as Tyhr was nothing more than a man.

Astrid went to the dressing table and righted the bottle, straightening the brushes, and tracing the pattern of vines on the handle. She sat with her back to the mirror, looking at the room, not bothering to shut the open door.

Home.

You have my deepest condolences.

Come to Siberia.

I'll be waiting.

Tyhr.

Three sentences and a name, that was all he'd given her. Astrid had read and reread the letter, wondering if something else might appear, holding it up to the light, hoping to expose some hidden message. The envelope had included money—enough to ransom a prince and train tickets, one for each stage of the journey from Sweden to Russia, but nothing else.

The ring on her finger had grown hot, burning when she'd opened the envelope, and she'd taken it off, staring as if seeing it anew. How could she have worn it all this time and forgotten it was there? But she had. All her life—since it had fit her finger, it had always been there.

A part of Astrid.

A token from him.

They had all gone by that point. Her family. One right after the other, leaving the rented house empty, the company in tatters. Her father's business partner told her how sorry he was but that he'd be moving back to England. It had been a mistake to bring Porter and Stern to the Netherlands.

There was no money there for them.

There had been no life either.

Her mother had been the catalyst for it all. Without her, it hadn't taken very long for her father and brother to fall apart. Astrid hadn't even been surprised. First cancer had taken her mother and the doctor had been unable to pinpoint her father's illness. Simply a broken heart. Antony had gone out gambling, gotten drunk, and fallen into the river. Officially he'd drowned. But he'd been halfway gone with grief for a long time already.

She'd been left alone—logical and refusing to let emotion get the better of her—to put what was left of her life into some kind of order.

Then a letter arrived as the furniture was being taken away. The books in her father's library. The painted dresser from her room. All the things that had been theirs. It still wasn't enough to cover the debt. But the envelope, thick with tickets, with her name written in bold black ink, had saved her.

Astrid traced the letters. *Come to Siberia.*

So, she had come, crossing continents, traveling to meet the man her father had promised her to. A marriage sealed in infancy. But how it had come to be—this tradition and classically arranged marriage was a mystery. Her father had never been clear on the details, only that it was a promise meant to be kept—imperative and unbreakable.

All her life, from the first moment in the morning to the

last in the evening, Astrid had wanted to make her father proud. Even as the idea of marrying a stranger chaffed, worrying at her, resentment knotting beneath her breast-bone, she would not go against him. They'd talked about it, talked circles around each other, and each time it had come down to one thing.

A promise.

There was nothing to go back to. No extended family and only strangers who might remember her in passing. They would tell her how familiar she looked but would never be able to recall her name.

Thunder boomed across the sky, rumbling through the house.

The candles she had lit shivered, the flames flickering. Astrid looked up, startled, surprised to see how dark the room had become. A half-eaten sandwich sat on the table, fruit and tea still on the tray, a glass of water and sugar-dusted cookies, all forgotten. The trunk sat open, contents spread across the bedroom, some of the books in the sitting room, one already on the desk in the office. She had been looking for something, anything, to keep her occupied and had come across the book she'd had on the train. And the letter.

Lunch had arrived when her back was turned. One moment the low table in the sitting area had been empty, and the next, the tray had been waiting. More magic. She had moved from one side of the bedroom to the other, the table in the sitting room out of sight for only minutes, yet the tray was there.

It tasted fine. It tasted like food. But her stomach was twisted, and Astrid hadn't eaten much. The blue morning had fled, driven away by dark clouds moving low over the valley. The air tasted of rain, the scent filling her rooms, but everything remained dry. Booming thunder, a flash of lightning across the sky. But no rain. It filled Astrid with expectation, an itchy sensation crawling across her skin, and she wanted the sky to crack open and let it all go.

Setting the letter down, she got up from the sofa, and crossed to the balcony, checking the sky again. The clock in the office chimed—a musical note—a little bell that would drive her mad if she didn't figure out how to turn it off soon. But it told her that it was four in the afternoon, despite the grim sky and dark clouds.

Astrid had time before dinner to do whatever she wanted, to explore the house or sit and read. She could find Chinook and ask questions. She could find the kitchen and eat cake. The whole house belonged to her.

CHAPTER EIGHT

The door directly across from her own opened into a darkened room—a wall of bookshelves with gold-embossed spines, a desk, and a chair. Like the ones in her rooms, the walls were covered in a pattern of flowers and vines, but here the colors were shades of evergreen with pops of plum and magenta. A small sofa, the color of the flowers, faced a pair of chairs with a low table between them. It felt like walking into a small clearing in the deep woods, everything seen through the filter of green shade.

There was a window on the far wall, its curtains pulled back, but its shutters closed. She crossed to it, wondering what the view might be on this side of the house. It faced the jungle here, the wall of green that seemed on the verge of overtaking the house. The carving on the wooden shutters was smooth, with more plants and animals—a leaping gazelle, and a fruit tree. She tugged on them, the hinges stiff, creaking as they opened wide.

Jungle.

A wind blew in, touching Astrid's face, and tugging her

hair. It brought the richness of the life outside, beyond the stone windowsill, beyond the wall of vegetation. Trees grew right up next to the house, within reach, several vines bridging the distance and attaching to the stonework.

Astrid leaned out through the window, no glass, nothing but the solid shutters she had opened, and looked out. The walls were covered in vines—no patch of stone was bare. It was as if the jungle were slowly eating the building, covering it, consuming it.

A bird called, a rolling song, fading and then picking up again. Leaves rustled as the wind became stronger. Thunder boomed, making her jump, and she turned, wondering if it had come from inside the house. It was so close, right on top of her.

All the hair on her body stood up, her skin prickling, as another crack rattled the room, the trees shivering with the noise. The light changed, dimming, and darkening as clouds moved to hide the sun. The trees swayed, stretching and pulling, leaves rattling. Something hit the roof, a falling limb, a crash that made her jump again.

A fat raindrop hit the windowsill—so heavy, she heard it. Then another, water falling from the sky suddenly, like a bucket being emptied over the house. Rain splashed through the open window, a violent wind whipping through the trees. They moved back and forth, rain blurring everything.

Water collected quickly on the tile below the window, coming into the room. Then the shutters shut with a snap, shut as if they'd always been closed, and the water on the floor was gone. More magic. Astrid stood breathless, listening as the rain pelted down—the sound of the jungle like an ocean, moving like waves breaking against the house.

A sigh escaped—relief at having something solid between her and the storm. The room was darker now, a twilight indoors, an invisible sun setting. She moved on, opening another door, and walking into a bedroom similar to hers. These rooms mirrored the rooms across the hall. One set dark, the other light—one in sunshine, the other in shade.

The conveniences were more modern than she had expected; the house was old, more castle than the house, and the exterior ancient and decaying. But the small bathroom was something she would have found in the newer parts of Stockholm or London. Close enough, even, to what she'd had before.

While she explored the storm passed—there and gone in a few breaths. The drumming on the roof quieted as a bird picked up a song, the house letting out a sigh. She went back to her suite of rooms to sit on the sofa and read. Soon sunlight traced patterns on the tile, picking out the titles of books stacked on the dresser, the clock chiming hours in an insanely sweet little tune.

———

THE CLOCK ANNOUNCED NINE.

Dinner.

Chinook had said there would be dinner and she was expected. But Tyhr had not mentioned dinner, nothing about required attendance. She glanced around the room— her open trunk with books stacked on the edge, a few items of clothing draped over the dressing table chair.

She'd started to unpack but stopped when she realized the wardrobe was full—everything in her size, a variety of colors and fabrics in several styles. So many things to choose from and all much nicer than anything she'd brought from home. But she crossed to the trunk now, digging through it until she found what she was looking for.

The gown was wrinkled, the velvet crushed in places, but she shook it out, hoping it would be suitable. Dark green, deep like the huge front doors and the jungle beyond, deep like the heart of an emerald in darkness, verging on black. She had always loved it, the squared-off shape of the neckline, the fitted bodice, and the flare of extra fabric at her waist. She went to the mirror above the dressing table, holding the dress in front of her, studying her reflection.

In the light of the candles, Astrid's eyes looked darker than usual, something in her expression wary. She shook her head, turning away, tossing the gown across the bed and pulling the pleated blouse she wore out of her skirt.

It had grown cool, and she turned to the fireplace in the room, searching the mantle for matches. She lit more candles when she found them and placed logs on the grate in the hearth, added kindling, but the fire wouldn't catch. She tried again but gave up after a third try.

"I would like a fire," she said aloud, looking around. Chinook had said the house was full, though she hadn't seen a soul. The room seemed expectant—as if someone might be listening so she added, "Please."

Nothing happened.

Astrid got up and grabbed the gown, crossing to the bathroom and pulling the door shut behind her. When she came out, wrapped in velvet and twisting her damp hair into a knot at the base of her neck, a fire was jumping cheerfully in the hearth.

CHAPTER NINE

The dining room was large with a ceiling covered in a mosaic that mimicked a canopy of trees—branches reaching across, leaves, tiles of golden sunlight peeking through. Astrid saw murals here as well—the whole room mimicking a forest glade. A long table ran down the middle, and an overly large fireplace on the opposite wall. No fire tonight—the hearth laid but unlit. Instead, the space glowed with dozens of candles throwing trembling light. They stood in a neat row along the mantel, and the table was covered in a forest of candelabras.

Only two chairs were at the table, facing each other, and both were empty.

Astrid hesitated, wondering if she was early or too late. The table was set—two places, plates and wine glasses, silverware, and napkins. Between them covered dishes and decanters of red and white wines. The stage was set—it waited only for the players to enter.

The house was silent at her back as she lingered in the doorway, wondering where Tyhr might be. She'd expected him to be here, waiting for her, as anxious to know her as she was to know him. But the room was empty. Her stomach twisted and she clenched her jaw tight.

It didn't matter.

She uncovered each platter, surprised to see an array of things she'd eaten at home—roast chicken, glazed carrots, potatoes, and a green salad. Like the sandwich, it was the last thing she'd expected to eat in a jungle. But here it was, a meal she would have shared with her family.

The chair scraped across the tile floor without her help, squeaking and filling the space, making her wince. The sound brought no one, nothing responded, the house swallowed the noise and returned to silence. She sat, perched on the edge of her seat, staring at the arched entrance to the room, expecting Tyhr to walk in at any moment.

Seconds stretched out painfully before she decided to eat. Astrid filled her plate, wondering where the chickens were kept and where the carrots grew. Or was it another thing, like everything here, that would be explained away by magic?

The chicken tasted like chicken. It was exactly as it should be. She had a few bites, chewing slowly, and studied the murals around the room.

At first glance, it seemed to be trees, trunk after trunk, underbrush and flowers tucked in near the baseboards. A stylized version of the real thing right outside the front door. Looking more carefully, though, she began to see the animals. They were painted in shades of brown and green, half hidden by the trees, sitting under leaves. Antelope, birds, monkeys, and tigers. Everywhere there were tigers.

The food grew cold. The candles on the table burning low, flames flickering, betraying the hour. Astrid felt as if she'd been at the table for a hundred years, waiting, growing anxious with each passing moment. The chair across from her remained empty. She pushed the plate away, standing, muscles stiff.

It was pointless to wait. Tyhr wasn't coming.

She took one of the candelabras, wax dripping across her hand and onto the tabletop, the sudden heat and flash of pain but she ignored it. The brass was solid, heavier than she'd expected, but she took it with her anyway. It would be enough to light the way back to her room.

Passing through the entryway, the space echoing with her steps, she paused at the foot of the stairs. The front door was open, as it always seemed to be, and she considered shutting it.

Was Tyhr out there? In the night? Or here in the house somewhere?

The brass clicked against the marble as she set the candelabra down. Astrid crossed to the door quickly, skirts swishing around her legs, something building inside her chest. She didn't feel like she was alone, the place didn't feel empty, despite the quiet. Chinook had been right; the house was full but silent.

She stepped in rainwater by the door; water pooled on the entryway tiles, seeping inside the house. With a noise of irritation, Astrid lifted up her skirts and stepped across the threshold.

Clouds clung to the far side of the valley, hiding the mountain ridges from view. The storm continued to rumble but it was receding, pulling back to leave the storm-washed valley drenched and quiet. Lightning flashed—not the crawling veins of electricity between clouds, but a boom of light—there and gone.

A cricket began to sing at the edge of the terrace—an invitation to come and be part of the night. She sucked in a breath of damp, green jungle, heavy with living, growing things that left the taste of foliage on her tongue. This place was like nowhere else. Nothing like what Astrid expected to find at the other end of the golden ring. She twisted it on her finger, wondering where Tyhr might be, wondering why he'd left her sitting at the table alone.

To have traveled so far, to have lived with the knowledge that her whole life was leading to him, and then to sit alone in this house? Anger and resentment filled Astrid—frustration at eating alone, in a strange place, in unusual circumstances—making it impossible to give him the benefit of the doubt. Actions spoke louder than words.

She went down the shallow steps, crossing the terrace to stand at the edge, trying to see past into the trees. Impossible. The darkness between the trunks was thick, and the dim glow from the open front door was distant. An impenetrable night.

For a moment—a blurred second flitting across her mind—Astrid considered stepping off the terrace to find the path to the glacier. But there was something in the jungle, the fear of the unknown and unseen eating at her. Beyond the edge of the terrace, where nature met manmade, there was danger.

Astrid turned away, going back up the steps, following the dim light thrown by the candles. Behind her thunder murmured the threat of more rain. A breeze followed her in, rustling the potted trees, sending spiked leaves swaying, and flowers bobbing.

———

NIGHTS AND DAYS PASSED. ONE RIGHT AFTER THE OTHER IN THE time-honored fashion of all calendars—an unending cycle of time. There were too many dinners alone. Chinook would flit through the house without a word, bright eyes resting on Astrid briefly before darting away.

She ate dinners in silence, watching the painted animals on the walls as if one night they might leap out of the murals in unison to run off into the house. Her last words to Tyhr haunted her, invading each thought and keeping her up at night.

Don't bother.

It had been exhaustion and frustration, uncertainty coming out with a sharp edge. But as much as she wished to apologize, to explain, the loneliness remained Astrid's constant companion. Even now, in the silence of predawn, loneliness was present.

She lay in bed, watching as dawn crept in to gently explore. It touched the edge of her balcony first and when not turned away came inside. Next, it touched the colorful patterned rug on the floor—intensifying muted colors, warming them with attention. The painted walls accepted the light greedily, flowers and green trees soaking it up, as if they could pull away from the walls to leap joyfully into the world outside.

Astrid lay in bed just watching the progression, morning giving way to afternoon. A sense of defeat filled her, the strange feeling of failing her father despite fulfilling a promise. She'd kept that promise, she was here, but there had to be more to it. There had to be a life here and not only existence.

She lay in bed until the sky turned gray—storm clouds rolling in—and shadows spread out from the corners, coming out from beneath the bed to reclaim the room.

———

Storms moved through the valley constantly—arriving in a rush to linger and then depart, only to return a few hours later. One moment the sky was clear, and the next, thunder rumbled, and gray clouds covered the valley. They were unusual, nothing like the weather patterns she'd experienced out in the world. She wondered where they came from and where they went after leaving this isolated jungle and strange house. Were they magic as well?

But there was no one to ask aside from Chinook, and he gave few answers.

The previous night she'd walked into the dining room, seen that it was empty, and gone straight back to her room. She'd slammed the bedroom door so hard, the sound had echoed down the hall, the wall vibrating.

Astrid lay in bed late the next morning, watching the shadows thrown by the stone lattice move across the floor, slow and steady, for over an hour. In the past she'd been an early riser, getting dressed in a rush to have breakfast with her mother. Sometimes her father and brother would join. They'd talk about their plans for the day, what the week had been like so far, or whatever they might be working on.

This silence in the morning, the quiet hush of the house around her, was unnatural.

She'd expected it to be the same here. She'd imagined breakfasts and conversations, shared plans and dreams, and building the connections it would take to get them through the rest of their lives.

Instead, Astrid ate alone—the house full and watchful, but always quiet. Chinook came and went, flying in and out of open doors and windows, looking in on her and moving on. He was constantly around without actually being present. A passerby on the stagnant accident of her life.

Astrid had only to think about breakfast and the scent

of it reached her. The trays appeared each morning, usually before she woke but sometimes between waking and a trip to the restroom. But it would arrive without noise, left on the table in the sitting room. The contents rarely varied— fruit, rolls, eggs, and thin slices of beef. At first, there had been tea and coffee, but when it became evident that she only drank the tea, the coffee disappeared. There was less food too, once the house learned her preferences. The first tray had held enough to feed several people, now it was just enough for her.

Do you always sleep all day?

Astrid sat up, searching the space until she saw Chinook perched on the back of the sofa.

"What're you doing here?"

Would you like to see more of the house?

She flopped back in bed. "I've seen the house. I've had a lot of time to myself, you know."

Obviously.

"Have you always been so charming, Chinook?" she asked, acid seeping into her tone. He was so smug and somehow managed, at all times, to be looking down his beak at her.

Yes, of course. I cannot help it if you are unable to see all of my many estimable qualities.

"You're a bird."

And you are a woman feeling sorry for herself and refusing to get out of bed.

Astrid glared at him as she threw the blankets back and stood up. She stomped to the restroom, anger coloring her cheeks, skin hot with his words. The door clicked softly behind her—she refused to give him the satisfaction of it slamming.

He wasn't wrong. That was why it stung, itching under

her skin, sticking to her like a leech. Astrid did feel sorry for herself. Alone in a house full of magic. A supposed husband, present but unavailable. A bird with a poor opinion of her checking in long enough to make sure she was breathing.

Astrid ran hot water in the sink until steam rose, blurring her face and the small room around her in the mirror. Heat filled the space quickly, and she sat on the edge of the tub, the surface cool beneath her.

This was nothing she could have planned for or expected.

But this life was what she had.

———

"You're still here," she said, pulling a dress from the wardrobe and slipping it over the cotton chemise. Mother-of-pearl buttons shone against fabric the color of holly leaves—a deep, clear green that brought out the color of her eyes. It had always been a favorite.

Do not sound so surprised.

Astrid shook her head, sitting at the dressing table to pin up her hair. "I'm not."

You do not hide it very well.

"My surprise or irritation?"

Both.

"Well," she said with a sigh, turning away from the mirror, "no one is perfect."

Except me.

Astrid laughed. It was exactly the response she'd expected. Chinook sounded so self-righteous.

"Possibly," she conceded, going into the sitting area and falling onto the sofa opposite him. The tea was lukewarm, but she drank it gratefully, eating rolls and fruit, waiting for

Chinook to break the silence. He seemed content to sit with her, ruffling his feathers and settling down on the cushion.

The book on the table was about Siberia. She'd thought it would be useful, would give her an idea about her new home, what it might be like. But of course, the information was useless. She was as far removed from Novgorod here as she had been in Sweden. Astrid picked it up anyway, flipping through the pages, reading scattered paragraphs, absorbing random facts.

Do you miss it?

"What?"

The world.

She stopped flipping pages, considering Chinook's question. "Yes and no. There isn't much left for me out there, no people to call my own. Did Tyhr tell you they were gone?"

A slow blink was her answer.

"Maybe family isn't everything to everyone. There is more to life than the people around you." Astrid shrugged, bringing her knees up and wrapping her arms around them. "But the world is a much emptier place with mine gone."

Would you like to see it again?

"What?"

The world.

CHAPTER TEN

Astrid followed him downstairs, bare feet on plush carpet and then cold marble. Daylight filled the entryway, catching the gold tile in the mosaic overhead. The front door stood open—always open—welcoming whatever might be passing inside with a silent invitation.

Though she had explored some, peeking behind doors and into closed-off rooms, she hadn't yet seen the whole house. Chinook took her down a hallway, farther than she had gone before. Past the dining room and several rooms dedicated to more sofas and chairs, small tables covered in potted plants, meaningless spaces.

Pausing at a blue door, perched on the brass handle, he waited for her to catch up.

In here.

The door opened into darkness, dim light from the hall barely penetrated the space, and it smelled closed off—air stale. She hesitated, uneasy about stepping forward, but Chinook darted ahead, disappearing inside.

There are candles on the table if you are afraid of the dark.

With the matches struck and candles lit, the room appeared like so many of the others—a copy of some other place, from some other time. There were more shelves here too but that wasn't surprising. The house had as many books as it did plants. Directly in front of her was a shuttered window—carved dark wood, more tigers observing her out of unblinking eyes.

Open the window and have a seat.

Astrid unfastened the wooden latch keeping the shutters closed and pushed it open before sitting. Sounds of a street came first—rattling harnesses and rolling carriages, church bells in the distance and murmured conversations. Swedish. Not her native tongue but still a pang of homesickness hit her. Then she recognized the street.

She sat on the window seat, mesmerized, staring at the street she'd looked at every day through the sitting-room window of the family townhouse. A carriage rattled past, horses neighing, the driver clicking his tongue. Blue sky stretched above the familiar rooftops—the color of new spring and warm weather. She'd left it in the cold, winter gripping the city, made even colder by their absence. But not enough time had passed—it should still be winter there, canals frozen over, icicles and snow drifts, wood smoke and red noses.

It was spring now.

"How long have I been here?" Astrid asked without taking her eyes from the glass, unable to break away from the mundane scene.

Time is different here.

"But is this now? Or a spring in the past? The future?"

Chinook landed on the seat beside her, walking back and forth, inspecting the world beyond the window.

"Do you even know?"

Things are slower here. They have always moved slowly. My guess is that it is now there, a now you might have occupied had you remained. But it is also now here, in this place, where spring is a distant hope.

Astrid touched the glass, the hard coolness, the world she'd left behind on the other side. She looked down at Chinook, perched on the windowsill and taking it all in.

"You can be very eloquent."

I'm glad you have begun to appreciate me.

"I'm not sure it's appreciation," she said.

He shot her a look, clearly unimpressed.

"Does it always show this street? Can I change it?"

You can. Think of what you want, clearly and calmly, a request, not a demand.

The window opened onto her father's offices. The dock where she'd stood with him and watched shipments come in—flags snapping from the masts, men at the ready to unload goods. It showed her the house her grandparents had lived in outside London, a place she'd only visited once but remembered vividly. Then Josephine's house—the young woman, Astrid's only friend, working on an embroidery hoop, her mother calling her down for lunch.

She should write to her. In the end, with her family gone and Porter and Stern disbanded, she hadn't sought Josephine out. Then the letter had come, Tyhr requesting her company, and nothing else had mattered.

"Do you visit this window?"

The little bird gave her a look, dry and condescending. *I do not have thumbs.*

"Won't the house open it for you?" she asked. "It closed the window itself the first day I was here."

The house sometimes lacks appreciation for all I do here and can be temperamental.

Astrid covered a smile, thinking about all the times Chinook has been acerbic and wondering how the invisible residents of the house might not appreciate his tone.

"Would you like me to open it for you? If there's a place you'd like to see again?"

A flash of surprise? Maybe. He gave her a nod but didn't say anything, leaving her to wonder whether he'd take her up on it and—someday—she'd see a place he missed.

———

A LONG, POLISHED BOX ARRIVED WITH THE BREAKFAST TRAY THE next morning. Brass inlay covered the top in a riot of leaves and flowers, and she traced the lines, marveling at the delicate details. Chinook waited expectantly on the back of the sofa, dark eyes bright and watchful.

"What is this?"

Seeds.

"From who?"

Tyhr.

She opened it to reveal neat rows of packets, all carefully labeled in handwritten cursive and sealed with wax. "He left me these?"

He said you enjoyed plants.

"I do," Astrid said with a nod, going through them, carefully reading the scientific names. "I have some seeds of my own as well. I'd planned to ask if I could start a garden here. There are so many plants, the whole house is full of them, and I didn't know where to start. Or if more would be welcome."

Chinook snorted. *We have enough plants.*

"You don't like them?"

They are plants.

"You say that as if they're uninteresting. But they aren't, not at all. There are so many uses and different species that have been around for thousands of years. It's all fascinating. Who takes care of them? The pots I mean, everything kept indoors." She shot him a glance, trying not to appear overcurious. The more interest she showed in things the fewer answers she was likely to get.

He fluffed his feathers, shaking it out, and looking around as if he hadn't heard her question.

"Why didn't he want to give these to me himself?"

Another careful question, another non-answer. She blew out a sigh, shuffling seed packets, dreaming of earth and sprouts, cool water. Pots would be best. Anything planted in the jungle would be overtaken and treated like the invasive species it was.

Several names were new to her, and she closed the lid with a snap, heading for the library to search for a book on plants.

"Coming?" she asked over her shoulder.

Chinook ruffled his feathers and followed.

He was a critical and sour companion, but welcome, nonetheless.

———

IT HAD TAKEN SEVERAL BOOKS TO FIND DESCRIPTIONS OF ALL THE seeds. She'd brought them all back to her suite—covering the desk in her office and the low table in the sitting room, other volumes were open beside her on the sofa. The books sat open, stacks of loose leaf pages tucked here and there— covered in scribbled notes and dotted with ink, lay scattered around the sitting room. She added another sheet, realizing her dress had ink spots on it now as well.

Chinook had followed her upstairs and lingered until he'd gotten bored—tired of inspecting things and her silence as she read. One moment he'd been there and when she'd next looked up from the pages he was gone. But she knew he'd be back at some point. Chinook was too nosey to stay away.

One of the books pulled from the shelf contained obscure lore and magical uses for various species. Each variety carried some kind of potential magic—protection from enchantments, clarity in a dangerous situation, or the ability to speak with animals.

What was he trying to convey with the gift of these seeds? She couldn't be sure and refused to make assumptions when he should have been here explaining for himself.

Where did Tyhr spend his days and nights? They never passed each other in the hall or crossed paths in the dining room. He sent her strange, but welcome gifts. And he had Chinook to defend and apologize for him. But where was the man himself?

Frustration filled her. Maybe she shouldn't have been so harsh that first night—her words hard and tone cutting. If she'd been on the receiving end, she might still be keeping her distance as well.

But he couldn't have wanted this limbo any more than she did. They'd been married by contract and proxy, but there had been no talk of an actual ceremony—a wedding that would truly be their own. She would have asked him about consummating the marriage but what was the point when she hadn't seen him since he'd shown her the house?

Astrid lived surrounded by the silence of this place. Virtually alone. Chinook came and went as he pleased, but there was no counting on him to linger with her for conversation. Tyhr should have been her companion. He should have been here, no matter what she'd said. He'd expected her to come, and she had. It was his turn to keep up his end of the promise.

Part of her was tempted to stand at the front door and yell for him—fill the jungle with the sound of her voice and his name. Bring him to her with nothing but willpower and determination. But he didn't seem like the kind of man who would respond to demands.

There was a scratching at the study door, soft, near the door handle. She stood, going over to it, half sure it would be Chinook. The sky was dark, the light in here provided by flickering candles and a single gas lamp.

Are you coming to dinner? Chinook asked when she opened the door, flying into her room uninvited.

"Will Tyhr be there? I'm tired of eating alone."

You will not be alone tonight.

Her heart picked up, sucking in a quick breath, taking a step toward Chinook she asked, "He'll be there?"

Chinook walked over to the book on the table, lifting a page, hopping to the next book, and staring down at the notes she'd scribbled in the margins.

It is very rude to write in other people's books.

"Is this not my home?" she asked, tartness on her tongue, bitterness behind it. Would Tyhr be there finally? Would any question, just one question, receive an answer?

Yes, Chinook's tone was patient, as if explaining something to someone who still would not understand the error of their ways. *It is indeed your home, yes technically these books are now yours. However, it is still extremely rude to write in the margins of books.*

"Don't tell me you're one of those snobby people who think books should always be kept pristine."

It is not snobby. Not at all.

"Books are made to be enjoyed, read, used."

Astrid reached out, shooing him off the book, closing it and the one beside it with a snap. He twittered at her, irritated at being shooed, and moved to the edge of the table. The stacks of paper were tapped into a neat pile, and she put the pen back in the drawer as he watched—gaze intent as if she might commit a crime against nature right before his eyes.

"Are you worried I'll write in the margins while you're looking?" she laughed, picking up a book and showing him the clean margins on the page. "You don't have to worry. I'm done for the night."

Probably for the best.

She nodded, exaggerating the motion, "Oh yes, probably."

Very well, he said, fluffing up, shaking out his wings.

"Chinook," she started, then paused, thinking about her words, not wanting to offend him. "You said I wouldn't be eating alone tonight and then you changed the subject very sneakily."

I did not sneak! You wrote in the margins of a beautifully illustrated book! That should be a crime.

"See?"

Can I help it if I am passionate about books?

She rolled her eyes, "Can you even read?"

His beak opened wide, black eyes narrowing. *Can I even read?*

She held up a hand, "I'm sorry. I'm sure you can. I've never met a bird who talked before so of course the one I meet also reads. I just want you to answer the question because now it seems like you're intentionally avoiding it."

His feathers settled—beak snapping shut as he looked away from her.

I had considered joining you, he said stiffly, *since you have grown tired of eating alone. Though I do not know why you would. The dining room walls are interesting to look at if you get tired of watching your plate.*

Astrid sighed, hugging the book to her chest, the quick pick up her heart had done slowing. It would be another night with a dinner table set for two with only one of the intended guests arriving.

"Thank you for the offer," she said, turning away, "but I don't think I'll be eating dinner tonight."

CHAPTER ELEVEN

Hunger twisted through her, stomach knotting and grumbling, refusing to be silent.

Astrid turned over, staring out of the window at a jungle lit by a full moon—a world touched with silver, edged with luminescent light. Frogs sang a constant low thrum, at once distant and near at hand. A breeze shifted the curtains, gliding across her face, bringing with it the scent of sweet flowers and damp earth. There were no storms slinking along the horizon tonight or low thunder coming across the valley.

Dinner.

Another one she would have spent alone if she'd bothered to sit down.

She'd chosen the window in the library instead, watching the shadows lengthen and the sun set on that other place. The house surrounding her had been so quiet. If anything had moved, if the stones had even shifted and settled, she would have heard it. But she'd remained alone.

Now she was hungry and wished she'd taken anything edible with her. Instead, she'd decided thoughtlessly that skipping dinner in silent protest would send a message. But when Tyhr was always absent, how would he know?

She could ask Chinook to pass on a message. It made her feel like a child though, sitting in a schoolroom and watching a boy out of the corner of her eye. Besides, Chinook would have some remark to make about it— cutting or curious, and no matter what unnecessarily judgmental.

Flinging back the sheets she grabbed her robe and a candle before heading downstairs. There would be something to eat in the kitchen. The pantry had to be well stocked for the fancy dinners that graced the table each night and the breakfast and lunch trays in her room.

Though she had not seen the kitchens yet, she had a rough idea about where they were. In the dining room, disguised by the mural, was a door. It was one of the few she'd not opened and now she pushed on it, letting it swing inward slowly and shielding the candle flame as she crept through.

What are you doing sneaking around? asked Chinook, flying in behind her—swift and sure.

"Don't do that!" Astrid yelped. "You scared the life out of me! Why are *you* lurking? I didn't even hear you!"

You were making a lot of noise. I came to see what you were up to.

Astrid nodded, looking around. The space was large and cavernous, obviously used and cleaned regularly. The terra- cotta tile floors were worn in places, as if feet had beat a memorized path from ovens to hearth, cabinets to cutting blocks. Copper pots hung from hooks around the room and there were nested bowls on the marble counter. The colors were warm and earthy—deep reds and rich browns, olive greens and dusky blues. Even here the walls were painted, the ceiling a riot of vegetables arranged in a pleasing pattern.

"Who cooks all the meals? I never see anyone."

Half ghosts, half memories.

"Is that what takes to keep a house like this running?"

Would you prefer I say it was magic?

She lifted a shoulder, "Maybe."

You would rather believe in magic than ghosts?

"I think they're all the same. All equally unbelievable."

And yet, Chinook fluttered his wings, the gesture managing to take in the room, the entirety of the house.

"And yet here I am," she agreed, going over to one of the cabinets and opening it.

The interior was sparkling clean and empty.

You will not find anything.

"Why?"

Astrid opened the next cabinet and the one beside it, moving on to the ice boxes, and then pulling open a door that led to a pantry. Everything was empty—shelves bare, nothing edible left at all. With a sigh she turned to Chinook, leaning against the counter, and crossing her arms.

"Is it like the fire? Do I have to ask?"

It would not do you any good.

With a groan she pushed away from the counter, looking around the room, searching for anything that might be edible, any sign that asking would get her a meal. "Please," she said, raising her hands, palms up, "I'm hungry and I would like something to eat."

Chinook chirped, a rhythmic noise that sounded very much like laughter.

"Are you laughing?"

Yes.

"Instead of laughing you could help me find something to eat."

I have told you. It will not work. The kitchen has always... his voice trailed off, stopping.

"Always?" she prompted.

Done what it pleased.

"So, what you're saying is you have temperamental ghosts?"

You said you did not believe in ghosts.

"I don't," she said with a sigh. "What are you doing up? If you know the kitchen won't be sharing anything with you at this hour?"

I thought you might come down after skipping dinner. He preened, lifting one foot and then the other.

"And you wanted to make sure the kitchen didn't take pity on me?"

Oh no, there was no danger of that ever happening. The kitchen pities no one.

She laughed, unable to stop herself.

I felt badly about the conversation earlier. They are your books. You should do with them as you please. Including filling the margins with your less than ideal penmanship.

"That's very generous of you."

Yes, I am.

Rolling her eyes, trying not to laugh again, she picked up the candle and headed back through the dining room. Chinook followed, flying a little ahead before circling back. She was grateful for the company in the night—a reprieve from loneliness. Halfway up the stairs, she paused, looking out over the entryway, the plants, and the open door. The scent of flowers clung to her and filled the room—rich and textured, green and sweet and sharp.

"Can I ask you something?"

I reserve the right not to answer.

"When will things be different?"

Different how?

The urge to throw the candle down and run for the door overwhelmed her. She would run and run, out into the jungle, to a door leading to a forest that never woke from its nightmares. She would escape. If he didn't understand what she meant by different, she wasn't sure how she could explain the gnawing feeling inside.

"Never mind," she said with a shrug.

CHAPTER TWELVE

Stacks of books in the library.

Countless meals eaten alone.

Chinook flitting in and out.

Too many quiet nights.

These things came together, woven carefully to make up the minutes and hours of her days here. Nothing seemed to change.

"I can't stay here. I can't keep living in this limbo."

You are betrothed.

"More than that," she said, waving a hand at the room, at the jungle beyond the window. "Married, but only in name. I expected it to be more, to have it be a real marriage. But now, having met him, having lived in this strange place, I don't believe it will be."

Chinook watched as she paced. *If you give it time—*

"Time? He hasn't even shown up for dinner. Night after night. It's been weeks. He picked me up at the station only to leave me alone in this house. He's had time."

Then what would you do? Where would you go? Out there in the world with no one, a woman on her own?

Astrid sat abruptly on the bed, arms limp at her sides, staring straight ahead. "I know. I understand it. But I can't do this if he won't even show up. I wander around an empty house night and day. I eat alone. I spend all my time talking to a bird."

His colorful feathers ruffled, indignation radiating outward, his beak open.

She held out a hand, stopping whatever further reaction he might have. "I'm grateful. You've quickly become a friend."

I am not sure that is a compliment, he huffed. *You simply lack choices.*

She laughed and shrugged, looking around the room and feeling lost.

Give it time, Chinook urged. *Sleep on it. You will feel better soon.*

When she nodded, he left, leaving her alone in the room, the house dark around her, the candles burning low.

Where had Tyhr gone with his silver mask and golden eyes?

The sun would rise soon, climb over the horizon and reach into this steep valley. Astrid would face the day on her own again.

She pushed the thought and the ripple of emotion that came with it away. The desire to open her heart to him—to build a bridge between two strangers—and leave the door open for love, was gone. The wound in her soul left by the deaths of her family had begun to heal, a messy scab that would one day be a jagged scar. She'd been willing to let Tyhr in while there was time, but it was gone now, and it was easier to pull away and keep herself apart.

Beyond the window, a bird called, and another farther away answered. Dawn. She looked around the room, wondering what she would take and what would be easy to carry. It was hard to know how long she'd been here and what the weather might be like beyond this place. When he'd picked her up from the station, it was deep winter, bitter and frozen, snowflakes melting on her lashes as they crossed into the Black Forest. Here, it was always summer, forever summer. But the window in the library had shown her spring.

She wanted to take everything and nothing.

It would all be too much or too little.

If she left wearing what she had on, cotton and muslin and silk, it would be enough in temperate weather. She would freeze otherwise. She went to the wardrobe, digging through the rows of clothes, gowns and day dresses, and mother-of-pearl buttoned blouses. At the back, out of sight, was a heavy, dark wool cloak with a silver clasp. She ran a hand across it—considering the warmth it offered but rejected it, a part of her wanting to carry nothing forward from this place.

Astrid moved to the dressing table, picking up one of the seed packets Tyhr had given her. They'd ended up everywhere. So had the books. Her rooms quickly became the disaster they had always been. You could see where her thoughts had stopped and her mind had picked up something new—a book set down, another chosen. Scraps of paper marked pages, torn and stuck in, a hairpin in an encyclopedia.

Her reflection in the dressing table mirror stopped her mid-step. The ring caught her eye, the band bending the light, the shape curving and catching, the surface worn but still etched with the faint traces of flowers and vines. It had felt right to wear it, all this time, like a piece of fate falling into place. She twisted it on her finger, around and around, the metal warm and so much a part of herself at this point. But it slipped off easily, and when it was sitting on the table, the world did not seem that different without it.

She left it there, left it all there—books, seed packets, and clothes.

All of it.

CHAPTER THIRTEEN

Astrid crossed the threshold into sunlight so bright, it blinded her. But she was out of the house and throwing herself down the stairs and across the terrace, crashing through the underbrush before her eyes had time to adjust. Her pulse pounded as the terrace vanished behind her—white stone obscured, the jungle a closing Venus flytrap, a closing deadly nightshade blossom.

Away.

To where? She didn't know. Just away. Tears gathered on her lashes, and the swelling loneliness and sorrow over what she thought her life would be came up—an unraveling knot spinning free.

This was nothing she'd expected—nothing she could have prepared for. A house in a strange land, not even a place on a map, full of ghosts, a talking bird, and a man in a mask. Her husband. The man her father had promised her to before she was even born. A promise she felt obligated to keep, that she couldn't bring herself to break because that would change the memory of her family and the life they had shared.

But none of it mattered if Tyhr was never there.

Astrid hadn't come all this way to live alone.

Trees towered over her—bushes reached in, leaning over. Small trees. More growth under those, layer after layer of green and living things. If she stopped and breathed, if she took the time, she could name each plant. But rushing through them now, she found they were nameless, out of place.

Astrid! Chinook called, his voice coming from behind her, following.

She didn't stop. He couldn't force her to return, couldn't compel her to stay.

Astrid, come back!

His voice in her head, heard without hearing, quieted the farther apart they were. Similar to sounds made with vocal cords, still something she wasn't used to. Over the noise he made were other noises—the sounds of birds and small mammals going about their lives, a rustle beneath some of last year's leaves.

When they quieted, she didn't notice. Astrid made too much noise, crashing and pushing, making her own path since there was none to follow. But when she paused—wondering where the door to the glacier was—it overtook her, crushing her with the force of silence.

The hair on the back of her neck rose.

She stopped, listening, straining to catch the slightest sound. Nothing. The silence was heavy, occupied by something unseen, filled out and owned. Fear crawled over Astrid, her hair rising, as certainty hit her.

Someone was here.

Overhead branches swayed, leaves rustling, moving in a

slow wave. A patch of blue sky came into view and was hidden again. Turning slowly, she studied each tree and bush separately, defining them and carrying on. If someone was there, she would see them, she would know.

But the jungle defied Astrid, coming together in a riot of colors, overwhelming in its variety. The undergrowth was thick, dense bushes and vines, with a taller understory of trees rising above those. Deep green shadows clung to the in-between places, concealing anything, giving nothing away.

A whisper in the back of her mind urged her to run. *Run!* But to where? And from what?

Nothing, no one, said her eyes.

But they were wrong. She could feel the danger here even if she couldn't see it.

Taking a step back, and continuing to scan the bushes around her, she turned and darted away. Branches whipped across Astrid's face as she went, stinging, biting at her hands when she stumbled and reached out to stop herself from falling. The growth was too thick to move through easily, too many things slowing her down, too many things to trip over.

Astrid could no longer tell which direction she had come from or where the house might be. It was all tall trees and bushes, vines and tree ferns, and flowers rioting. She stopped, wheezing a little, turning in a circle and straining to catch any sound. With an effort she held her breath, concentrating on calming her pulse. Buzzing filled her ears, then the thump of her heart, the gasp she let out when she couldn't hold her breath anymore.

A shape came together out of the underbrush directly in front of Astrid.

Tiger.

The animal was larger than any she'd ever seen in books. Bigger than the photographs she'd seen in the papers. It watched her, half hidden beneath a large brush—crouched and muscles tense. Light touched the face, the fur —orange, black, and white blending into the sunlit green. Intense golden eyes focused on her face. A noise escaped Astrid, and she slapped a hand over her mouth.

Gold eyes. The same color as those behind the silver tiger mask. She'd struggled to read them at the station, searching for something in the expression that would reveal any emotion. But Tyhr had studied her without giving anything away.

Now the tiger watched her.

Astrid!

Chinook's voice came from a distance, falling and rising, coming again. She wanted to answer, wanted to call out to him, to give him some idea of where she was. Any sound might unleash the tiger. Maybe her silence was the only thing keeping the beast from leaping toward her.

He called again, nearer now, and she urged him on silently.

The muscles beneath the sleek fur moved as the tiger shifted, bunched up and tight, eyes boring into her.

You fool! Chinook said, flying toward her in a flurry of feathers, anger in his bright black eyes. *What is wrong with you? It is dangerous!*

Astrid nodded without taking her eyes off the tiger. Chinook fluttered before her, voice shrill, a stream of frustration flowing over her. Then he slowed, realizing she wasn't looking at him. He landed on her shoulder, feet tiny and sharp, the weight of him nothing more than a leaf. The tiger had shifted slightly, muscles loosening.

I see, the bird said softly, tone calm and soothing. *Walk to your right and keep going. We will circle back to the house. Do not take your eyes off him. Do not turn your back.*

Astrid dreaded moving, terrified that the moment she lifted a foot, the tiger would spring. She hesitated, waiting, but Chinook squeezed her shoulder, tiny claws pricking, urging her into motion.

One step and then another, arm outstretched to feel what might come next without turning her head. The jungle floor was uneven, and she stepped into a bush, Chinook flapping his wings to stay upright when she stumbled. She had to look away then, had to see where they were going. Otherwise, she'd fall. And then the tiger would attack.

Go slowly, the bird urged.

She nodded, putting distance between herself and the threat, glancing back at the tiger. Was he less bunched now? In the same location? Astrid couldn't be sure. With care she navigated around trees and through bushes, wading through swaths of ferns. Chinook left her shoulder and went from branch to branch, looking ahead and behind, guiding her toward the house.

Finally, the jungle parted, falling away, and the house came into sight. The terrace was there, a blank expanse waiting for her feet, and the front door was open. Overhead a hot sun watched, a blinding eye. Chinook darted ahead, disappearing into the house, leaving Astrid alone.

Behind her came a low growl, rumbling through her, shaking the earth. She turned. The tiger was there, feet away.

She ran.

Branches slapped her face, the earth pulling at her heavy feet. She was getting nowhere, not able to put distance between herself and the threat. Each breath tasted of the humid head, sweat soaking into her clothes, but she kept moving, pushing forward.

Stopping meant death.

It was right behind her. So clear. The tiger's path was easy, put down by her own feet, a self-betrayal impossibly hard to forgive. With a sharp cry, she fell hard on one knee, a crack, a sharp pain. With a groan she tried to stand, unable to, falling back to the earth, flat on her face. A low growl came from behind, Astrid felt it in the earth, thrumming along each hair. Her breath came faster, sucking in a mouth full of dirt, shivering.

She felt the beast creep over her, unable to turn over, terrified to face it. One large paw entered her field of vision —orange and white, claws retracted, only hinted at. Squeezing her eyes shut, focusing on the blackness behind her lids, she tried to be calm.

Do not let him smell your fear.

It was too late.

The growl made her teeth ache, her brain screaming and urging flight, there was no fight here than she could win. But it was impossible to move. All Astrid could do was slowly roll over, easing into it, painfully slow with her eyes squeezed shut.

Hot breath on her face—predator's breath, meat and bone, a promise of what would come. One moment passed and then another, each second, she was sure would be the one, she would feel sharp teeth, a crushing bite, the world going dark around her in excruciating pain.

Nothing.

Not yet.

Soon.

Now.

When death didn't come, she opened her eyes slowly,

seeing the huge tiger's body over her, the white underbelly. How soft the fur looked, thick and luxurious. It would be a pleasure to run her hands over the creature, feel the beating heart, the chest expanding as the lungs worked. She brought her gaze up slowly, a millimeter at a time until there was only his face left.

Whose would it be? A familiar face? But why would a tiger's face be familiar?

Sucking in a breath, steeling herself for the moment coming, Astrid looked up.

A snarling face inches away, lips pulled back, mouth open—pink gums and red throat. A tiger, fearsome and hungry, mouth opening, jaws widening, teeth flashing.

She woke with a start, sitting up in bed, sweating, and searching the room wildly.

No tiger.

No threat.

At least not one she could see.

CHAPTER FOURTEEN

Astrid looked at herself in the mirror, turning, watching the way candlelight shifted the color of her hair, the shade of the dress. The afternoon, the tiger in the jungle, was too close—the fear collecting between her shoulders, the pressure building in her chest. She wasn't really seeing her reflection. Instead, her mind turned over the moment she'd realized she wasn't alone beneath the trees.

The tiger beyond the terrace had not been a dream. Not even a nightmare. The animal had been a cold, hard reality. Even now Astrid could feel its breath on the back of her neck, the expectant pressure of its paws.

With a flutter, Chinook entered her room. She'd begun to leave the door to her suite open a crack, a space wide enough for the small tanager to slip through and he'd gotten into the habit of using it. She'd been too exhausted, emotionally drained, to demand answers from Chinook earlier in the afternoon. But he'd promised to come back before dinner.

"I wasn't sure you were coming," she said, watching the

small bird flit around the room before finally coming to rest on the low table between the plush chairs. "Tell me about the tiger."

Not even a hello first?

"Chinook," Astrid let out a weary sigh, tucking a pin in her hair to keep the elegant knot in place. "You're changing the subject. And when have you ever cared for such niceties?"

And the subject is?

"Tigers."

There are not multiple tigers in this valley.

"One tiger then, a singular tiger. Are you being obtuse on purpose?"

Yes, there is in fact a tiger living in the jungle, he said, fluffing up his feathers in annoyance.

But there was a tiger living in the house too. One that wore a silver mask—prowling the halls and empty rooms, sharing the rooms with her without ever being seen. He'd avoided dinner with her, but she'd begun to wonder if the small changes she noticed—a dish moved, a book left on the window seat in the library—was Tyhr and not the ghosts and magic that made everything else happen.

That first morning, early before dawn, after the Black Forest, he'd left her to enter the house on her own. She'd been upset with him and now willing to admit a little scared in this new place. Maybe he'd left her there because he couldn't stay, not because her words had been so sharp.

"Is Tyhr the tiger?"

Chinook watched her, turning his head to the side, dark eyes bright.

"Is that part of the magic here?"

Do you believe in magic?

"I think I must," she said, waving around the room—

the fire that lit itself, the table where a breakfast tray appeared every morning without another soul coming into the space. Magic was a reality. But did Astrid truly, in the depths of her skeptical soul and logical mind, believe?

Do you know how to break curses?

Astrid paused, turning away from the mirror to consider him. "What do you mean exactly?"

Are you a curse breaker?

"I don't know," Astrid said, brow wrinkling.

Well, I would expect you to know.

"How?" She lifted her hands, eyebrows going up. "It's not as if these kinds of things are taught in school."

Well, obviously you had a poor education.

The clock in her study began to chime the hour—high and sweet, another clock in the house picking up the call, carrying it on in a deeper tone.

"Will you be joining me in the dining room?" she asked, hoping Chinook would say yes.

Not this evening. Possibly another time. If your manners improve.

"My manners are perfectly acceptable," Astrid glared at him. "You are the one that seems to be lacking in that area."

Nonsense.

She sighed. He would never admit if he were wrong. Chinook never doubted himself in the least. With a chirp— one she could not interpret—he left her alone, standing in a beautiful set of rooms that contained everything she could ever desire. But nothing she wanted.

Answers. She needed to understand.

Dinner. Food. A distraction. She wanted it, even if it meant eating alone, another meal in an empty room, another jungle with painted tigers instead of breathing ones. She got ready in a rush, running a cool cloth over her skin before changing, washing the dream away.

With a soft click pulled the bedroom door shut behind her—cutting off the light from the lamps that filled her rooms. The hall was completely black, the landing a faint pool of gray, a hint of candlelight coming up from the first floor. Astrid leaned back against the door, hesitating, the handle still in her hand. For a moment she considered going back in, not going downstairs at all, not even bothering to discover whether the table was set for two.

Stepping away from the door, she smoothed her dress, velvet soft against her palms, the golden ring warmer than usual. A sigh escaped, a small noise of acceptance and resignation, as she took the first few steps toward the stairs.

A shadow moved, a dark patch of nothing stepping forward, becoming Tyhr.

Astrid gasped, stumbling back, tripping on the edge of her gown.

"I'm sorry," he said, reaching out of the dark to steady her. "I didn't mean to frighten you."

His hand was warm on her bare upper arm as he leaned into her, barely visible, bringing the scents of the jungle with him. Heat. Green leaves. Rich earth. Her heart raced, her skin tingling with the contact. The closeness of him was something she had not known she was curious about—something she craved—until now.

"You didn't scare me," she lied.

The gloom made it impossible to see clearly—blurred features of the mask and a hint of height were all she could see. Tyhr seemed bigger, the hand on her arm larger, and the ring on her finger warmed with his presence.

"I came to see if you would be joining me for dinner."

His voice sounded stiff, too formal for a dark hallway, too formal for the heat that passed through his touch into her.

Astrid made a noise, a wave of irritation taking over—heart thumping, with his nearness and the shock. All these weeks he'd left her to sit at that table alone, hoping he'd come through those doors only to be disappointed night after night.

"Have one dinner with me," he said, as if he could read her expression in the dark.

"Of course, I will." She sighed, stepping back and giving herself room to catch her breath and steady her nerves. "Now that you've finally decided to show up, how could I resist?"

————

ASTRID SHIFTED IN HER SEAT, TAKING IN THE ROOM, POLISHED furniture, and gleaming dishes. It was all familiar at this point—each detail previously cataloged. All of it except him. How many times had she eaten alone? She couldn't be sure now. Too many. Now Tyhr sat across from her, not eating, the mask in place, virtually silent.

She regretted complaining to Chinook now about his absence because this was worse.

Tyhr sat across from her, an empty plate and glass before him. The mask had no opening for his mouth, there was no way to eat, and yet he'd joined her. Was that part of the reason he'd avoided this situation before? It was awkward to sit together with only one of them eating as the other watched.

"Why did you finally decide to join me?" she asked, fork tines tapping against the dish as she speared a nameless green vegetable. "Did Chinook tell you to?"

"He might have suggested it."

"So why did you keep away?"

Are you the tiger in the jungle? She almost asked—the question on the tip of her tongue but hesitated. How did you ask a man you didn't know if he became a tiger the moment sunlight touched him? It couldn't be that much stranger than the one who wore a silver tiger mask and refused to remove it.

"I thought you would appreciate the privacy." Tyhr glanced at her, a look Astrid couldn't read, before spreading his hands out in a gesture of defeat.

On the terrace she had been harsh—the journey too much, the grief too heavy. She'd regretted her words a thousand times since then, wishing more than anything she could take them back and start over. Here was her chance.

"Thank you," she said softly. "I'm sorry for making you feel the need to stay away."

"No, I—" he stopped and then cleared his throat. "Thank you."

She nodded, eating another bite, eyes drawn back to the mask. His gaze moved around the room, touching on her briefly. When she looked away, she felt the gentle pressure of his attention. Could he feel hers?

Setting her fork down she picked up the wine glass— clear golden liquid reminding her of spring afternoons in the park, picnic baskets, and parasols. She smiled to herself, flooded with memory, savoring the taste of past happiness.

"Are you enjoying dinner?" Tyhr asked.

"Yes," she nodded, picking up the fork and stabbing at the white fish on her plate. The tines squeaked against the porcelain, grating on raw nerves. He seemed to have nothing else to add, simply watching as Astrid ate, leaving her feeling as if she were a flower on display.

"How did you meet my father?" she asked, the abruptness taking them both off guard.

The question had not been answered before and she needed answers now. Growing up she could never understand how such a promise could have been made. No details had been shared, only that it would be an advantageous match, beneficial to the family and bringing great wealth.

Once, when she was young, she'd asked if her father cared for her happiness. His expression had shut down, *you'll see* had been the only response.

"Has Chinook spoken of me at all?"

"A little," she said, twisting a seed packet from her pocket around—Adiantum, the maidenhair fern. She hadn't realized it was in her pocket, stuffed there earlier absent-mindedly. She set it on the table beside her plate. "Not enough."

"What would be enough?" He leaned forward, earnestness in every motion—warm golden eyes, beautiful hands. "What would you like to know?"

"I don't know." She shrugged, looking down at her hands, avoiding the earnestness in his eyes. "So how did our engagement happen?"

"I used to go out more—"

"When you were younger."

It was his turn to shrug—one shoulder lifted, a quick tilt of the head. "You could say that. I would leave, go out into the world, search, and come back."

"What were you searching for?" She held her breath, expectant and afraid that the slightest distraction would keep the answers from reaching her ears. Now. It would have to be now.

"I came across your father," he skimmed over her question, carrying on, "and he needed help. He'd been traveling and attacked by bandits on an isolated road. It was the middle of winter, and the people were desperate."

"And you saved him for the price of a daughter."

Tyhr nodded, standing and walking around, pacing, seeing a past she could only imagine. Astrid waited, wondering what else he might share. The remains of dinner were cold, nothing she wanted to keep pretending to eat, her wine glass empty. Dinner was over. She could go if she wanted.

"Why?" she whispered, needing to know it all, to have the missing pieces of the story placed before her. Astrid needed to find the sense in all of this.

"There are some things I cannot share."

Because you're a tiger? She asked silently. But he'd requested only that she share a meal with him.

Now she had.

Tyhr came around and pulled her chair out, offering a hand as she stood. His touch was electric, the warmth of him like the promise of summer. Astrid wanted to feel it all over her skin, have it chase away the loneliness she'd kept at bay. But she pulled her hand back, stepping past him and making her way quickly to the entrance hall full of candle-light and the night.

Grief and homesickness came in waves as she left the dining room behind. The emotion overtaking her, drowning her, in an undertow that brought her again and again to the heart of it all. Grief. The hole in the fabric of her life, their absence. At times it felt so far away, with enough distance between herself and it—grief that was a force of nature—but not tonight.

There were some hours when the world felt like it had before, while she read, forgetting that when she looked up, they would not be there. At any moment Astrid would hear their voices—her mother's laugh, her brother's snort of derision, her father's exasperated complaint about sewing needles being left on the chairs in the sitting room.

But now, here in the entryway, surrounded by everything new—the things she had yet to become accustomed to. And a few things she had no desire to become accustomed to. The weight hit hard and fast, a sucking sensation, a bone-deep pain that knocked her down. Astrid leaned against the wall, half in a potted plant, tree branches in her hair, and slid to the floor—camouflaged.

Tyhr came out of the dining room, boots sharp on marble. The mask, a snarling tiger, surveyed the room. The plants rustled, giving her away. Tyhr looked around, spotting her in the greenery. The moment their eyes met she regretted being caught in a moment of weakness. But she stayed where she was, looking up at him as he came to stand before her.

"Hiding?" he asked softly—the tone that one of an adult speaking to a child.

"Not exactly," she said, fighting to keep her voice steady.

"No?"

"When I was little, I would hide in my mother's potted ferns. Usually, from my brother. Occasionally from my mother, who was very keen on the idea of improving my embroidery skills." She laughed softly, the sound barely there. "It's comforting."

With a chuckle, he eased down to sit beside her, his

back to the wall, his knee touching hers. The contact warmed her, the small connection with another person something she had missed terribly; more than she'd realized.

"I'm so sorry," Tyhr said, reaching out, touching her shoulder. "What can I do?"

Such a simple question, a simple offer. He'd said nothing about them beyond simple condolences and sharing a fraction of information about meeting her father. Tyhr gave nothing and Astrid had nothing to give. If she shared the memories, could it dilute them? Would they lose focus and blur away into nothingness?

"Did you have a family?"

"Yes," he said, voice soft between them.

"Do you miss them?" Astrid wiped at her eyes, pushing at the wave of grief, standing in the middle of it and fighting the undertow.

"Always."

She hadn't expected the emotion in his voice. The urge to reach out and comfort him was strong, but as she reached for him, Tyhr stood, holding out a hand.

"Would you like to go to the library?" he asked. "Chinook said you enjoy the view."

Astrid shook her head, not wanting to tell him that the window had stopped bringing her comfort. The days were better spent without staring through the glass, sometimes seeing a familiar face, sometimes not, watching seasons change there while everything here remained the same.

"Not tonight," she said, taking her hand back, smoothing down her skirt. "I'm tired and I have a book to finish."

"I'll escort you up," he said.

Astrid met his golden gaze, considering the offer, and

what else it might mean. He seemed to be holding his breath, waiting for a response, her confirmation or denial. What would happen between them in the dark? She needed there to be more between them in the light before she found out.

"Next time," she said, shaking her head.

She needed to think about what he wasn't telling her, what she needed to know, and the moment of connection amongst the potted plants. Astrid wanted to consider her reaction to him despite her anger with him.

"Tomorrow," Tyhr promised, taking her hand between his and smoothing his thumb over her wrist in a gentle caress.

She swallowed—heart jumping, skin heating with his touch—and nodded.

CHAPTER FIFTEEN

T he next night he wasn't in the dining room, in the library before the fire, or in any of the sitting rooms Astrid checked. After everything—the moments of connection the previous evening—the fear lingered that he would disappear.

There was still a barrier.

The things not spoken aloud.

Astrid paused in the entryway, looking around, the plants and mosaics overhead all so familiar now. Even the jungle beyond was a sight she'd grown used to—accepted and even admired the savage beauty of all. In those moments the loneliness was not too heavy, and the grief smaller. She moved to the front door, tempted to push it wider, to discover what might lay beyond beneath the stars.

But tonight, there were no stars. Fat raindrops hit the terrace, scattered and not yet serious rain and the air thrummed with the coming storm—expectant and ready. It would come. Part of her wanted to wait, be here when the clouds broke loose, stand beneath the onslaught, and let it wash sorrow and homesickness away—ease the doubt and growing fear that she would never truly understand the circumstance of her arrival in this summer place. Maybe the storm would take all of her doubt and fear—cloying and sticky as tar—and leave her with the peace she sought.

The trees stood motionless, expectant and for once there wasn't the rushing sound of crashing waves, the constant background noise of life beyond the house. It was unsettling and unnatural in the silence. The storm would come, and Astrid would withstand it, still be here after it rolled away grumbling into the distance into the night.

"What are you doing out here?"

Tyhr's voice washed over her—plucking at the strings in her heart, whispering into the lonely places of her soul. She didn't respond, not turning, waiting for him to come to her. Tyhr came down the steps to stand beside her. When Astrid glanced up, to see the silver mask and read the golden gaze, he was watching the sky too.

"I used to enjoy thunderstorms. How they smell, the electricity in the air. I would stand at my window and watch the lightning, thrilled with each boom that broke across the sky," Astrid said.

"Do you still?"

He touched her back, gentle pressure—tentative and warm.

"They're so constant here, scattered days of sunshine, so much muggy heat. I think I've come to miss the bright days more," she said, leaning into his touch.

"I always have as well," he said.

More raindrops fell, hitting stone, so fat she could hear them land—a patter over the terrace and house. The sky refused to light up though far off thunder came to them, breaking against them, engulfing them. A promise of what was to come. *I will come. I will drive you away,* it seemed to say.

"We'll be soaked if we stand here," he said.

"I don't mind." She shrugged, a wildness creeping in, a daring thrill.

"You'll mind if you catch a cold," he teased.

She laughed, looking at him, a soft moment blooming between them. Golden eyes, beautiful eyes, a gaze that worked to bring down Astrid's defenses whether he knew it or not. The homesickness retreated, easing away to watch from a distance, leaving space for another emotion—a different desire.

"Right now, I wouldn't mind," she said.

"I'll wait with you then," he said, voice roughing, catching her emotions.

"Aren't you worried about catching a cold?"

"Maybe being here with you is worth it," he said softly, facing the jungle, the stillness making his words possible, heard without the alive background noise.

She tingled all over, it left her skin warm and tight with awareness. He stood so close, brushing her arm, hand at his side just as hers was. She could reach out, brush against him, an invitation. Would he take her offer when she kept ignoring his own small efforts? He had softened from the man on the platform. Maybe he had realized it would push her farther away, tear down the beginnings of the bridge stretched tentatively between them.

Did she want to build bridges? What else was there to do in this place, with a man she'd been promised to all her life? It was why she'd come, to marry a stranger, to live a whole new life. Despite the unexpected mystery of him, the magic permeating everything about her new world, she did want there to be friendship at the very least. Someday there might be love. Last night had given Astrid hope.

More than anything she wanted that. *Love.* What had been between her mother and father was what she'd dreamed about. A love that meant if one went the other did too, death no barrier to emotion and devotion. The tenderness they had always shown each other, the simple daily things; a chair pulled out at dinner, a quick kiss if they passed each other in the hall, a small bunch of flowers, a hand-embroidered handkerchief. Each day, each hour the words spoken aloud and cemented into place, all those years. *I love you.*

Astrid turned to him, hand brushing his, lifting it to touch the mask, and Tyhr tensed with surprise. "Do you get tired of wearing it?"

That silver, snarling animal stared back at her. It meant to frighten Astrid away, intimidate and force her back—an intangible warning given life and form. A smooth surface beneath her fingertips, warm with Tyhr's body heat.

Take it off, she pleaded silently. *Let me see you*

It was a circle of thought, always turning, leaving her again and again in this place. She had no idea when it would stop or if it ever would. But their life couldn't begin until then, the gap too wide for any bridge and left them with half a life.

With a crack, lightning split the sky, thunder booming right on top of them. Astrid jumped, heart thumping, then laughed. The clouds gave up, cutting the rain loose, and a torrent fell all at once.

Tyhr grabbed her hand, pulling her up the steps, a laugh of his own escaping. The air following brought ozone and heat, a lightning struck the terrace, blinding them as sparks rose from the stone. She turned back, looking up at the sky, but Tyhr didn't let her go until he'd pulled her inside and they were safe beneath the roof.

The front door remained open, as always.

———

"You haven't told me much about your family," Tyhr said, curiosity woven through his words—a vine reaching out to her for support. He held the door to the library open, watching her hungrily as she moved past him and into the room.

"You haven't asked," Astrid said.

"I am now."

A fire burned in the hearth, jumping on the grate, and warming the room—the flames almost as warm as his voice. Restlessness touched her, keeping her from sitting, sending her from the window to the bookshelves. She'd discovered new favorites here, happily discovering books on botany and history, a handful of novels by new authors. Astrid ran a finger along the spines, leather and linen alternately rough and then smooth.

But she didn't want a book right now.

Moving to the overlarge desk she looked down at the maps spread across the surface, muted colors and carefully plotted lines—continents and countries, oceans and seas. The world as it had been presented to her as child. The known world, a place they were only tied to by the thinnest of threads here in the summer valley. The slightest motion would snap them free, releasing them into the unknown.

"My mother's family came from Norway." She traced a line across the map, the coastline of a forgotten shore. Astrid glanced at Tyhr who had come to stand beside her. "But that's not where they settled. We'd been in

Amsterdam for the last several years. But my father, he was from all over, or nowhere. He owned Porter and Stern, a shipping company. A hands-on kind of person, touching everything, always working."

"He didn't have someone he trusted to run the business?"

Was that curiosity or judgment in his tone? She couldn't be sure.

"He had a business partner, Mr. Porter, but they always kept their duties separate, two halves making up the whole. When my mother became ill, he brought someone in to help with his day-to-day workload. My brother could never be trusted with those things. But by the time she died, there wasn't much left of the company."

"And your father and brother?" he asked, his low voice coming from a distance, carrying an unknown grief.

Astrid shrugged, trying to brush it aside—smooth it down. In her mind, a dark sea rolled, a lighthouse cutting across the night. She looked down at the gold ring on her left hand, twisting it, a promise made and kept. Astrid turned to Tyhr, meeting his gaze in a challenge. "Don't you know? You must have found out. Otherwise, you wouldn't have written to me."

"What about the business partner?"

She studied the mask, wishing for the thousandth time that she could see his face—read his emotions. His words, his voice, gave nothing away.

"He took everything to cover the debt," Astrid said, voice lowering with each word until it became a whisper. "Even my bedroom furniture."

"I'm sorry," he said gently.

"Are you?" she asked, tone sharp, wondering why it had taken him so long to get here. This was a conversation she'd expected to have sooner; when the train journey was a fresh memory before the house became familiar. Instead, it was all overdue and exhausting.

"Why did you make a deal with my father?"

"Who would marry me otherwise?" he gestured to the mask. "I had to arrange my own."

"So, you willingly tied yourself to someone not even born yet?"

His eyes gleamed in the firelight, shifting with the dancing flame.

"How long have you been here Tyhr?" she whispered.

"There are things—"

"You can't say. Yes. You've said."

Her tone was dry, and he shrugged, the silence between them grating on her nerves.

"When will you tell me?"

Tyhr shook his head and Astrid sighed.

"So, until then I'm here because you're tired of being alone," she said quietly, pausing to let him speak, carrying on when he didn't. "Because I have nowhere else to go."

For a wild moment, she thought Tyhr would tell her to leave, and Astrid thought of the tiger in her dreams—green jungle shadows and orange stripes. Astrid would refuse to go and force him to face this, face her, and give her something worth holding on to.

Give me a reason to stay.

"I am glad you are here," he said, voice soft, looking down at his hands. "Even if it's only because I've been alone. Even if you had nowhere else to go. The circumstances have been unusual, extraordinary."

"Unbelievable."

"And yet you've stayed," he said, amusement and bitterness mixing.

She opened her mouth, something sharp on her tongue —tart and bitter. Nowhere else to go. The world beyond this place was difficult to navigate as a single woman— prey to any predator. But she could confront it, conquer it. Astrid remained for another reason, one she had not considered closely and had not yet fully acknowledged. Could she call it curiosity? A simple, uncomplicated emotion.

But there was something else there, too.

"Yes," she agreed. "I'm still here."

———

THE NEXT EVENING, ASTRID ARRIVED IN THE LIBRARY WELL BEFORE sunset, curling on the window seat and considering the conversation from the night before. She was still here. She remained. And she'd come to the library knowing Tyhr would be here, wanting to be with him.

Chinook followed, twittering to himself in a pleased way as he flitted around the room. A tea tray appeared between two blinks, a second of fizzing magic in the air, and then a steaming pot waited to be poured. Chinook flew to inspect it, pecking at the fruit biscuits the kitchen had learned she liked.

"You should ask first," Astrid said, putting one on a plate for him and setting it off to the side.

A good hostess would offer without the guest needing to ask.

"This is your house as much as mine," she said, letting out a sharp laugh.

You are the mistress of the house. Therefore, you should offer. Would you like me to find you a book on etiquette?

"Are you implying I lack manners?"

I do not believe there was any implication in my words. He paused in the devouring destruction of the food, tilting his head to one side. *I was very direct.*

"Chinook," she began, voice strained. She closed her eyes, breathing through her nose, resisting the urge to toss biscuit crumbs at him. "You are very forthright, aren't you?"

You are also very observant.

Astrid sighed, giving up. He would be himself, no matter what, and she respected any creature so wholly themselves. She gestured to the window seat in an invitation, and she was pleased when he joined her, perching on the ledge to watch the world beyond the glass go by. They sat together quietly as the evening grew longer, the night approaching like a wild thing.

When the sun was down and night insects sang the library door opened, drawing Astrid's attention away from the window. She hadn't realized she'd sat here there for so long. Tyhr came to stand beside her without making a sound, and she made room for him on the window bench, Chinook making a pleased chirp of welcome.

Awareness touched her, butterflies unfurling, a quick glance to see if he watched her. But Tyhr's gaze was directed at the window, looking out at the street, familiar to her and no one else in the room. That wasn't true though, Chinook had begun to familiarize himself, watching as she did only with more sharp judgment.

"Chinook said you come here most days," he said, glancing at her.

"Not all the time," she said. "Less and less now."

Astrid was surprised Chinook had shared that, though she realized she shouldn't be. But she'd counted that as private, her own tight emotions woven through her minutes here—observing the world going on, people living lives so alien to her own.

"Why?"

"At first it helped with the homesickness." One shoulder went up in a shrug. "But I think it's actually made it worse. I see these people, some of them neighbors for years, the trees I sat under to read, the streets I walked down. I do miss it."

"I'm sorry."

Tyhr's voice was soft, edged in tenderness, as he reached out to place a hand on hers. The touch warmed her, prickling along her nerves, an awareness creeping in of their closeness, of the intimacy shared here.

But she couldn't reassure him or minimize her emotion —the longing for a place she'd known so well. She couldn't promise that it would all be well in time. It would be untrue to herself and unfair to him. So, she didn't say anything at all and his hand retreated, leaving her cold.

———

THE CONSERVATORY WAS A CURE-ALL. A PLACE TO DISCOVER PEACE when she could find it nowhere else in the house. She'd begun the project of repotting the different plants from all over the house. It had become a quiet rhythm—counting out the hours of Astrid's days, the weeks that collected like water in a pail. It eased her soul and helped the restlessness that came over her.

Don't you get bored of messing with plants?

Astrid glanced up as Chinook came through the door connecting the conservatory to the rest of the house. He landed on the workbench, scratching through a pile of seed packets.

"Never," she said, half smiling.

I would.

"I'm glad I'm not you then."

Yes, well. You are missing out. I happen to be delightful.

"Oh yes," she said, making a face at him which he ignored. "Have you come to be critical? Bored of doing bird things?"

Never.

"Then can it be that the solitary Chinook is lonely? Desperate for my company?"

There was an edge of teasing in her tone, a surprising easiness between them. She put the pot down, the conservatory around them bright, Chinook's shadow moving beneath him as he hopped along her workbench.

Dirt caked her hands and lingered beneath her nails; a spot on her forearm, more on her dress. It was the most wonderful feeling, to be more herself than ever, enjoying the peacefulness of the conservatory and the lush plants.

I never said that.

"You didn't have to."

It is very rude of you to make assumptions about my feelings on any subject.

"Expect for when it comes to you lingering in my conservatory."

Possibly, he conceded.

"Definitely."

Or not at all if you plan to continue with that tone in your voice.

"You're just not enjoying being found out."

Very well. I might be willing to admit that you have proven yourself to be not nearly as annoying as I had feared, he fluffed up, a little round ball of colorful feathers with two beady eyes.

"Thank you." She smiled to herself, working a small fern from a pot and placing it in the larger one she had waiting. "You've turned out to be surprisingly decent company as well."

His feathers smoothed some.

"Especially since I never expected to make friends with a talking bird."

New experiences are good for people, they expand your horizons.

"Oh, I agree," she said.

And from what I've seen your horizons were in dire need of expansion.

"How is it that you manage to turn compliments in on themselves so that they are both insult and praise?" She sighed, going back to her pot, the small fern she'd taken from the hall moving from smaller to larger.

Natural talent and practice.

She threw her head back with a laugh. "You're very full of yourself."

Oh no, I have the exact right impression of myself.

"Well," she said, "I wish I could cultivate such confidence. Maybe you can teach me."

He ruffled his feathers, his version of a shrug, conveying his very obvious opinion that she was not teachable. But he remained with her, watching as begonias and ferns were repotted, watching as she picked through the stack of empty pots tucked into a far corner. He stayed until late afternoon when she decided that enough plants had been rehomed for the day and a bath before dinner was needed.

———

CHINOOK CAME AGAIN THE NEXT DAY. AND THE NEXT. CASUALLY appearing, inspecting the plants—that she'd come to think of as her own—and the corners of the conservatory searching for insects. The conversation began to flow more easily between them, a naturalness taking over that she'd not expected.

"Chinook, have you always been a bird?" she asked one day, glancing up from repotting a bleeding heart, double pink petals trembling with her words.

Have you always been a human?

"Of course!"

Well then?

"I think it's a fair question. Tyhr is not what he appears to be at first. Nothing here is as it seems. And here we are, talking. Most birds don't talk."

Maybe most people do not know how to listen.

"Or maybe you're avoiding the question."

I refuse to tell you my life story.

Astrid snorted, shooting him a look. "Why?"

I do not know you well enough. How do I know you are trustworthy?

She lay the plant down carefully, turning to him, a line between her brows. "You don't know me well enough? What would well enough entail exactly considering you come here every day?"

He ruffled his feathers, preening a wing, without responding.

"Trustworthy. Really?" she asked with a sigh.

She turned back to the plants in silence, more irritated with herself for being offended that he wouldn't share than his actual refusal. She shouldn't be hurt by it, it wasn't her business, everyone—even annoying little birds who criticized her love for plants—deserved their privacy.

If you must know, Chinook said, tone huffy, hopping along the workbench and through the dirt she'd spilled. *I've always been a bird and resident of the Summer Valley.*

"Have you always been able to talk?" she asked, concentrating on the plant, not wanting to distract him or discourage him from sharing by asking too many questions. "Or is that part of the magic at work here too?"

There is more than one kind of magic here.

———

ASTRID CHOSE A HISTORY OF THE ROMAN EMPIRE AFTER DINNER the next night—settling into the sofa in the library with a sigh of contentment. Tyhr sat across from her with a book of his own, the two of them comfortable with the silence. Chinook passed through, small and fast, there and gone as he looked around and moved on. Very much like a nosey sibling, reminding her of the way she'd lurked at the edges of her brother's conversations with friends.

Chinook. Tyhr. Astrid.

Slowly, they were coming together.

"Tell me about your family," she said, shutting the book abruptly and setting it aside.

"Mine?"

"Yes, don't sound so surprised." She leaned forward, the urge to reach across the space between them and touch him catching her off guard—a building siren song. "You know a little of mine and I know nothing of yours."

"Why don't I show you?"

———

TYHR MOVED THROUGH THE JUNGLE LIKE A TIGER, PASSING through the undergrowth without touching it—barely a rustle of leaves, no snapping twigs beneath his feet. Every branch caught her dress, the uneven earth tripping her up.

A sigh of frustration escaped Astrid, and Tyhr paused, glancing back, the light of the lantern catching the lines of the mask. In the half-light, it looked molten—moving, shifting.

"Would you like help?" he asked.

There was a smile in his voice, humor in his eyes. Not for the first time, she wondered about the face beneath the silver surface. She'd begun to dream about his voice, waking up with her name in the air, wondering if she'd imagined it or if in another part of the house, he was searching for her. But that was always in the daylight when the house contained only herself and Chinook.

"How would you be able to help?" she asked.

Tyhr held out his hand in invitation. It was always on offer, companionship and peace, friendship with the tantalizing hint of more. Astrid so rarely took it, even after months in this place, knowing she would never see the world again—never leave. She considered the hand, how warm he would be, and took it. Surprise flashed in his eyes.

"Well?" she prompted. "Do you plan to trample down the path ahead of me?"

"Come with me," he said, voice holding dark promises and mysteries.

Somehow the jungle drew back, letting her pass, no longer reaching for her—touching her. Tyhr guided Astrid, knowing the path better than she ever could. The lantern she carried only added to the darkness crouched beneath the leaves, tucked close to tree limbs and twisting vines.

Other shadows began to take shape beneath the vegetation—boulders, stones, and beneath her feet, the remnants of a paved path. The bulky shapes resolved into walls and arches leading onto trees, and stone cottages covered in vines. In several places stone walls stretched to the upper reaches of the trees, hinting at grander beginnings.

"What is this place?"

"Madytos," he said, holding the lantern higher. "It was a city."

"A city? Here?"

He nodded, considering the ruins. "My home wasn't always so small. It stretched far to the south and east. It's constricted over time, narrowing in on us."

"It was a big city?"

"Yes, as big as many of the ones now. Just older. A long time ago..."

She glanced at him, wondering how such a large city could have existed without making it into the history books, without ruins or artifacts. "Has it always been here?"

"Yes," he said, wistful with the memory. "It's always been on the other side of the Black Forest. We used to call it the Summer Valley."

"But," she said, hesitating, wondering how to ask, to express her confusion. "Never in my world. Never part of where I lived."

"Only in the way that the Black Forest is a part of the world now."

"In stories," Astrid confirmed.

He nodded, one shoulder going up, half a shrug.

"Then why have I never heard of it?"

"Maybe you haven't read the right books," he said, a teasing edge to his tone.

She laughed, the moment natural and easy between them. His hand around hers was warm, the touch prickling up her arm, easing into her heart. Being here with him, in this place, connected them more than anything yet had. This man felt like someone she would love, the emotion was there, waiting, hoping, ready. But not yet, she needed more.

This was a start.

Was it there for Tyhr, did he feel the flutter of it between them, the potential? Or had his moment been different or sooner? Had it arrived yet? She wanted to ask, the question died in her throat. Trapped like Tyhr's face beneath the mask. But the city began to grow around them, changing from what must have been outskirts to inner more heavily built areas. Even now, even in ruins with the jungle living within walls, and populating houses, she could see a difference.

They turned a corner and came into a small intimate area. In the center stood a large statue, worn white marble, a woman with her back to them, gazing at the world around them.

"A long time ago this plaza was filled with pink and white flowers. She loved the colors and would come here to sit amongst them. I would come with her."

Astrid looked at him, a quick peek, wishing again she could see his expression—catch the emotion there. But the loss, the deep grief, was in his voice, in how his accent thickened slightly. She'd grown so used to his accent and barely heard it now. But it was heavy here, in this place from him past—a history recalled and remembered.

He brought her around the statue, coming to stand before the stone woman—a beautiful face, even now, worn with countless years. The stone was patchy with moss, growing across the base, vines snaking up from the forest floor, and ferns taking root between the cracks. But the face remained clear, the marble white, as if someone cleared it regularly, lovingly.

"Do you come here often?" Astrid asked, wondering how closely he resembled his mother, if at all.

"Yes," he said after a long pause, voice thick.

She nodded. "I would too."

Turning, holding the lantern high, Astrid took in the ruins around them. He'd said it was a city, not just a town or village, but a huge bustling place. She wondered what had happened here, how much time had passed? Decaying buildings, windows and doors, the remains of a cobbled road. The jungle was taking it all back, reclaiming the land and space, stretching out with the sigh of growing things.

"What did it look like before?"

Tyhr was quiet for a moment, and Astrid wondered if she'd asked the wrong question. Were there ghosts here for him? Regret flashed through her. So many things were off-limits, subjects that were tender to the touch—bruising beneath clumsy questions—conversations where she said the wrong thing again and again.

"Tall."

His voice startled Astrid, coming so late.

"What?"

"This place was tall. White stone. Carved animals. Statues. There were flowers everywhere, huge pots of plants, and window boxes full of flowers. But all of it was cultivated and tidy. It's strange to see Madytos this way, covered in so much green. It's as if the city always wanted to look like this."

"Where's the rest of it?"

He turned, taking in what the light revealed, seeing something other than the present.

"Gone. It's taken some time. As fast as things grow here, they don't grow that fast."

"Hundreds of years?" she prompted.

He nodded.

"And you've been here all that time?"

Alone in the jungle, except for the sharp-tongued Chinook, watching everything you'd ever known being taken over, eaten, erased. And yet he seemed unchanged. Tyhr didn't appear to be hundreds of years old. His mannerisms, the way he spoke, and even the way his hands looked, gave her the impression of a young man.

"How old are you Tyhr?"

"Does it matter?" he asked, elusive and curious.

"Maybe I don't want to be married to an old man."

His laugh filled the air, genuine and delighted. "No, I don't blame you."

"So?" She drew the word out, waiting.

"Honestly? I stopped keeping track. So much time has passed, continues to pass, yet I remain the same."

"Will you tell me what happened here?"

"Someday," he said. "When the time is right."

"How do you know the time isn't right?" Exasperation crept into her tone, and Astrid worked to smooth it. "I want to know."

"And you will. That day is quickly approaching."

Tyhr didn't say more, focused on the statue of his mother, the lantern light catching his eyes and turning them into molten gold. Astrid watched him out of the corner of her eye, the way he stood, the way sizzle in the air of unspoken things. To have lived for so long, alone, the house closing in, the way the wind rushed through the trees—never changing.

How would she have handled it all? Retreated into herself, pushed at boundaries searching for escape, and then, discovering none, given up? Let it all go? Would she have managed to keep the pieces of herself together? She wasn't sure. There was no way to really know, not until it happened.

Tyhr was easier to understand knowing these things.

Now, Astrid needed the rest of the story, the pieces that would bring it all together. It was close, she could feel it, the way the story spiraled in on them. Soon, she'd understand all of it.

———

HE HELD HER HAND ON THE WAY BACK TO THE HOUSE. THEY shared a comfortable silence on the way back. Astrid embraced it, not feeling the need to fill the gap between them. When they reached the front door of the house, Tyhr paused, keeping her in the starlight.

"Are you tired? Would you like to return to your room?"

"Not yet," she said, even as sleep reached for her with tempting fingers.

"Library?"

She nodded.

A fire had been lit—by ghosts or magic, she never knew —and a tray with a decanter and wine glasses sat on the table, fruit and water too. She'd come to think of it as the standard and for the most part had stopped questioning it. There were never any answers.

They settled onto opposite sofas with their books—hers history of vegetable plants and his a copy of Greek myths. An easy kind of familiarity had come from a few shared hours in the library. They read, each self-contained but together. Soft sheets crossed her mind, blankets and pillows, a soft mattress to fall into. With the book in her hand and the warmth of the fire, the late hour seduced her, holding out welcoming arms.

Come. Sleep and I will hold you it said.

Keeping Tyhr's late hours was hard, he always slept a little toward dawn, but the late nights had been more difficult to adapt to than she'd expected. Even though she'd gotten into the habit of reading late at home and waking much later than her parents—skipping in at the end of breakfast to kiss cheeks on the way out the door to see friends or go shopping. Those hours hadn't seemed to wear Astrid down like these did.

That was a lifetime ago.

Here, after midnight, drowsiness lulled Astrid, welcoming her just as she welcomed it. Sleep came with heavy-lidded eyes, snuggled into velvet pillows, and the crackling fire filling her dreams.

———

HE STOOD WITH HIS BACK TO HER, TALL WITH BROAD SHOULDERS, long black hair pulled back in a knot at the base of his neck. The clothes he wore were navy and deep green, a jacket with a sharp cut and breaches, polished black boots, and a wide gold band on his left hand. She held her left hand up, a matching band—gold and gold—and Astrid smiled.

Around them the house was quiet, but the noises of a busy street came from beyond the green open door—carriages, chatter and laughter, someone yelling cheerfully. It sounded like the street she'd lived on, the one abandoned to come here.

But she knew that beyond those doors there would never be a bustling street, never anyone else to smile at or start a conversation with. This house was besieged by storms with an encroaching jungle on the other side of the threshold.

A fire burned behind her in a ring, surrounded by stones, crackling and jumping. Around the entryway potted plants swayed in a wind she could not feel—the force of it increasing and a post crashed to the floor, dirt spraying everywhere. A gardenia, white flowers crushed, already fading—hinting at some impending doom.

Astrid took a step forward, leaning into the wind she now felt, the force of it almost knocking her off her feet. Tyhr took a step forward as well, moving away easily, toward the open door without waiting for her. Calling out his name, panic building now, she found her voice didn't work. It belonged to the house with the wind, not to the house with the door facing a busy street.

Tyhr could not hear her.

Forcing movement, reaching for him, catching a sleeve, Astrid pulled until he turned to face her.

No tiger.

No mask.

A handsome face—a beautiful face—classical, the kind carved in marble and swooned over centuries later. A face Astrid wanted to take between her hands and kiss. His mouth opened, forming words, but his voice was indistinguishable from the ringing in her ears.

———

Astrid woke, pulse-pounding and throat tight. She kept her eyes closed, holding on to the image of his face, desperate to remember it and carry the shape with her into the light. Was it his true face? Would those be the features she saw when the mask finally fell away?

Would the mask ever come off?

The pages of a book turned, Tyhr reading on the sofa

opposite, unaware of her dream or nightmare. The warmth of the fire was still here, the room unchanged. Sleep did begin to come back, slowly, tiptoeing toward her, and she rested in limbo and her heart slowed.

Minutes passed, the night turning toward day. Astrid could feel it there, and the expectation that he would leave, abandoning her to sunlit hours weighed on her. Half asleep now, almost dreaming, she heard the book close, the creak of the sofa as he stood.

"Astrid?"

His voice came from far away. Her eyes were too heavy to open, body relaxed into the deep sofa, not wanting to give up the comfort. Footsteps came toward her. Gentle fingers brushed her cheek, tracing her brow, before combing through her hair. A soft touch—intimate.

"Sweet dreams," he murmured, the touch leaving, the sound of his boots retreating.

When she woke it was in daylight, the fire burned to nothing but embers.

CHAPTER SIXTEEN

A storm shook and rattled the windows—the world beyond the glass a blur of rain. Lightning lit the sky, there and gone in a heartbeat, thunder rumbling between each stark flash. The house felt under siege as the storm raged—the rain searching for a way inside, seeking a weak spot between the stones.

"Will the house withstand this?"

"It has before. It will again."

"What about the doors?"

They were always open—for good or bad—offering welcome to whatever might arrive.

Tyhr shook his head. "It can't come in."

It.

As if the storm lived—as if storms were creatures that rolled across the skies and would answer a call, that could be stopped with a gesture.

"Have the storms always been this bad?" Astrid asked, gaze pulled to the window as the sky lit up with lightning —the house shaking beneath the onslaught.

Tyhr gave a half shrug, neither confirming nor denying, simply accepting her curiosity.

"It seems like they've gotten worse," Astrid continued.

Tyhr looked around the sitting room—the elaborately painted ceiling and walls, noting details as if for the first time—before his eyes shifted back to the window. Absently, he ran a hand across the cover of the book he held, tracing the gold embossing on the cover—a travelogue about India with a tiger.

"It's possible," he said finally. A shadow lay beneath his words, the quiet tone hinting at something dark. He met her gaze, steady, a smile in his eyes, pushing the moment away. "I—"

He stopped and Astrid held her breath, tension blossoming, vibrating between them.

Tell me, she urged him silently. *Tell me about the magic here. Tell me something true.*

"Come to the baths tomorrow tonight," he said. "All the hot water you could ask for. Have you seen them yet?"

Astrid shook her head, caught off guard, her brain still focused on the conversation she'd thought they'd been having—on the answers she'd hoped would fill the space between them.

"Would you like to see them?"

"Yes," she closed the book in her lap, another history of the great outside world, and nodded. "Chinook told me little about them. Fed by hot springs?"

"Yes, the water is piped in, and the pool is continuously fed." There was a smile in his voice. "Always the perfect temperature."

"And you want me to come bathe with you?" She hesitated over the words, the images they brought to mind, as her cheeks began to warm.

He laughed. "Yes. Why not? I grew up in a culture where men and women traditionally bathed together in bath-houses. Like the Romans."

"How often were there separate pools though?"

"Most of the time."

"But we'd be together?" She raised an eyebrow, a smile tugging at her lips. "It doesn't sound very traditional."

"Well," he shook his head, a hint of laughter in his voice. "No, not exactly. Close maybe. I don't have a sauna either, but I could arrange a bucket of cold water and a birch branch to lash yourself with if that's what you'd like."

"No, thank you." She laughed. "I don't mind missing out on that part."

"And the rest?"

She studied his golden eyes—searching—wishing to peel the mask away, to read whatever expression his face might hold. She needed his features—needed more than the watchfulness of his gaze. He leaned forward, the snarling mask catching the light, earnestness conveyed in every muscle.

"Will you come?" he asked softly.

A challenge, a dare, and beneath it, a plea.

"Yes."

CHAPTER SEVENTEEN

Astrid stood at the top of the stairs, twisting the wedding ring on her finger, tracing the fading etched flowers. Change waited at the bottom, a shift in the small world turning around her. Something she longed for and feared. There was no way to know the future —to predict an outcome—but more than anything, she wished it were possible.

If she already knew what would happen next, would she go?

Yes.

She took the first step and then the next. The stairs wound down, a spiral that was brightly lit with lanterns— light flickered over the mosaics of plants and animals, forest scenes similar to the painted murals in the rest of the house. The dark, glossy eyes of antelopes and spotted, gleaming leopards observed Astrid. Birds of all colors crowded branches, flowered vines curving up trees, and deep red flowers were iridescent in the light. Every few feet an alcove held a frosted glass lantern with polished brass fittings.

Chinook had offered to bring her down to the baths. But she had a bath—a lovely white stone tub with painted orange blossoms and jasmine. Who needed Roman-style baths when you could read a book in a private tub? There had been no curiosity until now.

Not until Tyhr invited her.

Following the curve of the wall, Astrid kept her hand against the tile to steady herself as she continued down. Here and there the smooth surface dipped, catching at her fingers. Something made imperfectly, evidence of humanity, a hole in the magic. It was impossible to tell how much magic it took to hold the house together, whether it was all magic in places or at some points of the day more so than others. The house was very much like Tyhr—presenting a facade, hiding some kind of truth.

The stairs continued down, several stories into the earth, and she followed. The soft sound of water grew—a fountain bubbling and the fresh scent of wet stone. In the next curve, the stairs stopped and opened up onto an enormous room.

Lanterns lit the space, hung from the ceiling on delicate chains, shaped like the moon and stars—multifaceted and glimmering. The light caught the mosaics—blue and gold waves rolling across the ceiling in intricate patterns, coming together to paint a far-off ocean. Around the edges of the room sat carved benches, low with backs like palm leaves, the wood dark and smooth. A large pool filled the room, carved steps leading down into it, steam curling up from the surface.

"Hello?"

No one answered.

There was no one there.

He'd invited her. She'd come. But he wasn't here.

Disappointment bit into her sharply. She was startled by the savageness of her response, the pang of rejection. Was it too close to dawn? Would this be another night like so many before? When she'd sat at the dinner table eating alone and waiting, always waiting, for Tyhr?

Crossing to the nearest bench, she tugged at her robe with a sigh—silk, smooth and light, clung to her curves and then fell away with a whisper. The fabric pooled on the bench, flowing like liquid in the light. She loved the color—a deep purple, almost blue—that matched the color of the waves overhead.

Beneath the robe, she wore simple cotton chemise. Not something the house had given her, not one of the many things Tyhr had presented her with. This was from home. A piece to remind her of the world beyond the house opposite of paradise. If he'd been here, she'd planned to wear it into the water. The endless wardrobe in her suite had failed to produce a bathing suit but she wasn't brave enough to be nude in front of Tyhr.

Tyhr, her husband in name only.

Astrid hesitated, patting at the pins in her hair to make sure the bun was secure. He wasn't here, so what did it matter? With a shrug, she slipped the straps of the garment off her shoulders and tossed it on the bench with the robe. She shivered as the air touched her bare skin, goosebumps prickling along her arms and shoulders, as she moved to the edge of the pool.

Dipping a toe into the water she smiled. It was hot, but not uncomfortably so. With a sigh of pleasure, she stepped down into it, welcoming the release of tension in her back. Astrid waved her arms beneath the surface, enjoying the way the water felt as she moved through it, smiling to herself.

"I knew you'd love it." His laugh rippled out over the water, bouncing back from the tiled walls, shivering amongst the star-shaped lanterns. "It's wonderful, isn't it?"

She spun, searching for the source, and stopped when she saw Tyhr standing at the bottom of the stairs. His golden eyes were smiling and the pleasure in his voice was evident.

"You came!"

"Don't sound so surprised," he said, crossing to a bench at the opposite end of the pool from her own. He moved on bare feet, soundless as always, and filling up the room in a way no one else ever could.

"Well, it wouldn't be the first time you didn't show up for something," she said, sinking lower into the water, wondering how much was visible beneath the surface in the dim light. She'd felt so bold before but now she'd wished she'd kept the chemise on.

"I told you I'd be here."

"Yes, but you weren't here when I arrived." There was a sharp edge to her tone which she regretted immediately, and she hurried on, smoothing her voice out. "I thought you'd changed your mind."

"I won't stay if you don't want me to." His hand stopped on the tie of his robe, motionless, caught between untying or retying, waiting for her to make a choice.

"No." She shook her head. Even now, weeks after that moment on the edge of the terrace, they were still tentative around each other—slow and careful with the other's emotions. "I was only surprised when you weren't here. I thought I was going to have this place all to myself."

"You still can," he said softly.

She shook her head, stomach knotting, excitement and

unease coming together beneath her skin. "No, stay. Please."

Tyhr nodded, turning away as the robe slipped free. She turned as well but not before catching a glimpse of his muscled back, bare thighs, and backside. She sank lower in the water, warmth lapping around her neck as she moved her arms back and forth beneath the surface, watching the ripples. The lanterns flickered, light low, and she was grateful for the privacy they offered.

"This is one of my favorite places," he said, easing into the water, ripples reaching her, breaking against her body.

Astrid made a noise, interest and question all in one, as she turned to face him. Heat touched her, warmer than the water, filling her belly and burning her ears. Tyhr was waist deep, sinking and moving as she had, enjoying the warmth beneath false stars.

"I've always loved hot water. I think paradise is constant hot water and brandy."

"I wasn't expecting that." She said with a laugh. "I'd have thought you'd want a different kind of paradise."

"What do you imagine for me then?" he asked, moving through the water toward her, the space between them shrinking.

She could hear the smile in his voice, and it sent a delicious frisson through her.

"I don't know," she said thoughtfully, shrugging. "An endless party? Wine, women, and song? Maybe you would like to live in the sunshine."

She bit her lip, regretting the careless words the moment they were out. Of course, he wanted that—blue skies, to be his true self, without the mask, to feel sunshine on his face, searching out sunburns and squinted eyes against the highest point in the day. But they avoided the topic, dancing around it, getting closer every day without addressing it.

"I know your paradise," he said, ignoring her words out of kindness or for his own sake. "A garden full of every plant you've ever read about."

"Oh, well," she laughed, grateful that he'd skimmed over her thoughtlessness. "That's not a guess. It's obvious. I'm easy to figure out."

"You're not that easy," he said softly. "You're so self-contained. Encased in something solid I can't put a name to."

"Stubbornness?"

He laughed. "Maybe."

Astrid was surprised. She never considered herself hard to understand or difficult to reach. Any question he'd asked, she'd answered. While each question she asked him went unanswered. If there was a self-contained person in this room, it wasn't her.

The burble of the fountain seemed loud in their silence, the lanterns overhead flickering—patterned light rippling on the water. They were quiet together, the distance between them shrinking, the world easing them closer, waiting to see what would happen.

She wanted to see what would happen too.

"Are you glad you came?" he asked.

"To the baths or the Summer Valley?" she asked.

"Both."

She opened her mouth to respond, the answer on the tip of her tongue. But hesitated. Her instinct was *yes*. And it surprised her. If Chinook had asked her the same question an hour ago she wasn't sure what her response would have been. But now? With him?

"Yes." She nodded, swirling water around herself,

sinking into it. "I'm happy I came."

"If I asked you to come to the baths again, would you?"

"I would very much enjoy that."

He seemed pleased, though it was hard to tell. She watched him out of the corner of her eye, wondering if he watched her just as closely. If he did, it wasn't obvious. Steam curled from the surface of the pool, blurring everything slightly, giving the room a dreamy edge.

"Is this what you had in mind when you suggested a shared bath?" she asked, sending a ripple of water toward him.

"Honestly?"

She raised an eyebrow at him, waiting.

"I don't know," he admitted. "I don't think I had anything in mind. I just want—"

"To be closer?"

He nodded—eyes bright behind the mask.

"It's decided then," she said, stomach a knot of excitement, a soft smile touching her lips. "Because I would like that too."

They spoke about the conservatory and the plants she'd started and the others she was working to repot. The books in the library and how he brought new ones into the collection—he went into Novgorod periodically and placed a bulk order with a bookseller there. But when she asked how he could possibly move through the world without people noticing and reacting to his mask he shrugged.

"More magic?"

He nodded, again giving no true answer to the question.

"It will be dawn soon," he said. "I should go."

"You should," she agreed as frustration flared through her.

Don't go, she thought, wanting to reach for him,

wanting the daylight to hold off—give them a little more time. If she held on to him, if the sun rose with her arms around him, would it make a difference? Would that be the key? Something had changed. It was in the air around them, in the expression in his eyes—the way he looked at her. A barrier had come down.

Turning, Astrid made her way to the edge of the pool—not caring now that she was nude, needing to leave him wanting something, anything, as badly as she wanted answers. Astrid needed Tyhr to want her, she realized—to stay with her in the day as well as the night. It came into sharp focus, a blurry object in the distance resolving into a longed for object. And she wanted to find out if he wanted the daylight hours with her as well.

With a deep breath, she stepped out of the water, skin tingling. His gaze was on her, hot and focused, and she was thrilled with the attention. Throwing a glance over her shoulder, Astrid smiled, pleased with the intensity of his gaze.

"Astrid," he whispered.

"Tyhr," she said with a smile.

He didn't speak as she dressed—all reserve and shyness vanished. Words spun through her head—invitations and passionate pleas—but she kept them inside.

"Will I see you at dinner tomorrow?" she asked, keeping her smile, already moving toward the staircase.

His *yes* followed her up the stairs.

CHAPTER EIGHTEEN

"Did you know that the fire is only lit in this room when you're having dinner?" Astrid indicated the dining room fireplace, flames jumping merrily. "Each time I've eaten here alone, it's been unlit."

He glanced at it and back to her. "If you want something, anything, like fire, you've only to ask."

"I've discovered that."

"The house can be forgetful. It's been a long time with only me here."

"And Chinook."

Tyhr laughed. "I think he's as bad as I am. He doesn't spend a lot of time inside generally."

"So, the house is haunted?"

"Not exactly," Tyhr said with a shrug, studying the murals, the tigers watching a tiger. "I wouldn't call it that."

"What would you call it?"

"Maybe I would call it ghosts." He picked up a fork, turning it in the light before setting it down again. "But it's more like memory. At one point there was more here, a fullness. But it's faded over time, gone away."

"More magic," Astrid sighed.

"Why do you say it like that?"

"Because the answer to everything here is magic, and I'm tired of it."

The expression in his gaze was unreadable. She would have given anything for a raised eyebrow or pursed lips. Something, even an expression of irritation, would be better than the snarling silver mask.

"You don't enjoy magic?" His tone was soft.

"Not if I can't understand it."

"Not everything can be understood," he said, stiff with defensiveness.

"Or maybe it's not worth being understood," she snapped.

Tyhr reached for the fork again but stopped, bringing his hands together and resting them on the table. He met her gaze, steady and searching, and Astrid wondered what it was he saw on her face.

"You read fairytales when you were young," he said, continuing when she nodded. "What were some of the rules in them?"

"Never talk to an animal that can talk, good or bad. It's a sign of trouble. I think that one has already proven to be true." She counted them off on her fingers as she went. "Always be nice to old ladies. They're generally powerful enchantresses about to wreak havoc on some innocent person's life."

Tyhr laughed, the sound bursting out of him, surprising her.

"What?" she asked with a smile.

"Nothing." He waved a hand, wanting her to continue. "Your list is good. Exactly right. Do you have anything else?"

Astrid nodded, stomach doing a little flip with the words.

"A kiss will break a curse."

———

A KISS.

Astrid contemplated her answer as they finished dinner and moved into the library afterward. She'd finished her meal, shoulders pulled back and one foot tapping, waiting for him to confirm or deny. He'd done neither, simply suggested they carry on the conversation somewhere more comfortable.

They sat across from each other in the library now. Tyhr watched her with those beautiful golden eyes, lit by fire, casually draped across the sofa as if he cared nothing for the world or the people in it. Her words didn't seem to touch him, not in an obvious way.

"You need a kiss to break the spell?" She raised an eyebrow, a hint of laughter in her voice. It was the most fairytale idea out of all of them.

He stiffened, tension gathering between them before he spoke.

"You're mocking me," he said, voice soft, threaded with hurt.

"No," she said, lifting one shoulder—easing the stiffness, pushing it away. "More myself. This place becomes more like a fairytale every day. A kiss to break a curse isn't surprising."

A log popped, settling in the hearth, sparks flying up and away. He didn't respond, eyes sliding to the flames, drawn to the fire. Something cold lingered. She stood abruptly, not pausing to think, only pushing herself forward into action. Tyhr watched her come, wordless, and she couldn't read the expression in his eyes. Curiosity? Wariness? Astrid crossed to him, determined, and knelt beside him. Inches apart, the mask seemed to shift with her proximity—it caught the firelight, the snarling features softening.

"If a kiss will break this magic," she said, voice husky, "then let me kiss you."

What she had meant to sound lighthearted was serious, the air sucked from the room, pressure building with each breath. He said nothing, unmoved, propped up against the cushions. The room warmed around them, heat building, something rushing toward her that she could no longer avoid, something she didn't wish to.

Astrid reached out to touch the mask, and he grabbed her wrist—stopping her—surprise flashing in his eyes. He shook his head, barely, the movement more of a jerk—a loud refusal without words. But she moved, letting him hold her, easing forward until their faces were inches apart. Not their faces—her face and his mask—and he watched her come, pupils dilating, eyes becoming dark in the firelight.

A tiger's face. Stylized and snarling, lips pulled back, fangs exposed. A fierce face—meant to invoke fear, to build terror, to warn others away. An expression meant to keep the whole world at bay. But Tyhr's eyes did not match the expression, nor did the gentle way he held her wrist. Astrid leaned in with her eyes closed and pressed her lips to the mask.

A kiss made of metal and Tyhr's quick intake of breath beneath the surface.

But the mask remained—unchanged.

A moment passed, and another—she held herself still,

motionless, waiting. When he didn't move, she opened her eyes to meet his stare. With almost no space between them, his hand still wrapped around her own, they stared at each other—tension split between them. The silver tiger mask kept its snarl. Astrid leaned away, easing back on her heels, and Tyhr let her go.

"I guess it didn't work," she said, giving him a small smile, wanting to make a joke of it—pushing the heavy moment into lightness.

But it weighed too much. The instant she'd crossed the room, it had all become too real. Now she knew how badly she'd wanted it to work. A simple thing, so easy to bestow, a kiss from someone who might become a lover to break an enchantment.

It worked in the stories—it should have worked for her.

"No," he said softly, "it's not as easy as that."

"No." She sighed, pushing up on her feet and turning away. "Of course not."

Tyhr stood as well, the sofa creaking as his weight lifted, the rustle of velvet and silk.

"Leaving so soon?" she smiled, a little bitter, turning it inward. She reclaimed her spot on the opposite sofa, picking up the book she'd set aside, feeling the leather cover, the smooth pages. It was comforting in her hands, a steady weight, something to anchor herself to in a moment when she felt so lost.

"I'll let you finish your book," he said. "It'll be dawn soon. You must be tired."

"Believe it or not, I'm getting used to these late hours." She laughed, running a finger across the silver embossed title. *Rare Flora of the Tropics.*

"You should still try to get some sleep," he said, moving around the sofa, out of reach.

She nodded, lifting her eyes to the fire, watching him in the periphery of her vision.

"If I could, I would kiss you."

Tyhr's words rushed up her spine. Heat shot through Astrid, pooling in her stomach, as a flush spread across her cheeks. What would his mouth taste like? How would it feel with his arms tight around her?

She'd wondered about these things—even on the train station platform for a blistering moment. He was not the man her father had spoken of. Not the man she'd expected. It all left her not knowing how to feel about him, leaving her with curiosity and the growing desire to remove the mask and close the unknowable distance between them.

The distance he kept in place.

The fire in the hearth popped and crackled, cheerfully alive in the dark room, the night beyond the windows kept at bay. The light shifted over her—a wave of warmth and shadow—brushing the book on her lap, the low table with tea and fruit, the empty sofa across from her.

"Then kiss me," she whispered.

He touched her shoulder, sliding his hand up and across the bare skin of her throat, pausing against her rapid pulse. She wondered if he could feel it, how fast her heart raced—impossible to ignore, to resist, and she leaned into his touch.

"Kiss me," she said again, reaching up to wrap her fingers around his wrist—binding him to her.

"Astrid," he whispered, so softly it was almost unheard as the fire popped and crackled.

She waited, heart-pounding seconds, and then the warmth of his hand retreated, leaving goosebumps and a chill. He would come around the sofa, he would come to her, and finally remove the mask. A moment passed, her breathing coming faster with anticipation.

But he didn't kneel before her, didn't ease onto the sofa beside her. Disappointment stabbed her. He was gone. The room was emptier—she could feel the hole he left in the space, the way a chill crept in. But she had to be sure, to know it was true. Pushing down a curl of pain, rejection a solid mass in her chest, she looked around.

The library was empty and the door open. The space beyond the frame was as dark as the night watching through the windows. Astrid was alone, like so many times before.

"No," she said aloud, voice harsh in the silence.

She set the book aside, not bothering to mark the page, forgetting the life cycle of orchids. He didn't get to slip away, ignore her, and leave her with more unanswered questions.

Not again.

The contents of the low table rattled as she stood too quickly and bumped into it, spilling tea. She paused, an impulse to tidy it then moved on. It could wait. It didn't matter. The idea of picking up a candlestick to take with her was discarded. The night beyond the windows would be easing soon, going gray at the horizon—the day would slide in.

Another day. Hours lay ahead, full of nothing, his absence pressing on her, questions circling like vultures.

It was still night in the house, full dark, and she paused in the hall, listening. Which way had Tyhr gone? His rooms? To the hot springs? The kitchen? Or had he already left the house behind, melting into the jungle before light could touch him? She blinked, the firelight from the library failing to penetrate the darkness, leaving no difference between her eyes open or shut.

She turned toward the entryway and ran straight into his solid figure, a noise of surprise escaping her. His arms came around her, as she'd wanted them to do, and he pulled her into him, fitting their bodies together.

Astrid's hands pressed flat against Tyhr's chest, hard muscles, and the rise and fall of his breath passing into her, through her. Smoothing her hands over his shirt, his breathing quickened. It was too dark. Even this close, she couldn't make out the features of the mask, his shoulders, nothing beyond the flat blackness before her eyes.

"Why did you follow me?" he asked, voice soft, as he gripped her tightly, fingers digging into her upper arms.

"Why did you wait?"

Moving her hands up, finding the open collar of his shirt, she felt his pulse jump beneath her searching fingers. He swallowed. It thrilled her, his reaction, an opening in the armor he'd been so careful to keep between them.

In the library, in the light, this had seemed impossible. To have him hold her this way, to feel him so close without being pushed away.

"You said that it wasn't as easy as a kiss," she said, pressing closer, willing his hands to slide over every inch of her body. "There's something you're leaving out, something you're not saying. I can't tell if you can't or don't want to."

He made a noise—disagreeing or protesting—but she hurried on.

"Nothing here makes sense. You've given me no answers. And half the time I don't even know if you want me here. You have to give me something."

It was a plea—her soul exposed—and Astrid was

grateful for the darkness that hid her embarrassed blush. Tyhr moved, one arm remaining wrapped around her waist, as he brought her hand up to where his lips would have been without the mask.

"Astrid," he said, breathing out her name, putting so much emotion into it that it made her knees weak.

Then she realized she'd felt it. The exhale of her name. The heat of it against her cheek. She jerked back in surprise, but he held on, arm tightening for a moment and then letting go. Her hand hovered over his face as she let out a shaky breath, unable to stop the trembling that overtook her Slowly—achingly slow—she lowered her hand to his face, expecting at any moment the hardness of the mask—an unchangeable barrier between them.

Warm skin, the curve of his lips opening beneath her fingers with a soft gasp. She brought her other hand up, smoothing the line of his stubble roughened jaw, his sharp cheekbones. He was breathing fast, matching her, his hands moving over her now, searching as she did.

With a laugh, she threw her arms around him, pulling him down to her, pressing her mouth to his. She kissed him hungrily—pouring all of her heart into him—as his hands slid up her back to tangle in her hair. Astrid broke away, his kiss following, but questions were bubbling up, unstoppable, coming out jumbled.

"I don't understand! How? Why here? Not in the library? Did it work? Is it broken? Are you free?"

She brushed his face again, trying to feel how he might appear in the light, hungry to see the face of the man she was growing closer to day by day.

"No," he said, voice a low ache, something unsaid behind the simple reply.

"I don't understand," she said, keeping her voice soft to match his. "And I need to. I can't keep doing this."

The darkness in the hall was complete, total. She couldn't see anything, not even a hint of light. And the overwhelming need to see his eyes, to find something to hold on to in his golden gaze, swept through her.

"Tyhr," she whispered. "Please."

"I have to go."

His arms loosened. Disappointment filled his voice, the head of their kiss gone—vanished. She'd said the wrong thing again somehow, asked the wrong question at the wrong time. Touching her mouth, lips warm and tingling, she pushed down the desire to kiss him again. Not because it would be the right puzzle piece in the right spot, a way to accomplish a task and move forward, but because she *wanted* to.

"Wait," she said, reaching out for him, taking his face in her hands.

"Dawn is coming," he said, stepping back, out of her grasp.

"No," she said, following. "Not yet. You have to explain this."

"I *can't* Astrid."

"All this time you could have taken the mask off? And you've refused? Why?"

"I have to go," he said, voice full of resignation.

"Tyhr." She grabbed for him, touching him, grasping what might have been a sleeve. It slipped through her fingers, leaving her gasping and searching in the dark. "Stop."

But he didn't stop. She followed him down the long hall —the darkness barely lighter there, but lessened, enough light she might be able to make out his features if she could get him to wait for just a few seconds.

Astrid matched his pace, only a few steps behind when they reached the stairs, following him down in a rush. The entryway was only slightly less gloomy, the marble floor icy beneath her bare feet. The front door stood open and expectant, waiting as always for a visitor yet to appear.

Tyhr strode toward it, racing the dawn that even now rested poised on the horizon. Mere seconds between reaching the top of the stairs and the door, and already she could see so much more. He was a large shadow now, the shape of his shoulders clear, the elegant knot of dark hair at the base of his neck. She needed to see his face. If she could see him finally, she would know, it would answer the questions she hadn't put a name to, the doubts she'd been struggling with.

Astrid ran ahead of him, placing a hand on his chest, and stopped him.

"What are you leaving out?"

He met her gaze and she sucked in a breath—a knot twisting in her stomach. The silver tiger snarled at her, the hard lips of the animal pulled back, replacing the soft mouth she'd kissed only moments ago. He'd been cinnamon and pepper, mouth deliciously hot, warmth and as electric as lightning in her body as he'd gripped her tight. Golden eyes, always so intent, focused, waiting to catch a reaction, to discover how much she might understand.

The light around them brightened and began reaching into the shadows—collecting, pooling, a dam of light on the verge of buckling under pressure. The day was on the verge of breaking over the valley, over the jungle, over the house. Over Tyhr.

He sidestepped her, walking down the ribbon of growing light.

Around her the room cleared, coming into focus. But the sun had not yet broken over the horizon, not yet. A few seconds remained. She ran to the door, not bothering to call, to waste time or breath.

On the front steps of the huge house, the stone pale and pitted, she paused, looking around. There. At the edge of the terrace to the left. Tall bushes rustled as if someone had passed through them. She rushed down the steps, hitting the smooth stone terrace that ran right up to the jungle, the greenery leaning over, crowding in, and pushing through where she had seen movement.

It was darker under the trees and large leaves damp with dew brushed her face. An insect bit her arm, and Astrid slapped the spot, ignoring the sting. Birds chirped and warbled, light breaking into the upper canopy— emerald green and pale peridot. But it would be hours before it would touch her here, among the undergrowth and larger shrubs—the understory crouched beneath the reaching limbs of the upper canopy.

A branch cracked nearby—loud and sharp—stopping her in her tracks.

It had been a mistake to rush from the house in the daylight. There was no man in this jungle, no one she could ask questions of, no one she might be able to reason with. She searched the area around her. No path. No clear way. She had simply stumbled after him, hoping. But she could have been mistaken. Tyhr could have gone in the other direction.

Or, a small voice inside said, *he could be right here.*

But the man in the house was not the same as the tiger in the jungle. She had already seen that, felt the terror and threat—her own animal fear response to the predator had come to the surface. She'd promised Chinook she wouldn't go back into the jungle again during the day. She would keep to the front steps or, better yet, stay inside. He'd made her promise, not because Chinook wished to be contrary or keep Astrid inside out of spite, but for her safety.

Astrid turned, a sense of unease at her back—the pressure of a watchful eye on her skin—and began to pick her way to the house. She hurried, something jagged scraping her leg, but she didn't hesitate, didn't stop.

If the tiger observed her—hidden in plain sight, observing without being noted—she didn't want to know. Chinook had promised her that, that was how it would be. She would be nothing but food, bloody and broken, smeared across a large, striped face and enormous clawed paws.

Tyhr would never know her in the daylight.

He didn't even know himself.

CHAPTER NINETEEN

When she came down to dinner the next night he was already at the table, twisting an empty wine glass in his hand, brooding over his reflection in the crystal. It held nothing but light and shadow.

"Not drinking?" she asked, moving to take her seat. He stood but she waved a hand, "No need. Thank you though."

"Would you like a glass?"

She nodded, easing down in the chair, watching as he poured—a steady hand, focused on the glass, giving nothing away. The hours from dawn to dusk had dragged, weighted with worry and uncertainty, a thousand unanswered questions buzzing beneath her skin. Chinook had come and gone, saying little, as she'd repotted plants in the conservatory and started seeds.

"How was your day?" Tyhr asked, leaning back in his chair.

"Quiet," she said, removing the cover over her plate.

Chicken, vegetables, and rice with a creamy sauce thick

with herbs. She studied it, this perfectly cooked dinner, and considered how to bring up the previous evening. It felt strange to sit with him now, at a dinner table pretending to be something they weren't. She struggled to find the words, considering how to start, and knowing there would be little response.

"You kissed me," she said tentatively, wanting to reach across the table, stopping herself. Astrid needed Tyhr to do it, waiting for him to say something, anything, and added, "last night."

He watched her, eyes unreadable. What a difference a day made. He didn't seem to be the man who had kissed her now at all. Some of the stranger had returned—the mysterious man from the station—someone she would never know.

Astrid placed her fork next to the plate, precisely, perfectly straight—the silver highly polished, her finger-prints smudging the surface. She wanted to lean across the table and shake him, shake all the answers out. One for every question Astrid had ever asked. Another part, a smaller part, wanted to blow out all the candles and kiss him in the dark.

"I don't seem to know you at all. In the jungle, you're a tiger. In this house, you wear a mask and kiss me in the dark."

"It's hard," he said, looking down at his hands, "to go back and forth. Coming inside, remembering who I am. There have been times when I thought I'd grown used to it. Made a kind of peace with this place. But it never lasted long. I don't think any kind of peace is possible here, not for me. Not anymore. There's so much I can't tell you."

"You keep saying that," Astrid said, tone sharper than

she'd intended, a bubble of frustration expanding beneath her breastbone. "But there has to be something. I can't keep living without answers."

Tyhr watched her, searching her face, hidden beneath the mask. Unreadable. Unknowable.

"Say something," she urged, skin growing hot, a flush heating her face.

Answers. Just words. A response. Information. Everything she wanted.

Nothing he could give her.

"Or don't," she said with a sigh, pushing back from the table.

Tyhr remained seated, staring at his empty plate, letting her leave without a response. Her footsteps rang through the dining room and then the entryway—determined, angry. She'd had enough silence for the night.

If Tyhr couldn't—or wouldn't—answer her questions, there had to be someone who could.

———

ONCE UPON A TIME.

"That really can't be how it begins!"

I am telling this story, Chinook said, irritation coloring his tone. *Would you like to hear it or not?*

"I just want answers."

If you were quiet, you might get some.

"Some?" she asked, raising both hands in frustration.

Some is better than none.

She nodded.

Chinook watched her, waiting to see if Astrid would interrupt him again before continuing.

Once upon a time, there was a royal family in a failing kingdom with three sons. Two of the brothers were determined to rule next, believing they knew the way to turn the kingdom around. The third and youngest had no interest in power, and no desire to sit on the throne.

"Tyhr?" she asked.

Chinook gave her a look.

"Sorry," she whispered. "Continue."

Crops failed. Wells dried up. The birthrate declined. A woman appeared. A stranger, an enchantress, knowledgeable about magic and promising to help for a price. A deal was made, a bargain meant to be kept. But it did not work out the way the family had expected. Everything changed when the woman fell in love.

Chinook paused, focused on something far away.

"She fell in love?"Astrid prompted.

Yes. It changed everything.

"What was that everything?"

The price to save the kingdom was marriage.

"For Tyhr? Why hasn't he explained any of this?"

He is bound and unable to speak of it.

"Then how am I supposed to help?" Astrid threw her hands in the air, looking around the room. The gold ring on her left hand caught the light and she paused, studying it. "What am I even doing here?"

I have begun to wonder that myself.

"What is the curse? Exactly?"

Tyhr did not wish to marry a woman he had no love for. But what is love when the survival of a kingdom hangs in the balance?

"And the curse is tied to his refusal?"

It would appear so.

"You're not sure?"

I know what I have observed. Beyond that, I can only specu-late and that is a poor way to go about collecting information.

"Speculation is better than nothing," Astrid said, twisting the ring on her finger, considering its meaning. Husband and wife. Tiger and Enchantress. And Astrid, an orphan nobody in the middle of it. "I wish you'd said something sooner."

Would you have believed it before?

"It's all so fantastical. It's a fairytale."

See? Even now you have doubts.

"Anyone would have doubts!"

I do not.

"That's not fair. Any normal person would have doubts. You're a bird."

And you are rude. He fluffed up, feathers bristling.

"It's not rude if it's a fact."

He gave her a look, conveying clearly what he thought of her facts.

"What about the rest of it?" she waved her hand, wanting more information.

Maybe you should ask Tyhr.

"I have asked!"

Then maybe it was your rudeness that stopped him from responding.

"That's not fair!"

If not that, then maybe your obvious disbelief.

"I do believe. Just tell me how to break it."

A kiss.

"I have kissed him."

Chinook gave her a look, chest puffing up. *The right kind of kiss. The kind that would break a curse.*

"What does that mean?"

How should I know? I do not have lips! If he is still wearing the mask, then you must not have done it right.

"A kiss is just a kiss."

Is it?

CHAPTER TWENTY

The house was quiet—peaceful in the late hour—as dawn grew closer by the second. Astrid lay in bed, watching the window, thinking about dinner with Tyhr and the story Chinook had shared in private.

An Enchantress.

A curse.

And the need for someone to break it.

But Chinook hadn't told her how. He had stopped talking, leaving to go do bird things, whatever things those might be. But she could tell he knew more than he'd shared. There was a hesitation there not born of a lack of knowledge but of certainty and the need to tread carefully. The story of before had not been complete either—there were missing pieces everywhere.

A curse breaker. But *how*? How could a curse be broken if she didn't know what it was? Or how it had come about? Or what the price for it all might be?

Everything came back to the mask Tyhr refused to

remove. Always his eyes on her face—watchful, golden, and intent—how he lingered over her, on her. But all behind the tiger's face.

The mask.

She sat up, decision made, hurrying before she could change her mind. Cold air brushed her skin as she flung the covers back, and she slipped on the linen robe heavy with embroidery—vibrant colors muted in the darkness. But already the night beyond her windows was retreating as dawn approached.

Another dawn, another day, all of them blurring together. Astrid was tired of it all, tired of watching the sunrise with a heavy heart, tired of her life being determined by the heavens. And with first light, Tyhr would retreat to the jungle.

Soon she would be out of time, and he would disappear into the forest, becoming the tiger—forgetting those who waited for him. Chinook had given her that much. But she wouldn't see Tyhr again until sunset when he returned dressed as a man—as the man who made her heart beat a little faster.

But it would be too late then too. By then she might have lost her nerve.

The rooms on the other side of the house were his. Down the hall from hers, a set of six, identical to the layout of her own. Tyhr said he slept there occasionally because he missed beds and all things that came along with humanity—pillows and sheets and heaps of blankets. She hoped he would be sleeping now, that she'd arrive and his eyes would be closed. If not, if he was awake and reading, pacing the room, anticipating sunrise, she would have to come up with some excuse.

I don't want to sleep alone anymore.

It wasn't a lie.

The candle on her bedside had an inch or so left after her late night of reading. The book had failed to block out the circling questions. She took it out of the holder, slipping it and a box of matches into the pocket of her robe. A hazy idea was forming—taking shape—as she opened her bedroom door and made her way down the hall.

Faint gray light came up from the stairs, but the rest of the hall was dark. Beyond that point, deeper in the shadows, Tyhr's rooms waited. Pausing, listening, she tried to calm her racing heart. Nothing. No one. The rustle of her nightgown seemed loud, silk and linen, bare feet against tile as she moved down the hall. Astrid passed the head of the stairs, moving swiftly into an area of the house she'd dared not explore before.

Getting closer, she realized she didn't know which room he slept in. Six doors, three to the left and three to the right. But to the left, through windows that would be closed, the jungle waited, slowly overtaking the house and waiting to be invited inside. His rooms would be opposite that, facing out, like her own. He would want to know when the sunrise was coming. He would want to spend as much time as possible out of the trees, beyond the reach of the jungle.

She crept to the last door on the right, heart racing. The candle and matches were heavy in her pocket, weighing on her—something crept up, nervousness or unease. Pausing, listening for movement, trying to gauge if she could hear pacing or the rustle of paper. But it was quiet—she could hear only her rapid breathing. Gently, moving painfully slowly, she twisted the doorknob, easing it open. There was no creak, no giveaway that she was here.

The windows were open, the sounds of the valley

wandering in, moving around the room—tree frog songs and rustling branches, insects and night birds calling. The sky held the moon and stars, light silver and pale. In the half-darkness, she could make out a figure on the large bed, propped up on several pillows. She paused, watching for the telltale flicker of his golden eyes, the questions that would fall from his lips. He didn't move. He must be sleeping.

Astrid tiptoed in, pulling the candle from her pocket, careful not to rattle the box of matches. She had to know, needed to find out if this was what would set him free. If she was right and could save him—bring him back into the world—it would be saving herself as well.

Doubt flashed through her. But she shook it away, pushing it down, bringing in iron certainty to smother the emotion. Her fingers trembled as she struck the match and watched him, waiting for the slightest movement, any sign of waking. The fire burned bright, flickering, casting jumping shadows, highlighting the snarling mouth of the mask.

Even in his sleep, even here, it hid his face.

In the complete darkness of the hall, when he'd kissed her, there had been no mask. But why here? Was it the light from the moon? Was it any light that he had to hide his features from?

Chinook had given her so little information—barely hinting at a more complicated story. And she'd been so focused on the idea of breaking the curse that she'd failed to pick up on anything the bird was careful not to say. If there was anything at all.

What if she failed to remove it, the curse staying in place, part of his skin?

Another step brought her closer, and she could see his chest rise and fall, his closed eyes. The candle trembled, her hand shaking with adrenaline, as she drew in a shaky breath. He would be thankful she'd done this—taken the chance. He would kiss her and this time it would be in the daylight.

The desire to see his face had grown over the last few weeks. The itch to remove the mask, to see the man beneath it, burned through Astrid until she couldn't ignore it any longer.

Chinook said the curse needed to be broken.

Astrid had to become the curse breaker.

Edging closer, soft as she could move, acutely aware of the small noises she made—fabric rustling, bare feet whispering across the carpet. The warm, yellow light of the candle pushed back the silver moonlight, reminding her of the bubble of light they'd traveled in through the Black Forest to reach this place. A bubble of light and this man had changed her future forever.

He seemed to grow larger as she neared—the bulk of him, muscle and height. She found herself wondering again how he ended up here, in this place, locked behind a mask. She was hungry for the exact details, the full story. An Enchantress had fallen in love with a prince and when he chose love, she cursed him. Could it really be that simple?

Reaching the bedside, she looked down at the blankets tangled around his bare waist, candlelight shivering around them. Astrid wanted to touch him—run her hands across his chest—press her lips to the hollow at the base of his throat. A ribbon of hot wax touched her hand, the heat surprising her—a sudden sharp burn—and a small noise of surprise escaped.

Shadows moved over the mask—the lifeless thing alive, shifting in the candlelight. In the distance, from a clear sky, thunder rumbled as a storm approached. She glanced around for a place to set the candle, searching for a safe and out-of-the-way place where it would throw light on his face when the horrible thing was off.

Astrid tilted the candle over the bedside table until a little wax ran and pooled on the surface. Carefully she placed the candle on it, waiting until it hardened to let go. She studied the mask. There was no ribbon or sting keeping it in place, it appeared to be held on merely by will.

Or magic.

With both hands she reached out, trembling, her stomach a bottomless pit. She gasped when her fingers connected with the mask, the metal warm and smooth, the tiger's face half shadowed and seeming to shift. Doubt rose inside of her, filling her chest and gut, a wave of it so strong it almost knocked her off her feet.

But she could break the curse.

The mask came away easily, almost weightless in her hand—as if it had never been, and never would be again. Astrid smiled, thrilled as excitement spread through her, and Tyhr's lashes fluttered.

He was beautiful with a face from a classical painting—no one would believe he was real, that someone so handsome lived in the world. Her stomach flipped thinking about his mouth on hers, the way he'd held her to him, the way he'd looked at her in the baths. His golden eyes met hers, the eyes she'd grown so familiar with in such a strange face. She smiled and reached for him, ready to kiss him and seal his freedom.

But fear spread over his features, tinged with anger—brutal disappointment. It was a harsh look, not at all what she'd expected, and not the face of a man who had been freed from a terrible curse.

Tyhr's whisper chilled her, releasing the doubt she'd pushed down, yanking it from her soul.

"What have you done?"

CHAPTER TWENTY-ONE

The storm slunk nearer, lightning flashed, and thunder rumbled over the house, a loud boom rattling her bones. Astrid shook her head as his fear spread—catching in her chest, hollowing out her heart.

"The curse, to break it, I thought—"

"Not like this."

Quiet anguish, a groan. Without another word, he swung out of bed, throwing blankets back, dressed only in long silk pants the color of dark blood—heart's blood. He moved away from her, not toward her like she'd thought he would, but to the wardrobe, burying inside and pulling clothes out.

"Where are you going?"

"She'll be here any moment, might already be downstairs."

"Who?" Her voice shook.

"The woman who put me in the mask."

The house shook with more thunder, then a flash of bright light lit the room as clearly as day. In the thunder, a name was repeated—his name—and as if pulled by wire, he moved to the door, leaving her behind.

Astrid followed—left hand pressed to her chest, gold wedding ring over her heart.

"Wait!" she called, again and again, desperate to catch up with him.

But the wind howling through the house snatched the words from her lips, rushing into rooms and slamming doors—pots crashed, spilling dirt and plants across the floor. Somewhere deep in the house something cracked and split, the walls shuddering. If Tyhr heard Astrid over the noise, he didn't stop—he went relentlessly forward until he passed through the open front door and out into the storm.

Hurrying after him, taking the stairs two at a time, she stumbled at the bottom and righted herself. With his name in her mouth, Astrid threw herself forward, fighting the furious wind that worked to push her back. Reaching the door, she held on with both hands, focused on Tyhr standing in the middle of the steps, facing the terrace, the silver tiger mask in one hand.

"Tyhr!"

He didn't respond, didn't turn, and she went to him. She raised her voice to be heard over the storm but in that moment, it stilled, the wind vanishing. The clouds overhead split and lightning crackled through the air, striking the terrace, and out of the blinding flash a tall woman appeared.

She was striking, with light gray eyes and a lush figure. Wrapped in layers of flowing silk, the colors deep and rich —like opening a chest of jewels in a half-lit room, a fire sparkling in the center of each gem—she took in the scene and gave Astrid a vicious smile.

"Is this her?"

The Enchantress stepped forward, bringing ozone and rain with her, reaching out to run a finger down Astrid's cheek. Hard fingers grasped her chin, turning her one way and then the other—studying Astrid—searching for something. She let go, dismissing Astrid without another thought, turning to Tyhr.

"Are you ready?"

Tyhr nodded—silent as he looked out across the valley. Trees swayed with the storm the woman had summoned—an ocean of leaves and bark, twisted branches, and fallen limbs. The frost touched the air, the wind biting, as the temperature dropped.

"Who are you?" Astrid asked, stomach knotting as dread took hold.

But it was coming together. All of those nights where they had talked around what was really going on—a kiss to break a curse, an enchanted valley, and a man who was not a man in the daylight hours. Of course, there had to be something in the middle of all of it, a turning point, a location from which all else spun and circled.

This woman.

The Enchantress.

"My name is Livia Forza."

A cruel smile touched the women's mouth, spread over her perfect features.

"Why are you here?"

The woman laughed. "I've come to make sure a promise is kept."

"What promise?" Astrid demanded.

The woman turned to Tyhr, eyes glittering with intent, lips curved in a red smile. He stood with his back to Astrid, stiff, rigid in the storm. Without turning he spoke, the sound of his voice taken, words stolen by the wind. Astrid went to him, taking his arm, trying to tug him toward her. When he didn't move, she circled to stand in front of him.

"What did you say?" she asked, searching his eyes.

"I made a deal," he said again.

This time the words were clear, the hint of their meaning touching her.

"A promise!" The Enchantress cut in, anger in her tone.

"What deal?"

"I'm to be married," he said, looking beyond her.

Astrid shook her head and held up her hand. The golden band flashed, drawing the light and their gazes. Something like hope flashed in Tyhr's eyes, but he looked away, hiding it. Livia made a face, derision or disgust, or both. She grabbed his hand, feeling how warm and solid he was, and realized how much she had come to need him, to want to be near him, to hear the sound of his voice.

"It had conditions."

"You made a promise," Astrid said, squeezing Tyhr's hand. "You said you don't break your promises."

Golden eyes touched her and moved away in casual dismissal. "This was one I hoped I would never break. I'm sorry."

"What do you mean?"

The Enchantress laughed. "He means he made another promise. A bigger promise. Long before you came along. Long before you were even born. How long have you been in this valley now, Tyhr?"

"Almost a hundred years." He sighed, holding up the mask, turning it. He shot Astrid a look, one she couldn't read, and put the mask on. The familiar lines, the snarling face, her silver tiger.

"What are you doing?" Livia asked, voice sharp—slicing the air.

"A month remains."

"It's done." The Enchantress waved a hand in the air. "The terms have met."

He shook his head, silent behind the mask.

"Do you love him?" The Enchantress barked, turning her attention to Astrid.

The question cut into Astrid, the directness of the words, the sharp smile. She flinched, pulling back from the accusation in the question. Love. She opened her mouth to respond—say something, anything—but she froze, unable to respond.

"A month," the Enchantress confirmed, keeping her pointed smile. "Keep it for now if you wish, Tyhr. I'll remove it on our wedding day."

"He can't marry you," Astrid said, looking between the two. "He doesn't want to. I can see he doesn't. Whatever promise was made will have to be broken."

In two swift steps, the woman reached Astrid and grabbed her arm—digging into her flesh. She leaned over her, hissing into Astrid's face—spittle flecking the corners of her mouth, teeth clenched.

"Not all promises break, girl."

"I won't let you take him," Astrid whispered, jaw tight.

"You could have saved him." The woman lowered her voice—malice and pleasure shimmering in her eyes. "But you were the ruin of him."

"No," Astrid said, brows drawing together, denial bubbling beneath her skin.

"You destroyed his last chance."

Astrid shook her head, trying to pull away. But the woman held on, fingers digging in to the point of pain—going down to the bone. Her gaze shifted to Tyhr, searching for a clue, for a sign. But he didn't look at her, his eyes focused on the horizon.

"Impatient, stupid girl. If you hadn't tried to remove his mask, if you'd opened that small cold thing in your chest you profess to be a heart, you might have had a chance. Three words from your lips to his ears would have changed the world. The mask would have vanished—melted away, my magic defeated. The tiger would never have returned. But you failed."

The woman's laugh rang out, long and deep, and Astrid covered her ears.

"Even better, you broke the rules of the game."

"He isn't a game," Astrid whispered, tears blurring her vision.

"You've played without knowing the rules, and I won. Lucky me. Unlucky you." Her gaze swept over Astrid's form, eyes narrowing slightly. She raised her other hand to brush Tyhr's shoulder, her touch lingering "We've waited long enough and there was never a doubt how this would end, my love."

"What rules?" Astrid managed to pull her arm away, jerking out of the woman's grip.

The Enchantress smiled, eyes sliding between them now, laughter threatening like the storm.

"I'd forgotten you couldn't share the details. Seems very vindictive of me, doesn't it? But you were so stubborn. Tell her now," she said, voice lowering, cajoling. "Tell her now that it doesn't matter anymore, and she can't change it."

Tyhr sighed, shoulders sagging. "One hundred years beneath a mask without another living creature seeing my face. An easy enough thing. Or so I thought. I had a hundred years to find someone to love. To earn love, become deserving of it, before I could remove the mask. If I let someone see my face before that time, without it being spoken aloud, the terms of my..."

His voice trailed off, and he shot Livia a look. "I was given a hundred years to find something I wanted more than anything. If I couldn't find it, then I would marry the Enchantress."

"Why?"

"My kingdom was dying, my father too, and she saved it. She saved us all. Or it appeared that way at first. But it came at a price. I made a bargain, hoping I could find a way to change my future and choose a different course. But I doomed us all. It was selfish to choose the mask. I watched them all die." He lifted a hand, gesturing at the valley full of constant summer. "And the kingdom died with them."

Astrid turned to Livia. "You're powerful. You're beautiful. You could have any man in the world."

The women laughed, filling the room, "How charming you are. And yes, I could. As a matter of fact, the man I want is right here."

"He doesn't want you."

Anger flashed across the woman's face, coloring her cheeks and darkening her eyes. "Love is capable of developing in harsh circumstances, out of nothing. I think we will be as lucky."

"You're forcing something that isn't there. You can't force him to love you."

"No, you're right. I can't. But he'll keep his word. That's all that really matters."

"I won't let you go." Astrid turned to him, grabbing his arm, and squeezing until he looked down at her. "I'm not letting you go."

"You have to," he said, voice low, tenderness in his golden gaze.

Shaking her head, tears building in her eyes, she forced the word out. "No."

"I'll make a bargain," Livia purred, deathly sweet. "If he stays, you die. But if he keeps his promise and comes with me now, you live."

Tyhr cupped her face in the palm of his hand. "There's only one choice."

"But," she stammered, "what if I told you—"

"No," he said, voice cutting across her words, stopping her. "It's too late for that."

Tears fell down her cheeks, something inside tearing, breaking. "I won't let you go."

"You have to."

"Then I'll come for you," she said, holding on to him, trying to press into his skin her promise, what lay behind it. Three words. But powerless unless spoken aloud.

Something hot clutched her heart, digging into the muscle, stopping the frantic pounding. She gasped, hands to her chest, sucking in air, choking as pain shot through her. Buzzing filled her ears, and she fell, hitting the hard stone steps. From a distance their voices came, muddled together and meaningless, Tyhr's words angry.

Around Astrid the world grew dark, closing in, as her vision blurred.

Hold on, Chinook said, his voice coming from some distant place, a place she was losing touch with.

Hold on.

CHAPTER TWENTY-TWO

I t would have been easier to stay there, in the dark where nothing hurt, wrapped in silence. But it didn't last. Chinook's sharp tone came first, the hardness of the stone beneath her aching body, and then the cold. His voice swirled around her, words nonsense as she opened her eyes, focusing on his small brightly colored form.

It all came back then, memory sharp as knives and needles.

This was your fault, Chinook said, voice cold, lacking anger or inflection, holding disappointment and grief. *You stupid, selfish woman. One word. One. All this time you could have changed our fates and you never spoke it aloud. Maybe you do not even realize it. All this time you felt like you knew better. Like you could walk through our story without it touching you, without becoming part of it.*

"I didn't know," she began, fighting back tears, stomach aching, the pain threatening to spread. One word. She knew it but couldn't face it. Couldn't speak it aloud. Doubt hit Astrid, hurting, pounding with each beat of her heart, pain wailing beside it. "I'm sorry."

Apologies will buy you nothing here, not today. Not with me. Leave. You have wanted nothing else since you got here. Go. You are free to go out into the big, bright world. Maybe you will find happiness there.

A protest formed—mouth open to explain that her feelings had changed. Little by little, she realized she was no longer worried about what might be passing her by in the world, what life might be like outside this strange place. Over the last few weeks, she'd come to realize what her heart had always wanted was not out there.

It was here.

It had been here.

Chinook spread his wings, dropping from the stonework around the front door, a few swift beats carrying him out of sight.

With a groan she stood up, rubbing her elbow, body aching. The golden band on her finger warmed, reminding her of what she'd lost, of the promise she'd made to Tyhr. As she crossed the threshold, she could feel the house listening to her—empty now of all life but for her, the growing quiet breaking into her soul like an unwanted guest. No one else breathed here. She'd taken it all. One action, consequences rippling out, creating waves of destruction. At the center of it all was her curiosity.

But there had been impossible guidelines to live within. No questions. No answers. Just vague stories. A thousand *when the time is right* replies.

Instead of waiting, she'd forced the issue. Chinook was right. She'd thought she knew better.

Hot shame hit her, hard and heavy—falling stones burying her beneath their weight. She knelt, easing onto cool marble in the entryway, laying down inch by inch until she could press herself into the surface, trying to ease the pain. It hurt. It hurt so much worse than she could have ever imagined. To be here now, like this, knowing she'd made the choice. Tyhr's eyes, the harsh betrayal—the gut-wrenching moment—Astrid would give anything to take back.

The one thing she couldn't change.

Time passed.

Astrid didn't know how long she lay on the floor; it seemed to shift and move beneath her, subtle and then not at all. Snow began to blow inside the house, through the open door, touching her cheek, melting on her hands. But she couldn't bring herself to move. Movement meant dealing with the pain, with the future; it meant acknowledging and facing consequences.

She sat up, bones aching, head pounding with spent tears.

Are you done then?

Turning, she saw Chinook sitting on a table, out of the way of the door and blowing snow.

"I thought you were gone," she said, tears gathering, chest tightening.

Well, I thought you knew better than to spend so much time feeling sorry for yourself on a cold floor. He ruffled his feathers. *Are you done?*

Astrid nodded, rubbing her eyes, feeling as if she were waking up.

Have you decided what you will do?

"Yes," she said, pushing to her feet, muscles sore, bones creaking. "I need directions."

The bird eyed her, dark gaze curious, bright. *To where?*

"Wherever she's taken him."

The Glass Palace is not on any map.

"Someone must know how to get there. Don't you?"

Me? I have never been farther than this valley. It used to be wide, a kingdom, a land of many things. But shrunk, diminished. Since it became this, he looked around, wistful, *I have never left. I have never seen beyond the ice walls or the Black Forest.*

I'm sorry. I forgot the feeling of being removed from something and wishing it had not been so. In the beginning, I lost my shape, myself. I forgot that it has been so fresh for you. A new wound. I was harsh before, and I am sorry for how I said it.

Astrid shook her head, ready to tell Chinook he had nothing to apologize for.

He ruffled his wings, a shrug, a gesture that made her pause. *I am sorry for how I said it, but not what I said.*

"I'm sorry," she said, mouth dry, voice cracking. "You're right. I have to find the Glass Palace. You must know someone. There has to be someone who can tell me."

The bird looked her over thoughtfully, tilting his head. *Pack your things, whatever you can carry. Pick something that will wear well.*

"And then what?"

Then we ask the Black Forest.

PART TWO

EAST OF THE SUN, WEST OF THE MOON

CHAPTER TWENTY-THREE

S ilver scissors cut through her hair easily; small sections at a time, the long strands drifting away, curls gone. It hit harder than expected; the way her face sharpened in the mirror—the woman she'd been becoming unrecognizable. Tears collected in Astrid's eyes, poised to fall, and she wiped them away angrily. Her hair would grow back. It didn't change who she was.

Then it was done, and it didn't matter anymore. Becoming another piece of her past like the house in Stockholm, the warmth in the library fire in the evening, and the sound of Tyhr's laugh.

She turned her head, back and forth, up and down. It was a terrible haircut, shorter in some places, longer in others. The test would be putting on trousers and a jacket, a hat to cover the mess she'd made. Setting the scissors down on the sink, she stepped back, studying her reflection, wondering where this woman had come from, and whether she was strong enough to rescue Tyhr.

———

"Well?" she asked, holding her arms out and spinning around so that Chinook could see everything. The wardrobe had given her a light shirt and light jacket, as well as a cloak she'd discovered at the back. She'd hoped there would be a large overcoat, something thicker against the snow, but this was it. It would have to be enough. "What do you think?"

He watched her, not speaking, hopping this way and that as she moved.

"Do I look like a man?"

No.

"A boy? Will I pass?"

I cannot say.

Astrid stopped, frustrated and defeated. "That's it?"

Yes. Are you ready?

Astrid sighed, adjusting the strap of the bag on her shoulder, feeling the small weight of it. What did you take on a journey when you didn't know your destination? What distances would they cover? What would happen? She wanted these things answered, a solid black-and-white explanation. She would pack trunks, look at maps, and compare routes.

None of that was possible when she followed the pull of the golden ring. It had brought her here, warmed as the miles between them had dwindled, and maybe now it would be a compass—a guide.

They left the house behind, passing painted flowers and staring animal eyes, slipping through the open green door, and stepping away from it all without looking back. The months she'd lived here, as if dreaming, all of it hazy and indistinct, let her go. There were moments that stood out— Tyhr's laugh, the evening in the baths, but so much of it ran together, arrival to now only a small part of the story.

The end of the story was out there, not here. She believed that—needed it to be true.

At the edge of the terrace, unable to resist the urge any longer she paused, glancing at the house, snow collection on the steps.

"Will we be back?" But even as she asked the question, she knew the answer.

Who can say?

"Care to take a guess?"

Chinook ruffled his feathers in response, lifting up from the branch he'd perched on and leading the way into the jungle.

She had forgotten the sound snow made as it fell, the way it muffled other noises, a white susurration. It swirled around them, collecting on trees, and weighing down the underbrush. Overhead, the sky was heavy with it, the temperature dropping as it piled up. Already the plants wilted, leaves curling and blackening at the edges. Soon the snow would kill them all.

Before the door to the Black Forest had been invisible, hidden in a wall of tree trunks, blending into the surroundings. Now, where the door had been a tumble of boulders stood, a landslide of stone from the cliff's edge. A narrow path wound through it, leading into the rock face, into the tunnel that would take them to the glacier. From the opening came snow and cold wind—a howl like wolves in the distance, the world beyond pushing forward to invade the jungle.

Astrid hesitated. Beyond this point there were monsters frozen in ice, creatures wandering the Black Forest, hunting —blue eyes searching. There were so many things she hadn't seen, could not put a name to. Dangerous creatures.

Fear touched her, weighing down her feet, filling her lungs with ice.

We cannot stay. It is falling apart already. Soon there will be nothing left.

"I know."

A vibration came up through her boots, a tremble, faint now, but growing. It hinted at earthquakes and rockslides, the valley caving in on itself. She adjusted the cloak around her shoulders, pulling it tight, wishing the house had been able to provide warmer clothes. There was no way to know what time of year it would be out in the world—she'd lost track of life through the library window. But hoping for spring would not be enough to keep her warm if they arrived in the middle of a blizzard.

Chinook gripped her shoulder, huddled close to her for warmth, and she stepped between the boulders into the dark.

————

THE GLACIER HAD MELTED AND BROKEN APART. HUGE CHUNKS OF ice remained, large boulders scattered among the frozen lumps, the creatures inside gone. Free. Astrid moved carefully, slowly, careful not to make too much noise, worried they would return. Chinook rode on her shoulder, swaying with each step she took, looking around curiously. Astrid was able to follow the path, patches of it visible, circling around huge chunks of ice.

Ahead she could see the clearing where the sleigh had sat, the Dark Forest surrounding it, and in the middle sat a giant wolf. She stopped, stunned, unable to take another step. Fear—a solid, heavy thing, sat in her gut.

"Come forward," the creature said.

She went, her legs moving on their own, feet stumbling over ice and stone.

What are you doing? Chinook hissed. *Are you crazy?*

Astrid shook her head, clenching her jaw, trying to keep her teeth from chattering. She had no control over her legs, over the movements of her body. It called. She went. Haltingly, clumsy, and stumbling, she came to stand in the soft unmarked snow of the clearing.

The wolf walked toward them deliberately, one giant paw in front of the other, head down. Astrid stood frozen in place—heart rioting in her chest—as Chinook burrowed into the scarf around her neck.

The creature was huge, bigger than any wolf she'd ever seen, bigger than the elephant she'd seen at the circus as a child. In the darkness, there was only the absence of the stars where he stood, the constellations blocked by the fuzzy outline of his body. In his face—long and sharp—a pair of glowing blue-white eyes pierced the night, penetrating her soul. His snout, the fur around his face, was illuminated, the snow beneath him, around them, reflecting the glimmer.

"You smell," the wolf sniffed, bright, glowing eyes focused intently, hungrily on her, "like magic."

Astrid began to tremble, fighting to keep control, tempted to run—bolt like a hare into the forest. But she knew how that would go. Maybe, if she stood her ground here, it would not end with her blood all over the snow.

"Are you with the Enchantress?" the wolf asked.

"No," she whispered, fear choking out her voice.

The wolf towered over her now, staring down the length of his snout, eyes shining into her—through her. They stood together, one poised to run, the other to pounce and devour. She wanted to look away; she wanted to try to make herself small.

Chinook was a trembling tickle against her neck, his terror radiating through her skin. She tried to set herself apart from it, distance his fear from her own. She could not give up on Tyhr now. She could not let herself be stopped here, the journey over before they'd even begun. They hadn't even managed to leave the Black Forest behind.

"She took something from me," Astrid said, voice coming out stronger than she felt, loud and a little angry. She wouldn't be stopped here, not yet.

"Are you going to take it back?"

The wolf considered her, head coming up a little—the predator stance relaxing.

"Yes," she said, conviction solid in her voice.

"Good. I will help you."

She blinked, surprise shooting through her. *Help*. That wasn't something she'd been expecting. Help was much better than blood on the snow. Unless this was a trick of some kind.

"I will take you to the edge of the forest."

She nodded, grateful but still fighting an edge of fear. The creature was so large, looming over her, staring into her soul. She could see his teeth, huge and white in a dark mouth, as long as her arm and so close, she could have placed her hand against the smooth, white surface.

"But you must promise never to enter the Black Forest again. This place will be closed to you, all doors locked."

"I understand," she said. "I promise."

"Good," the wolf inched closer, his hot breath washing over her face. With it came the scents of burning wood, the sharp copper of fresh blood, and the cold frost of deep winter. "If you did find a way, for whatever reason, I would smell you again. I will eat you next time."

Astrid shook her head, trying to convey with her whole body that she'd never dare to enter the forest again. She wished to do nothing more than leave and never return. The wolf watched her, thoughtful, and she wondered what he thought of them. A woman and a small bird, trespassers —thieves in this quiet space, stealing into his territory and taking without leaving anything of worth behind.

"Come," he growled, wrinkling his snout. "Your smell. It makes my nose burn."

"Why?" The question was out before she could stop it, curiosity getting the better of her.

"Too much magic. The wrong magic. You stink of *her* magic." The wolf raised its nose, sniffing. "And something else. You stink of bird."

I do not stink, Chinook said from his spot beneath her scarf.

The wolf came closer as Astrid stiffened, and he placed his nose—his snout as big as her whole body—gently against her shoulder. Almost no pressure, just there, touching instead of crushing. Then the creature pulled in a great breath, rustling her hair and clothes, and let it out, warmth washing over her.

"Yes," he said, pulling away, and taking a step back. "Bird stench."

Chinook poked his head out, little body vibrating now with something besides anger. Indignation.

If anyone stinks, it is you, wolf!

"Yes," he agreed, "like a wolf. Not like you. Would you like to be a different shape?"

No!

The wolf sat, watching Chinook, head tilting. "What

were you before? There is something beneath your feathers, something like salt and lemons. You would be a sour bite."

Astrid put a calming hand on Chinook, smoothing down puffed-up feathers.

"You said you would help me," she reminded the creature, tone as gentle as the touch she gave Chinook.

"I will carry you as far as the path out." He looked over his shoulder, beyond the fir trees and the endless night. "At the end of that, you will find a door. A way out. Not a way back in."

"I understand," she said.

"Good, a deal. I will give you one thing to seal it."

"What do I give in return?"

"You? Give me something?" the creature laughed, a barking sound, low and half a growl. "What would I want of yours? Besides the small, salty bite."

"I don't know," Astrid said.

"Nothing. I want nothing from a human child. But I will give you something to keep you on the path, to let you through the door. Hold out your hand."

Astrid extended her arm, pleased that she shook only a little—a slight tremor—and not at all the quake shaking through the rest of her body. The wolf brought a paw to his mouth, his claws large and curved, and bit down. With a jerking motion, he pulled, drops of blood falling to the snow, the popping sound lodging deep in her brain. The wolf brought his muzzle—so large he could have swallowed her whole, yet gentle and careful when so close—to her hand and dropped it onto her palm.

A claw. Sharp and black, warm and smooth, it fit easily in her hand, much smaller than she would have imagined a claw from such a large creature would be. She looked up at the wolf, his size, and back to the claw in her hand.

"What?" he rumbled. "Too small? You want one as large as yourself to carry around?"

"No," Astrid said, surprised at the humor in his tone. "It's smaller than I imagined."

"Magic," he said, baring his teeth in a snarling grin.

"Thank you," she said, moving the cloak aside to put it in the bag slung across her body. She could feel it there, a hard lump, a gift from a creature made of darkness birth in the Black Forest.

"Come, I will take you to the edge of the forest now. We will go fast and far. You will have to ride." The wolf flattened himself in the snow, the crystals crunching and crushed beneath him, the smoky edges of his body bleeding out across the pale surface.

"Oh, no," she said. "I couldn't."

"You ride or I carry you," he said, baring sharp fangs, "in my mouth."

Astrid patted Chinook, whispering, "So we'll ride."

She hesitated only a moment before touching the giant wolf, wondering if he would be solid beneath her hands or if she would fall into the waving darkness of his body. But when she reached out, she felt warmth and softness. But it did not feel like fur; she imagined that he felt like what clouds might, soft and but insubstantial, something that could slip through your fingers. But he was real. She climbed up between his shoulder blades, holding tight as he stood, muscles shifting, the world suddenly very far beneath her.

With a leap, the wolf left the small clearing—bounding into the trees, taking them away. Astrid glanced back, taking one last look at the melting glacier. It receded, disappearing, as the trees closed in around them, tall and thick and full of secrets.

———

THEY SEEMED TO FLOAT THROUGH THE FOREST—AROUND LARGE boulders, across streams—without touching the ground. The wolf was smaller here, fitting into the landscape, and moving through it with fluid grace. Other wolves joined them, flowing between trees, bright eyes glancing at her and away. An escort, a pack of curious onlookers.

The forest around them changed—a way clearing, the trees easing back, arching overhead to create a tunnel. They raced down this path, wind whipping Astrid's face, pulling the air from her lungs— trees a blur as they sped forward. She closed her eyes, tears from the fierce wind slipping down her cheeks, the sound of paws on snow filling her head.

Then the wolf slowed, and she opened her eyes.

A crossroad with tunnels in the trees intersecting and overhead a bright white moon shining down through thick branches breaking through in pieces—points of light twinkling like stars. Ahead the path continued endlessly, reminding her of the road she'd first traveled with Tyhr.

But to the left and right the path was different; darker, the moon unable to break through, the snow beaten down, muddy in places from the passage of many feet. The wolf stopped, the smaller figures around them melting into the shadows beneath the trees.

"This is as far as I will take you," the wolf said, waiting patiently as Astrid slid down from his back. "Take the path to the left, you'll find the door."

Astrid nodded, smoothing down her jacket and adjusting the small bag. "Thank you for all your help."

But when she looked up, the path they stood on was

empty—the wolf gone, the forest silent and watchful around them.

That was not very friendly, Chinook said. *He should at least have said, you are welcome.*

"Friendlier than offering to eat you again though."

Astrid looked down the path the wolf had instructed her to take. The way was narrow and dark; trees to either side so close together they formed a wall, solid as any brick or stone. At the end a warm rectangle of light waited, beckoning.

That is it? Chinook asked.

"Must be."

I was expecting something grander. More interesting.

"How is a giant glowing rectangle of light boring?"

A branch broke somewhere in the forest behind them. Astrid froze, a cold sweat touching her, chest tightening. Slowly, afraid to move but afraid not to know, she glanced behind them. From beneath the trees, a figure stepped out. Small, childlike. The dark shadow from the sleigh, blue eyes glowing, focused on her. It took a step forward, beginning to grow.

What is it? Chinook asked, curious and unalarmed.

"A giant."

It is not very big.

"It will be."

Astrid turned to the rectangle of light that would lead her to the world she remembered, the one she was desperate to return to, and began to run. Astrid could feel the creature coming up behind her, the way the earth began to shake as it grew, the small figure expanding and giving chase.

Run! Chinook urged, fluttering around her face, tugging at her short hair. *Almost there!*

Astrid threw herself toward the door, desperate to pass into the warm, yellow light. Behind her, the reaching claws of the giant grasped, snagging the cloak, pulling. It had her. Holding onto her.

Do not stop, Chinook warbled, *just a little farther.*

"I can't," she screamed, fighting the steady pull, digging her heels in, reaching, fingers clutching at thin air.

The brooch! Undo the clasp!

He fluttered around her head, voice high, darting behind her to peck at the creature's curled fingers. The giant hissed, guttural words flowing over her in an unknown language, teeth gnashing. She knew what would happen if she couldn't break free. Scrabbling at the clasp, she felt the cloak tear, heard a sharp sound—shredding wool and silk, the lining separating. But the neck pulled taut, choking, tight against her windpipe.

"Let me go," she gasped. Her fingers caught and freed the clasp finally, and she was suddenly free and falling forward. The giant yanked the cloak backward, a cry of rage following.

She went into sunlight, through the door, falling into the unknown.

CHAPTER TWENTY-FOUR

A striding landed with a thud on her hands and knees, wheezing, tears falling into the grass, thankful for the warmth on her skin. It penetrated the clothes on her back, soothing the cold away, a gentle hand, comforting after the last moment of terror in the forest.

Never come back.

It was a promise she'd keep. She wouldn't survive another visit, not without Tyhr, possibly not even with him now that the Enchantress had called him to her, taking her magic and protection with her.

Chinook hopped into her line of sight, looking up into her face as a tear fell, landing on his head. *Are you all right?* His tone, always so sharp, was soft, laced with concern.

"Oh, Chinook," she said, easing back and reaching for him, unsure if he would jump out of her reach or not. But he stayed, letting her pick him up, his body soft and light, like blown glass and paper-mâché. She brought him close, smoothing her cheek against him, holding on for comfort, to chase away the fear–lingering like a black hand on her shoulder.

He stayed, motionless, and when another tear slipped down her cheek, he ruffled his feathers. She opened her hand as he stretched his wings, threatening departure, but he stayed, held against her face, and for the briefest moment, he ran his beak against her skin in a kiss of sorts.

Enough of this, he said, sharpness returned, briskness and efficiency taking over. *We need to find out where we are. Where to go from here? Can you feel a direction? Is the ring giving you any hints?*

He jumped out of her hand and onto her head, little claws pricking her scalp, turning this way and that, surveying the landscape.

They had come out on the side of a grassy hill spotted with wildflowers waving under a cloudless blue sky, bees buzzing. In the distance was a town; the church steeple beckoned, a beacon in the landscape, the glimmer of windows and movement of people living their lives. Mountains rose behind it, stepping up into exposed rock faces and white flashes of snow.

The world seemed empty from here, the green hills surrounding the town, far enough away that nothing but the sounds of the summer day reached her. Slipping a hand into the bag, she found the wolf claw there, smooth and warm and nestled against the seed packets she'd packed at the last minute. She missed the cloak, the warmth of it, the heavy weight, but she wouldn't have needed it here.

Novgorod.

"How do you know? You said you'd never left the valley."

It looks like the place described to me. Is it not familiar to you?

"I know it. But it looks different in the summer. When I

was here before, it was buried in several feet of snow, and it was the middle of the night."

Astrid looked down at her hand, remembering the click of metal against glass in the train car, moments before Tyhr had appeared. Now the ring was warm, soaking up the sun just as she had. She held up her hand, closing her eyes, waiting for it to tell her where to go. Faintly, barely there, it vibrated toward the west, over the mountains, to whatever lay beyond.

Well? The bird asked, jumping to her shoulder and settling down. *Let us go.*

Squinting at her shoulder, catching a glimpse of the black feathers iridescent in the sun, she asked, "And you'll go along for the ride? You can fly, you know."

I should conserve my energy, he replied primly. *You never know when I might need to scout ahead.*

"Yes," she said dryly, pushing up to her feet and dusting dirt off her hands and knees. "Of course. Very sensible of you."

It could prove vital.

With a nod she set off, moving downhill, careful to pick the easiest way, though there was no path to follow at first. Eventually, she found a sheep track, a narrow strip of bare earth, worn down by hooves and feet. She followed that down until the wild hillside became cultivated and cared for. A cow lowed in the distance, out of sight, another joining in. A lark called, sweet and high, as it drifted across the field. As she went, she picked a small bunch of wild-flowers, blue and yellow petals, the white of chamomile.

They passed a man cutting hay, a sharp scythe catching sunlight, throwing it against the blades of grass as he cut them, parted by light and steel to land at his feet. The raw scent crawled inside her nose—bright green, filling her lungs. He watched her wordlessly, tracking this young man coming out of the hills. She thought for sure he would call out, demanding answers to his questions. But the blade continued to move, the sound of cutting grass falling away as she left him behind.

Soon they reached the outskirts of town—small thatched-roof houses, weather-worn wood, kitchen gardens, and washing lines full of flapping clothes. Women worked, pulling down and hanging, pulling weeds from between vegetables; a few children ran ahead of her, their high screams full of delight. A cart stacked with barrels rattled by; the man driving gave her a nod and a curious look.

The houses changed sharply, thatch replaced by slate, the road going from dirt to cobbles and paving stones. Then the houses were gone, replaced with businesses, buildings stretching up, with restaurants on the bottom floors.

The city bloomed, opening, accepting them into its heart without a second thought. People moved past them and around them on the sidewalks; carriages rattled down the streets in all directions. Shouting and calls filled the air, chatter and laughter, the peaceful quiet of the hills now far behind them.

Someone bumped into her from behind; a murmured *pardon me* followed. It was too crowded for her after the valley, after the Black Forest. She stepped out of the flow, into the shadow of a building, leaning against the stone.

How long would it take to become part of it? To melt with the hard surface, to rest in ultimate stillness. How long would it take to forget her mistake and resign herself to loneliness and shame?

She'd never know. She'd never stop. The need to mend this mistake, to fix the delicate thing she had broken, drove her. Turning the ring on her finger, the unbroken circle, Astrid thought about the immediate future, and where it might take her.

———

A GILDED SIGN HUNG ABOVE THE TEA PARLOR; LOVELY GOLDEN flowers and more trailing vines had been painted on the window. People sat beyond the glass, ladies wearing hats and fashionable dresses, a few men in dark suits. But reflected in the glass was a rumpled young man. Her face was the same, even with her hair shorn so close, the color dulled, Astrid recognized the shape of herself.

The door opened, startling her as she realized she'd stood there for too long. A few of the faces nearest the glass windows watched her closely.

"Come in!" a woman said, cheerful and loud, keeping the door propped open with one foot and waving. She was short and dark hair piled in a bun on her head and friendly brown eyes. "Come in and have tea."

"Oh, no, I couldn't. I apologize for lingering." Astrid waved a hand, taking a step away. But the woman left the door, taking Astrid's arm firmly and insistently. "I really shouldn't. I need to be going."

"Nonsense," the woman replied, ushering her through the door and into a room filled with the clink of delicate cups and saucers and low conversation. The scents of bread and sugar, warm rich tea, and hints of savory spice wrapped around Astrid, enfolding her. Her stomach growled, louder than expected, and the woman laughed. "See? Your stomach has good sense."

The few curious faces that had turned toward her when she had entered lost interest as Astrid and the woman made their way to the back of the room. Astrid followed her through a door and into the steamy kitchen beyond. A large room filled with several stoves on one wall, covered in tall, bubbling pots and shallow pans, three or four cooks moving between the stoves and a preparation area.

The room was divided by several long workspaces, full of people chopping and ladling things onto plates, passing cutting boards full of cubed meat and potatoes to the cooks stationed at the stoves. Others made beet salads and worked seasoning meat, plating beautiful dishes of fruit and cakes. There was more here than just the sweets and small savory things for the tea room.

"It's a shared kitchen." The woman pointed to another door Astrid had not yet seen. "There are four restaurants, and we're right in the middle here. Please. Come sit."

The woman led Astrid to a desk in the corner, half protected from the riot of the kitchen by a shelf stacked high with mixing bowls and baking sheets, jelly molds, and rolling pins. On the wooden desk sat a small lamp and a jar with pencils, the surface worn and aged. Instead of a chair, a small, padded stool was pushed under and out of the way. The woman pulled it out, steering Astrid toward it.

"What do you like to eat?"

Stomach gurgling, she looked around, willing to take anything that might be offered. "I'm not picky."

"Good! I'll get you something," the woman said with a smile.

"Thank you," Astrid said, holding out her hand. "I'm—"

The woman raised an eyebrow, waiting as nothing came.

"Alastair," she decided. "I'm Alastair."

"It is a pleasure, Alastair. I am the North Wind. But here

I use Irina. Sometimes it is easier to go by another name. Irina is better anyway, don't you think?"

The woman's grip was strong, and she had a knowing twinkle in her eye, as if she knew where Astrid had come from and why. Irina turned away, calling to someone, ordering two dinner plates and tea. Astrid watched her for a moment, thankful to be out of the bustle of the kitchen, watching from the shelter of the shelves.

Chinook ruffled his feathers, poking out of the scarf around her neck, looking around.

The North Wind? I do not believe we would meet such a being here, in this little town.

"Why not here? Not a mile away there is a door to the Black Forest and beyond that place a magical valley you called home for almost a hundred years. Where you lived under a curse. From an enchantress."

When you say it like that it is unbelievable as well.

"I trust that she is who she claims to be."

You are too trusting.

"Maybe," she said. But Astrid had a good feeling about Irina—there was no malice in her, nothing lurking beneath the surface of the woman's smile, waiting to pounce.

Not maybe, the little bird said, wriggling from his shelter and onto the desk. *She could rob you. Lull you into a false sense of security. Take everything you have. Stick in me in a birdcage.*

"Hush," Astrid said, glancing around, watching Irina direct a chef filling two plates. "I've got nothing to steal."

She doesn't know that.

Astrid sighed, knowing he might be right but willing to trust her gut. "You've spent too long living in fear of the outside world, Chinook. We'll be fine."

He puffed up, obviously offended and getting ready to let loose when Irina returned with two plates. Behind her, a man balanced a tray with a small samovar, delicate porcelain cups, and two short glasses of water. There was sugar and jam, seashell-shaped spoons, and napkins with lace edges. Tea. Astrid was just as excited about the tea as the roast beef with turnips and greens and the rich scent of butter sauce and herbs. Her stomach rumbled in anticipation, mouth watering with anticipation.

"And who is this?" Irina asked, curious, a hint of a smile touching her face.

None of your business, he said, throwing a glance at Astrid.

"Chinook," Astrid said, gesturing to him, willing him to be silent.

Traitor.

"How lovely, such beautiful feathers. I did not realize you traveled with a companion." Setting the plates on the desk, she turned to take the tray from the man. "Will you get a bowl of fruit, whatever we have, please?"

With a nod the man turned, hurrying off into the chaos of the kitchen.

"Well," Irina looked around, "let me find a seat. Eat, do not wait for me."

In a moment the man returned with a shallow dish of melon and sliced apricots. He set it down silently, shooting Astrid a quick glance, taking in the bird and her appearance with curiosity.

"If you need anything else, I'm over there," he pointed to a preparation station nearby.

"Thank you."

He nodded, giving the bird one last glance, and returned to his station. Astrid watched him a moment—he was tall with golden hair and blue eyes and not much older than her. Looking around, she noticed that a few of the other staff had glanced her way, a quick flick of the eyes, an exchange of silent questions. But then she was dismissed, not nearly as important as getting orders out through the swinging kitchen doors.

Irina returned with a small cane chair from the tearoom, talking to someone over her shoulder, an instruction for another meal, and directing someone to take over the tearoom. With a smile she set the chair beside the desk, looking from Astrid to the untouched plate.

"Eat! Eat, and I will ask you questions after. We will have some tea, yes? You like tea?"

Astrid nodded, picking up a fork and taking a bite of roast. It was the most wonderful thing she had ever tasted —a sigh of pleasure escaped. "It's wonderful."

"Yes," Irina nodded, "Ivan is a very good cook. The best. Sometime, you will come back and have a proper meal, in the dining room, with dark red wine—very good wine, imported from France. It will taste much better then." The woman watched her eat for a moment, taking bites herself, spearing a piece of boiled turnips and using to pick up gravy. Chewing thoughtfully, gaze going over Chinook, she swallowed and asked, "You are not from here?"

Though it was phrased as a question, Astrid knew it was more of a statement. Shaking her head, agreeing, she reached for the water, taking a sip before replying. "Stockholm by way of England."

"Far from home," Irina said. She shot Chinook a look. "Eat! It is not poisoned. You should not waste food."

Astrid studied Irina, wondering if the woman might be able to hear him, if his voice appeared in her head like magic too. But Chinook chirped, high and sweet, keeping whatever opinion he might have to himself for once. She dared not ask him if Irina could understand him. She'd appear to be insane, a crazy person lingering on the streets and talking to birds. Chinook pecked at the melon, doing his best impression of a normal bird. Astrid smiled, covering the expression with another bite of food.

"How does an English woman come to the edge of Siberia?"

"Woman?" Her heart thudded painfully against her ribs, panic sloshing through her, stomach clenching around the food with a sickening twist. "I'm not—"

Irina held up a hand. "It is no matter. You may think you look like a boy, to some you will pass, but for many, no. Not at all. But maybe I see more than most."

"How could you tell?" Maybe it was something she could fix, put off discovery in the future.

"Good sight," the woman replied, tapping the corner of her left eye. "So, you came here because…"

"It's a long story," Astrid sighed, one shoulder going up in a shrug. How much could she say? What could she share? The minimum. Give nothing away.

"A love story?"

"A little bit of a love story," Astrid admitted, heart continuing to pound. Could she see that too? With her good sight?

"But you are traveling alone now?"

Astrid shook her head.

"No?" The woman looked from Chinook to her with a small laugh. "A bird is not much of a companion."

"Maybe not," Astrid admitted, ignoring Chinook's scowl.

They ate in silence for a while, Irina half turned to the kitchen, watching everyone move back and forth, meals coming together and going out beyond the swinging doors. The chatter and noise of the space filled whatever awkwardness there might have been. Astrid ate slowly, savoring each bite, the cold and fear of the Black Forest gone—a nightmare defeated and banished. When she was done, Irina motioned to one of the young boys doing dishes to take their plates.

"Leave the tea things and the fruit," she said, giving Chinook more time. He had eaten a little, but she obviously wanted him to eat more, just as she had urged Astrid to eat more. Irina turned to her, picking up a delicate cup. "Tea?"

"Yes, please," Astrid said.

"Strong? Weak?" Irina poured black tea from the pot, a rich deep color, and held the delicate cup beneath the samovar.

"Between the two."

With a nod Irina added boiling water to the cup, diluting the concentrated tea, and gestured at the sugar and jam. "Cherry? Or I can get you raspberry if you prefer. But I must tell you, the cherry is better. I made it myself last season. The raspberry my sister sent up from Italy. The flavor is not as good." She made a gesture, part shrug, part laugh.

"Cherry."

A dollop of jam was added to the cup and passed over. Black tea and cherries filled her nose, soaking into her lungs, into her bones. She stirred, watching it dissolve, little bits of fruit swirling, a few bits of tea leaves settling to the bottom. There had been tea in her life before. There had been tea in the jungle. But taking this first sip here, stuffed in the corner of a busy kitchen, it was as if she'd never tasted tea before.

"Good, yes?" Irina grinned with pleasure, making a cup for herself and easing back against the wall. "The tea comes overland. No sea-salt damp leaves in my kitchen. It comes dry, over the mountains, from China."

"It's very good."

No bitterness lingered in the cup, only hints of earth and sunlight, sweet, preserved cherries, and a lingering nutty note. Chinook helped himself to the water in Astrid's glass before settling on the edge of the desk farthest from Irina, where he could keep an eye on them both. Astrid was tempted to run a finger down his back, and offer some small comfort, but she knew it would only irritate him.

"So, your name is not Alastair."

"Astrid."

"Astrid," the woman repeated, as if she were beginning to read a story aloud, a sound to conjure the distant past and places that might never be. "I knew an Astrid once, a long time ago. A princess."

"My mother named me after a princess in a fairytale."

"So, you must be on an adventure then, a princess in search of her prince?"

"Do all princesses need a prince?"

"Not at all," Irina laughed, sipping tea and watching the young woman in front of her. "But you are searching for one."

Astrid shifted on the stool, uncomfortable. There was this feeling of knowledge, that Irina knew more than Astrid had intended to give away. The woman had seen through her disguise, though poorly thought out and executed, and seemed to know more. What had shown on her face? What sign was there on her clothes? She shook her head, denying whatever the woman might be implying, sipping tea so she would not have to speak.

Give nothing away, said Chinook.

"I should go," Astrid said, setting the cup down, porcelain rattling as the cup and saucer met. "I can't be late."

"I will tell you a story. A small part. So tiny. You have time for this. Afterward, you can go." Irina placed a hand on Astrid's arm, keeping her from rising, gentle but firm. There was no question of her leaving, not yet. "There was a land with three sons, long ago, so far back, people have forgotten. Or maybe they were made to forget, who knows? But the oldest and the second in line died. The remaining heir was cursed."

Astrid stared, transfixed, the hair on the back of her neck rising.

"A terrible thing, a curse, thought impossible to break. It takes a lot of care, to be thoughtful, to understand," the woman continued, gaze moving over Astrid and then on, giving her the space, she needed to swipe at sudden tears. "Once, long ago, I met a man in a mask. Fierce, with a tiger's snarl and something sad about his eyes. Defeat. Maybe longing."

"How long ago?" Astrid asked, wondering when Tyhr had passed through the town if it had been on a similar trip to the one where he met her father or the time when he picked her up from the station.

"Fifty years or more, who knows? It is impossible to keep track."

"But—" Astrid searched the woman's face, the lack of lines or wrinkles, the smooth plumpness of her cheeks, the delicate curve of her mouth. The woman didn't look over thirty if even that old.

"He is not the only one who knows the way through the Black Forest."

Be careful, Chinook hissed, hopping up.

But Astrid didn't look at him, couldn't tear her gaze away from the woman.

"You look like a woman at the start of an adventure," Irina said, kindness and a little pity in her voice. She took Astrid's cup—most of the liquid was gone, just a few bits of fruit and leaves swirling at the bottom. "One more sip," she nudged the cup forward, "and I will tell you what the leaves have to say."

Astrid took one more swallow—tiny leaf fragments swirled together in patterns that meant nothing to her. Irina accepted the offered cup with a nod, cradling it in her hands, turning it slowly, the few drops of liquid at the bottom rolling with the motion—a wave moving over the leaves, crossing and covering. Irina made a noise, a tutting sound, then grew silent.

Chinook jumped onto Astrid's shoulder, soft feathers brushing her cheek, a gesture of solidarity or comfort. He might only have been wanting a better vantage point, but she was grateful for his presence. Pinned to the chair, unable to look away, she couldn't even consider leaving now. The kitchen grew quiet, watching as Irina turned the cup.

From somewhere far away, a man called for wine, and someone dropped a tray—a glass broke, a sharp question, a low murmur of conversation. Irina set the cup down, eyes focused on something far away, the color of her irises deeper than the brown of seconds before. She watched an unfolding scene, brows together in concentration.

"What is it?" Astrid reached out, and touched the cup, searching the contents for any sign she might be able to interpret.

"You have much farther to go. Come. I will send you to the East Wind."

CHAPTER TWENTY-FIVE

Irina took her to the train station, only a few blocks away from the tea shop. She talked about the world, the people who came through her kitchen—more than just townsfolk and visitors. Astrid listened, trying to picture a woman who was also a stream, a certain flower, a man who moved as slowly as a tree, a creature that crossed mountain passes without breaking the crust on the fresh snow.

It didn't seem real to her. But in the kitchen, with the teacup in her hand, Irina had been all-knowing.

At the station, Astrid looked around, taking in the building, and the bustle of the place. It was strange to be here again, walking onto the platform in the middle of the day, the memory of the first night here so fresh in her mind. Months ago, when she'd been a different woman. It had all changed between then and now, the world around her was now steeped in magical things.

It had been hard to believe and at the same time so natural in the Summer Valley. And now, in what she'd once thought of as reality, she accepted the strangeness and magic that lay beneath the surface—discoverable for those willing to suspend their assumptions about the world.

And here she stood, with Irina the North Wind.

"I'll leave you here. You are going south to Rome, yes? Do not get off before then."

"I won't," Astrid said, patting her satchel, adjusting the cap down to conceal more of her face. She felt like people were watching; uneasiness filled her, and she tried not to look around.

"They don't know," Irina said, adjusting Astrid's collar, smoothing down the lapels of the jacket beneath the heavier coat she'd given her. "No one can tell. You are who you appear to be, nothing more, nothing less. Understand?"

Astrid nodded but the woman shook her head, "Repeat it."

"Nothing more or less than what I am."

"Then what you appear to be."

"Then what I appear to be."

Irina nodded. "You will be fine. Tell my sister I miss her when you see her."

"How will I know it's her?"

"I think she will find you." Irina laughed. "Go. Do not miss your chance."

"Thank you," Astrid said, grabbing the woman's hand impulsively. "I don't know what luck brought me to you but I'm so grateful."

"Fate," Irina said with a smile, raising Astrid's hand. The golden band warmed, catching the light, reminding her of the warmth of a golden gaze and promises yet to be kept. "Powerful fate. This ring is a compass, but I think you know. Yes?"

Astrid nodded—stomach tight with excitement at the confirmation.

"And you, Chinook," Irina said, turning her attention to the bird. "You are a good friend."

As if there were any doubt, he huffed, puffing up like a dandelion head.

———

ASTRID WAVED FROM THE DOOR OF THE TRAIN CAR, PAUSING FOR an instant before stepping inside, beginning a journey she had not expected to take. Leaving the house in the jungle might have been a start, but this, the first step in the real world, felt more solid. A true beginning.

Irina returned the gesture, smiling, and a pang of loss at this separation touched Astrid. The comfort and understanding for such a short time had brought relief and a sense of safety, and she hated to let it go.

You will never be ready, Chinook said from his spot beneath her scarf, the warmth of him soothing.

A laugh escaped. "Are you a mind reader, little bird?"

No, but I am not an idiot. I have eyes. You look as if you might cry. I would like to take this opportunity to remind you that my feathers are not absorbent, and I am not a handkerchief.

She didn't respond, moving into the car, a train whistle filling the air, announcing the imminent departure. There would be several stops along the way, a switch from one train to the next. But for now, they'd have an hour of quiet to themselves.

And she would do her best not to get Chinook's feathers damp.

———

"CHINOOK, JUST GET IN THE BIRDCAGE."

I have my dignity.

"Please."

I am not a pet.

"How else am I supposed to explain that I'm traveling with a bird?"

Pirates have birds on their shoulders.

"I am not a pirate!"

Pretend.

"Pirates don't ride trains."

You lack imagination.

He studied her from his perch on the highest stack of crates—poised to leap into the air if she reached for him—in a quiet area of the next station's platform. The crates concealed them but the sounds of people coming and going was only a few feet away.

"What do I say when they ask questions?" Astrid let out a sigh, closing her eyes.

Let them ask! I have never been in a birdcage. I am not a birdcage bird.

She twisted the small bamboo cage in her hands. It was a traveling cage meant to transport feathered creatures from point A to point B—only inches across, the interior tight and cramped. People would notice him. They *would* ask questions. This would be simpler, easier, but she had not counted on Chinook fighting the idea.

Do you want me to put you in a cage? he asked, going on. *No, of course not.*

Astrid shook her head, resigned, and set the cage on a trunk. "Fine, have it your way."

I will sit on your shoulder. Do not ask me to sing. I will keep the remains of my dignity.

————

It would be dawn soon. Another day. More hours between what she'd done and finding him and making it right. The longer it took, the more her heart ached. She wanted to fix it this instant, to gather up all the pieces, and fumble them back into shape. The look on his face, the face she had wanted to see for so many months—one she had dreamed about—the expression had broken Astrid. All the pain and anguish at her choice, her mistake, gnawed at her. She put a hand against her heart—beating the normal rhythm, unbroken and singing betrayal.

On the other side of the building, the train whistled, earsplitting in the silence, making her jump. It was now or never. Chinook would have to ride on her shoulder or in the scarf wrapped around her neck. If people asked, she would explain how well-trained he was, how she had raised him from a tiny egg. Would they believe it? Probably. But Astrid would still be the odd memorable boy they met on the train. She had this nagging feeling that she shouldn't be. She didn't want to stick out.

"Ready?" she asked, touching the small bag resting against her hip, making sure it was still there. Wolf claw and blessings from the North Wind. A talking bird. A golden ring.

Irina had given Astrid a little food, a flask of tea, and train tickets. One for over the Alps and the other to get her as far as Rome. If she was even going that far. Or in that direction. It was impossible to know. The ring kept tugging her south, Irina had told her to find her sister the East Wind, promising the woman would know which way Astrid had to go from there. But Irina had been unable to tell her *exactly* where she would find the woman.

You will know her. And she will know you.

It wasn't very reassuring.

Astrid patted her shoulder, an invitation to Chinook. He accepted, landing in a flutter; so light, she barely felt him there, digging in with tiny sharp claws. Straightening her spine, thinking about confidence and authority, she walked toward the waiting train.

In their train car, the conductor punched a hole in her ticket without looking at her or Chinook. He was a small man—dark and sleepy looking, with a thick mustache hiding his mouth—and indifferent as he waved her onto the train.

She had a ticket for one of the second-class cars, rows of wooden seats facing each other with no privacy. But the car was mostly empty, and she found a seat beside a window and slouched down into it.

Chinook moved to the narrow space between her and the window, settling down, and adjusting his wings. The strap on the bag pulled at her, and she struggled to get it off, putting it on the floor at her feet, the strap between her knees. The window faced opposite the platform, looking onto another train beside them headed in the other direction. It was empty as well, the interior dim.

A handful of other people arrived, choosing seats at a distance, glancing at her and away. Astrid tensed, waiting for someone to say something, but no one did.

You worry too much, Chinook grumbled, sounding half asleep.

"Not as much as you do," she said under her breath, impatient to be moving and on the way.

With a lurch, the train pulled away from the station, the huge iron wheels rolling to life beneath her. The car was only half full; people talked quietly or turned to watch the world roll by.

The rattle and thump as the train picked up speed was

soothing. It eased her aching bones and the soreness in her muscles. She watched the village pass as the sun rose, light touching the small farms rolling by. She closed her eyes, listening to the conversations, someone laughing toward the front.

Glancing down, she saw that Chinook's eyes were already closed.

———

ASTRID WOKE SUDDENLY—DREAMS CHASING HER, TYHR TURNING to watch her go. Sunlight hit her face, hot and bright, the memory of deserts and sand from the dream following her into reality, occupying space in her mind. The train swayed beneath her—around her—and it recalled the motion of water and blue-gray seas. She rubbed the sleep from her eyes, her mouth tasting of salt water.

With a sudden start, she realized a stranger sat across from her.

"Good morning," the man said. "Or should I say, good afternoon?"

He wore a gray suit and tie, a hat on the chair beside him with a red feather stuck in the brim. Blond hair and blue eyes, sharp features, attractive but cold, something about his posture hinting at impatience.

Astrid looked around. There were a few other passengers, but no one else nearby.

"Where's Chinook?" She sat up straighter, looking around, patting her shoulders, the scarf around her neck. A chirp caught her attention and brought her eyes up. He sat on the narrow baggage rail, looking down and hoping along the metal bar. She let out a sigh of relief.

"Is he yours, then?"

She nodded, pulling her bag into her lap, wishing the man would leave.

"I've never seen a bird like him," the man continued. "What species is he?"

"A tanager."

"Exotic for our area. A pet?"

"Yes," she said. "Is there something I can help you with?"

An eyebrow went up, "No. I just thought a young *man* traveling alone might want some company."

He put too much emphasis on young man, too much on traveling alone. Irina had warned her that anyone who looked at her too long would see that she was a woman. At a glance, yes, she might pass, but it was obvious the more you looked. Astrid had thought no one would take the time to notice. She'd been wrong.

"I don't need any company."

"Want, then," he said smoothly, motioning with his hand, an invitation, a welcome. "I have to admit that I was curious about your ring."

Her stomach dropped and she went cold. How could he know? It had never been obvious to her; it had never crossed her mind that it might be to someone else. Magic. If the North Wind moved through the world, if Tyhr traveled from place to place without being remembered, maybe this man did as well. Someone else who saw it all clearly, spotted her on a train, and wanted something she had.

"I don't know what you're talking about and don't want your company."

The smile on his face vanished.

"If you'll excuse me," Astrid said, standing and grabbing the bag at her feet. Chinook fluttered down, landing on her shoulder, and tucking himself against her neck.

The man didn't respond, but she could feel his eyes on her as she made her way down the center of the car. No one else noticed her, no second glances or questioning faces, and she was glad. There should be a dining car farther along, and she would spend the remaining part of her journey there.

He was not there very long, Chinook said, answering her unspoken question.

She nodded, worried he would follow now, that something more would come of it. But she passed through the doors at the end, crossing to the next car, cold wind pushing her, the sounds of the train deafening in the between place. Beyond the sound, the wind, mountains rose around them, and she realized for the first time, they were in the middle of the crossing, moving from Austria into Italy.

Once over, it would be all downhill toward the sea.

But how much farther to Tyhr? Where had Livia taken him?

All she could do was follow the pull of the ring.

CHAPTER TWENTY-SIX

A waiter in the dining car led her to a table toward the back, and she was grateful when she saw she wouldn't be sharing it. At least for now—if the car filled up, someone else would be bound to sit with her. But she would enjoy it for as long as it lasted.

She ordered soup and crusty bread, a glass of white wine, and smiled warmly at the waiter when he set it in front of her. Chinook had small pieces of the bread, and they watched the landscape slide by together, silent and content in each other's company.

More and more, she was grateful for his presence, even his sharp tongue and judgment.

A few strangers entered the car, a young woman in a maroon dress and a small, feathered hat. Behind her, a man in a dark suit, his hand on her elbow, steering her toward a table as they laughed together. Another woman dressed in blue, a beautiful color, mimicking the clear sky overhead. She glanced at Astrid, smiling, and motioned to her table— a silent question. Astrid nodded, inviting her with a hand.

Tired of my company already? Chinook asked, that tartness back in his tone.

"Hush," she said under her breath as the woman approached.

"Hello," the woman smiled warmly at her, extending a hand, "I'm Elaine. May I join you?"

"I would be delighted. I'm Alastair," she replied, taking the offered hand, gesturing for the woman to join her.

As they ate and talked, the train moved through the mountains and down the other side, the transition unnoticed. They passed through a tunnel, a few dark moments, and then into the sunshine again.

"May I be candid?" Elaine asked, leaning across the table.

Astrid's stomach dropped, expecting the worst, wondering how quickly she could excuse herself and get away. But she put a pleasant smile on her face. "Yes, of course."

"Well," the woman looked around the car, making sure no one could overhear them, "I don't think you're really fooling anyone."

"What do you mean?"

Elaine motioned to Astrid's clothes, and hair. "Maybe from far away you could pass for a young man, but up close, you are very much a woman."

"Oh?"

"And I don't mean to pry," she gave a delicate laugh, "but I am anyway. Are you in trouble? Is there something you're running from?"

Surprise touched her; she hadn't expected this to be the question from the woman. Relief followed closely, and her expression must have shown it.

"I don't know what to say," Astrid said.

Do not say anything then, Chinook muttered.

The woman waved a hand, "You don't have to say anything."

Quiet touched them, the noise of the train covering the moment. The meal lay half-eaten before them; Chinook watched the woman as if she might grow horns and breathe fire. Movement caught Astrid's eye, and she looked to see the man from earlier coming into the car, his gaze finding her at once. The color drained from her face as she looked away.

"Is that him? The man you're running from?"

She nodded. What else could she say? *I'm on my way to rescue a man I'm supposed to marry from an enchantress who cursed him by making him a tiger.* No. It was simpler to say this man was the issue. The problem was that it was also the truth. Danger radiated from him, a wave of malice. She was not safe with his attention focused on her.

Elaine glanced around casually as he moved down the center aisle, making his way toward them. There were empty seats all around them, places he could lurk and wait for the right time. A waiter intercepted him, getting his attention and steering him to a place toward the middle of the car. The stranger gestured, wanting a table near them, but the waiter shook his head, guiding the man to the middle section. A small piece of luck for which Astrid was grateful.

"Are you finished?" Elaine asked, inspecting the table. A scatter of crumbs, half-filled water glasses, and the remains of salad on a plate.

"Yes."

"Good," the woman nodded, "if you go through the door behind you, it leads to the private cabins. I'm in two-twenty-three, take my key."

The key slid across the tabletop, concealed beneath

Elaine's hand. Pity touched her face, kindness in her eyes. Astrid gave her a small smile, nodding gratefully, aware that the man watched them closely, attentive to everything spoken between them.

"Go," Elaine whispered. "I'll do what I can to distract him."

"I don't know how to thank you."

Do not, Chinook piped up. *It could be a trap.*

"Just know I understand."

See? Trap.

"Thank you," Astrid said, ignoring Chinook's smug irritation.

Turning away from the table, refusing to look back, she made her way to the end of the car. Sliding the door open let the noise of the wheels in, the wind rushing in to inspect food and passengers—see what it might be missing. The breeze was stiff, coming from the east, clean and fresh, touching Astrid with softness, and curiosity.

"Oh, my friend," Elaine said loudly, "it's been so long since we've seen each other! Please! Sit and tell me everything that's happened! Tell me how your dear sister is! I've missed you both so much."

"Madame," the man's voice was sharp, full of impatience and irritation, "I have no idea who you are. I have no sister."

Astrid slid the door shut, cutting off Elaine's answer, hoping that it would be enough time to reach the cabin and lock the door. Would a lock be enough? Would he pick it, and find a way inside? Would there be another way to get out of the tight space? Doubt crept through her, the idea of being confined in a small private space with that man sent a shiver through her.

Do not go into the cabin. You will not come back out.

They passed it without pausing, a pang of regret flashing by when she didn't use the key the woman had trusted her with. But the conductor would have another. Behind her, the door between cars slid open, again that curious east wind, and the pressure of a stranger's eyes on her back.

Go!

Hurrying now, on the verge of breaking out into a run, Astrid went toward the end of the car, to the next door between carriages. There was no way to know how many there would be left. She hadn't paid any attention to the number of cars, and now she regretted it.

"Stop!"

But reaching the door, she went through and turned to see him running toward her as she fumbled with the latch. Lock. Must be a lock, a way to cut off inquisitive passengers from going too far. There was none.

Hurry!

"There's no lock!"

Into the next car!

She moved, pulling at the opposite door just as the one behind her opened. A hard hand grabbed her, squeezing her skin and muscle, a hiss of some word half heard over the clatter of iron on iron. Chinook left her shoulder, twittering, flying at the man's face. He let her go—freed her—just as she threw herself back and out of his grip.

"The ring!" he shouted, anger and panic shooting toward her. "Give me the ring!"

Losing her balance, grabbing for the small rail between herself and the rushing ground, she missed them, tumbling past. There was a moment of falling, weightless, spinning. Then the ground arrived—hard and biting.

Then darkness.

CHAPTER TWENTY-SEVEN

"I s she badly hurt?"

"No broken bones. Bumps and scrapes. She was lucky, to have fallen and survived."

"How did you know she was coming?"

"Irina said there would be a young woman. An adventure, the leaves told her."

"It's been a long time since you've been interested in adventures." The woman's voice was soft, wistful, a moment of quiet filled the space. More briskly she asked, "But the train?"

"I was curious. I'd gone searching."

The voices circled around Astrid, faint but growing stronger—clearer. Her head ached, spiking pain shooting through her left elbow. She was listening for one voice; one she had not heard yet.

I can fly. You cannot. It was stupid to try to depart the train that way.

Relief. He had come too, escaped the man, and stayed with her.

"I didn't leave the train that way on purpose."

The women's conversation paused, and one said, "Of course not. Can I get you anything for the pain? What hurts?"

"My head," Astrid said, keeping her eyes closed, desperate for the throb to ease.

"I'll go get it," the other voice said.

"So," said the first voice, husky and tinged with an accent, one of Italy that sent a beautiful reverberation through the room. Rosemary and oregano came to her, the softness of the bed beneath her. "You've come from the north and are heading west. What do you hope to find there?"

Astrid opened her eyes, taking in the woman with light hair and pale green-gray eyes, shallow crow's feet, and smile lines around her mouth. She looked as if she could be carried away on the wind, tumbled through clouds, and skim the earth with open arms. Ethereal, not at all solid like Irina had been.

"Are you the East Wind?"

The woman laughed, throwing back her head. "Of course."

"Are you like Irina? Do you have a name?"

"No," she smiled softly. "I have never struggled with who I am. I have been and will always be, East."

"Where am I? I wasn't supposed to get off the train until Rome."

Astrid eased up on one elbow, searching for Chinook. He was perched on the end of the bed, settled down and watchful. She took in the rest of the space—the minimal room, the bed she lay on, the stool the woman sat on, the sheer white curtains over the window, an open door, and a slice of a bare hall beyond. All of it a creamy blue, the walls and floors, the doors and trim, like standing on the inside of a blue sky.

"My home. We're just over the border here, on the Italian side of the Alps. Rome is only a few hours away." East studied her, eyes going down to the ring on Astrid's finger. "Do you feel like standing up? Ophelia is making dinner if you're hungry."

Astrid nodded, sitting up slowly, a hand to her head. She hurt all over, muscles and bones, even her teeth. The expression on the man's face, the look he'd given her as she'd fallen backward out of his reach, surfaced.

"There was a man on the train," she began. "He was chasing me. I fell off because of him."

"Maybe it worked out for the best. Despite the bruises."

Astrid nodded. "Yes, I think so."

"What did he want?"

"This." Astrid held up her left hand. The man's desire for the ring had been physical, his curiosity a slimy pressing creature against her skin.

"He recognized it?"

"Yes," she said, twisting the ring on her finger. "He seemed to."

"A man with dark hair? Hunger in the way he moves?"

"Yes," Astrid nodded. It wasn't much of a description, but it fit him perfectly. Yes. He'd been hungry, not desperate and eager, it was beyond that—into starvation for what he coveted. "Do you know him?"

"If it is the same man, I did." She looked thoughtful beyond the window, considering the wide world. "Once."

"How did you know to look for me?"

"News travels fast on the North Wind, gusting south with Siberia in it. It came with spring this time, a refreshing change. She didn't give me a name, just a description, and that you'd be traveling by train. Also, that you'd have a bird."

Chinook twittered, more at ease with East than with North.

"I'm running out of time. I don't even know if I'm headed to Rome, or someplace beyond, I don't know where I'm going. Irina bought me tickets to Rome because she said the leaves pointed that way, and the ring is pulling me south. But beyond that? I have no idea." Astrid laid it out, opening up right away and admitting to the fear of not knowing what would come next. A month until he'd marry the Enchantress and seal whatever bargain they'd made.

Astrid would be too late and the fear of it was eating her alive.

"I have something for your headache," the other woman said, coming back with a bottle in her right hand.

Her left arm was gone from the elbow down and she wore her long sleeve pinned over it. Now she had a worry line between her brows, thoughtfulness in her expression. She was a plump woman, with a round face, someone who laughed and smiled, sang, and took advantage of all the daylight the sun had to offer. A compliment to East, who was relentless gales and gentle breezes, timeless and constant.

The new arrival held out a spoonful of sticky liquid— faint purple, tasting of lavender and honey. It worked at once, leaving Astrid clearheaded, and she sighed with relief.

"Better?"

She nodded.

"Good," the East Wind said with a sharp nod. She gestured to the woman. "This is Ophelia."

"Thank you for the medicine. It's a pleasure to meet you," Astrid replied.

"Likewise." Ophelia smiled. "Your friend has been very charming as well."

"My friend?"

Chinook perked up, flying from his perch at the end of the bed to Ophelia's shoulder, chirping and half singing, being a chirpy impression of a fairytale songbird. He picked at a strand of Ophelia's hair, twittering to himself.

"I'm surprised he likes you," Astrid said, tone dry, shooting Chinook a sour look. "He doesn't like anyone generally."

Chinook chirped and gave her a sideways glance.

"Well," Ophelia laughed, "I must be the exception. Come down and eat."

"And afterwards," East added, giving Astrid a pointed look, "we'll consider your future."

———

THE HALL AND STAIRS DOWN GOING DOWN, THE LIVING AREA AND kitchen, and even the ceilings, were all painted blue. Various shades, from the clearest azure sky to the deep indigo of evening, the colors moving through the stages of a day—dawn to dusk—tinted with violet and gold.

The table they sat at in the kitchen held salad and quiche, roasted asparagus, and stewed fruits. Drying herbs hung from the exposed rafters and brought the scents of basil and garlic, thyme, and mint to the room—trapped summers and springs, windswept hills, and walled kitchen gardens. Through the kitchen window, Astrid could see a green hillside—tall grass swayed, rippling like water.

Nothing important was talked about around the meal; only small talk filled the room. They discussed the weather and what last summer had been like, had she traveled much, did she have a favorite place. The obvious questions would have been the ring or Chinook. But the women skated around those topics, slipping over them easily, landing on common, everyday things.

Astrid was grateful that they talked as much to each other as to her. Time pressed on her, an elbow to the back, a sharp point telling her to move, to stand up, to run. *Go.* It took everything she had to sit at the table as the hillside grew dark beyond the window. She ate slowly, watching the two women, how comfortable they were with each other—how easy it was for one to reach out and the other meet her.

All of those times Tyhr had reached out. How often had Astrid taken his hand? Not enough.

Chinook began picking things off Astrid's plate after he'd gone through a bowl full of seeds and other green things that had been set out for him.

"Why don't you eat off your own plate?" she whispered.

Because I like what is on yours better.

"Come on, little bird," Ophelia said, standing and moving to the back door. "Let's go see what you might like to eat outside."

"Do you want to?" Astrid asked softly, looking up to Ophelia, who nodded. "I'll be here."

I will be back. Do not leave the house without me.

She nodded, watching as he lifted up to go flitting through the door Ophelia opened for him. She followed him into the dusk, humming to herself. Evening light changed the blue around them, the walls growing darker, the color deepening, mimicking the world outside.

"I think it works because of the ring," East said thoughtfully.

"What?" Astrid turned back to her, confused by the statement.

"The ring. I don't know why exactly, but he's tied to it. Or you are. Maybe both of you are. I can't understand what he's saying, can't really hear it, but it's obvious."

"Well," Astrid forced a laugh, "at least I don't look like a crazy woman talking to myself."

"Oh no," East said with a chuckle, standing. "You absolutely look like a crazy woman talking to herself. But it doesn't matter. Are you ready?"

"Ready?" Astrid asked, looking around. She'd promised Chinook she wouldn't leave the house without him. An edge of unease crept into her with East's gesture to leave the table.

"Come with me," the woman said, leading the way to a small door on the other side of the room. "It's through here."

————

THE LAST OF THE DAYLIGHT FILTERED DOWN THROUGH SKYLIGHTS, touching empty bottles, row after row, from floor to ceiling —cobalt blue, pale purple, brown, yellow, and crystal clear. In the center of the room sat an oak table and two chairs. The floor was dirt, hard-packed and swept clean—a smooth, solid surface after countless years of wearing it down.

Astrid didn't realize how dark the room was until East lit a candle and set it on the table. Flame danced, reflected in the glass surfaces, hundreds of tiny fires burning.

"What's in the jars?" Astrid asked, looking around. They all appeared empty, without labels or any other indication of what they might be for.

"Monsters. Ghosts. A few things that don't even have names." East considered the room, turning in a circle to take it all in. "Some have memories."

Astrid stepped closer to one of the shelves, staring, trying to see beyond the reflected flame to whatever might be beyond. Nothing. Emptiness. A room with hundreds of empty jars.

"Come and sit. I don't know why Irina still bothers with tea. Leaves can only tell you so much. What do dried-up old plants know about a person anyway? Let alone the future? It's better to read them."

"Read them?" Astrid sat, watching East settle opposite her, reaching across the table for her hands.

"Give me your hands."

———

EAST HELD HER HAND TIGHTLY, TURNING IT THIS WAY AND THAT, holding her palm close to the candlelight. Astrid held her breath, wondering what the woman saw, what might be revealed in the creases and patterns—a line for life, another for love, one for fortune. A scar that wasn't even a scar anymore, a way to open an invisible door.

A year ago, she would have thought it impossible. If she thought of it at all. Maybe she would have considered it a game at best, a con at worse. But these last few months had changed the world for her, shifted it, and altered reality. The world contained magic and now she knew it was all around her and inescapable.

If this woman could tell her something of the future, of the path in front of her, she would listen.

"You've come a long way," she said, tracing a crease, following it all the way to the edge of her palm. "But you're not done. I'm surprised to see so much traveling for you. It's not a common thing. But your father, he traveled, moving things from place to place."

Not a question. A statement. It surprised her and she nodded in confirmation. East turned her hand slightly, a line forming between her brows, lips pulling down in a frown. The woman sat back abruptly, keeping Astrid's hand, half pulling her out of her chair.

"Where have you come from?"

Pale eyes searched her face, a hint of accusation in her voice. Astrid didn't have time to answer before the woman grabbed her other hand, turning the palm up—searching intently.

"I thought you knew?" Astrid trailed off as she watched the woman examine her palm, and trace the lines back to the gold band. "You said the North Wind told you."

East laughed, not taking her eyes away from Astrid's palm. "Irina left a few things out, it seems. You've been through the Black Forest."

"You can see that?"

"Here," East traced a line, a faint crease. "You've been outside of time. Did you know that?"

"Not exactly," Astrid said, hesitated, and added, "but yes."

"It's not surprising he would want your ring—the man on the train. He's a magician. And it's powerful. People who know about these kinds of things know it when they see it. But it wouldn't mean anything without you. You are part of what makes it work now."

Firelight rolled over the ring, the band soaking up the light, twisting it into a golden reflection. A gift. A promise. Meaningless without the man who had given it and the woman who had received it.

"Will the man come back?"

"For your sake, I hope not. But others will smell the magic on you. You'll need to be aware of danger and do what you can to stay safe. You've got a long way to go."

"But where am I going?"

"Irina told you Rome, and I can't tell you any different. I think from there, you'll know where you're supposed to go. All I have to offer you tonight is a safe place to sleep and a ride in the morning."

CHAPTER TWENTY-EIGHT

A strid woke before dawn. Quiet filled the house and a few late stars were still visible in the sky through the open window. Cool air filled the room, a breeze ruffling the sheer curtains, touching her with gentle fingers. Chinook was settled down on the bedside table with his head tucked under a wing.

She lay there, listening to the house, the sounds of someone in the kitchen promising breakfast and company. For a moment, brief and almost too hot to touch, she wondered what her mother would have thought about this adventure. If her father would have been surprised. What her brother might have said. But she didn't want to think about them or that loss.

Pushing it away she sat up, stretching, stifling a yawn. She had no time for grief, not here, not now. She dressed quickly, checking the contents of her bag—wolf claw, seed packets, and a few other odds and ends. The claw was warm in the predawn light, heavy in her hand, and she wondered what magic waited within it.

With a squeak, Chinook fluffed up his feathers

becoming a round little ball before shaking out the night. He looked around with sleep blurred eyes, his gaze coming to rest on her.

"Did you sleep well?"

No. Did you?

"Better than on the train."

That is not saying much.

"Maybe you'll get a chance for a nap. I don't mind carrying you."

He brought his feathers up and down in a shrugging motion.

There was a knock at the door and East asked from the other side, "Ready?"

"Ready," Astrid asked Chinook softly. When he nodded, she raised her voice for East. "Yes."

With the door open a song rose to meet them, a sweet voice in a foreign tongue—Ophelia's voice. The words felt old, heavy with age, and Astrid wondered what they meant. As they went downstairs the boards creaked beneath them, making music of their own. The sound of the chickens clucking in the yard outside rounded it all out. The scent of fresh-baked bread filled the house, fresh lemons beneath it, and the sour bite of vinegar.

"We'll have breakfast and the Brentas will be by to pick you up. They're a lovely pair but very hard of hearing so don't expect a lot of conversation," East said, moving to help Ophelia with the food, setting a plate before Astrid and a bowl of seeds and fruit down for Chinook.

"I don't know if I can eat," Astrid said, easing down into the chair.

I can, Chinook trilled happily, landing on the table and pecking at a piece of toast covered in cherry jam on her plate. *You should never pass up the opportunity to eat.*

"Have some tea," Ophelia said, pouring her a cup with her right hand and handing it over carefully with a smile. "It always helps me."

"Thank you," Astrid said, cupping her hands around the warmth.

Tiny specks floated in the liquid, remnants of tea leaves, pulling up other memories—tea in the townhouse, tea in the jungle, tea on the train. A thousand cups throughout her life, all at different points, but the moments that lingered were the ones with Tyhr.

Where was he now? She glanced down at the ring, concentrating, trying to decern where it might lead her. Could she trust it? And would Tyhr want her at the end of the journey?

"Try not to worry. It will all work out," Ophelia said with a smile.

Or it will not, Chinook added, his beak full of her toast.

————

THEY STOOD TOGETHER ON THE FRONT STEPS OF THE EAST WIND'S blue house as a horse and cart creaked down the dirt road toward them. Chinook hopped through the flowers crowded around the front door—hunting bugs and pecking at the ground. A lump of excitement lodged in Astrid's throat, a ball of questions and worry she kept swallowing down.

More than anything Astrid wanted to know what came next—no doubt about their direction, no doubt about what they would find at the end of this journey. But she knew no one could tell her, not even the Winds.

When the cart neared Ophelia went to greet the pair

sitting on the driver's bench, leaving East and Astrid alone for a moment.

"Thank you—" Astrid began.

"You need to be careful," East reached out, placing a gentle hand on Astrid's arm. "If you see the Magician again, you must run. Even if it's in the opposite direction the ring is leading you."

"But—"

"Avoid him," East insisted, voice hard with warning. "Anyone who knows the ring for what it is, is dangerous."

Astrid studied the woman. An immortal as long as the winds moved around the world, connected to the earth and its millions of years. The warning East gave, the pressure on her arm, chilled her.

"What aren't you telling me?" Astrid asked, her voice low as the cart approached.

Ophelia raised her voice in greeting, raising it again to be heard over the jingle of the harness and clack of the wheels. The old woman on the cart was watching Astrid curiously and the old man beside her nodded to East.

"I think he might be someone from our past," East admitted, her eyes touching Ophelia before moving on to the horizon. "He was once very powerful. And if it is the same man, you run if you see him."

Astrid opened her mouth for another question or protest, but Ophelia was coming toward them, and East shook her head. The two women smiled at each other, such a brief and warm expression, the love between them a physical force.

"Well, here they are," Ophelia said, gesturing with her right arm to the cart. "It's been lovely having you here. Especially Chinook. I hope if you're ever in the country again you'll come for a visit."

"Thank you," Astrid said. "I would like that very much."

Did you hear that? Chinook preened. *She wants me to come back.*

"Not just you," Astrid said under her breath. "All of us."

"And your person, when you find him," Ophelia said with a smile. "Bring him too."

The thought of Tyhr twisted in her heart, sharp and insistent, reminding her that every moment spent lingering here was another moment they weren't any closer to rescuing him. But with that thought was the new fear. The unknown man and what connection he might have to East and the ring on her left hand.

"Please, tell me how you know him," Astrid pleaded quietly, needing to know about the stranger, worried that he'd be waiting for her out in the world. Chinook was on the edge of the cart, watching with an intent expression, impatience radiating outward. He shifted, the closest he could get to tapping a foot.

You are wasting time.

"Come back again," East said, pulling Astrid into a swift embrace, "and we'll tell you the story."

"You'll be back," Ophelia said, wrapping Astrid into an embrace next—pressing hopes and wishes and safe travels into her. "I know you will."

———

THE BRENTAS WERE BROTHER AND SISTER, TINY AND BENT DOUBLE with age. Both with thick white hair, a white beard for him, and dark sparkling eyes that reminded her of the North Wind. They smiled and gestured for her to get in the back of the wooden cart pulled by the large chestnut horse with white flowers embroidered in her bridle. The horse watched her curiously but beyond the first shouted introduction the siblings seemed uninterested in Astrid and Chinook.

"Thank you for the ride," Astrid said, getting into the back of the cart and settling in.

They both nodded, the brother picking up the reigns, the sister pulling a piece of knitting from beneath the bench seat. A word was never exchanged, only smiles and nods, as the horse took the first few steps away from the house.

The East Wind and Ophelia stood together on the back porch, arms around each other, and waving, a soft breeze rushing after them—urging them on, easing their way. Astrid returned the gesture, grateful for the safe place they'd provided. She hoped that she would see this place again—gently rolling hills and tall skinny trees, fields of lavender and olive orchards. She watched them all as they passed, avoiding the future, and thinking about the past.

"Chinook, what could scare the East Wind?"

I do not know.

"It's hard to believe that anything could."

No one, not even the Winds, can live without fear. Nothing is secure in this world.

Astrid considered his words, watching him, wondering what might be going through his mind. Tyhr had not been secure, not even in the Summer Valley hidden by the Black Forest. Someone with powerful magic had come and turned his life into a nightmare. Was this stranger, this man from the train, someone like that?

We can only keep going, Chinook said, a somber edge creeping into his voice. *We can only go forward.*

———

WITH A WAVE AND SILENT SMILE, THE BRENTAS DROPPED ASTRID and Chinook off on the outskirts of Rome—buildings collecting, coming together, rushing toward the pulsing humanity of the huge city. The ring pulled her toward it— urging her on. But she was wary, giving the ring time to adjust in case this was the wrong direction after all. Time pressed on her—a weight and worry—a constant tension between her shoulder blades.

Another part of her was worried about going into the city, about what might happen after the incident on the train. But the East Wind had said Rome and promised another meeting, another Wind to point her in the right direction. How would she find her?

Where are we going? Chinook asked.

"I'm not sure."

South? West?

Astrid shook her head, holding her left hand out in front of her like a woman in a dark room feeling through the space—light caught the band, warming it. Turning slowly, she tried to open herself to it, closing her eyes and concentrating, pushing the sound of Chinook's grumble away, the breeze rustling through the olive grove nearby, the buzz of bees through wildflowers.

South. Through the city, there was a sense of distance in the pull, an urging to cross the sea.

"Come on," she said, taking the first step forward, "let's skirt around the city and see where we end up. Maybe I'll be able to tell once we're past it."

And I will sit on your shoulder?

"If you'd like," she glanced at him pecking through the dirt a few yards away, inspecting the earth with a dedicated eye. He had stuck close to her since leaving the Black Forest behind, never too far away, his attitude softer toward her now than he'd ever been in the past. "You're always welcome to."

He didn't respond, merely pushing into the air and coming to perch on her right shoulder, looking out at the world, little claws gripping tight.

Onward then, he said, ruffling and settling his wings.

"Yes," she agreed. "Onward."

CHAPTER TWENTY-NINE

Astrid had never been to Rome. Porter and Stern Shipping had come and gone through the port here and her parents had visited once—a second honeymoon of sorts that took them all over the continent. They'd returned with stories that also included a list of what the company shipped—bulk dry goods—and what they'd chosen to bring home as souvenirs—painted dishes and paintings.

Each time her father had traveled he'd returned with treasures for each of them—books, delicate brass boxes, inlaid wooden trays. And stories. So many stories of strange and far off places. They would get the atlas out and track the progress of the ships and her father would point out where the goods came from and how far they traveled.

Her chest tightened with pain—dull and sharp at once —and she tried to clear her mind, focusing on the city around them. It was a relief to pass through a place with no memory of her family to color the streets, to wash the present in quick brush strokes grief and loneliness.

It struck her now, immersed in this strange and new

place, that she had no one to bring a gift back for, no one who would ask questions about her journey. And she never would if she couldn't find Tyhr. He was Astrid's only family now.

But Chinook had become family too, a friend she had not expected to find, another person she couldn't bear to lose. Reaching up she touched one clawed foot, an irritated noise coming from him as he adjusted and sidestepped her hand. She laughed, not minding his reaction. It didn't change how she felt and maybe someday he'd feel the same for her.

Clotheslines crisscrossed overhead on the smaller streets, doors opened onto houses full of chatter and laughter, the language foreign and indecipherable. They passed others—men and women, groups of children—but to Astrid, it felt as if they moved through the people unseen. They came to a square with a market on one end and shops of all kinds facing the large open space. It was bustling, as people came and went carrying bolts of fabric, pottery, silverware, and other household items.

They moved down other streets, crossing similar squares selling different items, some lined with cafes and restaurants. Others centered around fountains with old ladies dressed head to toe in black gossiping in the shade. Street after street, turning corners blindly, the city a seemingly endless maze, she followed the pull of the ring.

After the rustle of the jungle, the deep silences of the house, and the rumbling thunder building in the distance, all the noise of the city overwhelmed Astrid. But also, it was a relief, a small pleasure after so long without anyone else around her.

They passed through it all like ghosts.

"YOU MADE IT."

A woman's voice stopped Astrid, halting her progress as she made her way around the edge of another large square. Had she been here before? It seemed vaguely familiar, but the city had taken on that feel, an endless loop of similar places, all of them almost the same yet slightly different. Her head hurt and her stomach grumbled, hunger finally catching up with her.

Astrid turned, startled at the first English she'd heard spoken here, the familiarity in the tone. A woman sat at a café table a few feet away, a cup of coffee and pastry in front of her—white dishes, silver spoon. She was shaded by a small white lace parasol, the shadows moving strangely over her beautiful features. The woman beckoned to them with a smile, her dark eyes felt old—as if she'd seen everything the world had had to offer, and she'd chosen to accept only happiness and pleasure.

"Come!" she said, "Maybe you'd like a coffee? Pastry? Something small for your bird?"

Astrid could not have refused the woman even if she'd tried. She was magnetic, pulling Astrid forward irresistibly. Without question, this was the West Wind, the woman her sisters had promised she would find. Chinook let out a small chirp in greeting, knowing who this was without explanation. With a sigh of relief, Astrid sat and the West Wind moved the parasol until it shaded both of their faces.

"I wasn't sure how long it would take you and I've been here for several hours. I'm so glad you've made it without any trouble on the road."

"It was a relief," Astrid agreed with a nod.

"I'm sure. I hope that from here on out there will be no more."

"Me too," she agreed, the face of the man on the train surfacing in her mind. But already she was moving beyond those thoughts, the pull of the ring demanding now that she'd stopped. It was an itch, an inescapable insistence to get up and keep going forward.

"You're ready to go," the woman said with a laugh, holding up a hand when Astrid began to protest. "No, I don't blame you. I would be anxious too. This won't take long. I'm on my way out of the city as well, actually, so I've already taken a peek."

"A peek?"

"At your cards! They're my preference. Tea leaves can be unclear. Palms are a mystery. I prefer the answers found in the cards. My sisters think it's lazy. But they've never had the cards speak to them so possibly it's jealousy." She laughed, digging in a small, embroidered reticule in her lap.

A deck of small cards appeared; gold-edged with detailed bright art on one side and simple scrollwork on the other. The West Wind shuffled them quickly, deft with muscle memory, choosing three and laying them out one by one. Astrid studied them, unsure of their meaning.

"Ten of Cups. The Chariot. The Tower."

Each card was a piece of the future paired with the tea leaves and the creases on her palms. She curled her hands together in her lap, tracing what she had learned was her lifeline.

"Do you know what they mean?" the West Wind asked, shooting her a look.

Astrid shook her head.

The woman placed a finger on The Chariot, The Tower, and then the Ten of Cups. "Travel. Change. Love. Everything you've known and what my sisters have seen. But it's a reinforcement, a way to know you're on the right path."

The West Wind tapped her lip with one perfectly manicured finger.

"The Chariot indicates you still have far to go. You've not yet reached the end of your journey. The Tower is unstoppable, change that comes no matter what you do. Ten of Cups is love. The love you're searching for."

Love.

"Do you feel like it fits you now, right in this moment?"

"I think so," Astrid said, a thread of doubt winding around her words.

"Keep going. It will."

Astrid nodded and Chinook chirped.

"Are you ready? Let's send you on your way. Do you have an idea of the direction?"

They stood together, Chinook flapping to keep his perch, and the West Wind reached out and took Astrid's hand to pull her into the center of the square. A few people moved out of the way, the hot sun beating down, warming the top of her head, and Chinook was a weightless presence on her shoulder.

"Close your eyes," West urged, "and concentrate."

Astrid did as West gently turned her to face each direction of the compass. The square was quiet but beyond that, there was the noise of the huge bustling city. The scents of the café reached her here and below that the sour tang of garbage—an unseen fountain tinkled, a bird began to sing.

The ring tingled, warming against her skin.

"South and West," Astrid murmured, opening her eyes.

"My favorite directions!" West said with a smile. "You'll have fair traveling winds as you cross the sea."

Cross the sea. Chinook repeated, a thread of worry interwoven with his words.

Across the sea. Astrid hadn't really believed her search for Tyhr would end in Rome, but it would have been a relief if it had. For a moment she let panic and worry overwhelm her, accepting it, knowing there was nothing she could do to change it. She was going on, moving forward, no matter how much fear she felt. The ring would not lead her astray.

"You'll find plenty of ships down at the port. Choose the one that feels right." The West Wind patted her kindly on the shoulder. "Trust your gut."

I do not trust your gut, Chinook muttered. *You should use your head.*

Astrid bit her lip, wondering if she did either. She'd trusted her gut when she went into Tyhr's room with a candle and ruined everything. But she knew about ports and shipping vessels. Her father had taught her as much as Antony.

"I'll go down with you," West said easily, looping her arm through Astrid's to steer them in the right direction. "But then I really must be going. There's going to be a storm later that I just don't want to miss."

CHAPTER THIRTY

The bustling port was as familiar as home—they were all the same in a way, incoming and outgoing, goods and people, the world condensed into a small space. Wet rope and saltwater tickled her nose, the fishing boats bobbing away to the right adding their own scents to the mix. Men yelled instructions to each other as they unloaded and loaded vessels, passengers weaving through the maze of cargo and busy people.

There had been times when she'd gone with her father to inspect ships and cargo loads, wandering through crowded warehouses at his side. A young woman with a book under her arm, ready to hold his papers, and laughing when he shared silly shipping stories. It all felt so far away now, so far behind her—another woman, in another life.

She wasn't that person anymore.

Astrid, this Astrid, lived in a jungle and her best friend was a bird. The woman she'd become was following a man across the world, led by a golden ring, determined to see his face and tell him...

What?

Everything. All of it.

She would fix this mistake.

Which ship are we taking? asked Chinook, breaking across her thoughts.

"I don't know," she said, turning, concentrating on the faint pull coming from the ring.

Even *if* she found the right one—*when* she corrected—she had no idea how they would get aboard. There were only a handful of passenger vessels. Most were cargo ships, planks down, crates and huge bales being loaded into holds or placed and tied down on decks. Movers of goods, transporting raw materials from here to there.

But even working vessels sometimes took passengers. Porter and Stern Shipping had always discouraged it with a stiff frown and heavy fine. But some captains were willing to make room on their ships for the right price.

The ring pulled her down the dock, past larger vessels, as men shouted to be heard above the slap of water on hulls and the groan of machinery. Chinook tucked himself into the scarf looped around her neck, a small bundle of heat and prickly claws. Reaching the end of the dock she paused, the ring warm on her finger, certainty sinking in as she read the name of the last steamer on the pier.

The *Serendipity*.

"This one," she said, relieved to see a handful of travelers boarding. It would be easy enough to find a place among the other passengers. There would be no first or second class on a vessel like this one. They would blend right in.

You are sure? Chinook asked doubtfully, stretching out of his hiding place to look around. *It does not look like the one to me.*

"How would you know? She said to trust my gut."

What if I do not trust your gut?

"Why?"

The ship is small.

"It's not small!"

It is compared to the others here. Chose a different one.

"This is the one."

What if it sinks?

"It won't."

And if it does?

"Then you can blame me."

I will not hesitate, he replied with a sniff.

Astrid turned with a sigh, looking for someone who might be able to help add her name to the passenger list at the last minute—digging in the bag she carried for the envelope of money she'd packed along with the other things. Needing the luck that had carried her this far to get her a little farther.

Astrid, Chinook said, voice low, an edge to it.

"What's wrong?"

Is that the man from the train?

She turned, searching, heart quickening. It was less crowded here at the end of the pier, a few large crates still waiting to be loaded—men hurrying back and forth. It would be departing soon, impending departure hung in the air, and she couldn't miss this chance.

"Where?"

Then she saw him.

We need to go.

But the man was moving, striding toward her on long legs, taller than she remembered, eyes full of greed and anger. He crossed the distance between them before she could move, there in a flash, reaching for her with one long-fingered hand.

"Don't touch me," she said, stepping back, trying to avoid him. Chinook fluttered, trying to untangle himself from the scarf, chirping madly, but she hissed, "Stay there!"

The man's hand closed around Astrid's left wrist, cold and iron-tight, triumph on his face.

"You're not falling off any trains this time," he hissed, leaning over her, squeezing the bones in her wrist together. "Take it off."

"I don't know what you mean," she gasped, tugging, looking around wildly for help.

The pier was deserted now. All life and noise drained from their surroundings, the world containing only herself and this man.

"I want the ring."

Astrid shook her head. "No!"

"You don't even know what you're doing with it." His tone became persuasive, curling into her ear, offering release from her dangerous journey. "Why keep it?"

"It's mine," she said firmly.

"It was stolen from me centuries ago. It belongs to me. You've no claim on it."

"The East Wind knows you," Astrid whispered, heart pounding, chills shooting through her. Whatever the history

"And I know her." The man laughed darkly, mockingly. "Who do you think stole it?"

"You can't have it!"

"You don't have a choice," he hissed.

The man twisted her arm until she cried out, pain shooting through her elbow—sharp and hot—and grabbed her left hand. He pulled at the ring, trying to yank it free, muttering under his breath. The metal warmed, growing hot, and he yelped in pain, letting her go.

"If you won't take it off," he paused, looking around as if realizing for the first time they were in a public place, that anyone might see him. "You'll come with me."

Pain clutched her heart, pounding through her, a horrible echo of what she'd felt at the hand of the Enchantress. All of it was so sudden and harsh that it left her gasping, as her vision blurred, the world sliding out of focus, noises receding.

Hold on! Chinook whispered. *It is magic.*

Magic.

CHAPTER THIRTY-ONE

Wake up! Chinook's voice came from a distance, cutting through the fog, tearing away at the strands of tugging sleep. *The ship is sinking!*

Ship. Sinking.

Astrid blinked slowly, the world a blur, as she reached out searching for connection. Where was she? The last thing she remembered was the dock, the Magician, and Chinook. She sat up, hand flying to her temple as the world spun, blinking until she could see clearly.

"Chinook?"

Get up! Up! Get help!

"What happened?" she asked, looking around. She was on the top bunk in a tiny room—bare metal, nothing personal, not even a mattress or pillow. Only the bare metal sheet and the terrified bird perched on the rail.

The Magician locked us in here.

"But you said the ship is sinking?"

Are you blind? Deaf?

Astrid heard it then—a rushing sound, a low susurration of movement. She rolled onto her side, blinking at the floor. Water was coming in under the cabin door.

"The ship is sinking!"

Yes, so I said. Thank you for finally paying attention to me.

"How long have I been asleep?"

I do not believe you were sleeping.

"Knocked out then," Astrid said, sitting up and rubbing her hands together. Her fingers and toes were cold. Her bag was at the end of the bunk and she grabbed it, riffling through the contents quickly. Everything appeared to be there but she needed more time, a less stressful situation in which to make sure.

Long enough. Hurry, open the door!

"Give me a moment."

The cabin was bare, the bunks nothing but metal, all bedding gone. There was a high shelf with a tiny, burning oil lamp, light flickering. The walls were steel and coated in dull gray paint, thick and bumpy. The plates of the hull and whatever might be in the rooms to either side were riveted to the floor and ceiling, supported by metal beams. They were low down in the belly of the ship, possibly below the waterline. Astrid couldn't tell. She'd been unconscious for the trip down.

We do not have a moment. As you can see, with your now open eyes, the water is coming in. If you wish to remain in bed, I am positive it will rise to meet you. He lifted his wings, his version of throwing his hands in the air. *So, by all means, stay where you are.*

"I'm up," she said, swinging her legs over the metal bunk and looking down. She slipped the strap of her bag across her body, contemplating the rising water. Chinook hopped closer along the rail, and she reached for him, running a gentle finger down his back.

I tried to wake you, he said, voice small, a tenderness beneath the words. *I am relieved you are not dead.*

"Me too," she whispered. "Let's get out of here."

Pushing off the bunk Astrid leapt to the floor. The water rose, clear and cold, filling the cabin—ankle deep, then up to her knees. Her trousers were soaked, boots filling and becoming heavy weights at the ends of her legs quickly. Astrid tugged at the door while Chinook fluttered around her head, circling the sparse room before going back to the top bunk. She pounded on the door with the heel of her hand, yelling as she did, hoping that someone would hear her and open the door.

"Help! Someone!"

The water rushed, coming in, moving through the space beyond the locked door. It filled her ears, pounded in her head, and coursed through her bones. They could have struck another ship or been attacked. Or maybe the old ship had split at a weak point, the pressure of the sea too much to bear.

Astrid stopped pounding on the door, listening, the rush of water drowning out even her panicked breathing. The ship around her seemed large, big enough to cross oceans. They could be going anywhere. But if the ship was that large, then she would have to be out of sight, far below, stuck in an out-of-the-way spot, where the rest of the crew might never hear her. They might not even know she was there.

"What do you remember? What did you see?" Astrid raised her voice over the sound of water filling the space, coming in at an alarming rate.

Nothing. I saw nothing.

"What happened to the Magician?"

He carried you aboard. Someone called him Lucas.

"What else?"

I do not know! I hid! I stayed with you!

He sounded as panicked as she felt. Both of them jittery, a very real death by drowning facing them, here in this locked room.

"I don't know what to do." Astrid leaned against the door, palms flat, gold ring tapping against steel. The sound, heard above the rushing water and ragged breathing coming out of her throat, was loud. The band, her only tie to Tyhr, the only way to find him and fix what she had broken.

Now she would never get the chance.

"This might be it."

There must be something.

"I don't know what else to do."

I am not a fish, Astrid. I cannot fly in the sea.

"Oh, I am well aware that *you* are a very opinionated bird." She laughed, surprised that she could, and threw him a glance. "I'm not a fish either, you know."

Obviously. However, you can swim.

He watched her intently. It might have been an accusing glare. It might have been a stare of hope or love. It could have been fear and desperation. But accusation was what she felt. Astrid was the reason Tyhr had been forced from the valley, fulfilling the promise forced on him so many years before. Promises within promises, each peeled back like the layers of an onion, tightening, and growing closer, with the Enchantress at the heart of it all.

Astrid turned back to the door, hitting it hard with the palm of her hand, the ring connecting—resonating. Chinook startled into flight, fluttering around the space, tipping the oil lamp. Astrid smacked the door again, shouting at the top of her voice.

"Hello! We're down here!"

The water swirled above her knees now, crawling up the cabin walls, swirling eddies filling the room. Everything was wet, including Chinook.

"Hello?"

The voice, faint, came from far away. Was she imagining it? Was it a hallucination born of desperation? It came from down the hall, but closing in, and then a sloshing sound, like someone large wading through moving water, calling out, words indecipherable. Astrid thumped on the door, yelling—throat raw. Chinook flew to her shoulder, feet digging in and holding on. She adjusted the scarf around him, doubling it, giving him a safe place.

Are they coming for us?

"I hope so," she said, pounding on the door again, then yelling, "Can you hear me? Can you get us out?"

"Move back from the door."

A man's voice—older and rough—on the other side of the door. Something solid connected with the steel, the crash of metal on metal deafening. Again and again, he hit the door, and Astrid covered her ears. The cabin handle shivered and broke, falling into the water as the door eased open inch by inch, fighting the water. A man pushed it, his shoulder leaned into it, an ax in his hand. He was soaked as well, water turning the fabric of his clothing black, and it clung to his solid frame. A weather-worn face, buzzed dark hair. Blue eyes met hers with a question—curious—but there was no time for answers.

"Come on," he said, wading into the room and grabbing her arm. "We've got to get on deck."

The corridor beyond the cabin was too narrow to walk side by side. He moved her in front of him, heading to the left, pushing her against the rising water. She stumbled once, something large and unseen on the floor, but he jerked her up, keeping her from falling in over her head. Chinook clung desperately to her, claws biting into her skin, so sharp they might have drawn blood.

"Who are you?" she asked, glancing back.

"Simon. Keep moving," he said, gesturing for her to continue.

"Do you know what's going on?"

He shook his head, a line between his brows, "Up here we're going right and then up. There are ladders. We're going all the way up. Can you climb?"

"Yes."

"Good. We need to move fast. You understand?" His voice was hard and impatient.

At the end of the hall was a watertight hatch with a round window and a round wheel to seal it. Beyond, a tiny space waited, large enough for the ladder going up but little else. It disappeared into the ceiling and through another narrow opening.

"Up," he said, pushing her toward the ladder.

Astrid grabbed cold metal, tilting her head all the way back to look up. It was too hard to tell how many levels of the ship there were; the ladder went on, through too many hatches to count. Everything above her appeared dry, no water coming down the openings. But around her, beneath her, the water rose. Astrid climbed out of it, moving up, the man following. His steady breathing pushed her on, the thump of their boots ringing in the space as they went up.

Only once did she look down, past the man, to see swirling, dark water. It was deeper now, coming after them. The man, Simon, stopped at each hatch, slamming them into place and twisting them shut—metal crashing into metal, the squeal of metal grooves coming together.

"Keep going," he said, noticing she'd stopped.

She went through another hatch and another. New noises began to reach them—voices raised, an alarm blaring, and the sound of pounding feet. One more hatch to go through, but she had no idea what lay beyond.

They emerged into another tiny space, like the one so far below, a door with a round window looking out onto darkness. A shadow ran across it, shouting and waving arms—many voices shouting in an unfamiliar language. Simon came up behind her, turning to lower the final hatch, spinning it closed with a grunt of effort.

"How did you know I was there?" she asked. "Who are you?"

"There are lifeboats being lowered on the starboard side. Go out and to your right. Get in the first one you see." He reached past Astrid, opened the door, and pushed her out.

"Wait," she clutched his arm, feeling that it was important somehow. "How did you know I was there?"

"I overheard someone talking about a girl down below, someone they picked up on the docks. It's not the first time." With a gentle push, he sent her moving. "I couldn't let you drown."

The deck was dark, whatever lights the vessel might have had, gone, and it rocked violently in a choppy sea. Waves slapped the sides, spray catching her, clinging to her face. She'd thought she couldn't get any colder, but up here, in the open air, she began to freeze. The sea moved as if driven by a storm, but the skies were clear, each star a bright spot in the darkness.

Toward the stern of the ship, she could see figures, not very many, only a handful doing something with cargo on the deck. A man holding a lantern ran to them, throwing warm orange light over the work. More shouts came from out of sight, people running, a crash as a crate came loose and rolled across the deck.

Simon grabbed her arm again, pulling her in the other direction, around the cabin they'd come out of. He hustled her through more cargo strapped to the deck, huge barrels and crates roped in place, covered in spider webs of ropes. As the ship rolled, the bonds creaked, tensing, everything groaning as the ship moved, pitching forward.

"I heard some of them talking. The captain's men. A man brought you aboard. Bribed the captain. He asked to put you in the hold." He stopped, glancing around, and then searched her face. "There are a handful of passengers, women and kids too. They're by the lifeboats, and you can blend in. Stay with them."

Astrid nodded.

"Keep your back to anyone in uniform, hide your face."

She didn't have to ask who the man had been. The one from the train. The Magician. Lucas. The hissing pressure of his grip, fingers pulling at the gold ring he struggled to pry from her hand. He hadn't been able to. So, he'd taken her whole.

Getting as far away as possible from him was the priority. Then she'd worry about continuing in the right direction.

The wind picked up, blowing sea spray and the ozone scent of a storm coming over them. Clouds rolled in— covering the clear sky—fast, like a blinking eye. Astrid looked to the west at a wall of darkness cut by bolts of lightning. It would overtake them soon, the waves becoming more dangerous. With the water coming in from below, it wouldn't take long for the ship to sink.

Simon led her out from between the large shipping

crates, and Astrid saw the lifeboats and the crowd of about twenty people waiting to be loaded. Three boats in total on this side of the ship, more than enough room for the passengers and crew. She joined the group silently, head down. None of them noticed, all focused on the boats, clutching belongings and each other, fear in their faces.

A handful of men in blue uniforms were helping people into the boats one by one. As she watched, the first was filled and lowered into the churning ocean, a crewman at each end armed with oars, passengers between them. Rain began to fall, though Astrid couldn't feel the difference between what fell from the sky and what the wind blew up from below.

"All right!" One of the men shouted above the wind, cupping his hands around his mouth. "I want ten in this boat. We're going to load you one at a time. Who's first?"

Astrid was pushed forward, Simon getting her to the front of the group. Someone made a noise of protest—a woman's voice raised in sharp complaint. But it was too late. Astrid was at the railing with the wooden lifeboat, looking down over the side of the ship. Blue-black water rolled, cresting in white foam, crashing hungrily into the ship.

"You're first," the man said, not really looking at her, watching the way the lifeboat swayed suspended over the water. "You're going to hold on to this rope, and I'll help you over. Ready?"

"Yes," she said, glancing back at Simon, suddenly afraid to go on without him. He nodded, but she couldn't be sure if it was to say he would be right behind her or if it meant now she would be safe.

Grasping the rope, stretching over the gap between steel and wood—boat and ship—she reached, bracing for the crossing. With a gasp she held her breath, stomach dropping, the idea of falling into the sea so real, she could see it.

"Stop!"

Astrid froze, both feet still firmly on the deck.

"Not you," a man said—the man standing at the other lifeboat wench. He waved her away, back into the crowd. "You'll go last. You're traveling with someone."

Astrid shook her head.

"Get back! Who's next?" His sly dark eyes searched the crowd, head craning to see over the tallest people there. He seemed to be searching for someone.

"She's going," Simon said, putting a hand on the man's chest, stopping him from stepping forward to stop her.

Go now, Chinook said, voice rising shrilly in her mind, *while they are busy. Now!*

The people waiting looked from one to the other, distracted from the storm and their fear for a moment, uneasiness passing through them—a shared emotion. Astrid scrambled into the boat, sliding out of reach, and grasping one of the ropes attached to the bars keeping it tethered to the ship.

"Stop her!" a man called out, pushing from the back of the crowd. The Magician. "She can go with me in the next boat. I'll see she makes it safely."

"No," Simon said, tone hard, forceful. "She's in the boat now. You wait until the women and children are loaded in."

"She's mine." Lucas took two steps forward, hissing loudly enough for them all to hear. "You don't get a say in this."

"You left her to die. The cabin was half full of water. She almost drowned."

A mummer went through the group, looks exchanged,

faces full of curiosity and pity turned toward her. One of the sailors on deck studied her thoughtfully, and she wondered if he'd pull her out. Astrid turned to the rope, studying the pulley system meant to ease them down. It seemed easy to operate, it would only take one person to lower it. But the sailor held the end attached to the ship, fist tight, not ready to let go.

Lucas pushed Simon, sending him back into the crowd even as they moved out of the way. A woman screamed and a man reached out to help Simon up. But Lucas was there, fist raised and then connecting—a crunch that Astrid felt in her gut. Someone else shouted as they scuffled, punching and rolling across the deck. Simon got the upper hand, staggering up, kicking out and putting space between them.

"You bastard," he said, anger balled in his fists, creasing his face.

Lucas said nothing, breathing heavily, eyes narrowed. Then he smiled, straightened, and reached into the drenched jacket he wore. Lightning crackled overhead, illuminating pale faces—casting a hollow glow—exposed for an instant before being thrown into darkness again. Rain pounded down, the ship rolling lazily now, heavy and low in the water. A wave washed over the decks, knocking several people off their feet, and sending them clutching for the railing.

The man holding the rope to the lifeboat let go.

Now! Chinook insisted, digging his claws into her shoulder, fluttering wings against her neck.

But Lucas, staggering with the ship, kept his footing and pulled a gun from his jacket. A woman screamed as men rushed forward, but not before he pulled the trigger. Simon fell at once—boneless, lifeless, a dark shadow opening in his face, cracking through bone. Astrid screamed —horror and terror ripping through her.

She pulled at the rope, yanking it back, severing the connection to the ship, and sent the lifeboat free-falling into the sea.

CHAPTER THIRTY-TWO

Water slapped her face, the sounds of fighting breaking out, more screaming, and men yelling. Astrid looked up—the distance between herself and the ship growing as the lifeboat fell—to see Lucas leaping over the rail and falling toward her.

The boat hit the water, rocking violently, colliding with the hull of the ship. Chinook was thrown from her shoulder, fluttering in the rain, a high pitch note of fear coming from him. Lucas landed with a thud, knocking into her, and sending her into a bench seat. Her head cracked against hardwood, blackness washing over her for an instant. But it passed, leaving sharp pain and blood in her mouth.

Lucas was on top of her at once, fighting with one hand to grasp her arms as she thrashed, pushing at his chest. In his other hand was the gun. The rolling waves moved them swiftly away from the ship, sounds of distress coming from the deck, shouts and calls following after them. But she couldn't make out the words above the storm and the pounding in her head.

"Hold still, and I won't hurt you," he said through

clenched teeth. "I only want the ring back. After all this time. It's mine."

Astrid didn't respond, keeping her breath, her words, saving it all for the fight. Terror drove her, and she managed to get a knee up, connecting with his groin—hardness meeting tender flesh. He yelped—face reddening—falling to the side, away from her, and dropping the gun at the bottom of the boat. Ragged panting escaped him, as he sucked in air, fighting for breath until he finally released a groan.

"You brat," he hissed through clenched teeth, pain in his voice. "I'll cut the ring from your hand!"

Astrid snatched the gun up, shaking with adrenaline and cold, scrambling back over the bench.

"Stay away from me," she said, pointing the gun at him, keeping it there.

Shoot him! Chinook said from his hiding spot at the prow of the boat. *You will not get another chance!*

"I can't," she said. Rain blurred her vision, fear and panic, making her hand shake. The gun trembled in her hands.

Chinook hopped out onto the bench, furious, fluttering damp wings. Lucas still red in the face, but seemingly more in control, looked surprised to see the little bird.

We have to keep going. You cannot keep a promise if you are dead. He was angry, voice shrill in her head, accusing. *Shoot him and keep your word.*

Lucas lunged for Chinook, pouncing on the bird, a noise of triumph coming just as a squawk of surprise erupted. Lucas clutched the small delicate body, glaring, and then threw Chinook hard into the night, out to sea, away from the safety of the lifeboat.

Astrid screamed, wordless, pain coursing through her

veins—sharp and bitter—her eyes following Chinook, losing track of him almost at once. A wave crashed over the boat, water lingering in the bottom, sloshing over her feet. Blinking saltwater from her eyes and fighting to keep her footing, she swayed, moving with the ocean. Lucas lunged, reaching across the bench, closing the distance between them, fury burning in his gaze.

She pulled the trigger, more out of surprise than anything else; caught off guard, heart twisted into knots of sorrow. Lucas fell back onto a bench, blood welling from the chest wound, astonishment replacing anger. He touched the hole—large and gaping—hand coming away red.

He pushed to his feet, wobbling. He would keep coming. He would hurt Astrid, even as damaged as he was—this Magician intent on stealing her one tie to Tyhr. She lunged toward him, dropping the gun, palms out. They connected and the warmth of his blood startled her. But he went backward and fell into the water with a splash.

"Let the sea take you!" she said, voice shaking.

———

Landing on her knees, panting, she clutched the edge of the lifeboat. Lucas floundered, arms waving, thrashing as he sank below a wave and then rose, spluttering. A darker spot appeared on the water, black in the flash of lightning from the storm overhead. His face was turning blue, movements slowing.

In the distance, racing toward them, a sharp, white fin surfaced.

Lucas rolled in the water—desperate for his life— fighting to stay afloat. He followed her gaze, seeing the fin, the quickness, the intent. A harsh sound broke from his lungs; he made a feeble splash, then the animal was on him, rising from the water, enormous, bloody mouth open. Rows and rows of flashing teeth, black eyes, sharp snout. The shark was white as milk, the color of gardenias in a black pot, creamy and more alive than the surroundings. The huge mouth closed on the man's torso, jerking, diving back into the water, and pulling the man down with him.

Blood, a dark stain on a darker sea, rose and spread.

Astrid fell back, shaking, and crying with fear. Chinook was an aching hole in her gut, and she keened with loss, snot, and tears mixing. She stood shakily, looking around, yelling for him, sobbing, growing silent.

Chinook was gone. Gone like Tyhr. Because of her. Both of them, their lives altered because of her. Selfish and thoughtless, her actions only for herself. She'd killed Chinook, her only friend, her companion, her way of keeping loneliness at bay and keeping her sane, keeping her moving forward.

The huge shark surfaced and circled, fin above the water—long and sharp. Astrid panted, heart pounding, as another wave flowed over the boat—leaving it, filling it— and it sank lower. The shark continued to move around her slowly. It surfaced, rolling, watching her from a single black eye.

Thank you for the tribute.

His voice, deep and thumping, crashing like waves in her mind. She shook with it, terrified, the gold ring on her finger burning—a mark of failure.

You are searching for someone, the voice came again, the shark cutting through the water, rising and falling with the waves.

"Yes," she managed. "I lost someone."

A bird, thrown into the sea, not a tribute.

"My friend," Astrid said, clutching her stomach, and pushing at the hollow.

I will give you something. It has been many years without a tribute, without dedication. But you called to me. You gave him to the sea.

She shook her head, not understanding. The words she'd shouted had just been words, just sounds pulled up from her gut—anger and sorrow given breathing form.

It is no matter. You do not have to understand. It is done either way. So, I will give you a gift.

The shark rose to the surface again, black eye rolling, mouth gaping wide. The creature was so close, so near, he could have reached out with ease, grabbed her as he had the man to pull her beneath the waves. In his mouth, a limp colorful tangle of feathers—blue and green, jungle colors in this ocean place—the tiny body of Chinook. The shark waited, moving slowly in place.

Take him. A gift.

Astrid reached out—hesitated—meeting the black eye, seeing the coldness there, the alien life. Chinook would reach for her; he would have pecked this strange creature and been irritating. She refused to leave him to this horrible fate now. She snatched the small body from gaping jaws—the promise of death and terrible pain—expecting them to close, waiting and knowing it would happen. But the creature let her keep her arm, let her have the cold bundle of feathers.

With a sob she smoothed Chinook's face, gently touching his closed eyes, feeling for anything broken in his wings or delicate feet. He was so cold, so limp. Dead. Gone. She kissed him, knowing he'd hate it, pressing her cheek to his damp softness, hating everything about his moment of endless pain and knowing it would never leave her alone. She would carry this memory of Chinook to her grave.

She paused, gasping between sobs, and forced herself to be calm as she listened with her ear pressed to his body.

A heartbeat, fluttering, barely there, fast and faint.

He will live, the shark said, circling again, only the fin above the surface now, patiently waiting for the boat to sink—for her to have nowhere else to go.

"How do you know?" she asked, opening her vest and shirt, nestling Chinook against her skin, hoping her body heat would be enough to warm him. *Live,* she willed. *Don't leave me.*

You will have to trust me. I will give you another gift. I can smell the magic on you, a gift from a wolf. I smell quiet places on you.

"How?"

I am Akula, Guardian of the Sea, taker of tribute, collector of blood and sinking ships, sunrises, and glass-smooth seas. I will take you to a place where your feet will touch land.

Another creature from outside of time, outside of the world she'd been born into and grown up in—ancient, powerful, and thoughtful. She had begun to wonder if maybe it were the other way around, if the world she belonged to were not the real one, but a mirage over the surface of reality.

I will take you to where your feet will touch land. I will take you beneath the waves.

Chinook's words echoed in her mind: *But I am not a fish. I cannot live underwater.*

The shark swam closer, mouth open as it went by, a black eye fixed, row after row of sharp teeth in bloody gums

—darkness at the back of its throat. Around her the waves grew, rising like hills, threatening to become mountains, the sky a churning mix of rain and lightning. Circling back, brushing the lifeboat as it passed, the shark watched her, waiting for her decision.

"I'll drown if I go with you," she said, acceptance starting a slow spread, a decision coming.

A gift. A second gift. The ability to live beneath the waves.

Beneath her, the lifeboat floundered in the water, on the verge of disappearing completely. The shark rubbed against it, wooden planks shuddering, vibrating up her legs. Swift death. Biting, chomping death waited for her. Shoving down a scream, the urge to cry, she scrubbed at her face with both hands. She wanted something other than the hardness she needed to survive this moment.

"What gift?" she asked, swallowing hard, trying to still the shaking of her hands, the tremors shooting through her body.

A tooth, he said, coming around again, mouth opening slowly, water rushing over the jaws. *Take one.*

"How do I know it will work? That you won't eat me?"

Trust and nothing else.

Astrid waited for him to circle back, to come to her with an open mouth; the huge, white body moving through the water so easily. Strength and power—effortlessly, he returned, mouth opening once again, death in his jaws, terrifying and brutal.

Without thinking about it, she reached out, grasping one sharp tooth, the edge against her palm cutting into her skin as she tugged. It snapped off, breaking away from the jaw with a pop. She fell back into the bottom of the boat, waist deep in cold water. The white tooth, overlaying the edges of her palm, was smeared with blood.

"Now what?"

Swallow it.

Chinook stirred inside her shirt, close to her heart, easing the ache in her soul—relief sweeping across her to feel him living. She couldn't tell if he was awake and watching. She wanted to ask him what he would do, what he thought. She wanted a second opinion on the situation because she felt as if she were going over an edge—leaping blindly from another precipice, hoping that whatever lay in wait would not kill them.

But she knew what he'd think. *It is a trap.*

How was she supposed to swallow a shark tooth the size of her hand? Standing, swaying with the sea, with the shark circling, a constant figure wearing her down, she weighed it. It was heavy and solid in her hand, the hard bone impossible to swallow. But she brought it to her lips, watching the way water and blood swirled over the surface, mixing, becoming neither one thing nor the other.

Closing her eyes, she opened her mouth, the weight of the tooth staying the same, but the size shifting—changing —so that what she dropped on her tongue was the size of a sunflower seed. Strangely warm and pliant, dense with magic. Her throat worked, and she gagged, struggling to swallow, but managing to get it down, an odd weight in her belly.

Now come with me.

But even now she hesitated.

Or you drown and sink to the bottom of the sea to be eaten by crabs and fish, bones dissolving, becoming nothing.

Akula opened his mouth wide—huge, serrated, and hungry.

Astrid moved to the edge of the lifeboat, another vessel sinking beneath her, the sea determined to have her. With a pounding heart, cold with fear, she threw herself over the edge of the boat—body and soul—into the mouth of the great beast.

CHAPTER THIRTY-THREE

kula took her down into dark water in a swirl of cold and pressure. Astrid held her breath until the pressure built and she gasped, expecting to choke. But air filled her lungs, damp and tasting of brine and seaweed—a hint of oceanic wildness.

Akula gripped her arm, teeth taut against her flesh but without breaking the skin—capable of closing at any moment. He held her delicately, like something sweet, mouth, savoring the taste before crunching down. Beneath the waves, he was larger than he had been above. In his element he glowed white, illuminating the space around them, giving the dark water shape—highlighting the depth without penetrating it.

As they dove deeper, moving at a dizzying speed, she kept her free hand over Chinook, holding him in place and hoping he could breathe as well.

I can breathe, he said, *as long as you manage not to crush me.*

Astrid eased her grip with a smile—thankful for his acerbic tone, thankful they were together. A bird and a woman, breathing under the sea and at the mercy of the creature who ruled it.

Akula continued down, not toward some distant shore as she had imaged, but farther away from the surface. She twisted slightly, looking up, expecting light—even a little— and some indication of the surface. Nothing but darkness. She was no longer able to tell which way was up or down traveling in Akula's radiance. An uneasiness crept through her, a worry forming at the back of her mind—a suspicion that was becoming a conviction.

The darkness seemed to be shifting below them, growing lighter. Astrid blinked, the light intensifying. The water shifted from navy blue to sapphire, turning lighter by the second.

"Where are we going?"

The dark eye rolled, focusing on her, making her heart skip.

To my kingdom, his voice rumbled in her head—deep and blue like the water, threatening to crush her.

This was a mistake, Chinook said.

Hush, little bird, the Akula said. *You are a gift, a return to life. Do not throw it away now.*

"But—" she moved, the jaws easing down, putting pressure on her arm, and she hesitated before continuing. "You said you were going to take me to shallow water."

The shark didn't respond, remaining at a steady speed, continuing down. The weak light radiating from the ocean floor grew until Astrid could clearly see a manor house of coral and rock. They rushed toward it, a large opening like a courtyard at the center, the space dim and like an open maw ready to swallow them whole.

Chinook fluttered, wary of this new fate, of the shark pulling them along. Glowing, luminous fish and plant life swayed and swam in the current—seaweed, black and red, tall and green strands spiraling upward, drifting gently. An organic house, grown, expanded on with living creatures, unlike anything that might be found on dry land.

"What is this place?"

Shelter. Home. For my wives.

Cold touched Astrid—hard as ice, sharp as steel. Against her own rapid heartbeat, she could feel Chinook's, their joint pulses racing. The large black eye of the shark rolled, focusing on her, and the pressure on her arm increased. She fought to regain her calm—what little there had been—and took a deep breath, wondering if Akula could smell her adrenaline the way sharks could smell blood.

"I can't be your wife," she said, the gold ring warm, a reminder. "I'm married. I'm searching for my husband."

I have many wives, the shark said. *You can have many husbands.*

"No."

It does not matter to me. You will never leave.

Anger touched her then, enough to put an edge in her voice, her tone cutting. "You said you'd take me to where my feet could touch the sand."

I have, he said, and opened his mouth, releasing her to float, suspended high above the coral house.

He swam around her, a giant in the water—graceful and deadly—watching and waiting. Astrid didn't move, afraid that anything she did might be taken as a threat and acted on. But Akula seemed satisfied and pushed her with his snout—a tap, a test. She remained motionless. He pushed again, this time farther, faster, and down. He forced her down—like a dog corralling a sheep—until she hung suspended above what appeared to be the courtyard. Then he was gone with a swish of a fin.

Now what? Chinook asked.

Astrid looked around trying to make out the white shape of Akula. If she swam for the surface, would she make it? A white flash caught her eye, the shark cutting lazily through the water, circling back. With a kick, she propelled herself down—desperate now to avoid the gaping razor-lined maw—toward the sand and landed with a thump. A cloud of particles rose around her, blurring the water before the current carried them away. Overhead, the shark passed, black eyes calculating.

Coral towered around her, a web of reaching arms, woven together like thick trees. It reminded her, in a strange way, of the jungle, a solid surface made up of a million tiny lives—plant and animal, a network of life becoming one solid entity. From above it had looked like a fine manor house, and now, amongst the living stone, it made her think of some strange dream—a twisted version of reality.

Along the walls were arched openings all around her, and she turned, counting, wondering which she should take.

Eight arches, eight directions. She had no way of knowing which way to go.

What was expected of her in this place? What did a shark want with wives?

"What do you think?" she asked, continuing to turn slowly, little eddies of sand drifting around her feet.

I think you should figure out a way to get to the surface.

She nodded, mind spinning, scrambling to put together an escape plan. Moving through the water was difficult—limbs cumbersome and slow—as she pushed forward, planting her feet in soft sand. Her clothes floated around her, the bag slung across her body bobbing up. Chinook wriggled out of her shirt, planted his feet on her chest and pushed off, swimming away as if he were flying. Astrid smiled, watching him move easily as he twirled around her.

"You're a fish after all," she said with a smile. "You make it look so easy."

It is.

"For you, maybe."

For you too, if you tried.

She made a noise, half agreement and half disbelief, as they moved toward the nearest arch to the right. It held shade and dull, shifting light, more coral walls, and a sandy floor. The water was warmer here than it had been above. The coral grew out into the passage, coming down low in some places, the ceiling and walls swarming with sea life. Small fish darted in and out; a pale shrimp with long feelers moved slowly across her path, its many feet working furiously.

The path tunneled through the coral, following a curve, and moving out of sight. Here and there, groups of anemones and seaweed gave off greenish-blue light. But not enough to see anything clearly, just enough to give the surroundings a shape and shadow. Overhead there were openings, large enough that she might be able to squeeze through one of them if she tried.

Everything was blue and green, light playing along the ceiling—rippling and shifting—the motion of the water visible.

Chinook swam before her, sliding through the water, staying clear of the animals in the reef. He turned the corner ahead and vanished from sight. Astrid called after him, but he didn't return. She hurried to catch up, moving as fast as she could against the solid surface of the water, pushing back against the pressure.

Out of the corner of her eye, something moved—swift and sure—but when she turned to look, there was nothing there. The sound here was dull, but there was noise, a kind of throbbing silence. Right now, the water was full of things chattering in the coral, making small noises, and animal sounds.

A stray current of cold water touched her, a shock there and gone.

Astrid came to the corner where Chinook had turned and stopped. A cavern lay before her, carved and worn into pale stone; bubbles of air trapped in craggy places along the ceiling. It stretched back into darkness, going farther than she could see. Huge, striped black and peach shells were scattered around the cavern, grouped together as chairs and sofas might be in a room.

They sat like dishes, nestled in the sand, waiting for someone to settle into one, for a pearl or traveler to appear. Here and there along the walls, more seaweed glowed, waving; brightly colored fish darting back and forth, a long, pale-yellow shape slithering out of sight.

"Chinook!" Astrid called, hoping to be heard. But her voice came out distorted and thick

With nowhere else to go, only forward or backward, she went on. The bird would be here—must be. The life clinging to the rock walls swayed and brightened as she passed, like weak lamps being turned on. They came alive one by one, throwing faint light that failed to illuminate the farthest reaches of the cavern.

A startled squawk reached her, sending her heart racing, pulling her toward it.

Chinook raced out of the shadows, as swift and sure as a flying fish.

Back, he said, *go back!*

"Why?" she asked.

But she wasn't looking at him now.

From the dark recesses of the cavern, indistinct figures appeared—floating like wraiths, pale suggestions of people.

CHAPTER THIRTY-FOUR

Astrid and Chinook turned, only to be confronted by another figure—a woman.

She floated toward them from the corridor they'd traveled—pale and rotting, strips of skin peeling away, her dark hair a halo. One arm was missing, bitten off above the elbow, the marks of serrated teeth visible. Astrid took a step back, away from the searching, milky eyes, but there was nowhere else to go. The woman wore the remnants of silk underclothes, pale-pink chemise and pantaloons edged with decaying lace, all of it ripped and torn. Soon she would be naked, exposed completely to the sea.

"Who are you?" the woman asked, the words slurred and thick.

"Astrid," she whispered. "What's your name?"

The woman shook her head and lifted a shoulder, drifting closer, feet brushing the sandy bottom, a group of tiny silver fish darting toward her and away. Astrid stared, watching, trying to figure out what they were doing.

"They're eating you," she said, realization sinking in. She tried not to look at the place where the woman's arm had been, the bit of exposed bone, the washed-out gray muscle.

"Yes," the woman said, dead eyes surveying the fish.

"Don't you mind?"

"No, why would I? Everything is eaten here eventually." A pause as milky eyes studied Astrid and then rolled to Chinook. "Even you."

"I don't want to be eaten," Astrid said, horror growing, tightening in her chest.

"Neither did I," the woman said, boney shoulders going up in a shrug.

"Then tell me how to get out of here."

"Leave? And go where?" A hollow laugh vibrated from the dead throat, startling the little school of fish surrounding her.

"I can't stay here." Astrid raised her hands, pleading.

"You can."

The woman floated nearer, small pieces of flesh swaying, the torn silk of her underclothes rippling. A hundred years ago she would have been beautiful with her pale hair and delicate bones. Even now, as a dead thing, Astrid recognized the beauty.

How much of a person remained? How much humanity lingered?

"Please," Astrid said. "Tell me how I can escape."

"And go where? *He* is out there."

He. Akula.

"There must be a way," Astrid said. "It can't end here."

The woman didn't respond, her decaying face expressionless. Astrid could feel Chinook shivering, his tiny body tucked against the crook of her neck. He'd followed her all this way, even to the bottom of the sea. Delicately she brushed his back, smoothing down ruffled feathers with a soft murmur of comfort.

"I'm sorry," she whispered to him, throat tightening around the words. "I won't be able to save him."

Curiosity touched the dead face, the features shifting slightly. "Who do you have to save?"

"A man I love," Astrid said, the word exploding inside of her, the truth of it as hard as platinum. "He was taken. I need to find him."

"I loved someone," the woman said. "But I don't remember her face. Only the way she laughed, the sound of her voice. The way it made me feel." She touched her chest, where her heart might still be.

Astrid waited, not knowing what else to say, not wanting to interrupt the memory passing through the dead woman. She wanted it to be enough, to believe that love would bridge the gap between them.

"I think her name might have been Sarah."

"It's a beautiful name," Astrid said. "I'm looking for Tyhr."

The woman shook her head. "Not someone I know."

"He's tall, with broad shoulders, and gold eyes."

"Was he handsome?" the woman asked.

The memory of their final moments filled Astrid—the expression on his face, the disappointment and sorrow. Had he been handsome? He'd been kind. He'd been quiet. He'd been secretive. He'd been curious. He'd been a hundred thousand things, but his features were a blur in her memory now.

"I can't remember," Astrid admitted, haunted by golden eyes and the richness of his voice.

Of course he is handsome, Chinook muttered. *You have a bad memory.*

Astrid smiled sadly at him, running her finger down his back again. He scrunched down, shooting her an irritated glance.

"What's in your bag?"

"What?" Astrid asked, startled by the question.

The woman pointed to the satchel slung across her body. It had become part of her completely and she'd forgotten it was there. She placed a protective hand on it.

"Nothing important," she replied. "Just things."

"Can I have it?"

"No," Astrid said, shaking her head. "I need it."

"But you said it's not important."

She opened her mouth to respond and then shut it.

"The color," the woman spoke softly, reaching out with both hands—finger bones exposed. "It reminds me of her eyes."

"What about my jacket?" Astrid asked. "It's the same shade."

The woman's lips tilted upward in a soft smile, a flash of memory skating across her features. She gave a single nod, accepting Astrid's trade.

"It's yours."

Astrid shrugged it off, peeling it away, and held the sable jacket out. It was lined with satin the color of a clear lake, a cloudless sky. How long had it been since this woman had seen that color blue from the world above? Did she even remember it? Dead eyes stared, motionless, intent. The woman reached out, closing the space between them. Astrid could see the decay clearly, and she swallowed, holding in the urge to retch.

A woman, rotting and being eaten, dead and still alive,

the bride of a great white shark who demanded blood and tribute, wanted her jacket. Astrid would gladly give it to this woman, lost and doomed to this fate, trapped in the loneliness and horror of disappearing bite by bite.

The jacket was a remnant of humanity. A small piece of the world to hold the terror at bay. It wouldn't last. It couldn't in this place. But maybe it would be enough for the moment, for the flash of memory it contained.

The woman took it, the tips of her fingers worn down to bone, sharp claws emerging. An eel, olive green with yellow eyes, slipped out from a shadowed opening in the rock. It darted out, taking a bite of the woman's shoulder, a nip that left a small indentation. Ignoring it, she slipped on the jacket, overlarge on her spare frame, the color a contrast against blue-white flesh. Running her hand over the fabric, she made a sound of pleasure, something like a smile pulling at falling cheeks.

"Can you swim?" she asked, not taking her eyes from the sleeve.

Astrid blinked, caught off guard by the question. "A little."

"A little will have to be enough. Come with me."

Through all of this, she had followed and been led, at the whim of the ring and people she met along the way. Would this be another instance like the shark, or would the woman put her back on the path the North Wind had set her on, the right one, back to moving in the right direction? The woman must have sensed her hesitation, the silent doubt. She didn't speak, letting Astrid go over it, inspect it, and then make the choice.

Astrid would go where this woman took her, trusting a stranger because it was the only option she had. So, she followed her deeper into the house of coral, twisting through tunnels, passing through shafts of cool, green and blue light.

————

CHINOOK HELD ON TO HER NOW, AN APPENDAGE, AN EXTENSION OF herself. But after losing him to the sea, the image of his limp body burned into her mind, she never wanted him to let go.

Look behind you, he said, voice pitched low even in her mind, a curl of fear coming with it.

Astrid glanced back, the movement catching the woman's attention, and both came to a stop in the tunnel. Sand swirled up from beneath her feet, creatures in the walls pulling back, watchful.

Others approached—women in varying states of decay and consumption, a living death she dreaded facing. It was hard to look at them, see the missing limbs and chunks of flesh, the places where only bones remained.

We have to get out of here, Chinook said.

"I know."

"Do not tell them where we are going." The woman beside her whispered in a flat tone.

The women came forward in a swirl, surrounding her, a ring of lifeless eyes and blank faces.

"A new bride."

"A new wife."

"A fresh meal."

"Come," said one, short, dark hair swaying, a half-torn dress moving like a jellyfish around her body—a bite mark on her shoulder, scrapes on a once beautiful face. "Let us dress you in your finery, with pearls and red coral beads.

We will cover you in fish scales, glittering silver, with shark-teeth combs in your hair."

"He will find you beautiful. Tempting."

"I have somewhere to take her first," said the woman with her jacket.

They looked at Astrid then, seeing the jacket, the silk lining. They came forward, plucking at it, envious fingers tracing the lines, rubbing the brass buttons.

"You will share this, yes? And then," said the woman with the dark hair, turning to Astrid. "We will have the rest?"

"But first," said another, "a small thing, a ritual. A welcome."

One waved a bare arm, half her face eaten away, a hollow eye socket. "No, not this time. Never again."

"It's been so long," another agreed. "We don't need to keep the tradition."

Covetous eyes touched Astrid, lingering not only on her clothes but on the beauty of her intact flesh. But the gazes became curious when they finally noticed Chinook.

"A swimming bird," they laughed, gravel and croaks, gurgles and hisses. "You are far from your sky. Do you like it here? Will you remain with us at the bottom of the sea?"

Chinook didn't respond, watching them as they watched him, wary and repelled.

"We will not be dinner tonight," one said quietly.

The relief in the woman's voice twisted something inside Astrid, pulling pity from the panic.

———

THEY TOOK ASTRID BACK TO THE COURTYARD, THE OPENNESS OF IT making her skin crawl—the open water a threat. Akula was up there, circling, intending to come back. The women lingered in the shadows, eyes turning to the opening, waiting for something.

As Astrid watched, sharks began to arrive, crowding the water, hundreds of dark and light bodies, all sizes and shapes. The white one swam among them, huge compared to the others, snapping at those it passed. A striped shark came too close, brushing by, and Akula turned, grabbing the animal, tearing into it. Blood tinted the water as other sharks descended. They thrashed and tore, darting forward and ripping mouthfuls away, the blood cloud expanding, tiny pieces of shark sinking.

The women appeared unmoved, talking quietly among themselves, the one with the dark hair watching Astrid with a blank face.

"What's happening?" Astrid asked, leaning toward the woman she'd given her jacket to.

She had stayed close, an escort, a strange companion.

"He is coming."

At an unseen signal, the women moved into the center of the courtyard, faces turned upward, as Akula swam down. He circled, watching his harem, deciding fates and futures. Then he struck, faster than her eye could follow. Sharp jaws closed over the remnants of the woman with half a face. A shudder passed through the others—shared relief, part resignation. Astrid covered her mouth, fighting to keep the scream inside, the terrible retch threatening, her mouth watering, disgust bubbling.

The shark gulped and chewed once, twice, and the body was gone, swallowed almost whole, the sound of crunching bones lingering. The coral around them was motionless, each small life transfixed. No creature, no woman, wanted to draw attention to themselves, to become the next morsel.

With a flick of a fin, Akula came nearer, black eyes rolling to Astrid.

Tomorrow.

He didn't have to say more.

The sharks disbanded with swift flicks of their fins—vanishing into the sea—leaving the water above them empty and peaceful.

"Come," said the woman with the jacket.

Astrid let herself be pulled into another archway, into the narrow space where Akula couldn't follow. A few of the shark wives came with them, but the others went their own way, in solitude or silent pairs.

"Why does he eat you?" Astrid asked, looking back at the courtyard, wondering if he waited out there, circling out of sight.

"He knows no other way to love."

"This is love?" Astrid made a noise of disbelief, the sound echoed by Chinook.

"For something that has lived a hundred million years living only to swim and eat? Yes, it is a sort of love. What other way does he know? Only the snap of his jaws, the swallow as he takes you in to become part of himself."

"And this?" Astrid touched the woman's shoulder, above the missing lower arm, the place where bone jutted, and flesh ended.

"A love bite."

"I don't want it."

"Because you have your own love to find?"

"Yes." Conviction made Astrid's voice harder than she meant it to be. But she couldn't be here tomorrow, couldn't be here when Akula returned, watching her with those black eyes. She shuddered. "You said you'd help me."

The woman nodded. "You will do whatever it takes?"

Astrid stared into the milky eyes, wondering how much the woman could still see. If she could see at all. Did she move through this world navigating by water currents and temperature changes? What did she know that the others didn't? Whatever it was, it would be better than death.

"Whatever it takes," Astrid agreed.

CHAPTER THIRTY-FIVE

Another tunnel—a hall, coral and small striped fish, and transparent jellies floating near the ceiling. Astrid followed the woman through the maze until they came out suddenly, exposed to the open ocean. Sharks swam lazily overhead, a school of silver fish darting away, keeping close to the coral they had left behind.

They stood on rock—craggy and covered in depressions where bits of tiny coral formations were growing. A few yards away, a giant black hole gaped, striped fish darting around the sides, eating small things attached to the walls.

"What is this?" she asked, hesitation hitting her hard.

"The way out."

Do not go down there, Chinook said.

"There isn't another way?"

"It will go down until there is nowhere else to go and then up, up, and out."

"What's down there?"

The black maw waited—an invitation, a threat. The fish around them scattered, the movement catching her eye.

The sharks were swimming away in all directions, the ocean above them empty.

He is coming!

Akula swam toward them, speeding through the water, gnashing teeth, jaw snapping.

He was coming for Astrid.

"Go," said the woman, pushing Astrid toward the dark mouth in the rock. "He won't follow."

"But—"

The woman shook her head, shoving Astrid toward the opening, sending her stumbling. The shark came, mouth open wide, and she could see every single tooth.

Do not look back! Chinook urged, leaving her shoulder, shooting into the darkness.

Astrid reached the lip of the opening, stumbling down the sloped floor, as she threw herself into the pitch blackness. Crunching, ripping sounds followed her, the motion vibrating through the water, pushing her on, forcing her forward. Being on the verge of the unknown was better than what lay behind them—a shark wife, dinner.

The woman had helped her and sacrificed herself so that Astrid might escape. And Chinook had left her.

"You left me," Astrid said.

I refuse to be eaten.

"So do I!"

Then you should move faster.

"Can you see anything?" she asked, straining to see anything, opening her eyes wide.

Not enough, he mumbled.

"Where are you?" She fumbled, searching for him.

Stop that, he said, *you almost hit me.*

"Then come here. Sit on my shoulder and give me directions. You said you can see something." She felt him grab onto her shirt.

A very little. Like I said, not enough.

"Well, I can't see anything at all. I'd trade you total blindness for what you've got." She tried to look at him on her shoulder, but there was nothing. "What can you see?"

It is a dark tunnel, he said, sounding sullen.

"Steep? Are there stairs? Rocks?"

No, he said, thoughtfully, choosing his words. *Gently down. Like a den.*

Like a den. A home to some unknown creature.

"She said to go down. Down until there is nowhere else to go and then up."

Yes. I was there too.

Astrid bit her lip, keeping a response to herself, as they moved slowly forward. Chinook giving her small directions, the water warming around them. Soon a red-orange light began to ease the darkness, coming up from below, beckoning them forward.

―――――

A CAVERN, LOW CEILINGED, WITH STALACTITES REACHING FOR THE uneven floor, stalagmites stretching to meet them. The space glowed red, much hotter than the tunnel had been. The water here was warmer than the hot springs, warmer than a bath, and on the verge of being too uncomfortable to be in.

"Do you see a way through?" Astrid asked, trying to see around the obstructions.

No, he said, gripping her shoulder tighter. *And I am not going to go looking for one either.*

"Why not?"

Because anything could be in here. I am tired of being mistaken for someone's meal.

"Okay," she said, taking the first step, easing around a rock formation. "I don't want to force you to do anything you don't want to do."

I appreciate that. Very thoughtful.

"Even if it might help us."

Ahead there was a narrow gap in the rocky floor; warm light poured out. The water rippled there, a curtain of motion within the stillness. Heat. So much heat, it made her skin tight, her face burn. She wanted to gasp for air but pulled in scorching water, burning her throat and lungs. She swam back, pushing at the water with hands and feet, desperate to put distance between herself and the spot.

"What is that?" she asked.

I do not know. A vent maybe.

"A vent?"

Hydrothermal vent. We might be near a thin spot in the surface of the earth, near a volcano possibly. I read about it once... His voice trailed off thoughtfully before picking back up. *I cannot recall the exact details.*

"Those could be important."

He made a huffing sound. *Maybe you should read more about the oceans instead of plants. You are the one traveling across the world dragging a case of books around.*

"Not anymore," she said softly, a touch of sadness in her words.

She chose another route, working around more outcroppings, making slow progress through the forest of stone. There were more vents ahead, crisscrossing the cavern. She had to double back several times, desperate to avoid those areas and the unbearable heat.

Around the vents, small creatures moved—long,

narrow fish and white crabs, mussels and clams clinging to surfaces, a few bright red starfish. Pale shrimp swam through the water, searching out particles that floated up, an endless cycle of collecting and eating. A jellyfish with clear, pinkish insides floated toward her and she ducked out of the way. More floated near the ceiling.

As she wound through the room, Astrid saw a way out. A low, wide opening in the rock wall to the right, another dark, hungry mouth. Pushing against the water, leaning into the swirling currents, she headed for it. She wanted sunshine and rain, freezing wind whipping around her, cool fall breezes, anything but this warm, deep water. The liquid filled her lungs and ears, the pressure of it all building behind her eyes.

What are you?

The voice came out of the shadows of her mind, sharp and prickly, like claws and knives. Similar to Akula's, coming from the same place Chinook's did, but darker—hungry. It froze Astrid in place, her skin crawling, a slow dread spreading.

Not *who*. What.

"My name is Astrid," she said, turning slowly in place, scanning the cavern, searching for the source of the voice.

An Astrid?

Keep going, Chinook whispered, quivering.

"I'm a woman," she said.

A giant crab with long, thin legs—fiery orange and white—with black eyes on thin stalks came over the rocks to her left. It was the size of a horse, maybe larger, moving through the water easily, gracefully. The crab crossed a vent, stepping over it, gliding around a grouping of stalagmites. It stopped, staring.

Astrid took a step back, and it took a step forward.

Too close, Chinook hissed. *Too close!*

"I'm looking for a way out of the cave," she told the crab, taking a step sideways.

He mimicked her movement, a quick sidestep. *Why would you want to leave? It is very cold out there.*

"It's too warm in here for me," she replied, swaying to her left, the crab swaying with her.

I like the warmth.

"You should stay here then," she said, motioning Chinook to move. He nodded, a quick jerk of the head, and swam on, gliding through the water, flying in the direction of the opening leading out.

You should stay here as well. I've never had an Astrid.

The crab lunged forward, claws snapping. Astrid jerked backward, squeezing into a narrow gap between the rocks, the huge claws knocking into a rock formation, pieces breaking away, dislodging mussels and starfish. She jerked to the right, a claw missing her and crashing into rock. The water was full of sand, making it impossible to see more than a few feet away. Sand rose in clouds, the water turning murky. The crab pulled back, out of sight.

Easing between two rocks, kicking up sand as she went, Astrid tried to watch the path ahead and behind. Jagged rocks scraped her, tugging at her shirt, she winced at the sting of saltwater.

A claw came down from above, water moving around her head furiously, swirling, and she ducked, hunching her shoulders. The crab stood above her, straddling the crevice she'd squeezed into, crouched down, and determined to snag her. He snapped, forcing her down, sudden panic blinding her as the claw came again and there was nowhere else to go.

Chinook swooped in, darting forward, one black beady

eye, sharp-clawed feet extended. The crab knocked the bird away, and Chinook spun out of sight, trailing bubbles. He had given her a moment, a few seconds, to move and put some distance between herself and the crab. Kicking up more sand, pushing and pulling at the rock, she scrambled out of reach.

Small rocks fell from overhead, the sounds of the crab reaching, hard shell against stone—scrapping, clacking. She didn't look back, didn't dare turn only to discover that small movement would be what he needed to reach her.

Come back! I want to look at you! he called.

She moved quickly, continuing to kick up sand, clouding the water.

A horrible screech filled her mind, echoing through her, vibrating in her teeth. The crab made another noise of pain —gut-wrenching, anguished. It rocked the cavern, small stones rattling down the walls, the water around her shivering. She wanted to cover her ears. She wanted to get as far away from the noise as possible.

Swim! Run! Move! Chinook came up behind her, passing quickly, clutching one of the crab's eyestalks.

"Why did you do that! You've only made him angrier!"

Now he has one less eye to see you with as he eats you! Keep up!

Astrid shuddered, following Chinook, blood pounding in her ears.

The way out is up ahead, swim faster!

Behind them the sounds of the crab scrabbling at the rock grew weaker, his voice following her out of the cave, coming out of the red glow, refusing to leave her—plaintive and lonely.

Astrid.

Come Back.

THE WAVES ROLLED THEM TOWARD THE BEACH. ASTRID STUMBLED, pushed, and tumbled forward, coughing and fighting to breathe. Overhead the sun shone, bright and blinding after the depths of the ocean. She struggled to see anything beyond the tall dunes rising from the beach.

Almost there, Chinook said.

Astrid struggled to breathe around the lump in her windpipe, a pressure there she couldn't identify. Reaching the beach, clawing at her throat, she fell to her hands and knees and retched. Saltwater came up—burning her nose —more than any person could possibly hold—bits of seaweed followed, the flash of a silverfish scale.

Then a shark tooth.

It landed on the sand and grew, going from the size of her thumbnail to as big as her palm—vibrant white and bleached, a perfect specimen. More water came up, and she sobbed, sucking in air, collapsing onto the warm sand with relief.

Are you alive?

Astrid stared up at the blue sky—cloudless, perfect. There had been a moment down there when she'd wondered if they would see a sky ever again. If this color blue, the lightness of it, the pale quality that could only be wide-open sky over their head, would ever be in her life again. She laughed but stopped, wincing and sore from vomiting water.

So, that is a yes then?

"Yes."

Rolling to her feet, she dusted the sand from her hands only to spread it around—tiny grains clinging, impossible to shake off. Already sweat trickled down the back of her neck, between her shoulder blades, sliding down. The beach in either direction was empty, stretches of sand and small shells, nothing larger than the shark tooth.

She scooped it up, the saw-toothed edge rasping against her skin, reminding her of what waited in the ocean. But this was a weapon, a key, a bribe. It could be anything now. Or it could be nothing. Either way, she wasn't leaving it behind.

The small satchel she'd so carefully packed had survived. The contents—seed packets, paper money, and other oddments remained—and a sigh of relief escaped her. The leather was ruined—torn and ragged, waterlogged. But she still had it. Patting it down, searching for the wolf claw, she tensed until she found felt the hard shape and slipped the tooth in beside it.

What help would they be ahead? Or the seed packets for that matter. Up to this point, the whole bag had been useless aside from the money. But she wasn't ready to let it go. Something in it could still be useful and the idea of leaving behind felt wrong.

Stumbling away from the water and toward the dunes, Astrid paused, unable to tell which direction was north or south, east or west. Not that it would matter. The only direction that mattered was where the ring pointed her. The dunes inland, mimicking waves, obscured what might lay beyond. Holding out her hand, the gold ring burning in the harsh sunlight, she closed her eyes—waiting.

A pull to the right, stronger than it had ever been.

Tyhr.

Was that the reason she held onto these strange things? A magic ring. A talking bird. A claw. A tooth. If this was a fairytale those things would come together in the end— they would mean something. Tyhr had asked if she read fairytales, curious about what she'd learned. And the magic in them turned out to be reality, the creatures populating the stories alive and breathing.

But how would they get her across the desert?

What now?

"We keep going."

Do you think we will survive?

Astrid didn't look at him, afraid of what her eyes might reveal. The desert frightened her more than the ocean had. More like the Black Forest. The heat would kill them here, bake them under the clear sky; the sand would scour their bones, wear them away into nothingness. Astrid could feel it there—their deaths, the end, waiting in the open desert, patient and expectant.

"Yes," she said, looking up and down the empty beach one last time. "We have to."

She crawled up the first dune, slipping and sliding, progress made and then taken away, until finally she reached the top. Sticky with sweat, she paused, silent and stunned—stomach dropping.

An enormous, abandoned city drowning in sand spread out as far as she could see. Dunes washed over tall buildings, peaked roofs and towers reaching through the solid waves, the ruins wallowing and sliding apart. The structures glittered with chips of mica, stones crumbling. The doors and windows, squares and ovals, stared sightlessly, shocked into silence at their arrival.

The buildings and landscape under the harsh sun were all the same color, as if you could not have one without the other. A city slowly being worn down, erased, and returned to the desert. *Come back to me, I've missed you,* the earth said with a kiss of sand, an embrace of heat.

Some great place, a thriving home to thousands, maybe

hundreds of thousands, and now only bones. To the left and right, the buildings went on. They stretched backward into the desert, disappearing into dunes as large as mountains. There was no end, only dunes, only a dead civilization.

What is this place?

"I don't know." A hollow dread spread through her chest—a sucking wound. " A dead city."

Abandoned, Chinook corrected.

Astrid shook her head, the sensation of loss and devastation creeping over her. "No. Not abandoned."

Do we go through it?

"I think so," she said, gesturing around, taking in the whole landscape. "It goes on in either direction. We might walk for miles along the beach and never find the end. The ring is pulling inland, not along the coast."

The sand moved and shifted beneath her feet as she went. With each step, she sunk down and had to fight her way out, pushing up and reaching for the next step forward. Salt crackled on her skin, dried seawater and crusts of sand, a burn slowly appearing on her arms, the heat of it across her cheeks and forehead.

Water.

Where in this place would there be drinkable water? Licking her lips—tasting salt—Astrid waded through the sand toward a half-buried house. The roof was tiled with the same stone, solid and holding true after countless years. Only the upper stories were visible. It was impossible to tell how tall it might be. There were no doors, only large, open windows—a pair of eyes in an empty soul. Sand and wind had scoured it all clean. Tan stone remained, hinting at opulence, and suggestions of ornate features, all of it erased by the elements. No color, no life.

Chinook flew ahead, darting from one spot to another, landing briefly on a roof and coming back.

"What do you see?"

The same thing you do.

"Sand," Astrid paused, hands on hips, breathing heavily. "You'd be able to see more if you went higher. A little farther maybe?"

Chinook titled his head. *Are you asking me to abandon you?*

"No." She made a face. "I'm not asking you to abandon me you foolish bird. I'm telling you to go scout ahead and see if there's an easy way through all this."

What will you do?

"I'll be in the shade," she pointed to the building with the vacant eyes. "In there. Do you think you'd be able to find me again in all this?"

He made a noise. *I'm not blind.*

"Then prove it and go see what's out there."

Fine. I will. Do not go any further though. He stretched his wings, ruffling his feathers. *I do not want to have to go searching for you.*

She shook her head. "I won't. I promise."

In a flurry, Chinook was up, beating the air, swinging by her, and reaching out with a foot to grab playfully at her hair.

"Stop it, bird!" she said with a smile.

He laughed and tilted away, climbing into the air. Astrid watched as he spiraled upward, into the sky, going up in a tight circle until he became a black dot. Then he changed directions and flew from her line of sight.

CHAPTER THIRTY-SIX

With Chinook gone, an unbearable silence crowded around her. With a groan of effort, Astrid made her way to the house she'd pointed at. Reaching it, she sighed as shade engulfed her, welcoming the reprieve from the heat. Around her and with her, more sand spilled into the house through the open window.

It seemed like another world inside the structure—a cooler, gentler place. The silence here was deeper, without the wind rushing past her ears, without the sun beating down. The quality of the light shouldn't change the noise level in a room, but it did here. There was a lingering presence of dignity demanding silence and respect.

Astrid glanced around, pausing just inside the window, taking in the space. Sand slid into the room, piling at the openings but tapering off near a door on the far wall. There was almost no sand there, bits and pieces of red and purple tile peeking through—a pattern of twisting together. The color was so vibrant, shocking in this world of glittering tan, and she made her way down the slope, wanting to get a closer look.

With a foot, she brushed the sand out of the way to reveal flowers. Two varieties, one purple and the other red, twined around each other, forming a scrolling border. She didn't recognize the flowers, but maybe they hadn't been styled after a living species. Or maybe the variety had died out long ago.

"You've come a long way."

The voice came from farther inside the building, echoing strangely in the space.

"Who's there?"

"Come. I've been waiting."

Astrid crossed the room with the flowers, going through an arch in the far wall, and into another room. No flowers here, no decoration. A square empty space with a large round window facing the empty city.

A woman stood with her back to Astrid, small and frail, the clothes she wore blending into the surroundings. A bandage wound around her head several times, the fabric fraying at the edges. She turned and Astrid could see that the bandages covered her eyes completely.

"Who are you?"

"I am the South Wind. You've met my sisters?"

"Yes," she said. "They've all helped me."

All. Astrid wondered if that was the right word to use. The others had helped but this wind, the South Wind, hadn't made an offer yet. After Akula and the crab, the man from the train, all of it, she felt less inclined to trust the woman.

"Don't worry, I will help too. But I understand your hesitation and doubt." The South Wind said, a gentle smile touching her face. "You're searching for a way through the ruins?"

"Yes."

The old woman pulled out a black crystal pendulum from her robes, letting it sway before her until it began to move in a tight circle, patterns appearing in the sand at her feet—spirals moving and twisting. She spoke softly, the wind rising beyond the house, sand blowing through the air. The storm roared past the open window but not through it, an invisible barrier between the room and the blasting heat of the sandstorm.

"You're so close. Go southeast. There is a high spire topped with a starburst. Keep that always on your right until you have left the city. Beyond this place is the open desert. What you're searching for is there."

"Thank you," Astrid said, worried for Chinook but not wanting to appear ungrateful. "But I need to find my friend."

"Give the storm a moment and it will clear. He will find you." The woman's face tilted up, blind eyes searching her out. "He's waiting out the storm too."

The woman walked around Astrid, going toward the open window and the storm.

"This place can be dangerous. Do not linger."

The South Wind stepped out of the house, graceful and in her element, as the sandstorm swallowed her whole.

————

ASTRID LINGERED IN THE SHADOWS, GRATEFUL FOR THE SHELTER and reprieve from the heat. She wished she'd asked the South Wind where there was water. But the woman was gone before the thought had even crossed her mind. Now, she listened to the sandstorm dying down—the sound of a million tiny grains easing, slowing, and then gone.

Had Chinook been caught in it? Or had he flown high and far enough away while searching for a way through the city? Astrid refused to believe otherwise. They'd come too far together to be parted now.

When she felt that enough time had passed, she scrambled out of the house, over the new sand that had collected in the opening, and into the sunshine. She shaded her eyes as she emerged, searching the sky, but it was empty. Astrid turned her gaze to the city, searching for the tower the South Wind has spoken of. She found the flash of metal—a brilliant beacon glinting under the harsh sun—and began her trek through the city.

Astrid stuck to the shadows as much as possible. Exhaustion weighed each step, her feet sinking into the shifting sand as she pushed herself on. Sweat mingled with the dried salt of the sea, irritating her skin, and drying her out. Slowly she took the scarf from around her neck and wrapped it to shade her head and face. It helped but still the sun was merciless.

Behind her came a boom and she covered her ears, the pressure of the sound crashing through her. She stood frozen, listening to the sounds of falling masonry and the cascade of endless sand. A building collapsing, a wall going down, a floor giving out. It could have been any of those things.

Astrid waited until the sound stopped—heart racing—and the unearthly silence of the dead place returned. Continuing she kept the tower on her right, navigating the twisting maze of streets as best she could. She had to backtrack once, the path forward blocked by a huge building there was no hope of scrambling over or through.

Who had lived in this city? What kind of people made their home on the verge of an unforgiving desert washed by a tumultuous ocean? How long ago had they vanished, carrying their memories and possessions with them, beneath the burden of their failed civilization? Had they crossed the ocean or gone farther inland? The questions came one after another, as relentless as an incoming tide. Maybe she would find them, and maybe they'd have water.

Astrid scanned the sky, searching for the telltale speck of darkness that would be Chinook. Still, the air above her remained empty. She slowed, baking alive despite sticking to the shade as much as possible. Overhead the sun rose its peak, the little patches of soothing shade shrinking and then vanishing.

The dark openings in the buildings beckoned—dim doors and windows open and inviting her to experience the cool shade she wanted so badly. Chinook had instructed her to wait for him, but the South Wind had said this place was too dangerous to linger in.

Another question circled like a vulture. What kind of danger waited in this dead place? The danger of decay? Of falling buildings and collapsing floors? Possibly. If she was caught in something like that she could be smothered or crushed. It was better to keep moving, it was better not to linger too long in one place.

But the sun was too much to bear. At the next opportunity, Astrid ducked through a half filled opening—a round window—and slid into a cool, inviting interior. She entered another set of rooms filled with miniature drifting dunes— sand collected in the corners and flowing through other open doorways. One seemed to lead deeper into the house and the other to another room filled with sunshine.

Cautiously she moved, watching the ground and

hoping the surface beneath her was solid, she chose the door leading deeper into the cool space. More openings led to other spaces—more rooms, more halls, more of the building.

The temperature dropped as she entered the next room, a significant enough change that she wondered if there might be a water source nearby. Direct sunlight couldn't reach this space and with a sigh, she sat cross-legged in the center of the room. Astrid sat motionless for a moment, listening to the silence, and trusting that Chinook would find her when she left. But right now, she needed a respite from the relentless heat.

The Shark Wife had said the color reminded her of someone. Astrid was glad she'd traded the jacket instead. Her heart twisted at the fate of the woman and her final moments—the destructive form that Akula's love took. But she was glad it had not been her.

She opened her bag, amazed it had survived the crossing on the train, the sinking of the ship, and then a drowning by a shark. The sturdy brown leather and clasps had held up through it all. Inside the seed packets were mostly intact—thin wax paper crumbled and showing signs of wear but holding together. The carefully folded bills were now one solid block of paper. She wondered if she'd need money going forward and decided to keep it.

The East Wind had given her a bundle of dense bread and hard cheese wrapped in several layers of oilcloth—edges tucked in to create a packet. Unwrapping it carefully she was surprised at how well the contents had held up. She licked the cheese, expecting it to taste of the ocean but found it tasted of sharp cheddar. But the bread tasted of the ocean and was too salty to eat.

She dug a hole beside her and placed the bread inside,

covering it and hoping it didn't count as the desecration of a sacred space. After wiping her hands and trying to remove as much of the sand as possible she took small bites of the cheese, savoring each mouthful. Her stomach grumbled. Astrid hadn't realized how hungry she'd been until the cheese had touched her tongue. Now she was desperate—ravenous—but she would save it. There was no way to guess when their next meal might be. And Astrid wanted to share it with Chinook.

After replacing the oilcloth and shaking as much of the sand from it as possible she pulled the shark took and wolf claw out. She sat with one in each hand, considering where she'd been and where she needed to go. And who would be at the end of it.

Tyhr.

And the Enchantress.

There was no way to know what would happen at the end of this journey. Or even how much farther she had to travel. Astrid returned the tooth and claw to the bag, making sure they were secure and stood up, brushing sand from her backside.

Sand. And more sand. Sand as far as the eye could see. In her hair. Under her nails. In her shoes. Between her teeth. Under her clothes. She was tired of sand. She'd always loved the beach as a child. Now? She'd be happy to never stand on one again.

A sound she'd been hearing but hadn't fully comprehended broke through her thoughts.

A distant hushing flow, faint movement like water.

"Water," she whispered, jumping at the sound of her own voice. It sounded rough—parched and petrified.

Turning to the doorway leading deeper into the building she crept forward cautiously, watching the sand, ready for any tell-tale sign that it might shift beneath her. Astrid passed through another room, larger than the one she'd eaten in, the walls holding the faint shadows of what might have been murals before the wind had begun to wear them clean.

The sound that had drawn her grew louder—the rush becoming something else, not water as she'd hoped, but sand. But she could smell water. That cool scent of water moving under the earth—clear and deep, fresh and untouched. It sang to Astrid, leaving her desperate, pulled by the siren call.

The rooms grew larger with each threshold she passed through, the light dwindling—a faded twilight. She would stop when she couldn't see anymore. It would be pointless to carry on if she lost her way in the dark.

Please, please be in the light where the water is.

In the center of the next room was a huge hole—sand slid toward it, spilling over the edge into the unknown. It flowed around her boots, not deep here, less than an inch but a constant whispering cascade.

Beneath that sound was the burble of moving water.

With careful steps, she eased toward the hole in the floor, until she stood at the lip and could look down. The opening wasn't there because the floor had caved in. Steps lined the outside, spiraling down into the dark, but the center was open and the sound of running water echoed up and out—a promise and invitation.

Water.

"Oh my god," she whispered, tears gathering on her lashes.

Astrid looked around, scanning the room for anything that might hold water. But this room was as empty as all the others had been—as this whole place was. She patted her bag, but oilcloth and waxed paper wouldn't hold water for long. Not enough to get it out of the building and to wherever Chinook might be. She'd go down, get a drink, and then find Chinook and bring him back.

Taking the stairs one step at a time, a hand shielding her face from the cascade of sand, she held her breath until she reached the bottom and a narrow stone path that hugged the wall. It was a foot or so above the stream bed. Weak light came from above, barely touching the darkness at the bottom. The water was shallow, sweeping over a flat stone bed, rushing off beneath the city toward the sea.

Beyond the dim light from above the rest of the cavern was darkness. Astrid's footsteps echoed, the burble of water hitting high and distant walls before coming back. The space *felt* large. But the light only touched the walkway and a section of the stream. The far bank was in shadow. It could have been a few yards or a mile wide, it was impossible to know.

Astrid removed the bag, dropped it on the narrow lip of stone, and lay down in the stream. Cool water soaked into her clothes, washing sand and salt away, taking the memories and thirst with it. She scrubbed at her face and ran her fingers through her hair, luxuriating in the sensation.

Never again would she take the taste or feel of water for granted. Astrid might never step foot in the ocean again, but she would never pass a stream or lake or river without putting her feet in it. She'd spend whole weeks at a time in the bath from now on. Maybe months. Maybe she'd never be dry ever again.

Her laughter echoed through the room, coming up from her stomach, filling the air unexpectedly.

A rock tumbled in the darkness—a sharp series of cracks as it hit the floor and bounced. Astrid sat up, eyes wide and staring into the dark, heart pumping furious adrenaline-saturated blood.

She wasn't alone in the cool darkness.

Without thought Astrid stood and lunged for the stone wall and her bag. It wasn't safe. The South Wind had warned her it wasn't. But she'd ignored the woman's words. She *should* have ignored the temptation of shade, the call of water, she should have stayed where Chinook could find her.

Chinook.

Astrid unwrapped the thin scarf from around her neck and plunged it into the water, wringing it out and letting it soak up as much as possible. In a swift motion, she stuffed it in her bag, hoping it would hold on to some of the moisture, hoping there would be enough when she found her friend.

They would not be returning to this place.

Scrambling up the stairs, the falling sand clinging to her —gritty in her eyes, sticking to her skin—she promised herself she'd reach the top and find Chinook. It wouldn't end here, where he would never know what had happened.

She ran up the steps two at a time, no longer careful, concentrating on reaching the top.

Unable to resist the urge, knowing it would eat up precious seconds, she paused on the top step and looked down. A pair of emerald eyes, slitted like a snake or cat, larger and higher in the air than any eyes would be on a normal animal. But when had the animals she'd encountered been normal-sized? And they'd all wanted to eat her.

Slogging through the rooms she'd passed through only ten minutes before she followed the light. But its intensity had faded, the color shifting. The noise from the room behind her blended in with the one beyond the building and her stomach dropped when she realized why.

A sandstorm.

The sky had been clear, the world quiet and peaceful when she'd entered the building. Now it roared and raged, filling her ears and lungs, taking the city one long abrasive lick at a time. Astrid hesitated in an inner room, watching the wind blow past, eddies of sand that swept into the building, searching for a place to rest.

Behind her, rising from the well, came the sound of scales slithering—a heavy body shifting.

Astrid covered her face with an arm and darted into the room, sticking to the wall and following it. Reaching a corner she crouched down, eyes squeezed tight against the stinging sand, trying to calm her racing heart.

The unseen creature bumped the wall hard. It vibrated through her back, traveling across her body, raising the hair on the back of her neck. The pressure of it filled the space, sucking all the oxygen from the room. Astrid peeked through the shelter of her arms, unable to resist the urge to see what it was.

A wall of golden scales filled the circular door she'd come through. It moved, relentlessly on, as if it might stretch into forever and the rest of her life might be spent here, watching it go by. Snake. Lizard. Some cold-blooded creature who loved the punishing heat of this dead city. Maybe it was the reason it had died. She bit her arm, keeping the gasp of surprise and terror from escaping.

The movement slowed and then stopped. Slowly, ever so slowly, achingly slow it began to reverse, moving backwards. Astrid, already half buried in sand, the storm still raging beyond the window dug the hole she sat in deeper, frantic, fighting panic. She twisted into it, raking huge handfuls back toward her until most of her body was covered.

She lay there, face covered, listening to the breathing silence.

————

WHEN THE STORM DIED AND THE SAND SETTLED, ASTRID ventured out. A yellow-white sun hung high in the sky—suspended and shimmering—observing the world without being a part of it. Astrid squinted up, searching for a familiar shape, a black spot against the blue, but couldn't see Chinook.

Cautiously she began to move through the city, pausing to look behind her and then up, searching rooflines and peeking in windows. From inside the buildings came the sound of moving sand, waves of it crashing through lower floors, filling rooms, landslides and small currents filling in the cracks.

Each new crash rooted her to the ground, freezing her solid. Was it the creature she had seen? Was it merely decay? Astrid wanted to believe it was nature and time taking its toll. But she felt watched, moving through cool shadows cast by tumbled buildings, wading through drifts of sand. It moved constantly, her tracks disappearing behind her within a few minutes, leaving no trail—no path to follow.

Overhead the sun tracked across the sky and the day passed.

————

ANOTHER TIMELESS PLACE.

Not in the way the Summer Valley was, or the Black Forest, but in the way a scorching sun can draw out each second, sand blistering with each step. Astrid stopped, leaning against a rough wall in a patch of shade—even the stones burned. The spire with the starburst was to her right. It seemed an unreachable point, and she had no real idea of the distance between herself and it. It could have been five or ten miles; it could have been two.

With each pause, each small rest in a thin shadow, she listened for the sound of water. Her mouth was dry, tongue thick behind her teeth. She would have given anything for the thunderstorms that had filled the months shared with Tyhr. She would have sold her left arm for snow. Anything to escape the sensation of baking beneath an open sky.

Listening for water now—a trickle or murmur—something else caught her attention. A small sound—delicate feet scratching at stone. She looked up to see a brightly colored body against the washed-out backdrop of the abandoned city, perched on the edge of a building.

"Chinook!"

He saw her, leaping from the high roof to sweep down and circle her head.

Where have you been? After the sandstorm, I could not find you! You were not where you said you would be!

"I'm sorry." Astrid looked around, shaking her head. "I met the South Wind. And I found water. But we have to go, there's something here."

Water?

"We can't go back. There's something down there." Astrid pulled the soaked scarf from her pack. Already it was drying, the moisture evaporating. She groaned, aching with disappointment. "Come have a drink."

Chinook landed on her arm, and she squeezed the scarf

over his open beak until the little water that was left fell into his mouth. When it was gone, she smoothed the cool cloth over him, gently wiping down his feathers, and running the fabric over his small face. He sat quietly with eyes closed as she did.

"Better?"

Yes, he said softly. *But next time I would appreciate an invitation.*

"You'll be with me next time. But the South Wind said we shouldn't linger. And there's something out there. I saw something and it scares me."

Lucky for you I have found the way through. We are almost out of the city now. Over that wall ahead is a vast desert. I could not see the end.

"I know."

You know?

"The South Wind said to keep that spire on my right." Astrid pointed to the skinny tower stretching above the sand, a weathered metal starburst extending from the top.

Yes. That is fine. Wonderful. Next time you get to do the scouting and I get to rest in the shade and talk to the wind and drink water.

"But I don't have wings."

What does that have to do with it? I do not have hands.

"Wings make it easier to scout."

No. I am sure they do not. Hands are much more useful.

Astrid smiled. Wings would have made this journey much easier.

A booming crash echoed in the distance—thousands of pounds of sand moving, sliding to fill a new space. Astrid stopped, listening, until the rushing slowed and then stopped. A building collapse, a wall or floor giving out finally under the weight, maybe. Nothing more.

I do not think that sound is just sand, Chinook said softly.

"No, I don't either."

I thought I saw something earlier when I was looking for you.

She glanced at him. "What did you see?"

Not sure. I will go investigate.

"No," she said, shaking her head and pointing to a split in a ruined wall ahead. Beyond it lay an expanse of flat open desert—a mirage hovering over the sand. "We're almost out. See?"

Something is coming, Chinook hissed.

She ran for the break in the wall, sand sliding beneath her feet as the earth shivered. The remnants of the city shook, masonry grinding together, and she could feel it in her joints, in the back of her skull.

Astrid!

Chinook's voice buzzed in her head, an edge of terror sharpening it.

The wall of a building had broken apart, and large stone blocks had fallen to either side of the opening. A flash of color caught her eye, a tile like the one she'd seen in the house earlier. The same red and purple flowers. She stumbled, distracted, and Chinook let out a chirp of alarm.

A sliding, slithering sound filled the air.

Astrid threw herself toward the opening, gasping as she gripped the stone and looked out over the valley. The ground fell away—the city perched on the crest of a sea of dunes—into a flat expanse that stretched as far as she could see.

A land of nothing and no one.

A blur of movement caught her attention—something large, moving fast. The sand dunes slanted down, spilling out across a flat plain, and the city rose behind her. Astrid jumped down, slithering down the dunes, Chinook flying overhead and urging her on. She slipped and tumbled forward, sliding the rest of the way down in an uncontrolled heap.

Up! Get up!

"I'm trying."

Pushing to her feet with a groan, Astrid brushed at her eyes and face. Sand filled her nose and mouth; she could feel it inside of her clothes—gritting between her teeth. She brushed at her face, panicked, and desperate to see, skin crawling with expectation.

Move! Now!

"I can't see!" Astrid shouted, beginning to cry—welcoming the tears. Clumsily she wiped more sand away, blinking, and taking a staggering step forward. Chinook was chirping but not speaking, not making any kind of sense, and then she could see again—the world blurry but clearing quickly. She looked around, back up the dune, the city rising beyond with a hot baking sun overhead.

A golden snake—black tongue scenting the air—slithered out of the ruined city. The creature—sleek and armored, glinting in the light—glided down the dunes without appearing to move. The sand beneath it remained undisturbed, untouched by the monster's passage.

Astrid stood, transfixed, unable to look away as it came for them with astonishing speed. Sharp eyes, green with a black slash, pinned her to the ground. It moved with a hushing rustle like two dry palms being rubbed together, the sound growing as it neared, building in her chest with each pound of her inevitable heartbeat.

You could still run, Chinook said, settling on her shoulder, gripping her tight with two tiny feet.

"So could you," she whispered, raising a hand to shield him from the creature.

But it was too late. The snake was there, the arrow-shaped head as big as she was. The body circled around her in a wall of muscles and scales.

Who are you?

"A traveler," she said, remaining as motionless as possible.

I saw you with the old woman, the old Wind. You were in the well. What are you doing here?

"I need to cross the desert."

I will take you.

"For what price?" Astrid's brow wrinkled in surprise. There was no malice in the voice, no hunger that she could detect—only mild curiosity.

Dinner, Chinook hissed.

Astrid patted him, soothing ruffled feathers.

How can you be so sure I will have one?

"Because I'm not a fool," she said. "Everything comes at a price."

The snake watched Astrid, inscrutable, without speaking for a long moment. *Kill the Enchantress.*

"Why?" she asked. Astrid's heart raced. This creature knew the Enchantress? Was Tyhr that close? Her eyes shifted away to where the desert might be if the snake had not encircled her. On her shoulder, Chinook tensed.

I am tired of sharing my sand. One old woman is enough.

Astrid raised her chin. "Why haven't you done it yourself?"

The creature gave a slithering shrug. *I have not been able to breach her walls.*

"And you think I can?"

If you cannot, why do you want me to take you there?

"I don't know if I can promise that." Astrid bit her lip, considering the snake's request. She'd not imagined she'd get this far or what she'd do when she finally found Tyhr. "If I agree and can't, what happens then?"

And do not say you will eat us, Chinook said.

The snake blinked—a long slow blink. *I eat you.*

No, Chinook huffed, *unacceptable. I refuse.* He ruffled his feathers, opening and shutting his wings twice before darting forward in a flurry to land on the snake's snout. He pecked out each word. *I. Am. Not. Food.*

"Chinook! Have you lost your mind?" Astrid lunged for him, barely able to catch him but successfully snatching him away. He was light as air, beating at her hands, struggling to get away.

Let go!

"No!"

The black tongue flicked out, close to her face, tasting the air. The snake moved in, tightening the circle. There was nowhere else to go. Not that there would have been anywhere to go before. It would have caught them if they'd tried to run.

Let go of me! Chinook twittered, furious and feathered, a ball of anger and exhaustion.

Astrid clamped down on his wings and brought him close to her face, eye level, staring into this livid little face. Six months ago, she wouldn't have been able to read his expression; she would have sworn that birds lacked the ability to show emotion. Now she knew better.

"Stop," she said, voice soft. "Please."

His heart beat rapidly, as quickly as her own, and she tried to block out the sounds of scales moving on sand. The black tongue flicked around them, tasting the air, taking in their conversation.

You are brave, said the snake, green eyes fixed on the bird.

Chinook did not respond, and Astrid raised her shoulder slightly, prompting.

"I think—" she began.

I am not talking to you human, the snake hissed. *I will make my bargain with him.*

Fine, Chinook agreed. *We will kill the Enchantress. But I want more than safe passage to the oasis.*

What is your desire little bird?

Chinook stretched his neck, looking this way and that, nothing but sun and sand and snake within sight. *Something shiny and a drink.*

"Shiny?" Astrid asked.

Yes. Why not?

Yes, the snake agreed. *Why not?*

You will have to carry it for me, Astrid. Chinook shot her a look, humor glimmering in his eyes. *With your hands.*

She laughed, "It would be an honor. But what's shiny out here?"

The snake moved, pulling back to expose a section of smooth, pale underbelly.

Choose one, the snake said, *and then I will take you as far as the oasis.*

CHAPTER THIRTY-SEVEN

The clear blue water was a relief after the punishing sun. Astrid sank into it, completely submerging and washing the caked salt and sand away. Chinook bathed in the shallows, singing to himself, pleased with the result of his negotiations with the snake.

Fresh water. Shade. A single reflective snake scale.

And a promise to kill the Enchantress.

Chinook had agreed so easily, a hard edge to his tone. Astrid didn't blame him, not after years of living in fear of her in the jungle, his only friend and companion present only half the time. Chinook had never spoken about how it had been before Astrid came, how living with a tiger during the day worked. From what she had seen they were close, though the three were rarely in the same room together. Chinook, if it were possible, was even more private a person than Tyhr.

The oasis was small—the deep clear spring, a few dusty bushes, all between a handful of tall boulders. Beyond the sheltered spot a vast flat landscape spread out in either direction, the ruins of the beach miles behind them. The snake had taken them this far, no farther, with one word as to where they should go from there.

West.

"I want to wait until the sun sets before we set out," she said, coming out of the water and moving slowly to sit in the shade thrown by a boulder. Already her clothes and short hair were drying, water evaporating away. What would happen when they left this place? How far would they travel before finding water again?

That would have to be a later thought, saved for the person she would be in a few hours. Right now, she would think of other things. With a sigh, she pulled her bag toward her and took out the scale, tooth, and claw—snake, shark, and wolf. She tilted the scale, catching the light and sending a bright spot shivering over the rocks.

If you are not careful, you will blind yourself with that reflection.

Astrid tilted it slowly, centimeter by centimeter until her face filled the surface.

She didn't recognize the woman—thin features, sharp cheekbones, dark circles, and cracked lips. Her short hair was ragged, and uneven, patches sticking up here and there, and a reddening sunburn across her forehead and nose complimented the bloodshot look of her eyes.

She had never considered herself beautiful, pretty enough maybe, but not a beauty in the classical sense. There had never been anyone desperate to dance with her or call on her, no requests to go riding in the park or to escort her to a play. Not that it would have mattered if there had been. Her life, her destiny, had already been sealed with a ring.

It is not so bad, Chinook said, walking toward her, wings held out to dry.

"Maybe so," she said, forcing a smile and setting the scale aside.

The sunburn will fade. Your hair will grow back.

Astrid nodded, swallowing a lump in her throat.

Your hair was never the most beautiful thing about you.

"Thank you, Chinook."

After all, he went on, hopping up on a rock and turning this way and that as his feathers dried, *you were considered beautiful enough for a murderous shark to take you as a wife. I assume there are a lot of women in the world who would be very grateful for that.*

"And you've been told you would be a wonderful snack," she said, making a face at him, tempted to splash him with water.

I take it as a compliment.

She laughed, leaning back in the shade, watching the sky turn fiery as the world turned. It happened quickly, the sun there and gone, the stars impatient to fill the sky. They shared the last of the cheese, savoring each bite—eating quietly together.

"Do you think we'll ever want to eat cheese again?" she asked softly, hoping there would be a moment in the not-so-distant future when everything was different, and the world didn't hurt so much.

I do not want to eat cheese now.

"You don't have to," she said, making a face as him.

Oh no, it would be rude to refuse. Chinook pecked at his dwindling chunk, picking at it with a foot. *But I prefer bugs. The flavor is better. Or fruit. Next time, bring more fruit.*

"There won't be a next time." Her voice was firm, harsher than intended. But that was the fear lurking beneath the surface, Astrid's terror that this was a never-ending journey and at the end there would no glass palace

—no Tyhr. "We should sleep while we can. It's cool enough now."

Wake me when it is time to go, he said, hopping over and settling down in the crook of her elbow.

Astrid sat quietly for what felt like a long time, considering her past, wondering about her future, and grateful for the small warm spot in her life that was Chinook. When she finally fell asleep it was beneath the curious eyes of strange stars.

PART THREE
THE GLASS PALACE

CHAPTER THIRTY-EIGHT

Biting cold woke her.

"Chinook," she whispered, sitting up and adjusting her arm—the bundle of feathers burrowing farther into the warmth of her body. "It's time to go."

Wonderful. I will let you start.

"Too cold?"

What do you think?

"I think," Astrid said, groaning as she pushed herself up and shouldered her bag, "that I'm cold too. The walk will warm me up."

Good. You can share that warmth with me.

They set off in the dark. Astrid curled her hands up and tucked them under her arms, Chinook tucked against her chest. It was too cold to stop or sleep again. She ached all over, half frozen and exhausted from lack of sleep. Each step forward was a battle.

Before it had been too hot. She'd welcomed the setting sun and the relief it brought from the blazing sky. But now she wanted the warmth back. Overhead, millions of stars spangled the sky, the velvet night blue and violet. Not a single constellation was recognizable—not a single familiar grouping. Out here in the desert, it was all alien. Astrid had no way of knowing if this was a real place or somewhere like the Black Forest.

There must be stories about this place like there were about the black trees and the giant wolves. They'd washed up on a strange shore, passed through a dead city, and been set on the right path by a guardian of the desert. If that wasn't from a fairytale, she wasn't sure what was.

And here, in the middle of nowhere, at the heart of a vast desert, a glittering palace waited to be discovered.

———

THE SUN ROSE, BRINGING HEAT AND A SLOW BAKING SENSATION. Astrid squinted into the light, closing her eyes when it became too much, walking blind, the tug of the ring guiding her. Chinook had stopped talking as the day had gone on—retreating into himself. At first, he'd mumbled about missing the cold but then even his complaints slowed, before trailing off without being brought up again.

Astrid stumbled forward in almost silence—only her harsh breaths and shuffling feed over flat, hard packed earth filled the air. The terrain was a cracked and curled landscape of dirt that had once seen rain but not for a very, very long time. The dunes of the coast had vanished behind them hours ago, the little oasis was soon lost to sight. In either direction now was nothing but shimmering false promises and cracked earth.

Seconds were hours, hours were weeks. Astrid could not imagine spending another night and day this way— freezing and baking only to do it all over again. Had the shark been better? The Magician? The farther she walked the less it all made sense. The heat was killing her, stumbling step by stumbling step, cramping in her belly around thirst and hunger.

With a groan, Astrid sank to her knees.

You cannot give up now, Chinook said, voice soft.

"I'm not giving up," Astrid said, throat raw with thirst. "I'm tired."

You are not allowed to be tired.

"Oh?" A ghost of a laugh escaped. "And why is that?"

Because who would carry me then?

"Are you being serious or making a joke? I'm too exhausted to tell the difference."

I assure you, I would never jest about being carried.

Astrid swallowed. Her mouth was dry. Her skin stretched tight. Muscles ached, and her head pounded. If there had been tears, she would have cried, even now a dry sob, a whimper came from her—the croaking sound terrible in the silence.

"Chinook," she whispered, putting everything in his name—all of her fear, all of the pain.

You promised, he said, his unexpected gentleness there to meet her, more comfort than she deserved. *I will help you keep it. But for now, you are the one with hands and must keep walking.*

"And my hands are important because that means I can carry you, yes?"

Obviously.

It took everything to stand—the last shreds of her strength, all of Astrid's will. It was not her body that made it possible but her desperate need to find Tyhr and free him, to undo her mistake, to keep her promise.

Step after step, one foot in front of the other, she

watched the ground and when the light began to hurt her eyes, she closed them once again. It didn't matter. It was all the same. Nothing changed in this place. The ring continued to guide her, a subtle pull, a silent guide. It didn't matter if she could see or not as long as it knew the way.

When the sun shifted, coming down from the highest point, she opened her eyes and looked around. In the distance, something glittered—a point of light, a trap of sunshine and heat.

"There!" she shouted, knowing even without the instance of the ring that he was there.

Tyhr was there.

What is it? Chinook asked, head tucked beneath his wing. He didn't move, didn't look, trusting in Astrid's ability to describe the scene, or too tired to care. Possibly both. It was too hot, the sun punishing and relentless.

"The Glass Palace," Astrid said, studying the shape, the way light moved through it. "It's there."

The bird uncurled from the crook of her arm then, stretching one leg and then the other. He puffed up and out, shot Astrid a beady look, and jumped up to her shoulder, looking in the complete opposite direction. Chinook turned this way and that, chirping softly, feathers beginning to stick out.

I do not know what you are talking about. I do not see anything at all but a ruined nap with a nice dream about mango. Do you even remember what they taste like? I am not sure I do. Maybe I never did. I was about to find out. But no, you have to shout cryptically at the landscape and wake up a desperately tired bird.

Astrid sighed and pointed. "Over there."

Chinook turned and stared, feathers smoothing out,

feet digging into her shoulder at the sight of the palace rising up out of the desert.

"Well?"

Oh, you mean that giant glittering palace in the middle of an endless desert. Yes. You might be right. That could be the place we are searching for. But then again, we have so many options. He paused, preening, then added, *You know if you roll your eyes any harder, they might get stuck.*

"Would dreams about mangoes have been better?"

I will never know.

———

HER SKIN HURT.

There was no relief in this place, nothing but the night, and when it came, it brought extreme cold. Every inch of her skin was sunburnt, covered or uncovered didn't matter, the slightest movement was painful. Chinook clutched her shoulder, fanning his wings occasionally, moving the air around his body, and cooling her neck.

Astrid desperately craved water—clear, cool water from a spring or deep well, from a duckweed-filled lake or a muddy puddle. She would have taken anything. The water they'd filled their bellies with from the oasis was long gone —worse than a distant memory because now it felt like a dream. Like the mangoes.

The only place that might have water lay ahead.

Putting one foot in front of the other, Astrid focused on each lift and settle—the motion in her knees, the progress she made. Hard-packed sand and dirt, almost white, passed beneath her feet, huge cracks racing in all directions. Small pale stones had begun to appear, nothing larger than a marble, and she stooped to pick up the next one that caught her eye.

Hey! What are you doing? Chinook squawked and flapped, trying to maintain his balance.

She held up the rock, dull in the intense light, gritty between her fingers. "I wanted a rock."

Are you starting a collection?

"Maybe it will come in handy later when I need something to throw at you for being so rude."

Threats!

"Only when deserved."

Chinook twittered to himself, a little refrain she didn't catch, and then settled back into silence. They squabbled more under the sun, baking in the heat, with the past few days bearing down on them. A breaking point was coming. Astrid could feel it; she knew he did too. They were both struggling to maintain things—all of it had been so difficult. Too much danger, immense pressure and change, and the baking brutal sun to top it all off.

Looking ahead, hand up to shade her eyes, she squinted at the landscape.

It went on without end—stunning in simplicity, eternal. She couldn't imagine this place had ever been anything other than it was. But the earth was cracked as if once water had flowed. Maybe it rained here once every ten years and then this dead earth bloomed. She'd read about desert super blooms in her botany books—in places like the American West. Someday she would love to see something like that in person. Maybe when Astrid did, Tyhr would be at her side.

A shimmer on the horizon stopped her.

Crystal clear glass caught the sunlight, bending it into rainbows that raced across the desert—bright ribbons of light crisscrossing and merging. In another place it might have been lovely, a delicate crystal confection, a dream made real. But for her, it was bleak—harsh and soulless.

A palace of glass, surrounded by a forest of glass trees.

It came to her in pieces because she couldn't look at it all at once.

It burned Astrid's eyes and made her head throb.

Almost there.

Slowly, each footstep a thousand, each breath pulled from fire and expelled—her lungs a furnace—they reached the edge of the glass forest. It was a knot of delicate growth, a tangle of spun glass, piercing points. It was hard to tell how deep the trees were, how many of them stood between her and the destination. The glass warped the landscape—distorted reality.

"Will you find a way through?" she asked, searching but unable to make out a clear path.

You are very bossy when you are tired.

Astrid snorted, shading her eyes to look up at spires rising up behind high walls. Chinook propelled himself from her shoulder, dropping and then catching himself in a few swift beats. He rose in the air, gaining height, before darting away. But he was back after only a few minutes, landing on her shoulder, wings outstretched, and feathers fluffed out to cool his body.

It is not as bad as it looks, he said. *But there is no direct path. Very poor planning on the Enchantresses part. She should have expected visitors. I would not have been so sloppy in my design. Or so tasteless.*

A tight smile touched her face—there and gone—as she took the first step beneath the trees. Ribbons of light crawled over her as she walked beneath glass branches. It was worse than being out in the open desert. Out there the light was all the same, beating down on her all over. Here the light was like knives. Concentrated, sharp, piercing fabric and skin, sinking into her bones in a way she never thought possible.

Astrid avoided the bright spots as much as possible, twisting and turning through the nearly invisible maze. Chinook went ahead and came back, beak open, panting in the heat. He landed once on a branch and let out a squawk of surprise.

Hot! Hot! he complained, leaping back in the air and coming to rest on her shoulder.

"You silly bird," she said. "You should have known better."

Chinook stretched one wing, swiping at her face but Astrid ignored him. The walls of the palace warped and wavered through the trees. The upper stories were transparent, but she could see nothing in them, no one moved, no furniture sat waiting for occupants. The whole place would be enchanted. Someone could be watching them right now and Astrid would never know.

Who else lived within these walls?

There was no way to know.

But somewhere in there Tyhr and the Enchantress were together.

A pang of doubt hit Astrid for the first time. They'd come all this way to rescue a man who might no longer wish to be rescued. She stopped, motionless in the glass forest, breathing Placing a hand over her heart she concentrated on the sensation of blood pumping and lungs expanding, a swirl of worry and fear roaring through her.

"Chinook?"

Astrid?

"What if he doesn't want me?"

Want. This was the first time she'd even considered it. There had been something between them in the Summer Valley—a tension that might have become something solid given enough time. But with too many unanswered questions and a silver mask between them, what had they truly been able to build? A tentative friendship? The start of a romance? Was there love between them? Her heart raced in answer, her mind shying away from the word.

It didn't matter. She'd made a promise. If by some miracle they managed to make their way inside she would give him the choice. Astrid wasn't the Enchantress. She wouldn't deny Tyhr a voice in his future.

What is not to want? Chinook said with a shrug. *You are sunburnt and skinny and not always very friendly. You are also very nosey and do not listen to warnings.*

"Thank you so much," she said, a sour edge in her tone. Astrid let out a sigh and her shoulders slumped. Chinook dug tiny claws in and flapped to keep his balance.

You are also brave. You rescued me from a shark. I do not think any other human would do that. Maybe not even Tyhr. Chinook paused, a thoughtful expression in his dark eyes. *And I am nosey as well, so I believe we are matched very well in that area. Tyhr is lucky to have us. He is not nosey at all. Someone must keep him informed of things.*

Tears gathered in Astrid's eyes, trembling on her lashes before evaporating in the heat. He darted forward, rubbing his head against her cheek—soft feathers to roughed skin. She wanted to hug him, to hold on to him, and never let him go. And she knew it would annoy him to no end which only made her want to do it more.

"You are a very silly bird," Astrid said.

And you are wasting time. We have someplace to be.

———

TOGETHER THEY REACHED THE PALACE WALLS.

A palace of sand and glass, erupting out of the desert like a strange crystalline flower. Cloudy glass rose straight up from the sand, the solid surface the same color as the desert floor—a shade only slightly darker than white. Beyond the walls towers glittered, the opacity changing as they rose. At the highest point, the turrets were crystal clear like the trees.

She circled it, hand on the wall, feeling for a crack or break, a joint or dent. The surface was solid—impenetrable. There had to be a way inside, an entrance she couldn't see —an invisible door, a magic word. With a groan she leaned into the wall, the surface hot, the ground beneath her feet hot, the air hot.

"Open please," she said, voice croaky, throat dry.

The wall remained the same.

"Will you go up and look around?"

For what?

"A way in?"

And if there is not one?

"Then this is as close as we get to Tyhr."

What remained unspoken between were the words: *and we die here.*

Chinook threw himself into the air, beating his wings hard, and rising above the trees. Up and up he spiraled, climbing into the blue sky, circling and searching—a black speck wheeling across her vision.

"Who are you?"

The tone was sharp, an edge of broken glass—cutting through the feverish heat. Astrid jerked up from her slumped position against the wall, not sure how to respond, shaking her head at the strange woman who had appeared from nowhere. A stranger, and not someone who appeared to recognize Astrid. There was no plan beyond this. Show up, arrived, and be here. Astrid had never considered what would come next. She'd thought the hardest part was behind them.

"Astrid," she said, giving her name automatically and wishing the moment it came from her mouth she could take it back.

The woman looked her up and down—taking in the travel-worn clothes, the dirt under her nails and short hair, and the sunburned skin. Astrid no longer looked like the woman from the valley. She was much thinner now, with some of the youth worn away, luster faded. The last few weeks had been some of the hardest she'd endured. There was very little, if anything, left of the woman she'd been before the Summer Valley, before Tyhr.

"Aya-stride," the woman repeated, the name sounding strange and incomprehensible with her accent. She was wrapped in loose cream-colored garments, ageless with dark eyes—her expression flat, neither curious or suspicious.

"No." Astrid pronounced her name again slowly. "Like this, As-trid."

"Too difficult." The woman shook her head and waved a hand at Astrid to stand. "Aya will do. I'm Nora."

"Nora," Astrid repeated, turning to search the wall, looking for the door the woman must have arrived through. The wall was smooth, the same as it had been when she'd circled the palace looking for a way in. "How did you get out here?"

"You can't see it?" The woman tilted her head to the

side, looking from Astrid to the wall and back. "In the desert too long, yes?"

"Yes," Astrid agreed, squinting at the glass. "I'm lost."

"You've come a long way to be lost. Are you looking for work?"

"Work?" Her brain was fuzzy from the heat, eyes drifting to the pale sky in search of Chinook. How much time had passed? Where was he?

"Do you sweep? I need someone to sweep."

"I can sweep," Astrid said with a nod, excitement growing.

"We shall see." The woman looked Astrid up and down, lingering over the leather shoes that had once been beautiful—that even now hinted at luxury—in tatters, encasing sore feet. "You can get clean first."

Astrid nodded gratefully, glancing around again. Overhead, Chinook circled, high and distant. Astrid wanted to make some kind of signal, but the woman followed her look, squinting up into the sky. For a moment they both watched the gliding bird suspended on hot air currents.

"Won't last long out here," she said, eyes coming back to Astrid. "Not a lot of water. Not any water. Maybe, if you think about it, you might want to leave a dish out. If you like birds."

They shared a moment of silence as Astrid searched the woman's face—heart skipping. What would anyone in this place know of her? The Enchantress would not have spoken her name, would not have thought twice about her once the Summer Valley lay behind them. And maybe people and creatures arrived in this lonely place enough that strange faces were not unusual. Nora's face remained blank, dark eyes revealing nothing, offering only reflections.

"Come," she said. "We'll find you some water."

"How do we get in?"

Nora took Astrid's arm and positioned her until they stood side by side, facing the wall at a new angle. From this spot, only a few centimeters from where she'd sat moments before the wall was different. There was an opening—tall and narrow, barely wide enough for her to pass through. Astrid took a step to the side, and it vanished. An illusion—a wall that was not a wall, an opening only visible at a certain angle.

"But—" Astrid gestured at the palace, a wail threatening to break through. "I walked around the whole place. There were no doors before."

"Enchantments," Nora said with a shrug, gesturing Astrid inside, through the door in the glass, into the palace.

CHAPTER THIRTY-NINE

A week.

A week within strange walls.

A week living in the corners of the Enchantress's palace.

A week living with suspicious silent people and avoiding those that looked like glass.

Astrid swept relentless sand from one room to the next, fighting an unwinnable battle, hour by hour. The palace was home to only a handful of people—the rooms she swept clear were empty. It was the opposite of the house in the Summer Valley. There it had been full of plants and life, crowded with furniture and carpets, murals on every wall. Here the interior was like that of a snail shell—organic and smooth.

Chinook came and went as he pleased—a brightly colored speck in the sky or a distant figure resting in hard-to-reach places. Astrid left bowls of water and food in out-of-the-way locations for him—the two lingering to speak in whispers, huddling together in pale shadows.

Have you seen him? Have you found him?

There was no reason to ask *who* it was they'd seen or found.

Each time she had the urge to hold Chinook close—to rub a cheek against his feathers, to feel his solidness—had to be resisted. The solitude ate at her, the hope each day that she would see Tyhr crushed again and again. Chinook spent his days lurking in shady places or spinning high in the air, watchful and waiting, searching from above.

Astrid had not had any luck on her own. She wasn't permitted in the clearer reaches of the palace—the places Livia wandered through in her brightly colored gowns surrounded by crystal-clear halls with crystal-clear inhabitants.

The human servants were only allowed so far.

Beyond, in the halls of glass, other figures moved and performed duties. Glass figures, adult-sized, genderless, and without identity, moved through the world like iridescent bubbles. There was no way to know how many there were. The kitchen staff and sweepers refused to speak about them—turning their backs on her if she asked a question. Nora, the housekeeper, had warned her it would get her exiled—banished to the desert with nowhere else to go.

So, she watched as much as she could, sweeping into less traveled areas as far as she dared, alert for the flash of reflection thrown by a glass figure. Or the familiar shape of the man she was so desperate to find.

———

It was strange to work and have a routine.

Astrid had a bed—no more than a cot with a thin pillow —in a small, shared dormitory with three other women. Each day she put on a long shapeless robe, an apron, and a scarf to wrap around her head and face to keep the sun off. Her boots had been replaced with slippers; the burns treated with a cooling salve. The bag she'd carried for so long that it had almost fused to her skin now lay empty beneath the mattress.

When she worked the claw, tooth, scale, and the rock from the dessert stayed in the pocket of her apron— weights to her past, reminders of what was yet to be. When she slept, they lay beneath her pillow, filling her dreams with threats and promises.

Astrid swept fine sand constantly; little drifts collecting in corners and on stairs, gritty beneath her new slippers as she pushed it into piles. She spent hours sweeping a space, hauling pails of sand outside, dumping it beyond the walls, only to have the warm air carry it inside again.

There was a garden deep within the palace and open to the sky—a place only a few were permitted to go. Astrid had given Nora her seeds and explained how good she was with plants—how she could make anything grow. In time, Nora had promised Astrid would see the gardens. But not yet. First, she would master sweeping.

In the evenings Nora and the staff prepared meals for themselves and the prince—his covered dish was taken upstairs by a silent glass figure. The Enchantress never seemed to eat, and no one ever questioned it.

Astrid sat quietly at the shared table, gaze moving over the faces of her fellow residents. There had been no intro- ductions, no exchange of names when she'd arrived. Even though Astrid shared a room with three of the women present she only knew Uma because Nora used her name. Uma was one of the few who was permitted to tend to the gardens.

In total, there were only twenty of them—a few men, mostly women—each fighting a losing battle with the desert. Some had been kind—others too focused on some inner turmoil to acknowledge her. The people who ended up here were lost to the world—abandoned in the desert— with no real interest in her or each other.

Each day she worked to learn something new—to make a connection. Anything to get closer to the gardens.

Tyhr would be there.

But when the table spoke about the Enchantress, they never called her Livia or the Enchantress—it was always *her*. Just that, nothing more, because everyone knew who *her* was. It was strange to be in this place where the woman's name was never spoken. As if it were too fragile and might shatter like the glass walls around them.

For the past two evenings, Nora had Astrid help prepare the meal. The women worked together in silence, dicing carrots and small potatoes, water boiling on the stovetop. It reminded Astrid of home. Not the Summer Valley. But being with her mother in Amsterdam. The townhouse with the tiny kitchen at the back of the house, the door open to the back garden, and the alley beyond.

"Do you miss your home?" Astrid asked, voice abrupt, heavy with personal memory. "Where you came from?"

"No." Nora stirred the vegetable pot, watching it instead of looking at Astrid—maybe seeing some other place. "It's been a long time since I thought of home."

"I'm sorry," Astrid began, waving the carrot she was peeling. "I didn't mean—"

"No, no," the woman said, continuing to stir with a shrug. "No apology necessary. This place is home now."

"Have you been here a long time?" Astrid nodded,

peeling the carrot carefully, waiting for the older woman to speak.

"When I first came this place was smaller, very quiet. She was lonely, wandering the halls by herself, going in circles. The place was half full of sand and it kept building up. I couldn't take care of it by myself."

Lonely? Astrid fought to keep a sour expression from her face. The housekeeper spoke about the Enchantress, Livia Forza, with tenderness and respect. The only thing Astrid felt was anger, a strong dislike bordering on hatred, and more than a little fear. Fear of what the woman could do to Tyhr, fear of what she would do to Astrid. Even fear for Chinook.

"She let me take on more staff and in the last few years those..." her voice trailed off as she searched for words, brow furrowing, "glass men came. I haven't seen her this happy before. Not since the prince arrived. He's changed everything."

"Has he?" Astrid looked up, paring knife slipping and catching her thumb, blood welling up.

"Yes," Nora nodded, smiling happily. "They will be married the day after tomorrow."

———

Astrid! I found it! Chinook spun past her, looping around the hall, and coming back to land on the handle of her broom. *We have to leave right now. I will tell you where to go.*

"Found what?"

The entrance to the gardens.

Chinook directed her down empty echoing halls where sand collected in the corners, through arches, and across shining white-hot courtyards. They went up, circling out of the lower reaches of the palace, into an area where the glass was less opaque—translucent hints coming through.

He chattered the entire time, a stream of excited conversation that she struggled to hold on to. The pounding of her blood, the buzz of it in her ears, made it impossible to keep up with him. The only thought she had was *Tyhr*.

This is it. Chinook said. *Go down that hall there and take a left, follow it until you reach a double set of doors. I will be here if you need me.*

Astrid paused, looking around, really seeing their surroundings for the first time. It looked like anywhere else in this part of the palace, like a corridor she could have walked down a thousand times.

"What about you? Aren't you coming?"

I have decided to be kind and generous and allow you two a moment of privacy.

"Very thoughtful of you," she said with a smile. "Thank you."

Go, he urged, flapping his wings impatiently. *I will keep watch.*

Astrid started down the hall with her heart beating Tyhr's name.

———

"WHAT ARE YOU DOING HERE?"

Astrid jumped, turning to face the speaker, fighting to calm the tremor of fear shooting through her. A door she'd hurried past was open and a woman stood at the threshold, holding a dust rag and broom. Uma. One of the women from the dinner table—ever watchful, ever silent. Her blue eyes narrowed as she stepped into the hall, pulling the door shut behind her with a solid click, echoing click.

"I wanted to see more of the palace," Astrid said, looking beyond the woman for Chinook. "I was curious."

"*She* doesn't like us to wander around," Uma said, crossing her arms over her thin chest. "Did Nora give you permission to come to the gardens?"

Astrid shook her head.

"You need to go back."

The woman's voice was flat, definite.

"Please," Astrid said, keeping her voice low. "I know I shouldn't be here."

"Then what are you doing here?"

"I was curious. I've never seen a place like this."

"No excuse to go sneaking around."

"I know," Astrid put more pleading into her voice, growing desperate. The woman's posture had changed, moving away, tensing, preparing to yell. "I won't do it again. I promise I won't be here again. I can give you something, you can keep it, to seal the bargain."

"I'm not bargaining with you, and I don't take bribes."

"No! No!" Astrid waved her hands. "Not a bribe, a promise, just a way for me to prove to you that I won't be back here again." She dug in the pocket of the apron, the weight of her treasures there—with her always.

As she pulled the scale out it caught the light, a bright spot racing across the wall, moving as she turned the scale back and forth. Uma watched it, the pinched look fading. It was as reflective as a mirror, blurring what it showed, softening the images passing across its slick surface.

Astrid held it up, offering the woman her own reflection.

"You promise you won't come back?" Uma asked, reaching out, hesitating.

"I promise," Astrid said, meeting her gaze, putting

everything she had into it, hoping the woman would accept this offer and let her pass.

Uma took the scale and hid it in her apron. Without a backward glance, she turned and walked quickly back the way Astrid had come. Briefly, she wondered if she'd done the right thing with the gift from the serpent. What if there came another moment it might have been more useful? No, she shook her head, calming the swirl of questions. It felt like the right choice and there were other things to concentrate on now.

A breeze touched her, catching her off guard, and bringing with it a scent she'd forgotten. Green. A thousand little scents mingling into a swirl of alive, living green—plants and water, earth and vegetable decay. The desert had scrubbed it from her and left her raw with its absence. Tears filled her eyes, her heart picking up speed as excitement and relief flowed over her. The scent reminded her of home and all the good things she'd been afraid she would never see again.

It meant Tyhr was here.

Astrid turned a corner and there were the double doors Chinook had promised. They stood open, the hall between herself and them empty. Lush greenery filled the space beyond, the tinkling sound of a fountain reaching her, beckoning, promising a thousand cool dreams.

Passing over the threshold, she entered a huge conservatory.

It made the one in the Summer Valley small in comparison—a pale shadow of this much grander version. Tall trees rose to the glass ceiling, throwing patterned shadows on the plants and winding paths below. Flowering shrubs and pots of large-leafed plants—some familiar, others new —filled in the room. Smaller varieties crowded the areas between those until there was no room for anything else. Vegetation encroached on the paths, threatening to burst from this room to overtake the rest of the palace.

Paths fanned out in several directions, leading into the jungle, and Astrid hesitated only a moment before turning to the right. The pull of the ring was strong—stronger than it had been at any other time since she'd arrived—and she followed it, excitement building, hurrying now, almost running. Leaves brushed Astrid's face, reaching across the path, fern fronds touching her longingly. She pushed them aside, impatient, and saw a familiar figure walking on the path ahead.

She stopped, gulping in air, studying the line of his shoulders, the broadness of his back. Astrid would have known Tyhr anywhere—even with his back to her. He stood out in this place, a beacon, and the ring burned on her finger.

CHAPTER FORTY

"Tyhr?"

He turned, their eyes meeting—his golden gaze dull behind the silver mask—the sparkle she'd loved gone. *Love.* Yes, it was love. She'd avoided it, pushed it away, but it was true. Crossing oceans and deserts, facing magical creatures and fear, she had come all of this way not only to fix a mistake, but because love had crept up on her—consuming her.

Astrid needed him to know.

But his gaze was wary—flat. Not the eyes of someone who knew her, not the welcome she'd expected, not a moment of joyous relief. Her heart stuttered painfully in her chest, a heaviness filling her body. She pushed through it, going to him, closing the distance between them.

"Don't you know me?"

Astrid reached for Tyhr, wanting to touch him, shocked at how easily it came—the desire to make sure there would never be any distance between them again. But he took a step back, evading her hands.

It had come too late.

All those miles she'd ignored and denied the fear, trying not to look too far ahead. She was too late. Her chance had been in the Summer Valley, the wild jungle shrinking around them, the curse closing in. The love he needed had been there; growing but unrecognized, not yet strong enough to change their fate.

The wish Livia made was fulfilled. The husband she'd demanded was present, the years of his denial and refusal overcome—his sadness and resignation complete. And all because Astrid had made a stupid mistake. Selfish. Thinking she knew better, believing a kiss was all it would take. Only afterward had she accepted fully her misunderstanding of it all, lying on the cold marble floor, with the shade of Chinook's disappointment weighing on her soul.

"Tyhr," she said, teeth clenched tight around a sob. "You know me."

She grabbed his sleeve, stopping him as he turned from her, desperate to hold on, but he pulled away and kept walking. The fountain in the conservatory tinkled, bubbling and making enough noise to cover her whispers if anyone might be lingering at the edges of the room or between the trees.

Moving ahead of him, Astrid put her hands flat on his chest—halting his steps, leaning into him. So close. His warmth—skin and muscle beneath her hands. Curling her fingers into his shirt, she fought tears, putting everything she had into words. "You know me."

Tyhr's hands came up—achingly slow—and he laid them over her own. The gold ring burned, warming suddenly, going hot, caught between their skin. *Home.* All this time, it had been leading her here—to him. She had followed, hoping it would be enough, that it would not lead her astray. Astrid needed more from it now—getting here wasn't enough. She needed to reach his heart.

"She killed you," he said, squeezing her hand, present in a way he hadn't been before. Searching her face—gaze lingering on the thinness of it, her chopped hair, the difference between the woman in the jungle and the one before him now. "I thought you were dead. Astrid, how did you get here?"

"Chinook helped me," she said, holding on to him, a smile tugging at her lips. "It's been an adventure. We came for you."

He cupped her face, smoothing her cheek, and she could have cried with happiness.

"I came to tell you—"

A gong echoed through the space, the sound carrying on, vibrating through the glass. High above them the towers shivered, the deep tremor becoming a bright shivering tinkling.

"You have to go." He turned her around—the moment shattered; her words unspoken. The expression in his eyes had changed, the softness gone with something harder replacing it.

"No, I—" she began, but he cut her off.

"Through those doors there and down the stairs. Go now," he said, pointing across the courtyard to a set of doors opposite the ones she'd come through. "They can't find you here."

"But the wedding? The curse?"

"She's coming. You must leave. Please, Astrid. I can't bear to watch you die again."

Astrid turned, stumbling away, as the gong rang out again and the doors she'd arrived through opened. Chinook chirped from the arch Tyhr had pushed her toward, already waiting for her, and she hurried to him, tears welling in her eyes.

Hurry, he urged. *She is coming.*

Together they slipped through the doors and down the hall, the sound of voices following. A woman's laugh. Tyhr's low familiar tones. She glanced down at her hands, the golden ring, the creases in her palms that might predict her future, the place where there should have been a scar from opening a door in solid stone.

She hadn't been able to hold on to him at all.

Astrid turned a corner blindly, swiping tears from her eyes, and ran into a tall glass figure with a thud.

CHAPTER FORTY-ONE

The glass figure tottered and then steadied as a buzzing filled her head. A hole opened in the blurry glass face, the mouth opening wide—a slick maw. The figure darted forward, faster than Astrid thought possible, with grasping glass hands. Chinook darted away but the figure followed, leaping after the panicked bird. With a snap the mouth closed, Chinook trapped inside flapping wildly against the solid surface. His cries of distress were barely audible, muffled inside the glass.

The figure turned to Astrid, descending on her in a rush, Chinook bouncing around inside. Fumbling in her pocket she felt the claw and something else, something small and hard. She twisted away as the figure lunged for her, hands clutching at her robe, snatching at her arm.

Distantly Astrid heard others arrive—servants as well as the silent glass figures. Even if she managed to evade this one there would be others. If the Enchantress had not realized she was here, now she would.

Tomorrow they would marry, her plan for rescue

impossible. She had spent the last few days trying to work out a plan in which she and Tyhr escaped without confrontation, somehow making it across the desert, avoiding the great snake waiting at the edge, cross oceans, arrive somewhere far enough that they might be safe.

Nowhere would be far enough, the woman would pursue them, hunting Tyhr wherever he might go. Astrid would only lose him again.

She clutched the stone in her pocket, fist tight around it as she turned to face her attacker—refusing to run. Chinook beat in the creature's stomach, frantic, running into the glass again and again. The figure grabbed her, hand clamping onto her arm, fingers biting down into flesh. A noise escaped, pain and surprise, but her hand was already up, the rock gripped in her fist, and coming down hard.

A sharp crack of rock on glass, a shiver traveling up her arm, and hairline fractures appearing where the rock had connected. Astrid brought it down again and cracks spread, the grinding sound of glass on glass covering her whimper of pain as the creature put more pressure on her other arm.

Break!

Her voice or Chinook's she could not be sure.

Twisting, pulling her arm on one side and raising the other she hit the creature again. Abruptly its grip loosened, and it fell back with horrible inevitability. With a crashing, shattering it hit the floor and broke apart, pieces spinning away. Chinook flew up from the wreckage, speeding away down the hall, beyond the reaching fingers of more glass figures. Several gave chase and Astrid leapt to her feet, prepared to go after them, ready to smash them all.

"You!"

The cry cut through her like a shard of broken glass— slicing through her, trailing fear and panic. It brought her to a standstill—tense, stomach dropping. The Enchantress's voice echoed back from the walls, ringing in her ears. Astrid turned to face the woman, steeling herself for the confrontation, knowing what would have to come next.

The Enchantress's face was white, lips a bright red against pale skin, her dark hair twisted around a golden circlet on her head. She wore purple and gold, touches of deep red ribbons running through the skirts, touching the bodice. With crackling dark eyes, fire and lightning simmering in them, she looked every inch the powerful woman she was, a queen in her realm, a woman to be worshipped and feared.

But beneath all of that, something else flashed across Livia's face, an instant of uncertainty—there and gone— leaving Astrid unsure if she'd witnessed it at all.

"Take her," the Enchantress motioned to the glass figures, two of them stepping forward and grabbing Astrid. The woman looked around, seeing the crowd, the human servants lingering, faces carefully blank—eyes wide and watching. "Go back to where you came from!"

They all scurried away, Nora throwing a glance backward, mouth pressed into a thin line. Astrid watched her go, regret surfacing. She was sorry that she'd deceived the woman who had shown her so much kindness.

But that didn't matter—couldn't. Astrid was here for Tyhr.

"Where is Tyhr?"

"You've come all this way for nothing." Color touched the Enchantress's face, two red patches appearing high on her cheekbones, mouth twisting in a sneer.

"I want to see him."

"You will see for yourself how meaningless you are."

The smile turned sweet though her eyes remained hard. "Take her to the throne room."

The glass figures marched Astrid in front of the Enchantress, following a curving path that led upwards, out of the milky lower reaches of the palace and into the clear corridors and rooms of the upper stories.

Through the walls, Astrid could see empty rooms. Space after bare space with sunlight streaming through it all. The loneliness of it all overwhelmed her. All of these rooms with nothing in them—an enormous palace vacant of life. Nora's pity for the Enchantress touched Astrid for a fleeting moment, a flash of understanding that did nothing to diminish the distaste and anger she felt for the woman.

Astrid looked into each room they passed, the desert beyond the walls plain, stretching away around them endlessly. It was impossible to know in which direction the abandoned city lay and beyond that the coast, the sea, and across that ocean home.

Home.

The Summer Valley was gone. The way through the Black Forest closed to her forever.

The only home she had was here, with Tyhr.

Tears pricked her eyes, blurring the translucent world. Astrid pulled in a steadying breath, lifting her chin, not wanting to give Livia the satisfaction of seeing her cry. She turned her attention back to the space around her, concentrating on the light and the way it followed the curve of the glass around them, flowing up into the turrets over their heads.

Beneath Astrid's feet, the floor was transparent as well and she could see down several stories down, into the more solid regions where more was hidden from the eye. The height made her sweat. Uncomfortable with the free-floating feeling, she kept her eyes up after that, not looking down again.

The glass figures moved silently, the only sound her harsh breathing and the rustle of the Enchantress's skirts. She could feel the woman's gaze boring into her, a hot patch between her shoulder blades, and Astrid resisted the urge to look back.

Chinook was nowhere to be seen. She kept searching, straining to hear the beat of his wings—hoping that he hadn't been eaten again, hoping that he had gotten away. After everything they had been through together, she wanted him to escape.

They entered a short hall, the highest point in the palace, in the tallest tower—so thin and sharp it could pierce the sky. A set of closed doors filled the space before Astrid, large and imposing, the glass embossed with intricate patterns.

As they drew closer, she realized what they were. Tigers. Leaping, sitting, striding, some with their backs to the viewer, some facing head on. These glass doors were a copy of the green doors she'd come to know so well in the Summer Valley.

Beyond the glass, distorted by the bumps and dips in the glass, she could see a figure waiting.

Tyhr.

CHAPTER FORTY-TWO

A storm exploded around them as they passed through the doors—the punishing sun gone in an instant. Rain pelted and flowed over the glass, thunder shaking the earth, rattling the palace. Lightning lit the sky, bright light running along the interior, illuminating the rooms around them in one instant, leaving them in shadows the next.

Her storms, always *her* storms—brought on by strong emotions, crackling anger and twisting jealousy. It lit Livia's face up, the edges of her body blurring, her face incandescent with fury.

Astrid shook with anger and fear, terrified of what might come next but determined to face it. There would be pain, maybe Astrid would come to know the floor of this place as well as she had the one in the jungle house. But maybe she wouldn't have that long.

You are not alone.

Glancing around she spotted Chinook, perched high in the crystal chandler hanging from the domed ceiling over her head. She let out a sigh of relief, comforted by his presence. It gave her strength, knowing that after everything he was still here with her.

Behind Livia, Tyhr stood motionless—alert, watchful. Astrid took a step toward him, trying to convey with her whole body that she spoke the truth.

"I love you."

"What do you know of love?" Livia scoffed. "You don't know him. Nothing about his past or present, nothing about the man he was or could be. But I do. Tomorrow is August first. He'll no longer wear the mask. He'll be free."

"And you think he'll be grateful? You're the one who put him in the mask." Anger coursed hotly through her body, tingling in her fingertips, warming her cheeks.

"You wouldn't understand. You're a child." Livia shook her head. "You proved yourself to be cold and uncaring. Unworthy."

Astrid looked beyond the woman, taking in Tyhr, motionless beside the throne. Her mouth had gone dry, and she had to swallow the lump in her throat. The words crawled under her skin—planting doubts, working to convince her that he might feel the same. Those nights in the library before the fire, the moments at the dinner table when she'd scoffed at the magic, a curse she hadn't understood.

"Even you doubt yourself. It's written all over your face."

Livia grabbed her, and Astrid could feel it, the magic coming up her arm, tingling into her skin. A cruel smile covered Livia's face, red lips stretched wide.

"What animal would you like to be?" the Enchantress hissed. "Would you like to be a tiger? A bird? You could run off with your little friend. Would you like to try it?"

"No!" Astrid said, sweat breaking out, the smell of ozone filling her nose.

The fingers on the arm Livia gripped going numb. She dug in—inescapable, unbreakable, and squeezing down. Tyhr shouted, the wordless cry buzzing and ringing in her ears. The numbness spread, and with it came a shifting in her bones, nausea sweeping over her, skin pricking. Feathers. Hollow bones. Tiny, clawed feet. A beak. She could see them clearly in her mind, feel it in her muscles, contracting.

Fight! Chinook called. *Do not give up!*

Astrid shook her head, trying to clear it, shoving down the urge to vomit, the painful pinpoints crawling across her shoulders. *Bird*, her body said, warming to it, welcoming it even as she screamed, and her mind fought.

Out of the corner of her eye, Tyhr appeared, slamming into the Enchantress. The woman dropped Astrid's arm. Hollow bones and a beak receded, her skin forgetting to push out feathers. Astrid's head throbbed, and she clutched it, closing her eyes with a groan. Falling to her knees, the floor hard and jarring, the sounds of Tyhr and Livia scrambling together became distant. The storm grew louder, throbbing in her ears, rattling bones.

You are human! Not a bird! Chinook screamed, his voice in her head, pushing her, reminding her. *You have hands!*

What had she come here for? For love? To right a wrong?

Astrid's eyes snapped open, patting her pockets, feeling for the wolf claw she had brought all this way. The wolf had made her promise never to return, his dislike for the Enchantress enough to gift her with a claw, his magic. She had saved it for this moment.

Wobbling, Astrid got to her feet. Tyhr was beneath the woman, her hands on his throat. His figure blurred, changing, shimmering—tiger and man occupying the same space. There would be no breaking the curse this time. He'd remain a beast, a creature who wouldn't remember—he'd be lost to her.

Without thought, she sprung forward, slamming into the Enchantress, knocking her off Tyhr. The woman rolled beneath her, and Astrid managed to straddle her, the claw held high over Livia's head. A weapon, a knife, a way to stop all this madness.

Keep your promise.

It sang through Astrid—giving her the strength she needed.

Astrid brought her arms down. The claw plunged into the woman, parting silken robes, into flesh, puncturing the heart. It slipped in so easily, as if the woman were made of nothing, the claw finding a home inside Livia's body. Her face twisted, eyebrows rising, mouth open wide as the color drained away. Her heart beat once, twice, the movement traveling up the claw, into Astrid.

Tears gathered in Astrid's eyes, falling, and hitting Livia's face.

"I'm sorry," she whispered, though she wasn't sure it was true.

Astrid fell back, away from the Enchantress, scooting across the floor to put distance between them. Livia opened her mouth—eyes dim, no words coming, merely the crunch and shatter of breaking glass. Cracks appeared in the body, hairline fractures, splintering—a map of an unknown place, a forgotten language.

Thunder boomed, and Astrid covered her ears, the rattle shaking the palace around them. She looked up, through the glass to the world beyond, and already the storm was clearing. Clouds dissipated, patches of a starry night peeking through as the Enchantress began to crumble. Cracks widened, pieces of her—shards—falling away, hitting the floor to become a pile of painted glass.

Astrid sat under the weight of her emotion, unable to move.

You did the thing you came to do, Chinook said, voice soft and gentle.

Would she always feel like that? In the future, would she wake up sweating from a dream of a broken woman, the feel of her last heartbeat throbbing in her hands? Astrid looked down at them, bloodless and the same as they had always been. Would the East Wind read this death on her palms? Would the North see it in a cup of tea? She shivered —the brutal act imprinted on her soul.

"Astrid."

Tyhr stood over her, a hand extended to pull her up. He wore the silver snarling tiger face, a reminder of how his fate could have gone if she hadn't saved him. Would it be enough to keep the memory of Livia's face from the edges of her dreams?

His golden eyes, fixed on her were full of emotion, a silent plea in his hand. She took it, letting him pull her up, sinking into his embrace, his arms going tight around her. She'd come all this way to hold him, to apologize, to bring him home. To tell him that somehow, in that jungle, without her even realizing it, he had become her home.

Astrid eased back, and he held on to her waist, not ready to let go.

"May I?" she asked, reaching up, fingers brushing the familiar contours of the snarl.

Never again. Never again did she want to see this mask. Never again another tiger.

"Yes."

Astrid smiled, joy slipping through her, lingering, promising a future she so badly wanted. She found the edge of the mask and gently pulled it away—the magic in it gone —to reveal the face of the man she loved.

The mask dropped, slipping through her fingers, shattering like glass as it hit the floor.

EPILOGUE

W aves crashed against the rocks, rolling up the stone beach, saltwater misting her face and hair. It brought back the memory of deep water and wet sand—the sharp stabbing sensation of failure in a distant desert. But also, triumph.

From that moment to this, how far they'd come.

Astrid looked down at the shark tooth. It was as large as her palm, serrated and heavy, a solid reminder of the trials faced for love. Love. She could think it, say it, feel it without any reservation now—without any doubt. Astrid pulled her arm back and threw the tooth with everything she had into the churning waves, the hungry ocean swallowing it, accepting the offering.

Feel better? Chinook asked with a tilt of his head.

"Yes, I do actually."

Good. Can we go now?

"In a minute," she laughed. "You're so impatient. What's the hurry?"

I would have thought you would dislike the sea, Chinook said huffily, rustling his feathers.

"If you don't want to get damp you don't have to sit here with me," Astrid said, smiling but keeping her eyes on the water. He only came down to this rocky cove with her. And she was grateful for that—her favorite and most trusted travel companion, her dearest friend.

I did not say I would not sit here with you.

"Well then, what are you really complaining about?"

The fact that you are making us late for lunch. The East Wind has brought mango and Ophelia has the wine you enjoy. Though I do not know why, you have very expensive tastes for someone who does not know the difference between red and white.

"Me? Make you late for lunch?" Astrid put a hand to her chest, mock horror creasing her face. "You poor thing, how will you survive?"

Without any help from you, that is obvious.

The sound of boots on stone made them turn. Astrid smiled, her stomach twisting with excitement, taking in the sight of Tyhr in his work clothes—handsome tan face, hairline damp. He'd been cutting hay in the hills—sweat darkened the shirt and there were bits of grass everywhere. The flat cap he wore to keep the sun off was pushed back, his golden eyes intent on her. The intense gaze had once been so familiar behind a silver tiger mask, now it was hers without it, and there was nothing between them in the dark.

"What are you two doing?" Tyhr asked, coming down the winding path from the East Wind's house. "East sent me to let you know lunch is ready."

See? As I told you.

"Nothing really," Astrid said, holding out a hand for him. "I just wanted to see the ocean."

Tyhr took her hand, pulling her toward him to kiss her cheek, then the corner of her mouth—lingering as their eyes met. Astrid grinned, breathless and expectant, still thrilled to have him this close without the mask between them. She would never get tired of studying his handsome features—the way he was quick to smile and laugh— dimples flashing—tenderness in every expression. She savored them all, revealing in them—in him.

Come on, Chinook said, annoyance in each word. *You will be late for the mango.*

"You go on without us, Chinook," Tyhr said, his arm tightening around Astrid.

I had forgotten how annoying you were, the bird said with a huff. *Being late is rude.*

"Do you mind?" Tyhr asked Astrid, mouth hovering over hers, the hint of a smile tugging at his cheeks. "We'll only be a little late. So, it's not very rude."

Astrid threw her arms around him, pressing close, covering his face with kisses as they both laughed. They'd found a home here, sheltered by the East Wind, at the edges of the world. A strange little family living out a happily ever after. She kissed him fiercely, ignoring the disgruntled sound Chinook made as he leaped into the air and headed to lunch on his own, his final remark ignored as Tyhr returned the kiss.

Lunch could wait.

So rude!

ABOUT THE AUTHOR

Kathryn Trattner is an award-winning author who has loved fairy tales, folk stories, and mythology all her life. Her hands-down favorites have always been East of the Sun, West of the Moon and the myth of Persephone and Hades. When not writing or reading, she's traveling as much as possible and taking thousands of photos that probably won't get edited later. She lives in Oklahoma with her wonderful husband, two very busy children, one of the friendliest dogs ever, and three cats who think they're in charge.

If you enjoyed this book, please consider leaving a review and signing up for my newsletter. You'll get information on new releases and exclusive content!

sign up for Kathryn's Newsletter
https://www.kathryntrattner.com/newsletter

ALSO BY KATHRYN TRATTNER

Deep Water and Other Stories

Mistress of Death

The Scent of Leaves

Magic and Myth: Short Stories

Magnolia House

The Glass Palace

The Blood and Rubies Series

The Dead Saint

The Living Saint

Steel and Starlight

Printed in Great Britain
by Amazon

31841189R00216